The
Andrew Lang
Fairy Tale Treasury

Edited and with an Introduction by
Cary Wilkins

With Numerous Illustrations by H. J. FORD, G. P. JACOMB HOOD,
and LANCELOT SPEED

"And going where this pathway goes,
You too, at last, may find, who knows
The Garden of the Singing Rose."

AVENEL BOOKS
NEW YORK

The illustrations on pages 307 and 321, originally drawn by H. J. Ford, have been redrawn by Cary Wilkins.

Special material copyright © MCMLXXIX by Crown Publishers, Inc.
All rights reserved.
This edition is published by Avenel Books,
distributed by Crown Publishers, Inc.
a b c d e f g h
AVENEL 1979 EDITION
Manufactured in the United States of America

Library of Congress Cataloging in Publication Data

Main entry under title:

The Andrew Lang fairy tale treasury.

   ''The illustrations on pages 307 and 321, originally
drawn by H. J. Ford, have been redrawn by Cary Wilkins. ''
   SUMMARY: A collection of more than 50 familiar
fairy tales originally published in Andrew Lang's color
fairy book series.
   1. Fairy tales. [1. Fairy tales. 2. Folklore]
I. Lang, Andrew, 1844-1912. II. Wilkins, Cary.
III. Ford, Henry Justice, 1860-1941. IV. Jacomb-Hood,
George Percy, 1857-1929. V. Speed, Lancelot, 1860-1931.
PZ8.A5617 1979   398.2'1   79-10836
ISBN O-517-27928-2.

CONTENTS

INTRODUCTION

Perhaps no one has done as much for the fairy tale as Andrew Lang. In 1889, *The Blue Fairy Book* was published and became an instant success. Thereafter, Lang had a new children's story book published every year until 1913. Out of these twenty-five books, twelve were fairy tale collections. Lang knew instinctively what children liked and realized how much this vast, imaginative field of literature had to offer.

His own childhood helped to prepare him for the delightful task of opening children's eyes to the wonderful world of fairies and elves, princes and princesses. Born in the Scottish border country at Selkirk on 31 March 1844, he and his five brothers and one sister lived in a haunted land of romance and legend. On Saturday evenings, an old shepherd would entrance him and his companions with tales of the strange and fantastic. Lang's nurse also captivated him with a wealth of local stories and folk tales.

Little else is known of Lang's early years, because he kept no letters, left no reminiscences, and asked his wife to destroy all of his papers after his death. We do not know the reason for this. We do know, however, that his interest in folklore and fairy tales remained with him throughout his life. Studying at the University of St.

Andrews, Glasgow University, and Balliol College at Oxford, he acquired much knowledge of ancient and modern literature. He was a poet, critic, essayist, and journalist, but his chief interest was cultural anthropology, including mythology, folklore, fairy tales, psychic phenomena, and superstitions. Although Lang wrote many scholarly books on these subjects, he is best known for collecting and editing the fairy books.

Lang and his publishers, Longmans, Green, and Company, were taking a risk with *The Blue Fairy Book* in 1889. Although there was much interest in folklore in the early and middle nineteenth century (the Grimms and Andersen were popular), by the late 1800s, critics and educators considered the unreality of fairy tales to be harmful for children. There were also the beliefs that children were no longer interested in fairy tales and that such stories were beneath serious consideration as literature. The success of Lang's first fairy tale book, however, proved at least that the interest was still there.

Proponents of fairy tales have been fighting these objections—the unreality of fairy tales and their inferiority as literature—ever since then. And when psychoanalysts and child psychologists discovered that a child's imagination can be violent and destructive, the cruelty and violence in fairy tales came under attack. Also, some believe that certain fairy tales may terrify a child and be psychologically harmful. Most recently, women's groups have denounced fairy tales as sexist, claiming they depict women in passive, submissive roles. Fortunately, the land of happily-ever-after has had some excellent defenders along the way: Andrew Lang, hundreds of thousands of children, the master of Middle-earth J. R. R. Tolkien, and child psychologist Bruno Bettelheim.

Some critics and parents believe that fairy tales are not healthy for young readers, because they give an untruthful, unrealistic view of life. In a review of some contemporary fairy tales, Lang eloquently argued against this belief:

> In the old stories, despite the impossibility of the incidents, the interest is always real and human. The princes and princesses fall in love and marry—nothing could be more human than that. Their lives and loves are crossed by human sorrows. ... The hero and heroine are persecuted or separated by cruel stepmothers or enchanters; they have wanderings and sorrows to suffer; they have adventures to achieve and difficulties to overcome; they must display courage, loyalty and address, courtesy, gentleness and gratitude. Thus they are living in a real human world, though it wears a mythical face, though there are giants and lions in the way. The old fairy tales which a silly sort of people disparage as too wicked and ferocious for the nursery, are really "full of matter," and unobtrusively teach the true lessons of our wayfaring in a world of perplexities and obstructions.[1]

From a modern psychological viewpoint, Bruno Bettelheim, in his book *The Uses of Enchantment: The Meaning and Importance of Fairy Tales,* reminds us that a child's concept of truth is different from that of adults. Truth of the imagination is what fairy stories are all about. They do not attempt to describe the real world, and children are aware that these stories are make-believe. Bettelheim explains that fairy tales conform to the way a child thinks and experiences life: for instance, he sometimes believes that everything that can move is alive. Children do not always understand realistic explanations of life, because they cannot think abstractly about things. Fairy tales, however, offer solutions to a child's problems and dilemmas in imaginative ways that he can understand. For example, as Bettelheim points out, a young child cannot fully comprehend that the earth revolves around the sun and is held in place by gravity. He is much more comfortable with the explanation that the earth rests on the shoulders of a giant. Such explanations are not lies; they are the child's frame of reference for dealing with reality.

Fairy stories are not just for children, however. J. R. R. Tolkien points out, in his book *Tree and Leaf,* that a false connection has been made between children and fairy tales. How it happened is not known, but it is conjectured that, with the wave of realism in art and literature in the nineteenth century, these tales were dismissed as silly and frivolous and were "relegated to the 'nursery'," as Tolkien says.2 But those who understand the importance of imagination and fantasy, he continues, know that the fairy story is as valid an art form as any other branch of literature.

The third objection to fairy tales—the presence of violence and cruelty—is responsible for much of the anemic, antiseptic children's literature today. When psychologists discovered the violent, destructive, and sadistic tendencies in a child's imagination, parents were concerned that violent fairy tales would aggravate these tendencies. They didn't realize, Bettelheim argues, that the monsters in the stories help the child to know the monster within himself better. He sometimes hates his parents, even wishing to kill them; if he has no imaginative way to deal with these feelings and no consolation that he is not alone in feeling this way, his anxiety increases. The fairy tale can reassure the child that there are ways to handle these problems and that things will work out happily in the end. In response to those who think fairy tales are harmful because of their terrifying aspects, Bettelheim agrees with Tolkien that a child can be easily reassured that he is safe from giants and ogres.

Most recently, fairy tales have been shouted down by cries of ''Sexist!'' Cinderella, the Sleeping Beauty, and Snow White supposedly perpetuate the stereotype of the passive, submissive woman. In his work with children, Bettelheim has found that children identify themselves with both sexes in fairy tales. If female characters are concerned with inward struggles and males deal aggressively with the outside world, they symbolize together the ways in which a child must learn about himself. But even if this were not true, claims of sexist stereotyping do not hold up. There are just as many stories (and they are included in this volume) where the man is passive and helpless and the woman takes an active role in saving him.

Despite all these objections to fairy tales, they have managed to survive, and Andrew Lang has played a large part in this survival. The stories in this collection have been selected from nine of his fairy books—the Red, Blue, Green, Yellow, Brown, Grey, Violet, Pink, and Olive. Lang chose stories from all over the world and used the original printed or oral sources whenever possible. He refused to censor or bowdlerize them, insisting that their magic and horror were important in keeping the imagination of children alive. Lang himself retold hardly any of the stories. In fact, most of the retelling and translating was done by his wife, his cousins, his wife's nieces, and other literary young women.

Some stories in these fairy books are not true fairy tales, as Tolkien and many others define them. These include travelers' tales, beast fables, and myths. Tolkien describes fairy tales as being "about the adventures of men in the Perilous Realm or upon its shadowy marches."3 The most important characteristic of the fairy tale, according to Tolkien and Lang, is the happy ending—the joy that gives us "a sudden glimpse of the underlying reality or truth."4 In selecting the tales for this volume, I have tried to follow these two definitions of fairy tales. And, in addition to selecting the most popular tales, I have usually weeded out stories in which the same faces reappear with different names.

Most of the illustrations are by Henry Justice Ford, with a few others by Lancelot Speed and G. P. Jacomb Hood. H. J. Ford's (1860–1941) graphic, realistic illustrations of fanciful subjects have a grace, beauty, and charm, which make them excellently suited to fairy tales —where reality exists in the mind, and truth is found in the imagination.

CARY WILKINS

1. Roger L. Green, *Andrew Lang* (London: Bodley Head, 1962), p. 48.
2. J. R. R. Tolkien, *Tree and Leaf* (Boston: Houghton Mifflin Co., 1965), p. 34.
3. Ibid., p. 9.
4. Ibid., p. 71.

THE MASTER CAT; OR, PUSS IN BOOTS

THERE was a miller who left no more estate to the three sons
he had than his mill, his ass, and his cat. The partition was
soon made. Neither the scrivener nor attorney was sent for. They
would soon have eaten up all the poor patrimony. The eldest had
the mill, the second the ass, and the youngest nothing but the cat.

The poor young fellow was quite comfortless at having so poor
a lot.

'My brothers,' said he, 'may get their living handsomely enough
by joining their stocks together; but, for my part, when I have
eaten up my cat, and made me a muff of his skin, I must die of
hunger.'

The Cat, who heard all this, but made as if he did not, said to
him with a grave and serious air:

'Do not thus afflict yourself, my good master; you have nothing else to do but to give me a bag, and get a pair of boots made
for me, that I may scamper through the dirt and the brambles, and
you shall see that you have not so bad a portion of me as you
imagine.'

The Cat's master did not build very much upon what he
said; he had, however, often seen him play a great many cunning
tricks to catch rats and mice; as when he used to hang by the
heels, or hide himself in the meal, and make as if he were dead;
so that he did not altogether despair of his affording him some
help in his miserable condition. When the Cat had what he asked
for, he booted himself very gallantly, and, putting his bag about
his neck, he held the strings of it in his two fore paws, and went
into a warren where was great abundance of rabbits. He put bran
and sow-thistle into his bag, and, stretching out at length, as if he
had been dead, he waited for some young rabbits, not yet acquainted
with the deceits of the world, to come and rummage his bag for
what he had put into it.

Scarce was he lain down but he had what he wanted: a rash and foolish young rabbit jumped into his bag, and Monsieur Puss, immediately drawing close the strings, took and killed him without pity. Proud of his prey, he went with it to the palace, and asked to speak with his Majesty. He was shown upstairs into the King's apartment, and, making a low reverence, said to him:

'I have brought you, sir, a rabbit of the warren, which my noble Lord, the Master of Carabas' (for that was the title which Puss was

pleased to give his master) 'has commanded me to present to your Majesty from him.'

'Tell thy master,' said the King, 'that I thank him, and that he does me a great deal of pleasure.'

Another time he went and hid himself among some standing corn, holding still his bag open; and, when a brace of partridges ran into it, he drew the strings, and so caught them both. He went and made a present of these to the King, as he had done before of the rabbit which he took in the warren. The King, in like manner, received the partridges with great pleasure, and ordered him some money, to drink.

The Cat continued for two or three months thus to carry his Majesty, from time to time, game of his master's taking. One day in particular, when he knew for certain that he was to take the air along the river-side, with his daughter, the most beautiful princess in the world, he said to his master:

'If you will follow my advice your fortune is made. You have nothing else to do but go and wash yourself in the river, in that part I shall show you, and leave the rest to me.'

The Marquis of Carabas did what the Cat advised him to, without knowing why or wherefore. While he was washing the King passed by, and the Cat began to cry out:

'Help! help! My Lord Marquis of Carabas is going to be drowned.'

At this noise the King put his head out of the coach-window, and, finding it was the Cat who had so often brought him such good game, he commanded his guards to run immediately to the assistance of his Lordship the Marquis of Carabas. While they were drawing the poor Marquis out of the river, the Cat came up to the coach and told the King that, while his master was washing, there came by some rogues, who went off with his clothes, though he had cried out: 'Thieves! thieves!' several times, as loud as he could.

This cunning Cat had hidden them under a great stone. The King immediately commanded the officers of his wardrobe to run and fetch one of his best suits for the Lord Marquis of Carabas.

The King caressed him after a very extraordinary manner, and as the fine clothes he had given him extremely set off his good mien (for he was well made and very handsome in his person), the King's daughter took a secret inclination to him, and the Marquis of Carabas had no sooner cast two or three respectful and somewhat tender glances but she fell in love with him to distraction. The King would needs have him come into the coach and take part of the airing. The Cat, quite over-joyed to see his project begin to succeed, marched on before, and, meeting with some countrymen, who were mowing a meadow, he said to them:

'Good people, you who are mowing, if you do not tell the King that the meadow you mow belongs to my Lord Marquis of Carabas, you shall be chopped as small as herbs for the pot.'

The King did not fail asking of the mowers to whom the meadow they were mowing belonged.

'To my Lord Marquis of Carabas,' answered they altogether, for the Cat's threats had made them terribly afraid.

'You see, sir,' said the Marquis, 'this is a meadow which never fails to yield a plentiful harvest every year.'

The Master Cat, who went still on before, met with some reapers, and said to them:

'Good people, you who are reaping, if you do not tell the King that all this corn belongs to the Marquis of Carabas, you shall be chopped as small as herbs for the pot.'

The King, who passed by a moment after, would needs know to whom all that corn, which he then saw, did belong.

'To my Lord Marquis of Carabas,' replied the reapers, and the

King was very well pleased with it, as well as the Marquis, whom he congratulated thereupon. The Master Cat, who went always before, said the same words to all he met, and the King was astonished at the vast estates of my Lord Marquis of Carabas.

Monsieur Puss came at last to a stately castle, the master of which was an ogre, the richest had ever been known; for all the lands which the King had then gone over belonged to this castle. The Cat, who had taken care to inform himself who this ogre was and what he could do, asked to speak with him, saying he could not pass so near his castle without having the honour of paying his respects to him.

The ogre received him as civilly as an ogre could do, and made him sit down.

'I have been assured,' said the Cat, 'that you have the gift of being able to change yourself into all sorts of creatures you have a mind to; you can, for example, transform yourself into a lion, or elephant, and the like.'

'That is true,' answered the ogre very briskly; 'and to convince you, you shall see me now become a lion.'

Puss was so sadly terrified at the sight of a lion so near him

that he immediately got into the gutter, not without abundance of trouble and danger, because of his boots, which were of no use at all to him in walking upon the tiles. A little while after, when Puss saw that the ogre had resumed his natural form, he came down, and owned he had been very much frightened.

'I have been moreover informed,' said the Cat, 'but I know not how to believe it, that you have also the power to take on you the shape of the smallest animals; for example, to change

yourself into a rat or a mouse ; but I must own to you I take this
to be impossible.'

'Impossible ! ' cried the ogre ; ' you shall see that presently.'

And at the same time he changed himself into a mouse, and
began to run about the floor. Puss no sooner perceived this but
he fell upon him and ate him up.

Meanwhile the King, who saw, as he passed, this fine castle of
the ogre's, had a mind to go into it.   Puss, who heard the noise
of his Majesty's coach running over the draw-bridge, ran out, and
said to the King :

'Your Majesty is welcome to this castle of my Lord Marquis of
Carabas.'

'What ! my Lord Marquis,' cried the King, ' and does this castle
also belong to you ?   There can be nothing finer than this court
and all the stately buildings which surround it ; let us go into it, if
you please.'

The Marquis gave his hand to the Princess, and followed the
King, who went first.   They passed into a spacious hall, where they
found a magnificent collation, which the ogre had prepared for
his friends, who were that very day to visit him, but dared not to
enter, knowing the King was there.   His Majesty was perfectly

charmed with the good qualities of my Lord Marquis of Carabas, as was his daughter, who had fallen violently in love with him, and, seeing the vast estate he possessed, said to him, after having drunk five or six glasses:

'It will be owing to yourself only, my Lord Marquis, if you are not my son-in-law.'

The Marquis, making several low bows, accepted the honour which his Majesty conferred upon him, and forthwith, that very same day, married the Princess.

Puss became a great lord, and never ran after mice any more but only for his diversion.[1]

[1] Charles Perrault.

THE SLEEPING BEAUTY IN THE WOOD

THERE were formerly a king and a queen, who were so sorry that they had no children; so sorry that it cannot be expressed. They went to all the waters in the world; vows, pilgrimages, all ways were tried, and all to no purpose.

At last, however, the Queen had a daughter. There was a very fine christening; and the Princess had for her god-mothers all the fairies they could find in the whole kingdom (they found seven), that every one of them might give her a gift, as was the custom of fairies in those days. By this means the Princess had all the perfections imaginable.

After the ceremonies of the christening were over, all the company returned to the King's palace, where was prepared a great feast for the fairies. There was placed before every one of them a magnificent cover with a case of massive gold, wherein were a spoon, knife, and fork, all of pure gold set with diamonds and rubies. But as they were all sitting down at table they saw come into the hall a very old fairy, whom they had not invited, because it was above fifty years since she had been out of a certain tower, and she was believed to be either dead or enchanted.

The King ordered her a cover, but could not furnish her with a case of gold as the others, because they had seven only made for the seven fairies. The old Fairy fancied she was slighted, and muttered some threats between her teeth. One of the young fairies who sat by her overheard how she grumbled; and, judging that she might give the little Princess some unlucky gift, went, as soon as they rose from table, and hid herself behind the hangings, that she might speak last, and repair, as much as she could, the evil which the old Fairy might intend.

In the meanwhile all the fairies began to give their gifts to the Princess. The youngest gave her for gift that she should be the most beautiful person in the world; the next, that she should have the wit of an angel; the third, that she should have a wonderful grace in everything she did; the fourth, that she should dance perfectly well; the fifth, that she should sing like a nightingale; and the sixth, that she should play all kinds of music to the utmost perfection.

The old Fairy's turn coming next, with a head shaking more with spite than age, she said that the Princess should have her hand pierced with a spindle and die of the wound. This terrible gift made the whole company tremble, and everybody fell a-crying.

At this very instant the young Fairy came out from behind the hangings, and spake these words aloud:

'Assure yourselves, O King and Queen, that your daughter shall not die of this disaster. It is true, I have no power to undo entirely what my elder has done. The Princess shall indeed pierce her hand with a spindle; but, instead of dying, she shall only fall into a profound sleep, which shall last a hundred years, at the expiration of which a king's son shall come and awake her.'

The King, to avoid the misfortune foretold by the old Fairy, caused immediately proclamation to be made, whereby everybody was forbidden, on pain of death, to spin with a distaff and spindle, or to have so much as any spindle in their houses. About fifteen or sixteen years after, the King and Queen being gone to one of their houses of pleasure, the young Princess happened one day to divert herself in running up and down the palace ; when going up from one apartment to another, she came into a little room on the top of the tower, where a good old woman, alone, was spinning with her spindle. This good woman had never heard of the King's proclamation against spindles.

'What are you doing there, goody ? ' said the Princess.

' I am spinning, my pretty child,' said the old woman, who did not know who she was.

' Ha ! ' said the Princess, ' this is very pretty ; how do you do it ? Give it to me, that I may see if I can do so.'

She had no sooner taken it into her hand than, whether being very hasty at it, somewhat unhandy, or that the decree of the Fairy had so ordained it, it ran into her hand, and she fell down in a swoon.

The good old woman, not knowing very well what to do in this affair, cried out for help. People came in from every quarter in great numbers ; they threw water upon the Princess's face, unlaced her, struck her on the palms of her hands, and rubbed her temples with Hungary-water ; but nothing would bring her to herself.

And now the King, who came up at the noise, bethought himself of the prediction of the fairies, and, judging very well that this must necessarily come to pass, since the fairies had said it, caused the Princess to be carried into the finest apartment in his palace, and to be laid upon a bed all embroidered with gold and silver.

One would have taken her for a little angel, she was so very beautiful ; for her swooning away had not diminished one bit of her complexion : her cheeks were carnation, and her lips were coral ; indeed her eyes were shut, but she was heard to breathe softly, which satisfied those about her that she was not dead. The King commanded that they should not disturb her, but let her sleep quietly till her hour of awaking was come.

The good Fairy who had saved her life by condemning her to sleep a hundred years was in the kingdom of Matakin, twelve thousand leagues off, when this accident befell the Princess ; but she was instantly informed of it by a little dwarf, who had boots of seven leagues, that is, boots with which he could tread over seven leagues of ground in one stride. The Fairy came away immediately, and she arrived, about an hour after, in a fiery chariot drawn by dragons.

The King handed her out of the chariot, and she approved everything he had done; but as she had very great foresight, she thought when the Princess should awake she might not know what to do with herself, being all alone in this old palace; and this was what she did: she touched with her wand everything in the palace (except the King and the Queen)—governesses, maids of honour, ladies of the bedchamber, gentlemen, officers, stewards, cooks, undercooks, scullions, guards, with their beefeaters, pages, footmen; she likewise touched all the horses which were in the stables, as well pads as others, the great dogs in the outward court and pretty little Mopsey too, the Princess's little spaniel, which lay by her on the bed.

Immediately upon her touching them they all fell asleep, that they might not awake before their mistress, and that they might be ready to wait upon her when she wanted them. The very spits at the fire, as full as they could hold of partridges and pheasants, did fall asleep also. All this was done in a moment. Fairies are not long in doing their business.

And now the King and the Queen, having kissed their dear child without waking her, went out of the palace and put forth a proclamation that nobody should dare to come near it.

This, however, was not necessary, for in a quarter of an hour's time there grew up all round about the park such a vast number of trees, great and small, bushes and brambles, twining one within another, that neither man nor beast could pass through; so that nothing could be seen but the very top of the towers of the palace; and that, too, not unless it was a good way off. Nobody doubted but the Fairy gave herein a very extraordinary sample of her art, that the Princess, while she continued sleeping, might have nothing to fear from any curious people.

When a hundred years were gone and passed the son of the King then reigning, and who was of another family from that of the sleeping Princess, being gone a-hunting on that side of the country, asked:

What those towers were which he saw in the middle of a great thick wood?

Everyone answered according as they had heard. Some said:

That it was a ruinous old castle, haunted by spirits;

Others, That all the sorcerers and witches of the country kept there their sabbath or night's meeting.

The common opinion was: That an ogre lived there, and that he carried thither all the little children he could catch, that he might eat them up at his leisure, without anybody being able to follow him, as having himself only the power to pass through the wood.

The Prince was at a stand, not knowing what to believe, when a very aged countryman spake to him thus:

'May it please your royal highness, it is now about fifty years since I heard from my father, who heard my grandfather say, that there was then in this castle a princess, the most beautiful was ever seen; that she must sleep there a hundred years, and should be waked by a king's son, for whom she was reserved.'

The young Prince was all on fire at these words, believing, without weighing the matter, that he could put an end to this rare adventure; and, pushed on by love and honour, resolved that moment to look into it.

Scarce had he advanced towards the wood when all the great

trees, the bushes, and brambles gave way of themselves to let him pass through; he walked up to the castle which he saw at the end of a large avenue which he went into; and what a little surprised him was that he saw none of his people could follow him, because the trees closed again as soon as he had passed through them. However, he did not cease from continuing his way; a young and amorous prince is always valiant.

He came into a spacious outward court, where everything he saw might have frozen up the most fearless person with horror. There reigned over all a most frightful silence; the image of death everywhere showed itself, and there was nothing to be seen but stretched-out bodies of men and animals, all seeming to be dead. He, however, very well knew, by the ruby faces and pimpled noses of the beefeaters, that they were only asleep; and their goblets, wherein still remained some drops of wine, showed plainly that they fell asleep in their cups.

He then crossed a court paved with marble, went up the stairs, and came into the guard chamber, where guards were standing in their ranks, with their muskets upon their shoulders, and snoring as loud as they could.   After that he went through several rooms full of gentlemen and ladies, all asleep, some standing, others sitting. At last he came into a chamber all gilded with gold, where he saw upon a bed, the curtains of which were all open, the finest sight was ever beheld —a princess, who appeared to be about fifteen or sixteen years of age, and whose bright and, in a manner, resplendent beauty, had somewhat in it divine.   He approached with trembling and admiration, and fell down before her upon his knees.

And now, as the enchantment was at an end, the Princess awaked, and looking on him with eyes more tender than the first view might seem to admit of:

'Is it you, my Prince?' said she to him.   'You have waited a long while.'

The Prince, charmed with these words, and much more with the manner in which they were spoken, knew not how to show his joy and gratitude; he assured her that he loved her better than he did himself; their discourse was not well connected, they did weep more than talk—little eloquence, a great deal of love.   He was more at a loss than she, and we need not wonder at it: she had time to think on what to say to him; for it is very probable (though history mentions nothing of it) that the good Fairy, during so long a sleep, had given her very agreeable dreams.   In short, they talked four hours together, and yet they said not half what they had to say.

In the meanwhile all the palace awaked; everyone thought upon their particular business, and as all of them were not in love they were ready to die for hunger.   The chief lady of honour, being as sharp set as other folks, grew very impatient, and told the Princess aloud that supper was served up.   The Prince helped the Princess to rise; she was entirely dressed, and very magnificently, but his royal highness took care not to tell her that she was dressed like his great-grandmother, and had a point band peeping over a high collar; she looked not a bit the less charming and beautiful for all that.

They went into the great hall of looking-glasses, where they supped, and were served by the Princess's officers; the violins and hautboys played old tunes, but very excellent, though it was now above a hundred years since they had played; and after supper, without losing any time, the lord almoner married them in the chapel of the castle, and the chief lady of honour drew the curtains. They had but very little sleep—the Princess had no occasion; and the Prince left her next morning to return into the city, where his father must needs have been in pain for him. The Prince told him :

That he lost his way in the forest as he was hunting, and that he had lain in the cottage of a charcoal-burner, who gave him cheese and brown bread.

The King, his father, who was a good man, believed him ; but his mother could not be persuaded it was true ; and seeing that he went almost every day a-hunting, and that he always had some excuse ready for so doing, though he had lain out three or four nights together, she began to suspect that he was married, for he lived with the Princess above two whole years, and had by her two children, the eldest of which, who was a daughter, was named *Morning*, and the youngest, who was a son, they called *Day*, because he was a great deal handsomer and more beautiful than his sister.

The Queen spoke several times to her son, to inform herself after what manner he did pass his time, and that in this he ought in duty to satisfy her. But he never dared to trust her with his secret ; he feared her, though he loved her, for she was of the race of the Ogres, and the King would never have married her had it not been for her vast riches ; it was even whispered about the Court that she had Ogreish inclinations, and that, whenever she saw little children passing by, she had all the difficulty in the world to avoid falling upon them. And so the Prince would never tell her one word.

But when the King was dead, which happened about two years afterwards, and he saw himself lord and master, he openly declared his marriage ; and he went in great ceremony to conduct his Queen to the palace. They made a magnificent entry into the capital city, she riding between her two children.

Soon after the King went to make war with the Emperor Contalabutte, his neighbour. He left the government of the kingdom to the Queen his mother, and earnestly recommended to her care his wife and children. He was obliged to continue his expedition all the summer, and as soon as he departed the Queen-mother sent her daughter-in-law to a country house among the woods, that she might with the more ease gratify her horrible longing.

Some few days afterwards she went thither herself, and said to her clerk of the kitchen :

' I have a mind to eat little Morning for my dinner to-morrow.'

' Ah ! madam,' cried the clerk of the kitchen.

' I will have it so,' replied the Queen (and this she spoke in the tone of an Ogress who had a strong desire to eat fresh meat), ' and will eat her with a *sauce Robert.*'

The poor man, knowing very well that he must not play tricks with Ogresses, took his great knife and went up into little Morning's chamber.   She was then four years old, and came up to him jumping and laughing, to take him about the neck, and ask him for some sugar-candy.   Upon which he began to weep, the great knife fell out of his hand, and he went into the back yard, and killed a little lamb, and dressed it with such good sauce that his mistress assured

him she had never eaten anything so good in her life.   He had at the same time taken up little Morning, and carried her to his wife, to conceal her in the lodging he had at the bottom of the court-yard.

About eight days afterwards the wicked Queen said to the clerk of the kitchen, ' I will sup upon little Day.'

He answered not a word, being resolved to cheat her as he had done before.   He went to find out little Day, and saw him with a little foil in his hand, with which he was fencing with a great monkey, the child being then only three years of age.   He took him up in his arms and carried him to his wife, that she might conceal him in her chamber along with his sister, and in the room of little Day cooked up a young kid, very tender, which the Ogress found to be wonderfully good.

This was hitherto all mighty well ; but one evening this wicked Queen said to her clerk of the kitchen :

' I will eat the Queen with the same sauce I had with her children.'

It was now that the poor clerk of the kitchen despaired of being able to deceive her. The young Queen was turned of twenty, not reckoning the hundred years she had been asleep; and how to find in the yard a beast so firm was what puzzled him. He took then a resolution, that he might save his own life, to cut the Queen's throat; and going up into her chamber, with intent to do it at once, he put himself into as great fury as he could possibly, and came into the young Queen's room with his dagger in his hand. He would not, however, surprise her, but told her, with a great deal of respect, the orders he had received from the Queen-mother.

' Do it ; do it ' (said she, stretching out her neck). ' Execute your orders, and then I shall go and see my children, my poor children, whom I so much and so tenderly loved.'

For she thought them dead ever since they had been taken away without her knowledge.

' No, no, madam ' (cried the poor clerk of the kitchen, all in tears) ; ' you shall not die, and yet you shall see your children again ; but then you must go home with me to my lodgings, where I have concealed them, and I shall deceive the Queen once more, by giving her in your stead a young hind.'

Upon this he forthwith conducted her to his chamber, where, leaving her to embrace her children, and cry along with them, he went and dressed a young hind, which the Queen had for her supper, and devoured it with the same appetite as if it had been the young Queen. Exceedingly was she delighted with her cruelty, and she had invented a story to tell the King, at his return, how the mad wolves had eaten up the Queen his wife and her two children.

One evening, as she was, according to her custom, rambling round about the courts and yards of the palace to see if she could smell any fresh meat, she heard, in a ground room, little Day crying, for his mamma was going to whip him, because he had been naughty ; and she heard, at the same time, little Morning begging pardon for her brother.

The Ogress presently knew the voice of the Queen and her children, and being quite mad that she had been thus deceived, she commanded next morning, by break of day (with a most horrible voice, which made everybody tremble), that they should bring into the middle of the great court a large tub, which she caused to be filled with toads, vipers, snakes, and all sorts of serpents, in order to have thrown into it the Queen and her children, the clerk of the kitchen, his wife and maid ; all whom she had given orders should be brought thither with their hands tied behind them.

They were brought out accordingly, and the executioners were just going to throw them into the tub, when the King (who was not so soon expected) entered the court on horseback (for he came post) and asked, with the utmost astonishment, what was the meaning of that horrible spectacle.

No one dared to tell him, when the Ogress, all enraged to see what had happened, threw herself head foremost into the tub, and was instantly devoured by the ugly creatures she had ordered to be thrown into it for others. The King could not but be very sorry, for she was his mother ; but he soon comforted himself with his beautiful wife and his pretty children.

CINDERELLA
OR THE LITTLE GLASS SLIPPER

ONCE there was a gentleman who married, for his second wife, the proudest and most haughty woman that was ever seen. She had, by a former husband, two daughters of her own humour, who were, indeed, exactly like her in all things. He had likewise, by another wife, a young daughter, but of unparalleled goodness and sweetness of temper, which she took from her mother, who was the best creature in the world.

No sooner were the ceremonies of the wedding over but the mother-in-law began to show herself in her true colours. She could not bear the good qualities of this pretty girl, and the less because they made her own daughters appear the more odious. She employed her in the meanest work of the house: she scoured the dishes, tables, etc., and rubbed madam's chamber, and those of misses, her daughters; she lay up in a sorry garret, upon a wretched straw bed, while her sisters lay in fine rooms, with floors all inlaid, upon beds of the very newest fashion, and where they had looking-glasses so large that they might see themselves at their full length from head to foot.

The poor girl bore all patiently, and dared not tell her father, who would have rattled her off; for his wife governed him entirely. When she had done her work, she used to go into the chimney-corner, and sit down among cinders and ashes, which made her commonly be called *Cinderwench*; but the youngest, who was not so rude and uncivil as the eldest, called her Cinderella. However, Cinderella, notwithstanding her mean apparel, was a hundred times handsomer than her sisters, though they were always dressed very richly.

It happened that the King's son gave a ball, and invited all persons of fashion to it. Our young misses were also invited, for they cut a very grand figure among the quality. They were mightily delighted at this invitation, and wonderfully busy in choosing out such gowns, petticoats, and head-clothes as might become them. This was a new trouble to Cinderella; for it was she who ironed her sister's linen, and plaited their ruffles; they talked all day long of nothing but how they should be dressed.

'For my part,' said the eldest, 'I will wear my red velvet suit with French trimming.'

'And I,' said the youngest, 'shall have my usual petticoat; but then, to make amends for that, I will put on my gold-flowered manteau, and my diamond stomacher, which is far from being the most ordinary one in the world.'

They sent for the best tire-woman they could get to make up their head-dresses and adjust their double pinners, and they had their red brushes and patches from Mademoiselle de la Poche.

Cinderella was likewise called up to them to be consulted in all these matters, for she had excellent notions, and advised them always for the best, nay, and offered her services to dress their heads, which they were very willing she should do. As she was doing this, they said to her :

'Cinderella, would you not be glad to go to the ball ? '

'Alas!' said she, 'you only jeer me; it is not for such as I am to go thither.'

'Thou art in the right of it,' replied they; 'it would make the people laugh to see a Cinderwench at a ball.'

Anyone but Cinderella would have dressed their heads awry, but she was very good, and dressed them perfectly well. They were almost two days without eating, so much they were transported with joy. They broke above a dozen of laces in trying to be laced up close, that they might have a fine slender shape, and they were continually at their looking-glass. At last the happy day came; they went to Court, and Cinderella followed them with her eyes as long as she could, and when she had lost sight of them, she fell a-crying.

Her godmother, who saw her all in tears, asked her what was the matter.

'I wish I could—I wish I could—;' she was not able to speak the rest, being interrupted by her tears and sobbing.

This godmother of hers, who was a fairy, said to her, 'Thou wishest thou couldst go to the ball; is it not so ? '

'Y—es.' cried Cinderella, with a great sigh.

'Well,' said her godmother, 'be but a good girl, and I will contrive that thou shalt go.' Then she took her into her chamber, and said to her, 'Run into the garden, and bring me a pumpkin.'

Cinderella went immediately to gather the finest she could get, and brought it to her godmother, not being able to imagine how this pumpkin could make her go to the ball. Her godmother scooped out all the inside of it, having left nothing but the rind; which done, she struck it with her wand, and the pumpkin was instantly turned into a fine coach, gilded all over with gold.

She then went to look into her mouse-trap, where she found six mice, all alive, and ordered Cinderella to lift up a little the trap-door, when, giving each mouse, as it went out, a little tap with her wand, the mouse was that moment turned into a fine horse, which altogether made a very fine set of six horses of a beautiful mouse-coloured dapple-grey. Being at a loss for a coachman,

'I will go and see,' says Cinderella, 'if there is never a rat in the rat-trap—we may make a coachman of him.'

'Thou art in the right,' replied her godmother; 'go and look.'

Cinderella brought the trap to her, and in it there were three

huge rats. The fairy made choice of one of the three which had the largest beard, and, having touched him with her wand, he was turned into a fat, jolly coachman, who had the smartest whiskers eyes ever beheld. After that, she said to her:

'Go again into the garden, and you will find six lizards behind the watering-pot, bring them to me.'

She had no sooner done so but her godmother turned them into six footmen, who skipped up immediately behind the coach, with their liveries all bedaubed with gold and silver, and clung as close behind each other as if they had done nothing else their whole lives. The Fairy then said to Cinderella :

' Well, you see here an equipage fit to go to the ball with ; are you not pleased with it ? '

' Oh ! yes,' cried she ; ' but must I go thither as I am, in these nasty rags ? '

Her godmother only just touched her with her wand, and, at the same instant, her clothes were turned into cloth of gold and silver, all beset with jewels. This done, she gave her a pair of glass slippers, the prettiest in the whole world. Being thus decked out, she got up into her coach ; but her godmother, above all things, commanded her not to stay till after midnight, telling her, at the same time, that if she stayed one moment longer, the coach would be a pumpkin again, her horses mice, her coachman a rat, her footmen lizards, and her clothes become just as they were before.

She promised her godmother she would not fail of leaving the ball before midnight ; and then away she drives, scarce able to contain herself for joy. The King's son, who was told that a great princess, whom nobody knew, was come, ran out to receive her ; he gave her his hand as she alighted out of the coach, and led her into the hall, among all the company. There was immediately a profound silence, they left off dancing, and the violins ceased to play, so attentive was everyone to contemplate the singular beauties of the unknown new-comer. Nothing was then heard but a confused noise of :

' Ha ! how handsome she is ! Ha ! how handsome she is ! '

The King himself, old as he was, could not help watching her, and telling the Queen softly that it was a long time since he had seen so beautiful and lovely a creature.

All the ladies were busied in considering her clothes and head-dress, that they might have some made next day after the same pattern, provided they could meet with such fine materials and as able hands to make them.

The King's son conducted her to the most honourable seat, and afterwards took her out to dance with him ; she danced so very gracefully that they all more and more admired her. A fine collation was served up, whereof the young prince ate not a morsel, so intently was he busied in gazing on her.

She went and sat down by her sisters, showing them a thousand civilities, giving them part of the oranges and citrons which the

Prince had presented her with, which very much surprised them, for they did not know her. While Cinderella was thus amusing her sisters, she heard the clock strike eleven and three-quarters, whereupon she immediately made a courtesy to the company and hasted away as fast as she could.

Being got home, she ran to seek out her godmother, and, after having thanked her, she said she could not but heartily wish she might go next day to the ball, because the King's son had desired her.

As she was eagerly telling her godmother whatever had passed at the ball, her two sisters knocked at the door, which Cinderella ran and opened.

'How long you have stayed!' cried she, gaping, rubbing her eyes and stretching herself as if she had been just waked out of her sleep; she had not, however, any manner of inclination to sleep since they went from home.

'If thou hadst been at the ball,' says one of her sisters, 'thou wouldst not have been tired with it. There came thither the finest princess, the most beautiful ever was seen with mortal eyes; she showed us a thousand civilities, and gave us oranges and citrons.'

Cinderella seemed very indifferent in the matter; indeed, she asked them the name of that princess; but they told her they did not know it, and that the King's son was very uneasy on her account and would give all the world to know who she was. At this Cinderella, smiling, replied:

'She must, then, be very beautiful indeed; how happy you have been! Could not I see her? Ah! dear Miss Charlotte, do lend me your yellow suit of clothes which you wear every day.'

'Ay, to be sure!' cried Miss Charlotte; 'lend my clothes to such a dirty Cinderwench as thou art! I should be a fool.'

Cinderella, indeed, expected well such answer, and was very glad of the refusal; for she would have been sadly put to it if her sister had lent her what she asked for jestingly.

The next day the two sisters were at the ball, and so was Cinderella, but dressed more magnificently than before. The King's son was always by her, and never ceased his compliments and kind speeches to her; to whom all this was so far from being tiresome that she quite forgot what her godmother had recommended to her; so that she, at last, counted the clock striking twelve when she took it to be no more than eleven; she then rose up and fled, as nimble as a deer. The Prince followed, but could not overtake her. She left behind one of her glass slippers, which the Prince took up most carefully. She got home, but quite out of breath, and in her nasty old clothes, having nothing left her of all her finery but one of the little slippers, fellow to that she dropped. The guards at the palace gate were asked:

If they had not seen a princess go out.

Who said: They had seen nobody go out but a young girl, very meanly dressed, and who had more the air of a poor country wench than a gentlewoman.

When the two sisters returned from the ball Cinderella asked them: If they had been well diverted, and if the fine lady had been there.

They told her: Yes, but that she hurried away immediately when it struck twelve, and with so much haste that she dropped one of her little glass slippers, the prettiest in the world, which the King's son had taken up; that he had done nothing but look at her all the time at the ball, and that most certainly he was very much in love with the beautiful person who owned the glass slipper.

What they said was very true; for a few days after the King's son caused it to be proclaimed, by sound of trumpet, that he would marry her whose foot this slipper would just fit. They whom he employed began to try it upon the princesses, then the duchesses and all the Court, but in vain; it was brought to the two sisters, who did all they possibly could to thrust their foot into the slipper, but they could not effect it. Cinderella, who saw all this, and knew her slipper, said to them, laughing:

'Let me see if it will not fit me.'

Her sisters burst out a-laughing, and began to banter her. The gentleman who was sent to try the slipper looked earnestly at Cinderella, and, finding her very handsome, said:

It was but just that she should try, and that he had orders to let everyone make trial.

He obliged Cinderella to sit down, and, putting the slipper to her foot, he found it went on very easily, and fitted her as if it had been made of wax. The astonishment her two sisters were in was excessively great, but still abundantly greater when Cinderella pulled out of her pocket the other slipper, and put it on her foot. Thereupon, in came her godmother, who, having touched with her wand Cinderella's clothes, made them richer and more magnificent than any of those she had before.

And now her two sisters found her to be that fine, beautiful lady

CINDERELLA'S FLIGHT.

whom they had seen at the ball. They threw themselves at her feet to beg pardon for all the ill-treatment they had made her undergo. Cinderella took them up, and, as she embraced them, cried :

That she forgave them with all her heart, and desired them always to love her.

She was conducted to the young Prince, dressed as she was ; he thought her more charming than ever, and, a few days after, married her. Cinderella, who was no less good than beautiful, gave her two sisters lodgings in the palace, and that very same day matched them with two great lords of the Court.[1]

[1] Charles Perrault.

RUMPELSTILTZKIN

THERE was once upon a time a poor miller who had a very beautiful daughter. Now it happened one day that he had an audience with the King, and in order to appear a person of some importance he told him that he had a daughter who could spin straw into gold. 'Now that's a talent worth having,' said the King to the miller; 'if your daughter is as clever as you say, bring her to my palace to-morrow, and I'll put her to the test.' When the girl was brought to him he led her into a room full of straw, gave her a spinning-wheel and spindle, and said: 'Now set to work and spin all night till early dawn, and if by that time you haven't spun the straw into gold you shall die.' Then he closed the door behind him and left her alone inside.

So the poor miller's daughter sat down, and didn't know what in the world she was to do. She hadn't the least idea of how to spin straw into gold, and became at last so miserable that she began to cry. Suddenly the door opened, and in stepped a tiny little man and said: 'Good-evening, Miss Miller-maid; why are you crying so bitterly?' 'Oh!' answered the girl, 'I have to spin straw into gold, and haven't a notion how it's done.' 'What will you give me if I spin it for you?' asked the manikin. 'My necklace,' replied the girl. The little man took the necklace, sat himself down at the wheel, and whir, whir, whir, the wheel went round three times, and the bobbin was full. Then he put on another, and whir, whir, whir, the wheel went round three times, and the second too was full; and so it went on till the morning, when all the straw was spun away, and all the bobbins were full of gold. As soon as the sun rose the King came, and when he perceived the gold he was astonished and delighted, but his heart only lusted more than ever after the precious metal. He had the miller's daughter put into another room full of straw, much bigger than the first, and bade her, if she valued her life, spin it all into gold before the following

morning.   The girl didn't know what to do, and began to cry; then
the door opened as before, and the tiny little man appeared and
said : ' What'll you give me if I spin the straw into gold for you ? '

' The ring from my finger,' answered the girl.   The manikin took
the ring, and whir ! round went the spinning-wheel again, and
when morning broke he had spun all the straw into glittering gold.
The King was pleased beyond measure at the sight, but his greed

for gold was still not satisfied, and he had the miller's daughter brought into a yet bigger room full of straw, and said : ' You must spin all this away in the night; but if you succeed this time you shall become my wife.' ' She's only a miller's daughter, it's true,' he thought; 'but I couldn't find a richer wife if I were to search the whole world over.' When the girl was alone the little man appeared for the third time, and said : ' What'll you give me if I spin the straw for you once again ? ' ' I've nothing more to give,' answered the girl. ' Then promise me when you are Queen to give me your first child.' ' Who knows what mayn't happen before that ? ' thought the miller's daughter ; and besides, she saw no other way out of it, so she promised the manikin what he demanded, and he set to work once more and spun the straw into gold. When the King came in the morning, and found everything as he had desired, he straightway made her his wife, and the miller's daughter became a queen.

When a year had passed a beautiful son was born to her, and she thought no more of the little man, till all of a sudden one day he stepped into her room and said : ' Now give me what you promised.' The Queen was in a great state, and offered the little man all the riches in her kingdom if he would only leave her the child. But the manikin said : ' No, a living creature is dearer to me than all the treasures in the world.' Then the Queen began to cry and sob so bitterly that the little man was sorry for her, and said : ' I'll give you three days to guess my name, and if you find it out in that time you may keep your child.'

Then the Queen pondered the whole night over all the names she had ever heard, and sent a messenger to scour the land, and to pick up far and near any names he should come across. When the little man arrived on the following day she began with Kasper, Melchior, Belshazzar, and all the other names she knew, in a string, but at each one the manikin called out : ' That's not my name.' The next day she sent to inquire the names of all the people in the neighbourhood, and had a long list of the most uncommon and extraordinary for the little man when he made his appearance. ' Is your name, perhaps, Sheepshanks, Cruickshanks, Spindleshanks ? ' but he always replied : ' That's not my name.' On the third day the messenger returned and announced : ' I have not been able to find any new names, but as I came upon a high hill round the corner of the wood, where the foxes and hares bid each other good night, I saw a little house, and in front of the

house burned a fire, and round the fire sprang the most grotesque
little man, hopping on one leg and crying :

> To-morrow I brew, to-day I bake,
> And then the child away I'll take ;
> For little deems my royal dame
> That Rumpelstiltzkin is my name !

You may imagine the Queen's delight at hearing the name, and
when the little man stepped in shortly afterwards and asked : ' Now,
my lady Queen, what's my name ? ' she asked first : ' Is your
name Conrad ? ' ' No.' ' Is your name Harry ? ' ' No.' ' Is
your name, perhaps, Rumpelstiltzkin ? ' ' Some demon has told you
that, some demon has told you that,' screamed the little man, and in
his rage drove his right foot so far into the ground that it sank in up
to his waist ; then in a passion he seized the left foot with both hands
and tore himself in two.[1]

[1] Grimm.

THE STORY OF PRETTY GOLDILOCKS

ONCE upon a time there was a princess who was the prettiest creature in the world. And because she was so beautiful, and because her hair was like the finest gold, and waved and rippled nearly to the ground, she was called Pretty Goldilocks. She always wore a crown of flowers, and her dresses were embroidered with diamonds and pearls, and everybody who saw her fell in love with her.

Now one of her neighbours was a young king who was not married. He was very rich and handsome, and when he heard all that was said about Pretty Goldilocks, though he had never seen her, he fell so deeply in love with her that he could neither eat nor drink. So he resolved to send an ambassador to ask her in marriage. He had a splendid carriage made for his ambassador, and gave him more than a hundred horses and a hundred servants, and told him to be sure to bring the Princess back with him. After he had started nothing else was talked of at Court, and the King felt so sure that the Princess would consent that he set his people to work at pretty dresses and splendid furniture, that they might be ready by the time she came. Meanwhile, the ambassador arrived at the Princess's palace and delivered his little message, but whether she happened to be cross that day, or whether the compliment did not please her, is not known. She only answered that she was very much obliged to the King, but she had no wish to be married. The ambassador set off sadly on his homeward way, bringing all the King's presents back with him, for the Princess was too well brought up to accept the pearls and diamonds when she would not accept the King, so she had only kept twenty-five English pins that he might not be vexed.

When the ambassador reached the city, where the King was waiting impatiently, everybody was very much annoyed with him for not bringing the Princess, and the King cried like a baby, and nobody could console him. Now there was at the Court a young man, who was more clever and handsome than anyone else. He

was called Charming, and everyone loved him, excepting a few
envious people who were angry at his being the King's favourite
and knowing all the State secrets. He happened one day to be with
some people who were speaking of the ambassador's return and
saying that his going to the Princess had not done much good, when
Charming said rashly :

'If the King had sent me to the Princess Goldilocks I am sure
she would have come back with me.'

His enemies at once went to the King and said :

'You will hardly believe, sire, what Charming has the audacity
to say—that if *he* had been sent to the Princess Goldilocks she
would certainly have come back with him. He seems to think that
he is so much handsomer than you that the Princess would have
fallen in love with him and followed him willingly.' The King was
very angry when he heard this.

'Ha, ha!' said he; 'does he laugh at my unhappiness, and
think himself more fascinating than I am? Go, and let him be
shut up in my great tower to die of hunger.'

So the King's guards went to fetch Charming, who had thought
no more of his rash speech, and carried him off to prison with great
cruelty. The poor prisoner had only a little straw for his bed, and
but for a little stream of water which flowed through the tower he
would have died of thirst.

One day when he was in despair he said to himself ·

'How can I have offended the King? I am his most faithful
subject, and have done nothing against him.'

The King chanced to be passing the tower and recognised the
voice of his former favourite. He stopped to listen in spite of
Charming's enemies, who tried to persuade him to have nothing
more to do with the traitor. But the King said :

'Be quiet, I wish to hear what he says.'

And then he opened the tower door and called to Charming, who
came very sadly and kissed the King's hand, saying :

'What have I done, sire, to deserve this cruel treatment ?'

'You mocked me and my ambassador,' said the King, 'and you
said that if I had sent you for the Princess Goldilocks you would
certainly have brought her back.'

'It is quite true, sire,' replied Charming; 'I should have drawn
such a picture of you, and represented your good qualities in such a
way, that I am certain the Princess would have found you irresistible. But I cannot see what there is in that to make you angry.'

The King could not see any cause for anger either when the matter was presented to him in this light, and he began to frown very fiercely at the courtiers who had so misrepresented his favourite.

So he took Charming back to the palace with him, and after seeing that he had a very good supper he said to him:

'You know that I love Pretty Goldilocks as much as ever, her refusal has not made any difference to me; but I don't know how to make her change her mind: I really should like to send you, to see if you can persuade her to marry me.'

Charming replied that he was perfectly willing to go, and would set out the very next day.

'But you must wait till I can get a grand escort for you,' said the King. But Charming said that he only wanted a good horse to ride, and the King, who was delighted at his being ready to start so promptly, gave him letters to the Princess, and bade him good speed. It was on a Monday morning that he set out all alone upon his errand, thinking of nothing but how he could persuade the Princess Goldilocks to marry the King. He had a writing-book in his pocket, and whenever any happy thought struck him he dismounted from his horse and sat down under the trees to put it into the harangue which he was preparing for the Princess, before he forgot it.

One day when he had started at the very earliest dawn, and was riding over a great meadow, he suddenly had a capital idea, and, springing from his horse, he sat down under a willow tree which

grew by a little river.   When he had written it down he was looking round him, pleased to find himself in such a pretty place, when
all at once he saw a great golden carp lying gasping and exhausted
upon the grass.   In leaping after little flies she had thrown herself
high upon the bank, where she had lain till she was nearly dead.
Charming had pity upon her, and, though he couldn't help thinking
that she would have been very nice for dinner, he picked her up
gently and put her back into the water.   As soon as Dame Carp
felt the refreshing coolness of the water she sank down joyfully to
the bottom of the river, then, swimming up to the bank quite boldly,
she said:

'I thank you, Charming, for the kindness you have done me.
You have saved my life; one day I will repay you.'   So saying,
she sank down into the water again, leaving Charming greatly
astonished at her politeness.

Another day, as he journeyed on, he saw a raven in great distress.   The poor bird was closely pursued by an eagle, which would
soon have eaten it up, had not Charming quickly fitted an arrow to
his bow and shot the eagle dead.   The raven perched upon a tree
very joyfully.

'Charming,' said he, 'it was very generous of you to rescue a
poor raven; I am not ungrateful, some day I will repay you.'

Charming thought it was very nice of the raven to say so, and
went on his way.

Before the sun rose he found himself in a thick wood where it
was too dark for him to see his path, and here he heard an owl
crying as if it were in despair.

'Hark!' said he, 'that must be an owl in great trouble, I
am sure it has got into a snare;' and he began to hunt about, and
presently found a great net which some bird-catchers had spread
the night before.

'What a pity it is that men do nothing but torment and persecute
poor creatures which never do them any harm!' said he, and he took
out his knife and cut the cords of the net, and the owl flitted away
into the darkness, but then turning, with one flicker of her wings,
she came back to Charming and said:

'It does not need many words to tell you how great a service
you have done me.   I was caught; in a few minutes the fowlers
would have been here—without your help I should have been killed.
I am grateful, and one day I will repay you.'

These three adventures were the only ones of any consequence that befell Charming upon his journey, and he made all the haste he could to reach the palace of the Princess Goldilocks.

When he arrived he thought everything he saw delightful and magnificent. Diamonds were as plentiful as pebbles, and the gold and silver, the beautiful dresses, the sweetmeats and pretty things that were everywhere quite amazed him ; he thought to himself : ' If the Princess consents to leave all this, and come with me to marry the King, he may think himself lucky ! '

Then he dressed himself carefully in rich brocade, with scarlet and white plumes, and threw a splendid embroidered scarf over his shoulder, and, looking as gay and as graceful as possible, he presented himself at the door of the palace, carrying in his arm a tiny pretty dog which he had bought on the way. The guards saluted him respectfully, and a messenger was sent to the Princess to announce the arrival of Charming as ambassador of her neighbour the King.

' Charming,' said the Princess, ' the name promises well ; I have no doubt that he is good-looking and fascinates everybody.'

' Indeed he does, madam,' said all her maids of honour in one breath. ' We saw him from the window of the garret where we were spinning flax, and we could do nothing but look at him as long as he was in sight.'

' Well to be sure ! ' said the Princess, ' that's how you amuse yourselves, is it ?   Looking at strangers out of the window ! Be quick and give me my blue satin embroidered dress, and comb out my golden hair.   Let somebody make me fresh garlands of flowers, and give me my high-heeled shoes and my fan, and tell them to sweep my great hall and my throne, for I want everyone to say I am really " Pretty Goldilocks." '

You can imagine how all her maids scurried this way and that to make the Princess ready, and how in their haste they knocked their heads together and hindered each other, till she thought they would never have done. However, at last they led her into the gallery of mirrors that she might assure herself that nothing was lacking in her appearance, and then she mounted her throne of gold, ebony, and ivory, while her ladies took their guitars and began to sing softly.   Then Charming was led in, and was so struck with astonishment and admiration that at first not a word could he say. But presently he took courage and delivered his harangue, bravely ending by begging the Princess to spare him the disappointment of going back without her.

'Sir Charming,' answered she, 'all the reasons you have given me are very good ones, and I assure you that I should have more pleasure in obliging you than anyone else, but you must know that a month ago as I was walking by the river with my ladies I took off my glove, and as I did so a ring that I was wearing slipped off my finger and rolled into the water. As I valued it more than my kingdom, you may imagine how vexed I was at losing it, and I vowed never to listen to any proposal of marriage unless the ambassador first brought me back my ring. So now you know what is expected of you, for if you talked for fifteen days and fifteen nights you could not make me change my mind.'

Charming was very much surprised by this answer, but he bowed low to the Princess, and begged her to accept the embroidered scarf and the tiny dog he had brought with him. But she answered that she did not want any presents, and that he was to remember what she had just told him. When he got back to his lodging he went to bed without eating any supper, and his little dog, who was called Frisk, couldn't eat any either, but came and lay down close to him. All night long Charming sighed and lamented.

'How am I to find a ring that fell into the river a month ago?' said he. 'It is useless to try; the Princess must have told me to do it on purpose, knowing it was impossible.' And then he sighed again.

Frisk heard him and said:

'My dear master, don't despair; the luck may change, you are too good not to be happy. Let us go down to the river as soon as it is light.'

But Charming only gave him two little pats and said nothing, and very soon he fell asleep.

At the first glimmer of dawn Frisk began to jump about, and when he had waked Charming they went out together, first into the garden, and then down to the river's brink, where they wandered up and down. Charming was thinking sadly of having to go back unsuccessful when he heard someone calling: 'Charming, Charming!' He looked all about him and thought he must be dreaming, as he could not see anybody. Then he walked on and the voice called again: 'Charming, Charming!'

'Who calls me?' said he. Frisk, who was very small and could look closely into the water, cried out: 'I see a golden carp coming.' And sure enough there was the great carp, who said to Charming:

'You saved my life in the meadow by the willow tree, and I promised that I would repay you. Take this, it is Princess Goldilock's ring.' Charming took the ring out of Dame Carp's mouth, thanking her a thousand times, and he and tiny Frisk went straight to the palace, where someone told the Princess that he was asking to see her.

'Ah! poor fellow,' said she, 'he must have come to say goodbye, finding it impossible to do as I asked.'

So in came Charming, who presented her with the ring and said:

'Madam, I have done your bidding. Will it please you to marry my master?' When the Princess saw her ring brought back to her unhurt she was so astonished that she thought she must be dreaming.

'Truly, Charming,' said she, 'you must be the favourite of some fairy, or you could never have found it.'

'Madam,' answered he, 'I was helped by nothing but my desire to obey your wishes.'

'Since you are so kind,' said she, 'perhaps you will do me another service, for till it is done I will never be married. There is a prince not far from here whose name is Galifron, who once wanted to marry me, but when I refused he uttered the most terrible threats against me, and vowed that he would lay waste my country. But what could I do? I could not marry a frightful giant as tall as a tower, who eats up people as a monkey eats chestnuts, and who talks so loud that anybody who has to listen to him becomes quite deaf. Nevertheless, he does not cease to persecute me and to kill my subjects. So before I can listen to your proposal you must kill him and bring me his head.'

Charming was rather dismayed at this command, but he answered:

'Very well, Princess, I will fight this Galifron; I believe that he will kill me, but at any rate I shall die in your defence.'

Then the Princess was frightened and said everything she could think of to prevent Charming from fighting the giant, but it was of no use, and he went out to arm himself suitably, and then, taking little Frisk with him, he mounted his horse and set out for Galifron's country. Everyone he met told him what a terrible giant Galifron was, and that nobody dared go near him; and the more he heard the more frightened he grew. Frisk tried to encourage him by saying:

'While you are fighting the giant, dear master, I will go and bite his heels, and when he stoops down to look at me you can kill him.'

Charming praised his little dog's plan, but knew that his help would not do much good.

At last he drew near the giant's castle, and saw to his horror that every path that led to it was strewn with bones. Before long he saw Galifron coming. His head was higher than the tallest trees, and he sang in a terrible voice:

> ' Bring out your little boys and girls,
> Pray do not stay to do their curls,
> For I shall eat so very many,
> I shall not know if they have any.'

Thereupon Charming sang out as loud as he could to the same tune:

> ' Come out and meet the valiant Charming,
> Who finds you not at all alarming;
> Although he is not very tall,
> He's big enough to make you fall.'

The rhymes were not very correct, but you see he had made them up so quickly that it is a miracle that they were not worse ; especially as he was horribly frightened all the time. When Galifron heard these words he looked all about him, and saw Charming standing, sword in hand ; this put the giant into a terrible rage, and he aimed a blow at Charming with his huge iron club, which would certainly have killed him if it had reached him, but at that instant a raven perched upon the giant's head, and, pecking with its strong beak and beating with its great wings, so confused and blinded him that all his blows fell harmlessly upon the air, and Charming, rushing in, gave him several strokes with his sharp sword so that he fell to the ground. Whereupon Charming cut off his head before he knew anything about it, and the raven from a tree close by croaked out :

'You see I have not forgotten the good turn you did me in killing the eagle. To-day I think I have fulfilled my promise of repaying you.'

'Indeed, I owe you more gratitude than you ever owed me,' replied Charming.

And then he mounted his horse and rode off with Galifron's head.

When he reached the city the people ran after him in crowds, crying :

'Behold the brave Charming, who has killed the giant ! ' And their shouts reached the Princess's ear, but she dared not ask what was happening, for fear she should hear that Charming had been killed. But very soon he arrived at the palace with the giant's head, of which she was still terrified, though it could no longer do her any harm.

'Princess,' said Charming, 'I have killed your enemy; I hope you will now consent to marry the King my master.'

'Oh dear ! no,' said the Princess, 'not until you have brought me some water from the Gloomy Cavern.

'Not far from here there is a deep cave, the entrance to which is guarded by two dragons with fiery eyes, who will not allow anyone to pass them. When you get into the cavern you will find an immense hole, which you must go down, and it is full of toads and snakes ; at the bottom of this hole there is another little cave, in which rises the Fountain of Health and Beauty. It is some of this water that I really must have : everything it touches becomes wonderful. The beautiful things will always remain beautiful, and the ugly things become lovely. If one is young one never grows old, and if one is old one becomes young. You see, Charming, I could not leave my kingdom without taking some of it with me.'

'Princess,' said he, 'you at least can never need this water, but I am an unhappy ambassador, whose death you desire. Where you send me I will go, though I know I shall never return.'

And, as the Princess Goldilocks showed no sign of relenting, he started with his little dog for the Gloomy Cavern. Everyone he met on the way said:

'What a pity that a handsome young man should throw away his life so carelessly! He is going to the cavern alone, though if he had a hundred men with him he could not succeed. Why does the Princess ask impossibilities?'

Charming said nothing, but he was very sad. When he was near the top of a hill he dismounted to let his horse graze, while Frisk amused himself by chasing flies. Charming knew he could not be far from the Gloomy Cavern, and on looking about him he saw a black hideous rock from which came a thick smoke, followed in a moment by one of the dragons with fire blazing from his mouth and eyes. His body was yellow and green, and his claws scarlet, and his tail was so long that it lay in a hundred coils. Frisk was so terrified at the sight of it that he did not know where to hide. Charming, quite determined to get the water or die, now drew his sword, and, taking the crystal flask which Pretty Goldilocks had given him to fill, said to Frisk:

'I feel sure that I shall never come back from this expedition; when I am dead, go to the Princess and tell her that her errand has cost me my life. Then find the King my master, and relate all my adventures to him.'

As he spoke he heard a voice calling: 'Charming, Charming!'

'Who calls me?' said he; then he saw an owl sitting in a hollow tree, who said to him:

'You saved my life when I was caught in the net, now I can repay you. Trust me with the flask, for I know all the ways of the Gloomy Cavern, and can fill it from the Fountain of Beauty.' Charming was only too glad to give her the flask, and she flitted into the cavern quite unnoticed by the dragon, and after some time returned with the flask, filled to the very brim with sparkling water. Charming thanked her with all his heart, and joyfully hastened back to the town.

He went straight to the palace and gave the flask to the Princess, who had no further objection to make. So she thanked

Charming, and ordered that preparations should be made for her departure, and they soon set out together. The Princess found Charming such an agreeable companion that she sometimes said to him:

'Why didn't we stay where we were? I could have made you king, and we should have been so happy!'

But Charming only answered:

'I could not have done anything that would have vexed my

master so much, even for a kingdom, or to please you, though I think you are as beautiful as the sun.'

At last they reached the King's great city, and he came out to meet the Princess, bringing magnificent presents, and the marriage was celebrated with great rejoicings. But Goldilocks was so fond of Charming that she could not be happy unless he was near her, and she was always singing his praises.

'If it hadn't been for Charming,' she said to the King, 'I should never have come here; you ought to be very much obliged to him, for he did the most impossible things and got me water from the Fountain of Beauty, so I can never grow old, and shall get prettier every year.'

Then Charming's enemies said to the King:

'It is a wonder that you are not jealous, the Queen thinks there is nobody in the world like Charming. As if anybody you had sent could not have done just as much!'

'It is quite true, now I come to think of it,' said the King. 'Let him be chained hand and foot, and thrown into the tower.'

So they took Charming, and as a reward for having served the King so faithfully he was shut up in the tower, where he only saw the gaoler, who brought him a piece of black bread and a pitcher of water every day.

However, little Frisk came to console him, and told him all the news.

When Pretty Goldilocks heard what had happened she threw herself at the King's feet and begged him to set Charming free, but the more she cried the more angry he was, and at last she saw that it was useless to say any more; but it made her very sad. Then the King took it in his head that perhaps he was not handsome enough to please the Princess Goldilocks, and he thought he would bathe his face with the water from the Fountain of Beauty, which was in the flask on a shelf in the Princess's room, where she had placed it that she might see it often. Now it happened that one of the Princess's ladies in chasing a spider had knocked the flask off the shelf and broken it, and every drop of the water had been spilt. Not knowing what to do, she had hastily swept away the pieces of crystal, and then remembered that in the King's room she had seen a flask of exactly the same shape, also filled with sparkling water. So, without saying a word, she fetched it and stood it upon the Queen's shelf.

Now the water in this flask was what was used in the kingdom

for getting rid of troublesome people. Instead of having their
heads cut off in the usual way, their faces were bathed with the
water, and they instantly fell asleep and never woke up any more.
So, when the King, thinking to improve his beauty, took the flask
and sprinkled the water upon his face, *he* fell asleep, and nobody
could wake him.

Little Frisk was the first to hear the news, and he ran to tell
Charming, who sent him to beg the Princess not to forget the poor
prisoner.   All the palace was in confusion on account of the King's
death, but tiny Frisk made his way through the crowd to the
Princess's side, and said:

  ' Madam, do not forget poor Charming ! '

Then she remembered all he had done for her, and without
saying a word to anyone went straight to the tower, and with her
own hands took off Charming's chains. Then, putting a golden
crown upon his head, and the royal mantle upon his shoulders, she
said :

  ' Come, faithful Charming, I make you king, and will take you
for my husband.'

Charming, once more free and happy, fell at her feet and
thanked her for her gracious words.

Everybody was delighted that he should be king, and the
wedding, which took place at once, was the prettiest that can be
imagined, and Prince Charming and Princess Goldilocks lived
happily ever after.[1]

[1] Madame d'Aulnoy.

BEAUTY AND THE BEAST

ONCE upon a time, in a very far-off country, there lived a merchant who had been so fortunate in all his undertakings that he
was enormously rich. As he had, however, six sons and six daughters,
he found that his money was not too much to let them all have
everything they fancied, as they were accustomed to do.

But one day a most unexpected misfortune befell them. Their
house caught fire and was speedily burnt to the ground, with all the
splendid furniture, the books, pictures, gold, silver, and precious
goods it contained; and this was only the beginning of their
troubles. Their father, who had until this moment prospered in all
ways, suddenly lost every ship he had upon the sea, either by dint
of pirates, shipwreck, or fire. Then he heard that his clerks in distant countries, whom he trusted entirely, had proved unfaithful;
and at last from great wealth he fell into the direst poverty.

All that he had left was a little house in a desolate place at least
a hundred leagues from the town in which he had lived, and to this
he was forced to retreat with his children, who were in despair at
the idea of leading such a different life. Indeed, the daughters at
first hoped that their friends, who had been so numerous while they
were rich, would insist on their staying in their houses now they
no longer possessed one. But they soon found that they were left
alone, and that their former friends even attributed their misfortunes to their own extravagance, and showed no intention of offering them any help. So nothing was left for them but to take their
departure to the cottage, which stood in the midst of a dark forest,
and seemed to be the most dismal place upon the face of the earth.
As they were too poor to have any servants, the girls had to work
hard, like peasants, and the sons, for their part, cultivated the fields
to earn their living. Roughly clothed, and living in the simplest
way, the girls regretted unceasingly the luxuries and amusements
of their former life; only the youngest tried to be brave and cheer-

ful. She had been as sad as anyone when misfortune first overtook
her father, but, soon recovering her natural gaiety, she set to work
to make the best of things, to amuse her father and brothers as well
as she could, and to try to persuade her sisters to join her in dancing
and singing.   But they would do nothing of the sort, and, because
she was not as doleful as themselves, they declared that this miserable life was all she was fit for.   But she was really far prettier and
cleverer than they were ; indeed, she was so lovely that she was
always called Beauty.   After two years, when they were all beginning to get used to their new life, something happened to disturb
their tranquillity.   Their father received the news that one of his
ships, which he had believed to be lost, had come safely into port
with a rich cargo.   All the sons and daughters at once thought that
their poverty was at an end, and wanted to set out directly for the
town ; but their father, who was more prudent, begged them to wait
a little, and, though it was harvest-time, and he could ill be spared,
determined to go himself first, to make inquiries.   Only the youngest
daughter had any doubt but that they would soon again be as rich
as they were before, or at least rich enough to live comfortably
in some town where they would find amusement and gay companions once more.   So they all loaded their father with commissions for jewels and dresses which it would have taken a fortune to
buy ; only Beauty, feeling sure that it was of no use, did not ask for
anything. Her father, noticing her silence, said : ' And what shall I
bring for you, Beauty ? '

' The only thing I wish for is to see you come home safely,' she
answered.

But this reply vexed her sisters, who fancied she was blaming
them for having asked for such costly things. Her father, however,
was pleased, but as he thought that at her age she certainly ought
to like pretty presents, he told her to choose something.

' Well, dear father,' she said, ' as you insist upon it, I beg that
you will bring me a rose.   I have not seen one since we came here,
and I love them so much.'

So the merchant set out and reached the town as quickly as
possible, but only to find that his former companions, believing him
to be dead, had divided between them the goods which the ship had
brought ; and after six months of trouble and expense he found
himself as poor as when he started, having been able to recover
only just enough to pay the cost of his journey.   To make matters
worse, he was obliged to leave the town in the most terrible weather,

so that by the time he was within a few leagues of his nome he was almost exhausted with cold and fatigue.   Though he knew it would take some hours to get through the forest, he was so anxious to be at his journey's end that he resolved to go on ; but night overtook him, and the deep snow and bitter frost made it impossible for his horse to carry him any further.   Not a house was to be seen ; the only shelter he could get was the hollow trunk of a great tree, and

there he crouched all the night, which seemed to him the longest he had ever known.   In spite of his weariness the howling of the wolves kept him awake, and even when at last the day broke he was not much better off, for the falling snow had covered up every path, and he did not know which way to turn.

At length he made out some sort of track, and though at the beginning it was so rough and slippery that he fell down more than

once, it presently became easier, and led him into an avenue of trees
which ended in a splendid castle. It seemed to the merchant very
strange that no snow had fallen in the avenue, which was entirely
composed of orange trees, covered with flowers and fruit. When
he reached the first court of the castle he saw before him a flight of
agate steps, and went up them, and passed through several splendidly
furnished rooms.   The pleasant warmth of the air revived him,
and he felt very hungry ; but there seemed to be nobody in all this
vast and splendid palace whom he could ask to give him something to
eat. Deep silence reigned everywhere, and at last, tired of roaming
through empty rooms and galleries, he stopped in a room smaller
than the rest, where a clear fire was burning and a couch was
drawn up cosily close to it.   Thinking that this must be prepared
for someone who was expected, he sat down to wait till he should
come, and very soon fell into a sweet sleep.

When his extreme hunger wakened him after several hours,
he was still alone ; but a little table, upon which was a good dinner,
had been drawn up close to him, and, as he had eaten nothing for
twenty-four hours, he lost no time in beginning his meal, hoping
that he might soon have an opportunity of thanking his considerate
entertainer, whoever it might be.   But no one appeared, and even
after another long sleep, from which he awoke completely refreshed,
there was no sign of anybody, though a fresh meal of dainty cakes
and fruit was prepared upon the little table at his elbow.   Being
naturally timid, the silence began to terrify him, and he resolved
to search once more through all the rooms ; but it was of no use.
Not even a servant was to be seen ; there was no sign of life in the
palace ! He began to wonder what he should do, and to amuse
himself by pretending that all the treasures he saw were his own,
and considering how he would divide them among his children.
Then he went down into the garden, and though it was winter
everywhere else, here the sun shone, and the birds sang, and the
flowers bloomed, and the air was soft and sweet.   The merchant,
in ecstacies with all he saw and heard, said to himself :

'All this must be meant for me. I will go this minute and bring
my children to share all these delights.'

In spite of being so cold and weary when he reached the castle,
he had taken his horse to the stable and fed it.   Now he thought
he would saddle it for his homeward journey, and he turned down
the path which led to the stable.   This path had a hedge of roses
on each side of it, and the merchant thought he had never seen or

smelt such exquisite flowers.   They reminded him of his promise
to Beauty, and he stopped and had just gathered one to take to her
when he was startled by a strange noise behind him.   Turning
round, he saw a frightful Beast, which seemed to be very angry and
said, in a terrible voice :

'Who told you that you might gather my roses?   Was it not

enough that I allowed you to be in my palace and was kind to
you?   This is the way you show your gratitude, by stealing my
flowers!   But your insolence shall not go unpunished.'   The
merchant, terrified by these furious words, dropped the fatal rose,
and, throwing himself on his knees, cried : ' Pardon me, noble sir.   I
am truly grateful to you for your hospitality, which was so magni-

ficent that I could not imagine that you would be offended by my
taking such a little thing as a rose.'   But the Beast's anger was
not lessened by this speech.

'You are very ready with excuses and flattery,' he cried ; 'but
that will not save you from the death you deserve.'

'Alas ! ' thought the merchant, 'if my daughter Beauty could
only know what danger her rose has brought me into ! '

And in despair he began to tell the Beast all his misfortunes,
and the reason of his journey, not forgetting to mention Beauty's
request.

'A king's ransom would hardly have procured all that my other
daughters asked,' he said ; 'but I thought that I might at least take
Beauty her rose.   I beg you to forgive me, for you see I meant no
harm.'

The Beast considered for a moment, and then he said, in a less
furious tone :

'I will forgive you on one condition—that is, that you will
give me one of your daughters.'

'Ah ! ' cried the merchant, 'if I were cruel enough to buy my
own life at the expense of one of my children's, what excuse could
I invent to bring her here ? '

'No excuse would be necessary,' answered the Beast.   'If she
comes at all she must come willingly.   On no other condition will
I have her.   See if any one of them is courageous enough, and loves
you well enough to come and save your life.   You seem to be
an honest man, so I will trust you to go home.   I give you a month
to see if either of your daughters will come back with you and stay
here, to let you go free.   If neither of them is willing, you must
come alone, after bidding them good-bye for ever, for then you will
belong to me.   And do not imagine that you can hide from me, for
if you fail to keep your word I will come and fetch you ! ' added the
Beast grimly.

The merchant accepted this proposal, though he did not really
think any of his daughters would be persuaded to come.   He promised to return at the time appointed, and then, anxious to escape
from the presence of the Beast, he asked permission to set off at
once.   But the Beast answered that he could not go until the next
day.

'Then you will find a horse ready for you,' he said.   'Now go
and eat your supper, and await my orders.'

The poor merchant, more dead than alive, went back to his room, where the most delicious supper was already served on the little table which was drawn up before a blazing fire. But he was too terrified to eat, and only tasted a few of the dishes, for fear the Beast should be angry if he did not obey his orders. When he had finished he heard a great noise in the next room, which he knew meant that the Beast was coming. As he could do nothing to escape his visit, the only thing that remained was to seem as little afraid as possible ; so when the Beast appeared and asked roughly if he had supped well, the merchant answered humbly that he had, thanks to his host's kindness. Then the Beast warned him to remember their agreement, and to prepare his daughter exactly for what she had to expect.

' Do not get up to-morrow,' he added, ' until you see the sun and hear a golden bell ring. Then you will find your breakfast waiting for you here, and the horse you are to ride will be ready in the courtyard. He will also bring you back again when you come with your daughter a month hence. Farewell. Take a rose to Beauty, and remember your promise ! '

The merchant was only too glad when the Beast went away, and though he could not sleep for sadness, he lay down until the sun rose. Then, after a hasty breakfast, he went to gather Beauty's rose, and mounted his horse, which carried him off so swiftly that in an instant he had lost sight of the palace, and he was still wrapped in gloomy thoughts when it stopped before the door of the cottage.

His sons and daughters, who had been very uneasy at his long absence, rushed to meet him, eager to know the result of his journey, which, seeing him mounted upon a splendid horse and wrapped in a rich mantle, they supposed to be favourable. But he hid the truth from them at first, only saying sadly to Beauty as he gave her the rose :

' Here is what you asked me to bring you ; you little know what it has cost.'

But this excited their curiosity so greatly that presently he told them his adventures from beginning to end, and then they were all very unhappy. The girls lamented loudly over their lost hopes, and the sons declared that their father should not return to this terrible castle, and began to make plans for killing the Beast if it should come to fetch him. But he reminded them that he had promised to go back. Then the girls were very angry with Beauty, and said it was all her fault, and that if she had asked for something sensible this would never have happened, and complained bitterly that they should have to suffer for her folly.

Poor Beauty, much distressed, said to them :

' I have indeed caused this misfortune, but I assure you I did it innocently. Who could have guessed that to ask for a rose in the middle of summer would cause so much misery ? But as I did the mischief it is only just that I should suffer for it. I will therefore go back with my father to keep his promise.'

At first nobody would hear of this arrangement, and her father and brothers, who loved her dearly, declared that nothing should make them let her go ; but Beauty was firm. As the time drew near she divided all her little possessions between her sisters, and said good-bye to everything she loved, and when the fatal day came she encouraged and cheered her father as they mounted together the horse which had brought him back. It seemed to fly rather than gallop, but so smoothly that Beauty was not frightened ; indeed, she would have enjoyed the journey if she had not feared what might happen to her at the end of it. Her father still tried to persuade her to go back, but in vain. While they were talking the night fell, and then, to their great surprise, wonderful coloured lights began to shine in all directions, and splendid fireworks blazed out before them ; all the forest was illuminated by them, and even felt pleasantly warm, though it had been bitterly cold before. This lasted until they reached the avenue of orange trees, where were statues holding flaming torches, and when they got nearer to the palace they saw that it was illuminated from the roof to the ground, and music sounded softly from the courtyard. ' The Beast must be very hungry,' said Beauty, trying to laugh, ' if he makes all this rejoicing over the arrival of his prey.'

But, in spite of her anxiety, she could not help admiring all the wonderful things she saw.

The horse stopped at the foot of the flight of steps leading to the terrace, and when they had dismounted her father led her to the little room he had been in before, where they found a splendid fire burning, and the table daintily spread with a delicious supper.

The merchant knew that this was meant for them, and Beauty, who was rather less frightened now that she had passed through so many rooms and seen nothing of the Beast, was quite willing to begin, for her long ride had made her very hungry. But they had hardly finished their meal when the noise of the Beast's footsteps was heard approaching, and Beauty clung to her father in terror, which became all the greater when she saw how frightened he was. But when the Beast really appeared, though she trembled at the sight of him, she made a great effort to hide her horror, and saluted him respectfully.

This evidently pleased the Beast. After looking at her he said, in a tone that might have struck terror into the boldest heart, though he did not seem to be angry :

'Good-evening, old man. Good-evening, Beauty.'

The merchant was too terrified to reply, but Beauty answered sweetly :

'Good-evening, Beast.'

'Have you come willingly?' asked the Beast. 'Will you be content to stay here when your father goes away?'

Beauty answered bravely that she was quite prepared to stay.

'I am pleased with you,' said the Beast. 'As you have come of your own accord, you may stay. As for you, old man,' he added, turning to the merchant, 'at sunrise to-morrow you will take your departure. When the bell rings get up quickly and eat your breakfast, and you will find the same horse waiting to take you home ; but remember that you must never expect to see my palace again.'

Then turning to Beauty, he said :

'Take your father into the next room, and help him to choose everything you think your brothers and sisters would like to have. You will find two travelling-trunks there ; fill them as full as you can. It is only just that you should send them something very precious as a remembrance of yourself.'

Then he went away, after saying, 'Good-bye, Beauty ; good-bye, old man ; ' and though Beauty was beginning to think with great dismay of her father's departure, she was afraid to disobey the Beast's orders ; and they went into the next room, which had shelves and cupboards all round it. They were greatly surprised at the riches it contained. There were splendid dresses fit for a queen, with all the ornaments that were to be worn with them ; and when Beauty opened the cupboards she was quite dazzled by the gorgeous jewels that lay in heaps upon every shelf. After choosing a vast quantity, which she divided between her sisters—for she had made a heap of the wonderful dresses for each of them—she opened the last chest, which was full of gold.

'I think, father,' she said, 'that, as the gold will be more useful to you, we had better take out the other things again, and fill the trunks with it.' So they did this; but the more they put in, the more room there seemed to be, and at last they put back all the jewels and dresses they had taken out, and Beauty even added as many more of the jewels as she could carry at once; and then the trunks were not too full, but they were so heavy that an elephant could not have carried them!

'The Beast was mocking us,' cried the merchant; 'he must have pretended to give us all these things, knowing that I could not carry them away.'

'Let us wait and see,' answered Beauty. 'I cannot believe that he meant to deceive us. All we can do is to fasten them up and leave them ready.'

So they did this and returned to the little room, where, to their astonishment, they found breakfast ready. The merchant ate his with a good appetite, as the Beast's generosity made him believe that he might perhaps venture to come back soon and see Beauty. But she felt sure that her father was leaving her for ever, so she was very sad when the bell rang sharply for the second time, and warned them that the time was come for them to part. They went down into the courtyard, where two horses were waiting, one loaded with the two trunks, the other for him to ride. They were pawing the ground in their impatience to start, and the merchant was forced to bid Beauty a hasty farewell; and as soon as he was mounted he went off at such a pace that she lost sight of him in an instant. Then Beauty began to cry, and wandered sadly back to her own room. But she soon found that she was very sleepy, and as she had nothing better to do she lay down and instantly fell asleep. And then she dreamed that she was walking by a brook bordered with trees, and lamenting her sad fate, when a young prince, handsomer than anyone she had ever seen, and with a voice that went straight to her heart, came and said to her, 'Ah, Beauty! you are not so unfortunate as you suppose. Here you will be rewarded for all you have suffered elsewhere. Your every wish shall be gratified. Only try to find me out, no matter how I may be disguised, as I love you dearly, and in making me happy you will find your own happiness. Be as true-hearted as you are beautiful, and we shall have nothing left to wish for.'

'What can I do, Prince, to make you happy?' said Beauty.

'Only be grateful,' he answered, 'and do not trust too much to your eyes. And, above all, do not desert me until you have saved me from my cruel misery.'

After this she thought she found herself in a room with a stately and beautiful lady, who said to her :

' Dear Beauty, try not to regret all you have left behind you, for you are destined to a better fate. Only do not let yourself be deceived by appearances.'

Beauty found her dreams so interesting that she was in no hurry to awake, but presently the clock roused her by calling her name softly twelve times, and then she got up and found her dressing-table set out with everything she could possibly want ; and when her toilet was finished she found dinner was waiting in the room

next to hers.   But dinner does not take very long when you are all by yourself, and very soon she sat down cosily in the corner of a sofa, and began to think about the charming Prince she had seen in her dream.

' He said I could make him happy,' said Beauty to herself.

' It seems, then, that this horrible Beast keeps him a prisoner. How can I set him free ?   I wonder why they both told me not to trust to appearances ? I don't understand it.   But, after all, it was only a dream, so why should I trouble myself about it ? I had better go and find something to do to amuse myself.'

So she got up and began to explore some of the many rooms of the palace.

The first she entered was lined with mirrors, and Beauty saw herself reflected on every side, and thought she had never seen such a charming room. Then a bracelet which was hanging from a chandelier caught her eye, and on taking it down she was greatly surprised to find that it held a portrait of her unknown admirer, just as she had seen him in her dream. With great delight she slipped the bracelet on her arm, and went on into a gallery of pictures, where she soon found a portrait of the same handsome Prince, as large as life, and so well painted that as she studied it he seemed to smile kindly at her. Tearing herself away from the portrait at last, she passed through into a room which contained every musical instrument under the sun, and here she amused herself for a long while in trying some of them, and singing until she was tired. The next room was a library, and she saw everything she had ever wanted to read, as well as everything she had read, and it seemed to her that a whole lifetime would not be enough even to read the names of the books, there were so many. By this time it was growing dusk, and wax candles in diamond and ruby candlesticks were beginning to light themselves in every room.

Beauty found her supper served just at the time she preferred to have it, but she did not see anyone or hear a sound, and, though her father had warned her that she would be alone, she began to find it rather dull.

But presently she heard the Beast coming, and wondered tremblingly if he meant to eat her up now.

However, as he did not seem at all ferocious, and only said gruffly:

'Good-evening, Beauty,' she answered cheerfully and managed to conceal her terror. Then the Beast asked her how she had been amusing herself, and she told him all the rooms she had seen.

Then he asked if she thought she could be happy in his palace; and Beauty answered that everything was so beautiful that she would be very hard to please if she could not be happy. And after about an hour's talk Beauty began to think that the Beast was not nearly so terrible as she had supposed at first. Then he got up to leave her, and said in his gruff voice:

'Do you love me, Beauty? Will you marry me?'

'Oh! what shall I say?' cried Beauty, for she was afraid to make the Beast angry by refusing.

' Say " yes " or " no " without fear,' he replied.

' Oh ! no, Beast,' said Beauty hastily.

' Since you will not, good-night, Beauty,' he said.   And she answered :

' Good-night, Beast,' very glad to find that her refusal had not provoked him.   And after he was gone she was very soon in bed and asleep, and dreaming of her unknown Prince.   She thought he came and said to her :

' Ah, Beauty ! why are you so unkind to me ?   I fear I am fated to be unhappy for many a long day still.'

And then her dreams changed, but the charming Prince figured in them all ; and when morning came her first thought was to look at the portrait and see if it was really like him, and she found that it certainly was.

This morning she decided to amuse herself in the garden, for the sun shone, and all the fountains were playing; but she was astonished to find that every place was familiar to her, and presently she came to the brook where the myrtle trees were growing where she had first met the Prince in her dream, and that made her think more than ever that he must be kept a prisoner by the Beast. When she was tired she went back to the palace, and found a new room full of materials for every kind of work—ribbons to make into bows, and silks to work into flowers.   Then there was an aviary full of rare birds, which were so tame that they flew to Beauty as soon as they saw her, and perched upon her shoulders and her head.

' Pretty little creatures,' she said, ' how I wish that your cage was nearer to my room, that I might often hear you sing ! '

So saying she opened a door, and found to her delight that it led into her own room, though she had thought it was quite the other side of the palace.

There were more birds in a room farther on, parrots and cockatoos that could talk, and they greeted Beauty by name ; indeed, she found them so entertaining that she took one or two back to her room, and they talked to her while she was at supper ; after which the Beast paid her his usual visit, and asked the same questions as before, and then with a gruff ' good-night ' he took his departure, and Beauty went to bed to dream of her mysterious Prince.   The days passed swiftly in different amusements, and after a while Beauty found out another strange thing in the palace, which often pleased her when she was tired of being alone.   There was one room which she had not noticed particularly; it was empty, except that under each of the windows stood a very comfortable chair; and the first time she had looked out of the window it

had seemed to her that a black curtain prevented her from seeing anything outside. But the second time she went into the room, happening to be tired, she sat down in one of the chairs, when

instantly the curtain was rolled aside, and a most amusing panto-
mime was acted before her ; there were dances, and coloured lights,
and music, and pretty dresses, and it was all so gay that Beauty was
in ecstacies. After that she tried the other seven windows in turn,
and there was some new and surprising entertainment to be seen
from each of them, so that Beauty never could feel lonely any
more. Every evening after supper the Beast came to see her, and
always before saying good-night asked her in his terrible voice :

'Beauty, will you marry me?'

And it seemed to Beauty, now she understood him better, that
when she said, ' No, Beast,' he went away quite sad. But her
happy dreams of the handsome young Prince soon made her forget
the poor Beast, and the only thing that at all disturbed her was to
be constantly told to distrust appearances, to let her heart guide her,
and not her eyes, and many other equally perplexing things, which,
consider as she would, she could not understand.

So everything went on for a long time, until at last, happy as
she was, Beauty began to long for the sight of her father and her
brothers and sisters; and one night, seeing her look very sad, the
Beast asked her what was the matter. Beauty had quite ceased to be
afraid of him. Now she knew that he was really gentle in spite of
his ferocious looks and his dreadful voice. So she answered that
she was longing to see her home once more. Upon hearing this
the Beast seemed sadly distressed, and cried miserably.

'Ah! Beauty, have you the heart to desert an unhappy Beast
like this? What more do you want to make you happy? Is it
because you hate me that you want to escape ? '

'No, dear Beast,' answered Beauty softly, 'I do not hate you,
and I should be very sorry never to see you any more, but I long
to see my father again. Only let me go for two months, and I
promise to come back to you and stay for the rest of my life.'

The Beast, who had been sighing dolefully while she spoke, now
replied :

'I cannot refuse you anything you ask, even though it should
cost me my life. Take the four boxes you will find in the room
next to your own, and fill them with everything you wish to take
with you. But remember your promise and come back when the
two months are over, or you may have cause to repent it, for if you
do not come in good time you will find your faithful Beast dead.
You will not need any chariot to bring you back. Only say good-
bye to all your brothers and sisters the night before you come away,

and when you have gone to bed turn this ring round upon your
finger and say firmly : " I wish to go back to my palace and see my
Beast again." Good-night, Beauty. Fear nothing, sleep peacefully,
and before long you shall see your father once more.'

As soon as Beauty was alone she hastened to fill the boxes with
all the rare and precious things she saw about her, and only when
she was tired of heaping things into them did they seem to be
full.

Then she went to bed, but could hardly sleep for joy. And
when at last she did begin to dream of her beloved Prince she was
grieved to see him stretched upon a grassy bank sad and weary,
and hardly like himself.

' What is the matter ? ' she cried.

But he looked at her reproachfully, and said :

How can you ask me, cruel one ? Are you not leaving me to
my death perhaps ? '

' Ah ! don't be so sorrowful,' cried Beauty ; ' I am only going to
assure my father that I am safe and happy. I have promised the
Beast faithfully that I will come back, and he would die of grief if
I did not keep my word ! '

' What would that matter to you ? ' said the Prince.   ' Surely
you would not care ? '

' Indeed I should be ungrateful if I did not care for such a kind
Beast,' cried Beauty indignantly.   ' I would die to save him from
pain.   I assure you it is not his fault that he is so ugly.'

Just then a strange sound woke her—someone was speaking
not very far away ; and opening her eyes she found herself in a room
she had never seen before, which was certainly not nearly so
splendid as those she was used to in the Beast's palace.   Where
could she be ?   She got up and dressed hastily, and then saw that
the boxes she had packed the night before were all in the room.
While she was wondering by what magic the Beast had transported
them and herself to this strange place she suddenly heard her
father's voice, and rushed out and greeted him joyfully.   Her
brothers and sisters were all astonished at her appearance, as they
had never expected to see her again, and there was no end to the
questions they asked her.   She had also much to hear about what
had happened to them while she was away, and of her father's
journey home.   But when they heard that she had only come to
be with them for a short time, and then must go back to the
Beast's palace for ever, they lamented loudly.   Then Beauty asked

her father what he thought could be the meaning of her strange
dreams, and why the Prince constantly begged her not to trust to
appearances. After much consideration he answered : 'You tell
me yourself that the Beast, frightful as he is, loves you dearly, and
deserves your love and gratitude for his gentleness and kindness ;
I think the Prince must mean you to understand that you ought to
reward him by doing as he wishes you to, in spite of his ugliness.'

Beauty could not help seeing that this seemed very probable ;
still, when she thought of her dear Prince who was so handsome, she
did not feel at all inclined to marry the Beast. At any rate, for
two months she need not decide, but could enjoy herself with her
sisters. But though they were rich now, and lived in a town again,
and had plenty of acquaintances, Beauty found that nothing amused
her very much ; and she often thought of the palace, where she
was so happy, especially as at home she never once dreamed of her
dear Prince, and she felt quite sad without him.

Then her sisters seemed to have got quite used to being without her, and even found her rather in the way, so she would not
have been sorry when the two months were over but for her
father and brothers, who begged her to stay, and seemed so
grieved at the thought of her departure that she had not the
courage to say good-bye to them. Every day when she got up
she meant to say it at night, and when night came she put it off
again, until at last she had a dismal dream which helped her to
make up her mind. She thought she was wandering in a lonely
path in the palace gardens, when she heard groans which seemed
to come from some bushes hiding the entrance of a cave, and running quickly to see what could be the matter, she found the Beast
stretched out upon his side, apparently dying. He reproached
her faintly with being the cause of his distress, and at the same
moment a stately lady appeared, and said very gravely :

'Ah ! Beauty, you are only just in time to save his life. See
what happens when people do not keep their promises ! If you
had delayed one day more, you would have found him dead.'

Beauty was so terrified by this dream that the next morning
she announced her intention of going back at once, and that very
night she said good-bye to her father and all her brothers and
sisters, and as soon as she was in bed she turned her ring round upon
her finger, and said firmly :

'I wish to go back to my palace and see my Beast again,' as she
had been told to do.

Then she fell asleep instantly, and only woke up to hear the clock saying, 'Beauty, Beauty,' twelve times in its musical voice, which told her at once that she was really in the palace once more. Everything was just as before, and her birds were so glad to see her! but Beauty thought she had never known such a long day, for she was so anxious to see the Beast again that she felt as if supper-time would never come.

But when it did come and no Beast appeared she was really frightened; so, after listening and waiting for a long time, she ran down into the garden to search for him. Up and down the paths and avenues ran poor Beauty, calling him in vain, for no one

answered, and not a trace of him could she find; until at last, quite tired, she stopped for a minute's rest, and saw that she was standing opposite the shady path she had seen in her dream. She rushed down it, and, sure enough, there was the cave, and in it lay the Beast—asleep, as Beauty thought. Quite glad to have found him, she ran up and stroked his head, but to her horror he did not move or open his eyes.

'Oh! he is dead; and it is all my fault,' said Beauty, crying bitterly.

But then, looking at him again, she fancied he still breathed, and, hastily fetching some water from the nearest fountain, she sprinkled it over his face, and to her great delight he began to revive.

'Oh! Beast, how you frightened me!' she cried. 'I never knew how much I loved you until just now, when I feared I was too late to save your life.'

'Can you really love such an ugly creature as I am?' said the Beast faintly. 'Ah! Beauty, you only came just in time. I was dying because I thought you had forgotten your promise. But go back now and rest, I shall see you again by-and-by.'

Beauty, who had half expected that he would be angry with her, was reassured by his gentle voice, and went back to the palace, where supper was awaiting her; and afterwards the Beast came in as usual, and talked about the time she had spent with her father, asking if she had enjoyed herself, and if they had all been very glad to see her.

Beauty answered politely, and quite enjoyed telling him all that had happened to her. And when at last the time came for him to go, and he asked, as he had so often asked before:

'Beauty, will you marry me?' she answered softly:

'Yes, dear Beast.'

As she spoke a blaze of light sprang up before the windows of the palace; fireworks crackled and guns banged, and across the avenue of orange trees, in letters all made of fire-flies, was written: 'Long live the Prince and his Bride.'

Turning to ask the Beast what it could all mean, Beauty found that he had disappeared, and in his place stood her long-loved Prince! At the same moment the wheels of a chariot were heard upon the terrace, and two ladies entered the room. One of them Beauty recognised as the stately lady she had seen in her dreams; the other was also so grand and queenly that Beauty hardly knew which to greet first.

But the one she already knew said to her companion:

'Well, Queen, this is Beauty, who has had the courage to rescue your son from the terrible enchantment. They love one another, and only your consent to their marriage is wanting to make them perfectly happy.'

'I consent with all my heart,' cried the Queen. 'How can I ever thank you enough, charming girl, for having restored my dear son to his natural form?'

And then she tenderly embraced Beauty and the Prince, who had meanwhile been greeting the Fairy and receiving her congratulations.

'Now,' said the Fairy to Beauty, 'I suppose you would like me to send for all your brothers and sisters to dance at your wedding ? '

And so she did, and the marriage was celebrated the very next day with the utmost splendour, and Beauty and the Prince lived happily ever after.[1]

[1] *La Belle et la Bête.* Par Madame de Villeneuve.

THE BRAVE LITTLE TAILOR

ONE summer's day a little tailor sat on his table by the window in the best of spirits, and sewed for dear life. As he was sitting thus a peasant woman came down the street, calling out: 'Good jam to sell, good jam to sell.' This sounded sweetly in the tailor's ears; he put his frail little head out of the window, and shouted: 'Up here, my good woman, and you'll find a willing customer.' The woman climbed up the three flights of stairs with her heavy basket to the tailor's room, and he made her spread out all the pots in a row before him. He examined them all, lifted them up and smelt them, and said at last : 'This jam seems good, weigh me four ounces of it, my good woman; and even if it's a quarter of a pound I won't stick at it.' The woman, who had hoped to find a good market, gave him what he wanted, but went away grumbling wrathfully. 'Now heaven shall bless this jam for my use,' cried the little tailor, 'and it shall sustain and strengthen me.' He fetched some bread out of a cupboard, cut a round off the loaf, and spread the jam on it. 'That won't taste amiss,' he said; 'but I'll finish that waistcoat first before I take a bite.' He placed the bread beside him, went on sewing, and out of the lightness of his heart kept on making his stitches bigger and bigger. In the meantime the smell of the sweet jam rose to the ceiling, where heaps of flies were sitting, and attracted them to such an extent that they swarmed on to it in masses. 'Ha! who invited you?' said the tailor, and chased the unwelcome guests away. But the flies, who didn't understand English, refused to let themselves be warned off, and returned again in even greater numbers. At last the little tailor, losing all patience, reached out of his chimney corner for a duster, and exclaiming : 'Wait, and I'll give it to you,' he beat them mercilessly with it. When he left off he counted the slain, and no fewer than seven lay dead before him with outstretched legs. 'What a desperate fellow I am!' said he, and was filled with admiration at his

own courage. 'The whole town must know about this;' and in great
haste the little tailor cut out a girdle, hemmed it, and embroidered
on it in big letters, 'Seven at a blow.' 'What did I say, the town?
no, the whole world shall hear of it,' he said; and his heart beat
for joy as a lamb wags his tail.

The tailor strapped the girdle round his waist and set out into
the wide world, for he considered his workroom too small a field
for his prowess. Before he set forth he looked round about him,
to see if there was anything in the house he could take with him
on his journey; but he found nothing except an old cheese, which
he took possession of. In front of the house he observed a bird

that had been caught in some bushes, and this he put into his wallet beside the cheese. Then he went on his way merrily, and being light and agile he never felt tired. His way led up a hill, on the top of which sat a powerful giant, who was calmly surveying the landscape. The little tailor went up to him, and greeting him cheerfully said : ' Good-day, friend ; there you sit at your ease viewing the whole wide world. I'm just on my way there. What do you say to accompanying me ? ' The giant looked contemptuously at the tailor, and said : ' What a poor wretched little creature you are ! ' ' That's a good joke,' answered the little tailor, and unbuttoning his coat he showed the giant the girdle. ' There now, you can read what sort of a fellow I am.' The giant read : ' Seven at a blow ; ' and thinking they were human beings the tailor had slain, he conceived a certain respect for the little man. But first he thought he'd test him, so taking up a stone in his hand, he squeezed it till some drops of water ran out. ' Ncw you do the same,' said the giant, ' if you really wish to be thought strong.' ' Is that all ? ' said the little tailor ; ' that's child's play to me,' so he dived into his wallet, brought out the cheese, and pressed it till the whey ran out. ' My squeeze was in sooth better than yours,' said he. The giant didn't know what to say, for he couldn't have believed it of the little fellow. To prove him again, the giant lifted a stone and threw it so high that the eye could hardly follow it. ' Now, my little pigmy, let me see you do that.' ' Well thrown,' said the tailor ; ' but, after all, your stone fell to the ground ; I'll throw one that won't come down at all.' He dived into his wallet again, and grasping the bird in his hand, he threw it up into the air. The bird, enchanted to be free, soared up into the sky, and flew away never to return. ' Well, what do you think of that little piece of business, friend ? ' asked the tailor. ' You can certainly throw,' said the giant ; ' but now let's see if you can carry a proper weight.' With these words he led the tailor to a huge oak tree which had been felled to the ground, and said : ' If you are strong enough, help me to carry the tree out of the wood.' ' Most certainly,' said the little tailor : ' just you take the trunk on your shoulder ; I'll bear the top and branches, which is certainly the heaviest part.' The giant laid the trunk on his shoulder, but the tailor sat at his ease among the branches ; and the giant, who couldn't see what was going on behind him, had to carry the whole tree, and the little tailor into the bargain. There he sat behind in the best of spirits, lustily whistling a tune, as if carrying the tree were mcre sport.

The giant, after dragging the heavy weight for some time, could get on no further, and shouted out : ' Hi ! I must let the tree fall.' The tailor sprang nimbly down, seized the tree with both hands as if he had carried it the whole way, and said to the giant : ' Fancy a big lout like you not being able to carry a tree ! '

They continued to go on their way together, and as they passed by a cherry tree the giant grasped the top of it, where the ripest fruit hung, gave the branches into the tailor's hand, and bade him eat. But the little tailor was far too weak to hold the tree down, and when the giant let go the tree swung back into the air, bearing the little tailor with it. When he had fallen to the ground again without hurting himself, the giant said : ' What ! do you mean to tell me you haven't the strength to hold down a feeble twig ? ' ' It wasn't strength that was wanting,' replied the tailor; ' do you think that would have been anything for a man who has killed seven at a blow ? I jumped over the tree because the hunstmen are shooting among the branches near us. Do you do the like if you dare.' The giant made an attempt, but couldn't get over the tree, and stuck fast in the branches, so that here too the little tailor had the better of him.

' Well, you're a fine fellow, after all,' said the giant; ' come and spend the night with us in our cave.' The little tailor willingly consented to do this, and following his friend they went on till they reached a cave where several other giants were sitting round a fire, each holding a roast sheep in his hand, of which he was eating. The little tailor looked about him, and thought : ' Yes, there's certainly more room to turn round in here than in my workshop.' The giant showed him a bed, and bade him lie down and have a good sleep. But the bed was too big for the little tailor, so he didn't get into it, but crept away into the corner. At midnight, when the giant thought the little tailor was fast asleep, he rose up, and taking his big iron walking-stick, he broke the bed in two with a blow, and thought he had made an end of the little grasshopper. At early dawn the giants went off to the wood, and quite forgot about the little tailor, till all of a sudden they met him trudging along in the most cheerful manner. The giants were terrified at the apparition, and, fearful lest he should slay them, they all took to their heels as fast as they could.

The little tailor continued to follow his nose, and after he had wandered about for a long time he came to the courtyard of a royal palace, and feeling tired he lay down on the grass and fell asleep.

While he lay there the people came, and looking him all over read on his girdle: 'Seven at a blow.' 'Oh!' they said, 'what can this great hero of a hundred fights want in our peaceful land? He must indeed be a mighty man of valour.' They went and told the King about him, and said what a weighty and useful man he'd be in time of war, and that it would be well to secure him at any price. This counsel pleased the King, and he sent one of his courtiers down to the little tailor, to offer him, when he awoke, a commission in their army. The messenger remained standing by the sleeper, and waited till he stretched his limbs and opened his eyes, when he tendered his proposal. 'That's the very thing I came here for,' he answered; 'I am quite ready to enter the King's service.' So he was received with all honour, and given a special house of his own to live in.

But the other officers resented the success of the little tailor, and wished him a thousand miles away. 'What's to come of it all?' they asked each other; 'if we quarrel with him, he'll let out at us, and at every blow seven will fall. There'll soon be an end of us.' So they resolved to go in a body to the King, and all to send in their papers. 'We are not made,' they said, 'to hold out against a man who kills seven at a blow.' The King was grieved at the thought of losing all his faithful servants for the sake of one man, and he wished heartily that he had never set eyes on him, or that he could get rid of him. But he didn't dare to send him away, for he feared he might kill him along with his people, and place himself on the throne. He pondered long and deeply over the matter, and finally came to a conclusion. He sent to the tailor and told him that, seeing what a great and warlike hero he was, he was about to make him an offer. In a certain wood of his kingdom there dwelt two giants who did much harm; by the way they robbed, murdered, burnt, and plundered everything about them; 'no one could approach them without endangering his life. But if he could overcome and kill these two giants he should have his only daughter for a wife, and half his kingdom into the bargain; he might have a hundred horsemen, too, to back him up.' 'That's the very thing for a man like me,' thought the little tailor; 'one doesn't get the offer of a beautiful princess and half a kingdom every day.' 'Done with you,' he answered; 'I'll soon put an end to the giants. But I haven't the smallest need of your hundred horsemen; a fellow who can slay seven men at a blow need not be afraid of two.'

The little tailor set out, and the hundred horsemen followed

him. When he came to the outskirts of the wood he said to his
followers : ' You wait here, I'll manage the giants by myself ; ' and he
went on into the wood, casting his sharp little eyes right and left
about him. After a while he spied the two giants lying asleep
under a tree, and snoring till the very boughs bent with the breeze.
The little tailor lost no time in filling his wallet with stones, and
then climbed up the tree under which they lay. When he got to

about the middle of it he slipped along a branch till he sat just
above the sleepers, when he threw down one stone after the other
on the nearest giant. The giant felt nothing for a long time, but
at last he woke up, and pinching his companion said : ' What did
you strike me for ? ' ' I didn't strike you,' said the other ' you
must be dreaming.' They both lay down to sleep again, and the
tailor threw down a stone on the second giant, who sprang up and
cried : ' What's that for ? Why did you throw something at me ? '

'I didn't throw anything,' growled the first one. They wrangled on for a time, till, as both were tired, they made up the matter and fell asleep again. The little tailor began his game once more, and flung the largest stone he could find in his wallet with all his force, and hit the first giant on the chest. 'This is too much of a good thing!' he yelled, and springing up like a madman, he knocked his companion against the tree till he trembled. He gave, however, as good as he got, and they became so enraged that they tore up trees and beat each other with them, till they both fell dead at once on the ground. Then the little tailor jumped down. 'It's a mercy,' he said, 'that they didn't root up the tree on which I was perched, or I should have had to jump like a squirrel on to another, which, nimble though I am, would have been no easy job.' He drew his sword and gave each of the giants a very fine thrust or two on the breast, and then went to the horsemen and said : 'The deed is done, I've put an end to the two of them ; but I assure you it has been no easy matter, for they even tore up trees in their struggle to defend themselves ; but all that's of no use against one who slays seven men at a blow.' 'Weren't you wounded ? ' asked the horsemen. 'No fear,' answered the tailor ; ' they haven't touched a hair of my head.' But the horsemen wouldn't believe him till they rode into the wood and found the giants weltering in their blood, and the trees lying around, torn up by the roots.

The little tailor now demanded the promised reward from the King, but he repented his promise, and pondered once more how he could rid himself of the hero. 'Before you obtain the hand of my daughter and half my kingdom,' he said to him, ' you must do another deed of valour. A unicorn is running about loose in the wood, and doing much mischief; you must first catch it.' ' I'm even less afraid of one unicorn than of two giants ; seven at a blow, that's my motto.' He took a piece of cord and an axe with him, went out to the wood, and again told the men who had been sent with him to remain outside. He hadn't to search long, for the unicorn soon passed by, and, on perceiving the tailor, dashed straight at him as though it were going to spike him on the spot. 'Gently, gently,' said he, 'not so fast, my friend ;' and standing still he waited till the beast was quite near, when he sprang lightly behind a tree ; the unicorn ran with all its force against the tree, and rammed its horn so firmly into the trunk that it had no strength left to pull it out again, and was thus successfully captured. ' Now I've caught my bird,' said the tailor, and he came out from behind the tree, placed the cord round its neck first, then struck the horn out of the tree with his axe, and when everything was in order led the beast before the King.

Still the King didn't want to give him the promised reward, and made a third demand. The tailor was to catch a wild boar for him that did a great deal of harm in the wood; and he might have the huntsmen to help him. 'Willingly,' said the tailor; 'that's mere child's play.' But he didn't take the huntsmen into the wood with him, and they were well enough pleased to remain behind, for the wild boar had often received them in a manner which did not make them desire its further acquaintance. As soon as the boar perceived the tailor it ran at him with foaming mouth and gleaming teeth, and tried to knock him down; but our alert little friend ran into a chapel that stood near, and got out of the window again with a jump. The boar pursued him into the church, but the tailor skipped round to the door, and closed it securely. So the raging beast was caught, for it was far too heavy and unwieldy to spring out of the window. The little tailor summoned the huntsmen together, that they might see the prisoner with their own eyes. Then the hero betook himself to the King, who was obliged now, whether he liked it or not, to keep his promise, and hand him over his daughter and half his kingdom. Had he known that no hero-warrior, but only a little tailor stood before him, it would have gone even more to his heart. So the wedding was celebrated with much splendour and little joy, and the tailor became a king.

After a time the Queen heard her husband saying one night in his sleep: 'My lad, make that waistcoat and patch these trousers, or I'll box your ears.' Thus she learnt in what rank the young gentleman had been born, and next day she poured forth her woes to her father, and begged him to help her to get rid of a husband who was nothing more nor less than a tailor. The King comforted her, and said: 'Leave your bedroom door open to-night, my servants shall stand outside, and when your husband is fast asleep they shall enter, bind him fast, and carry him on to a ship, which shall sail away out into the wide ocean.' The Queen was well satisfied with the idea, but the armour-bearer, who had overheard everything, being much attached to his young master, went straight to him and revealed the whole plot. 'I'll soon put a stop to the business,' said the tailor. That night he and his wife went to bed at the usual time; and when she thought he had fallen asleep she got up, opened the door, and then lay down again. The little tailor, who had only pretended to be asleep, began to call out in a clear voice : 'My lad, make that waistcoat and patch those trousers, or I'll box your ears. I have killed seven at a blow, slain two giants, led a unicorn captive, and caught a wild boar, then why should I be afraid of those men standing outside my door?' The men, when they heard the tailor saying these words, were so terrified that they fled as if pursued by a wild army, and didn't dare go near him again. So the little tailor was and remained a king all the days of his life.

THE WHITE CAT

ONCE upon a time there was a king who had three sons, who
were all so clever and brave that he began to be afraid that
they would want to reign over the kingdom before he was dead.
Now the King, though he felt that he was growing old, did not at
all wish to give up the government of his kingdom while he could
still manage it very well, so he thought the best way to live in
peace would be to divert the minds of his sons by promises which
he could always get out of when the time came for keeping them.

So he sent for them all, and, after speaking to them kindly, he
added :

' You will quite agree with me, my dear children, that my great
age makes it impossible for me to look after my affairs of state as carefully as I once did. I begin to fear that this may affect the welfare
of my subjects, therefore I wish that one of you should succeed to
my crown ; but in return for such a gift as this it is only right that
you should do something for me. Now, as I think of retiring into
the country, it seems to me that a pretty, lively, faithful little dog
would be very good company for me ; so, without any regard for
your ages, I promise that the one who brings me the most beautiful
little dog shall succeed me at once.'

The three Princes were greatly surprised by their father's sudden
fancy for a little dog, but as it gave the two younger ones a chance they
would not otherwise have had of being king, and as the eldest was
too polite to make any objection, they accepted the commission with
pleasure. They bade farewell to the King, who gave them presents
of silver and precious stones, and appointed to meet them at the
same hour, in the same place, after a year had passed, to see the
little dogs they had brought for him.

Then they went together to a castle which was about a league
from the city, accompanied by all their particular friends, to whom
they gave a grand banquet, and the three brothers promised to be

friends always, to share whatever good fortune befell them, and not
to be parted by any envy or jealousy ; and so they set out, agreeing
to meet at the same castle at the appointed time, to present themselves before the King together. Each one took a different road,
and the two eldest met with many adventures; but it is about the
youngest that you are going to hear. He was young, and gay, and
handsome, and knew everything that a prince ought to know ; and
as for his courage, there was simply no end to it.

Hardly a day passed without his buying several dogs—big and

little, greyhounds, mastiffs, spaniels, and lapdogs. As soon as he
had bought a pretty one he was sure to see a still prettier, and then
he had to get rid of all the others and buy that one, as, being alone, he
found it impossible to take thirty or forty thousand dogs about with
him. He journeyed from day to day, not knowing where he was
going, until at last, just at nightfall, he reached a great, gloomy forest.
He did not know his way, and, to make matters worse, it began to
thunder, and the rain poured down. He took the first path he could
find, and after walking for a long time he fancied he saw a faint light,

and began to hope that he was coming to some cottage where he might find shelter for the night. At length, guided by the light, he reached the door of the most splendid castle he could have imagined. This door was of gold covered with carbuncles, and it was the pure red light which shone from them that had shown him the way through the forest. The walls were of the finest porcelain in all the most delicate colours, and the Prince saw that all the stories he had ever read were pictured upon them ; but as he was quite terribly wet, and the rain still fell in torrents, he could not stay to look about any more, but came back to the golden door. There he saw a deer's foot hanging by a chain of diamonds, and he began to wonder who could live in this magnificent castle.

They must feel very secure against robbers,' he said to himself. ' What is to hinder anyone from cutting off that chain and digging out those carbuncles, and making himself rich for life ? '

He pulled the deer's foot, and immediately a silver bell sounded and the door flew open, but the Prince could see nothing but numbers of hands in the air, each holding a torch. He was so much surprised that he stood quite still, until he felt himself pushed forward by other hands, so that, though he was somewhat uneasy, he could not help going on. With his hand on his sword, to be prepared for whatever might happen, he entered a hall paved with lapis-lazuli, while two lovely voices sang :

> The hands you see floating above
> , Will swiftly your bidding obey ;
> If your heart dreads not conquering Love,
> In this place you may fearlessly stay.

The Prince could not believe that any danger threatened him when he was welcomed in this way, so, guided by the mysterious hands, he went towards a door of coral, which opened of its own accord, and he found himself in a vast hall of mother-of-pearl, out of which opened a number of other rooms, glittering with thousands of lights, and full of such beautiful pictures and precious things that the Prince felt quite bewildered. After passing through sixty rooms the hands that conducted him stopped, and the Prince saw a most comfortable-looking arm-chair drawn up close to the chimney-corner ; at the same moment the fire lighted itself, and the pretty, soft, clever hands took off the Prince's wet, muddy clothes, and presented him with fresh ones made of the richest stuffs, all embroidered with gold and emeralds. He could not help admiring everything he saw, and the deft way in which the hands waited on him, though they sometimes appeared so suddenly that they made him jump.

When he was quite ready—and I can assure you that he looked very different from the wet and weary Prince who had stood outside in the rain, and pulled the deer's foot—the hands led him to a splendid room, upon the walls of which were painted the histories of Puss in Boots and a number of other famous cats. The table was laid for supper with two golden plates, and golden spoons and forks, and the sideboard was covered with dishes and glasses of crystal set with precious stones. The Prince was wondering who the second place could be for, when suddenly in came about a dozen cats carrying guitars and rolls of music, who took their places at one end of the room, and under the direction of a cat who beat time with a roll of paper began to mew in every imaginable key, and to draw their claws across the strings of the guitars, making the strangest kind of music that could be heard. The Prince hastily stopped up his ears, but even then the sight of these comical musicians sent him into fits of laughter.

'What funny thing shall I see next?' he said to himself, and instantly the door opened, and in came a tiny figure covered by a long black veil. It was conducted by two cats wearing black mantles and carrying swords, and a large party of cats followed, who brought in cages full of rats and mice.

The Prince was so much astonished that he thought he must be dreaming, but the little figure came up to him and threw back its veil, and he saw that it was the loveliest little white cat it is possible to imagine. She looked very young and very sad, and in a sweet little voice that went straight to his heart she said to the Prince:

'King's son, you are welcome; the Queen of the Cats is glad to see you.'

'Lady Cat,' replied the Prince, 'I thank you for receiving me so kindly, but surely you are no ordinary pussy-cat? Indeed, the way you speak and the magnificence of your castle prove it plainly.'

'King's son,' said the White Cat, 'I beg you to spare me these compliments, for I am not used to them. But now,' she added, 'let supper be served, and let the musicians be silent, as the Prince does not understand what they are saying.'

So the mysterious hands began to bring in the supper, and

first they put on the table two dishes, one containing stewed
pigeons and the other a fricassée of fat mice. The sight of the
latter made the Prince feel as if he could not enjoy his supper
at all; but the White Cat seeing this assured him that the dishes
intended for him were prepared in a separate kitchen, and he might
be quite certain that they contained neither rats nor mice; and the
Prince felt so sure that she would not deceive him that he had no
more hesitation in beginning. Presently he noticed that on the
little paw that was next him the White Cat wore a bracelet con-

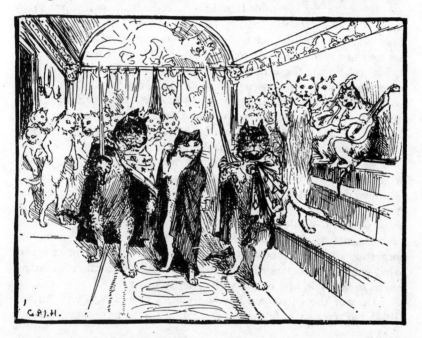

taining a portrait, and he begged to be allowed to look at it. To his
great surprise he found it represented an extremely handsome young
man, who was so like himself that it might have been his own portrait! The White Cat sighed as he looked at it, and seemed sadder
than ever, and the Prince dared not ask any questions for fear of
displeasing her; so he began to talk about other things, and found
that she was interested in all the subjects he cared for himself, and
seemed to know quite well what was going on in the world. After
supper they went into another room, which was fitted up as a
theatre, and the cats acted and danced for their amusement, and

then the White Cat said good-night to him, and the hands conducted
him into a room he had not seen before, hung with tapestry worked
with butterflies' wings of every colour; there were mirrors that
reached from the ceiling to the floor, and a little white bed with
curtains of gauze tied up with ribbons. The Prince went to bed in
silence, as he did not quite know how to begin a conversation with
the hands that waited on him, and in the morning he was awakened
by a noise and confusion outside his window, and the hands came
and quickly dressed him in hunting costume. When he looked out
all the cats were assembled in the courtyard, some leading greyhounds, some blowing horns, for the White Cat was going out
hunting. The hands led a wooden horse up to the Prince, and
seemed to expect him to mount it, at which he was very indignant;
but it was no use for him to object, for he speedily found himself
upon its back, and it pranced gaily off with him.

The White Cat herself was riding a monkey, which climbed even
up to the eagles' nests when she had a fancy for the young eaglets.
Never was there a pleasanter hunting party, and when they returned
to the castle the Prince and the White Cat supped together as before, but when they had finished she offered him a crystal goblet,
which must have contained a magic draught, for, as soon as he had
swallowed its contents, he forgot everything, even the little dog that
he was seeking for the King, and only thought how happy he was
to be with the White Cat! And so the days passed, in every kind
of amusement, until the year was nearly gone. The Prince had
forgotten all about meeting his brothers: he did not even know
what country he belonged to; but the White Cat knew when he
ought to go back, and one day she said to him:

'Do you know that you have only three days left to look for the
little dog for your father, and your brothers have found lovely
ones?'

Then the Prince suddenly recovered his memory, and cried:

'What can have made me forget such an important thing? my
whole fortune depends upon it; and even if I could in such a short
time find a dog pretty enough to gain me a kingdom, where should
I find a horse who could carry me all that way in three days?'
And he began to be very vexed. But the White Cat said to him:
'King's son, do not trouble yourself; I am your friend, and will make
everything easy for you. You can still stay here for a day, as the
good wooden horse can take you to your country in twelve hours.'

'I thank you, beautiful Cat,' said the Prince; 'but what good will it do me to get back if I have not a dog to take to my father ? '

' See here,' answered the White Cat, holding up an acorn ; ' there is a prettier one in this than in the Dog-star ! '

' Oh ! White Cat dear,' said the Prince, ' how unkind you are to laugh at me now ! '

' Only listen,' she said, holding the acorn to his ear.

And inside it he distinctly heard a tiny voice say : ' Bow-wow ! '

The Prince was delighted, for a dog that can be shut up in an acorn must be very small indeed. He wanted to take it out and look at it, but the White Cat said it would be better not to open the acorn till he was before the King, in case the tiny dog should be cold on the journey. He thanked her a thousand times, and said good-bye quite sadly when the time came for him to set out.

' The days have passed so quickly with you,' he said, ' I only wish I could take you with me now.'

But the White Cat shook her head and sighed deeply in answer.

After all the Prince was the first to arrive at the castle where he had agreed to meet his brothers, but they came soon after, and stared in amazement when they saw the wooden horse in the court-yard jumping like a hunter.

The Prince met them joyfully, and they began to tell him all their adventures ; but he managed to hide from them what he had been doing, and even led them to think that a turnspit dog which he had with him was the one he was bringing for the King. Fond as they all were of one another, the two eldest could not help being glad to think that their dogs certainly had a better chance. The next morning they started in the same chariot. The elder brothers carried in baskets two such tiny, fragile dogs that they hardly dared to touch them. As for the turnspit, he ran after the chariot, and got so covered with mud that one could hardly see what he was like at all. When they reached the palace everyone crowded round to welcome them as they went into the King's great hall ; and when the two brothers presented their little dogs nobody could decide which was the prettier. They were already arranging between them-selves to share the kingdom equally, when the youngest stepped for-ward, drawing from his pocket the acorn the White Cat had given him. He opened it quickly, and there upon a white cushion they saw a dog so small that it could easily have been put through a ring. The Prince laid it upon the ground, and it got up at once and began to dance. The King did not know what to say, for it was impossible

that anything could be prettier than this little creature.   Nevertheless, as he was in no hurry to part with his crown, he told his sons
that, as they had been so successful the first time, he would ask them
to go once again, and seek by land and sea for a piece of muslin so fine
that it could be drawn through the eye of a needle.   The brothers
were not very willing to set out again, but the two eldest consented
because it gave them another chance, and they started as before.
The youngest again mounted the wooden horse, and rode back at
full speed to his beloved White Cat.   Every door of the castle

stood wide open, and every window and turret was illuminated, so
it looked more wonderful than before.   The hands hastened to meet
him, and led the wooden horse off to the stable, while he hurried
in to find the White Cat.   She was asleep in a little basket on a
white satin cushion, but she very soon started up when she heard
the Prince, and was over-joyed at seeing him once more.

   ' How could I hope that you would come back to me, King's son ? '
she said.   And then he stroked and petted her, and told her of his
successful journey, and how he had come back to ask her help, as

he believed that it was impossible to find what the King demanded. The White Cat looked serious, and said she must think what was to be done, but that, luckily, there were some cats in the castle who could spin very well, and if anybody could manage it they could, and she would set them the task herself.

And then the hands appeared carrying torches, and conducted the Prince and the White Cat to a long gallery which overlooked the river, from the windows of which they saw a magnificent display of fireworks of all sorts; after which they had supper, which the Prince liked even better than the fireworks, for it was very late, and he was hungry after his long ride. And so the days passed quickly as before; it was impossible to feel dull with the White Cat, and she had quite a talent for inventing new amusements— indeed, she was cleverer than a cat has any right to be. But when the Prince asked her how it was that she was so wise, she only said :

'King's son, do not ask me ; guess what you please. I may not tell you anything.'

The Prince was so happy that he did not trouble himself at all about the time, but presently the White Cat told him that the year was gone, and that he need not be at all anxious about the piece of muslin, as they had made it very well.

'This time,' she added, 'I can give you a suitable escort;' and on looking out into the courtyard the Prince saw a superb chariot of burnished gold, enamelled in flame colour with a thousand different devices. It was drawn by twelve snow-white horses, harnessed four abreast; their trappings were of flame-coloured velvet, embroidered with diamonds. A hundred chariots followed, each drawn by eight horses, and filled with officers in splendid uniforms, and a thousand guards surrounded the procession. 'Go !' said the White Cat, 'and when you appear before the King in such state he surely will not refuse you the crown which you deserve. Take this walnut, but do not open it until you are before him, then you will find in it the piece of stuff you asked me for.'

'Lovely Blanchette,' said the Prince, 'how can I thank you properly for all your kindness to me ? Only tell me that you wish it, and I will give up for ever all thought of being king, and will stay here with you always.'

'King's son,' she replied, 'it shows the goodness of your heart that you should care so much for a little white cat, who is good for nothing but to catch mice ; but you must not stay.'

So the Prince kissed her little paw and set out.   You can
imagine how fast he travelled when I tell you that they reached
the King's palace in just half the time it had taken the wooden
horse to get there.   This time the Prince was so late that he
did not try to meet his brothers at their castle, so they thought
he could not be coming, and were rather glad of it, and displayed their pieces of muslin to the King proudly, feeling sure of
success.   And indeed the stuff was very fine, and would go through
the eye of a very large needle; but the King, who was only too glad
to make a difficulty, sent for a particular needle, which was kept
among the Crown jewels, and had such a small eye that everybody

saw at once that it was impossible that the muslin should pass
through it.   The Princes were angry, and were beginning to complain that it was a trick, when suddenly the trumpets sounded
and the youngest Prince came in.   His father and brothers were
quite astonished at his magnificence, and after he had greeted them
he took the walnut from his pocket and opened it, fully expecting
to find the piece of muslin, but instead there was only a hazel-nut.
He cracked it, and there lay a cherry-stone.   Everybody was looking
on, and the King was chuckling to himself at the idea of finding the
piece of muslin in a nutshell.

However, the Prince cracked the cherry-stone, but everyone

laughed when he saw it contained only its own kernel. He opened that and found a grain of wheat, and in that was a millet seed. Then he himself began to wonder, and muttered softly:

'White Cat, White Cat, are you making fun of me?'

In an instant he felt a cat's claw give his hand quite a sharp scratch, and hoping that it was meant as an encouragement he opened the millet seed, and drew out of it a piece of muslin four hundred ells long, woven with the loveliest colours and most wonderful patterns; and when the needle was brought it went through the eye six times with the greatest ease! The King turned pale, and the other Princes stood silent and sorrowful, for nobody could deny that this was the most marvellous piece of muslin that was to be found in the world.

Presently the King turned to his sons, and said, with a deep sigh:

'Nothing could console me more in my old age than to realise your willingness to gratify my wishes. Go then once more, and whoever at the end of a year can bring back the loveliest princess shall be married to her, and shall, without further delay, receive the crown, for my successor must certainly be married.' The Prince considered that he had earned the kingdom fairly twice over, but still he was too well bred to argue about it, so he just went back to his gorgeous chariot, and, surrounded by his escort, returned to the White Cat faster than he had come. This time she was expecting him, the path was strewn with flowers, and a thousand braziers were burning scented woods which perfumed the air. Seated in a gallery from which she could see his arrival, the White Cat waited for him. 'Well, King's son,' she said, 'here you are once more, without a crown.' 'Madam,' said he, 'thanks to your generosity I have earned one twice over; but the fact is that my father is so loth to part with it that it would be no pleasure to me to take it.'

'Never mind,' she answered; 'it's just as well to try and deserve it. As you must take back a lovely princess with you next time I will be on the look-out for one for you. In the meantime let us enjoy ourselves; to-night I have ordered a battle between my cats and the river rats, on purpose to amuse you.' So this year slipped away even more pleasantly than the preceding ones. Sometimes the Prince could not help asking the White Cat how it was she could talk.

'Perhaps you are a fairy,' he said. 'Or has some enchanter changed you into a cat?'

But she only gave him answers that told him nothing. Days go by so quickly when one is very happy that it is certain the Prince would never have thought of its being time to go back, when one evening as they sat together the White Cat said to him that if he wanted to take a lovely princess home with him the next day he must be prepared to do as she told him.

'Take this sword,' she said, 'and cut off my head!'

'I!' cried the Prince, 'I cut off your head! Blanchette darling, how could I do it?'

'I entreat you to do as I tell you, King's son,' she replied.

The tears came into the Prince's eyes as he begged her to ask him anything but that—to set him any task she pleased as a proof of his devotion, but to spare him the grief of killing his dear Pussy. But nothing he could say altered her determination, and at last he drew his sword, and desperately, with a trembling hand, cut off the little white head. But imagine his astonishment and delight when suddenly a lovely princess stood before him, and, while he was still speechless with amazement, the door opened and a goodly company of knights and ladies entered, each carrying a cat's skin!

They hastened with every sign of joy to the Princess, kissing her hand and congratulating her on being once more restored to her natural shape. She received them graciously, but after a few minutes begged that they would leave her alone with the Prince, to whom she said :

'You see, Prince, that you were right in supposing me to be no ordinary cat. My father reigned over six kingdoms. The Queen, my mother, whom he loved dearly, had a passion for travelling and exploring, and when I was only a few weeks old she obtained his permission to visit a certain mountain of which she had heard many marvellous tales, and set out, taking with her a number of her attendants. On the way they had to pass near an old castle belonging to the fairies. Nobody had ever been into it, but it was reported to be full of the most wonderful things, and my mother remembered to have heard that the fairies had in their garden such fruits as were to be seen and tasted nowhere else. She began to wish to try them for herself, and turned her steps in the direction of the garden. On arriving at the door, which blazed with gold and jewels, she ordered her servants to knock loudly, but it was useless ; it seemed as if all the inhabitants of the castle must be asleep or dead. Now the more difficult it became to obtain the fruit, the more the Queen was determined that have it she would. So she ordered that they should bring ladders, and get over the wall into the garden ; but though the wall did not look very high, and they tied the ladders together to make them very long, it was quite impossible to get to the top.

'The Queen was in despair, but as night was coming on she ordered that they should encamp just where they were, and went to bed herself, feeling quite ill, she was so disappointed. In the middle of the night she was suddenly awakened, and saw to her surprise a tiny, ugly old woman seated by her bedside, who said to her :

' " I must say that we consider it somewhat troublesome of your Majesty to insist upon tasting our fruit ; but, to save you any annoyance, my sisters and I will consent to give you as much as you can carry away, on one condition—that is, that you shall give us your little daughter to bring up as our own."

' " Ah ! my dear madam," cried the Queen, " is there nothing else that you will take for the fruit ? I will give you my kingdoms willingly."

' " No," replied the old fairy, " we will have nothing but your little daughter. She shall be as happy as the day is long, and we will give her everything that is worth having in fairy-land, but you must not see her again until she is married.''

' " Though it is a hard condition,'' said the Queen, " I consent, for I shall certainly die if I do not taste the fruit, and so I should lose my little daughter either way.''

' So the old fairy led her into the castle, and, though it was still the middle of the night, the Queen could see plainly that it was far more beautiful than she had been told, ' which you can easily believe, Prince,' said the White Cat, ' when I tell you that it was this castle that we are now in. " Will you gather the fruit yourself, Queen ? " said the old fairy, " or shall I call it to come to you ? "

' " I beg you to let me see it come when it is called,'' cried the Queen; " that will be something quite new." The old fairy whistled twice, then she cried :

' " Apricots, peaches, nectarines, cherries, plums, pears, melons, grapes, apples, oranges, lemons, gooseberries, strawberries, raspberries, come ! "

' And in an instant they came tumbling in, one over another, and yet they were neither dusty nor spoilt, and the Queen found them quite as good as she had fancied them. You see they grew upon fairy trees.

' The old fairy gave her golden baskets in which to take the fruit away, and it was as much as four hundred mules could carry. Then she reminded the Queen of her agreement, and led her back to the camp, and next morning she went back to her kingdom ; but before she had gone very far she began to repent of her bargain, and when the King came out to meet her she looked so sad that he guessed that something had happened, and asked what was the matter. At first the Queen was afraid to tell him, but when, as soon as they reached the palace, five frightful little dwarfs were sent by the fairies to fetch me, she was obliged to confess what she had promised. The King was very angry, and had the Queen and myself shut up in a great tower and safely guarded, and drove the little dwarfs out of his kingdom ; but the fairies sent a great dragon who ate up all the people he met, and whose breath burnt up everything as he passed through the country ; and at last, after trying in vain to rid himself of the monster, the King, to save his subjects, was obliged to consent that I should be given up to the fairies. This time they came themselves to fetch me, in a chariot of pearl drawn by sea-horses, followed by the dragon, who was led with chains of

diamonds. My cradle was placed between the old fairies, who loaded
me with caresses, and away we whirled through the air to a tower
which they had built on purpose for me. There I grew up surrounded with everything that was beautiful and rare, and learning
everything that is ever taught to a princess, but without any companions but a parrot and a little dog, who could both talk ; and receiving every day a visit from one of the old fairies, who came
mounted upon the dragon. One day, however, as I sat at my
window I saw a handsome young prince, who seemed to have been
hunting in the forest which surrounded my prison, and who was

C.P.J.H.

standing and looking up at me. When he saw that I observed him
he saluted me with great deference. You can imagine that I was
delighted to have some one new to talk to, and in spite of the height
of my window our conversation was prolonged till night fell, then
my prince reluctantly bade me farewell. But after that he came
again many times, and at last I consented to marry him, but the
question was how I was to escape from my tower. The fairies
always supplied me with flax for my spinning, and by great dili-
gence I made enough cord for a ladder that would reach to the foot
of the tower; but, alas! just as my prince was helping me to

descend it, the crossest and ugliest of the old fairies flew in. Before
he had time to defend himself my unhappy lover was swallowed
up by the dragon. As for me, the fairies, furious at having their
plans defeated, for they intended me to marry the king of the
dwarfs and I utterly refused, changed me into a white cat. When
they brought me here I found all the lords and ladies of my father's
court awaiting me under the same enchantment, while the people
of lesser rank had been made invisible, all but their hands.

'As they laid me under the enchantment the fairies told me all
my history, for until then I had quite believed that I was their
child, and warned me that my only chance of regaining my natural
form was to win the love of a prince who resembled in every way
my unfortunate lover.'

'And you have won it, lovely Princess,' interrupted the Prince.

'You are indeed wonderfully like him,' resumed the Princess —
'in voice, in features, and everything; and if you really love me all
my troubles will be at an end.'

'And mine too,' cried the Prince, throwing himself at her feet,
'if you will consent to marry me.'

'I love you already better than anyone in the world,' she
said; 'but now it is time to go back to your father, and we shall hear
what he says about it.'

So the Prince gave her his hand and led her out, and they
mounted the chariot together; it was even more splendid than
before, and so was the whole company. Even the horses' shoes
were of rubies with diamond nails, and I suppose that is the first
time such a thing was ever seen.

As the Princess was as kind and clever as she was beautiful, you
may imagine what a delightful journey the Prince found it, for
everything the Princess said seemed to him quite charming.

When they came near the castle where the brothers were to
meet, the Princess got into a chair carried by four of the guards; it
was hewn out of one splendid crystal, and had silken curtains,
which she drew round her that she might not be seen.

The Prince saw his brothers walking upon the terrace, each
with a lovely princess, and they came to meet him, asking if he
had also found a wife. He said that he had found something much
rarer—a little white cat! At which they laughed very much, and
asked him if he was afraid of being eaten up by mice in the palace.
And then they set out together for the town. Each prince and
princess rode in a splendid carriage; the horses were decked with

THE PRINCE'S BRIDE.

plumes of feathers, and glittered with gold. After them came the youngest prince, and last of all the crystal chair, at which everybody looked with admiration and curiosity. When the courtiers saw them coming they hastened to tell the King.

'Are the ladies beautiful?' he asked anxiously.

And when they answered that nobody had ever before seen such lovely princesses he seemed quite annoyed.

However, he received them graciously, but found it impossible to choose between them.

Then turning to his youngest son he said:

'Have you come back alone, after all?'

'Your Majesty,' replied the Prince, 'will find in that crystal chair a little white cat, which has such soft paws, and mews so prettily, that I am sure you will be charmed with it.'

The King smiled, and went to draw back the curtains himself, but at a touch from the Princess the crystal shivered into a thousand splinters, and there she stood in all her beauty; her fair hair floated over her shoulders and was crowned with flowers, and her softly falling robe was of the purest white. She saluted the King gracefully, while a murmur of admiration rose from all around.

'Sire,' she said, 'I am not come to deprive you of the throne you fill so worthily. I have already six kingdoms, permit me to bestow one upon you, and upon each of your sons. I ask nothing but your friendship, and your consent to my marriage with your youngest son; we shall still have three kingdoms left for ourselves.'

The King and all the courtiers could not conceal their joy and astonishment, and the marriage of the three Princes was celebrated at once. The festivities lasted several months, and then each king and queen departed to their own kingdom and lived happily ever after.[1]

[1] *La Chatte blanche.* Par Madame la Comtesse d'Aulnoy.

HANSEL AND GRETTEL

ONCE upon a time there dwelt on the outskirts of a large forest a poor woodcutter with his wife and two children; the boy was called Hansel and the girl Grettel. He had always little enough to live on, and once, when there was a great famine in the land, he couldn't even provide them with daily bread. One night, as he was tossing about in bed, full of cares and worry, he sighed and said to his wife: 'What's to become of us? how are we to support our poor children, now that we have nothing more for ourselves?' 'I'll tell you what, husband,' answered the woman; 'early to-morrow morning we'll take the children out into the thickest part of the wood; there we shall light a fire for them and give them each a piece of bread; then we'll go on to our work and leave them alone. They won't be able to find their way home, and we shall thus be rid of them.' 'No, wife,' said her husband, 'that I won't do; how could I find it in my heart to leave my children alone in the wood? the wild beasts would soon come and tear them to pieces.' 'Oh! you fool,' said she, 'then we must all four die of hunger, and you may just as well go and plane the boards for our coffins;' and she left him no peace till he consented. 'But I can't help feeling sorry for the poor children,' added the husband.

The children, too, had not been able to sleep for hunger, and had heard what their step-mother had said to their father. Grettel wept bitterly and spoke to Hansel: 'Now it's all up with us.' 'No, no, Grettel,' said Hansel, 'don't fret yourself; I'll be able to find a way of escape, no fear.' And when the old people had fallen asleep he got up, slipped on his little coat, opened the back door and stole out. The moon was shining clearly, and the white pebbles which lay in front of the house glittered like bits of silver. Hansel bent down and filled his pocket with as many of them as he could cram in. Then he went back and said to Grettel: 'Be comforted, my dear little sister, and go to sleep: God will not desert us;' and he lay down in bed again.

At daybreak, even before the sun was up, the woman came and woke the two children : ' Get up, you lie-abeds, we're all going to the forest to fetch wood.'   She gave them each a bit of bread and spoke : 'There's something for your luncheon, but don't you eat it up before, for it's all you'll get.'   Grettel took the bread under her apron, as Hansel had the stones in his pocket.   Then they all set out together on the way to the forest.   After they had walked for a little, Hansel stood still and looked back at the house, and this manœuvre he repeated again and again.   His father observed him, and spake : ' Hansel, what are you gazing at there, and why do you always remain behind ?   Take care, and don't lose your footing.' ' Oh ! father,' said Hansel, ' I am looking back at my white kitten, which is sitting on the roof, waving me a farewell.'   The woman exclaimed : ' What a donkey you are ! that isn't your kitten, that's the morning sun shining on the chimney.'   But Hansel had not looked back at his kitten, but had always dropped one of the white pebbles out of his pocket on to the path.

When they had reached the middle of the forest the father said : ' Now, children, go and fetch a lot of wood, and I'll light a fire that you mayn't feel cold.'   Hansel and Grettel heaped up brushwood till they had made a pile nearly the size of a small hill.   The brushwood was set fire to, and when the flames leaped high the woman said : ' Now lie down at the fire, children, and rest yourselves : we are going into the forest to cut down wood ; when we've finished we'll come back and fetch you.'   Hansel and Grettel sat down beside the fire, and at midday ate their little bits of bread. They heard the strokes of the axe, so they thought their father was quite near.   But it was no axe they heard, but a bough he had tied on to a dead tree, and that was blown about by the wind. And when they had sat for a long time their eyes closed with fatigue, and they fell fast asleep.   When they awoke at last it was pitch-dark.   Grettel began to cry, and said : ' How are we ever to get out of the wood ? '   But Hansel comforted her.   ' Wait a bit,' he said, ' till the moon is up, and then we'll find our way sure enough.' And when the full moon had risen he took his sister by the hand and followed the pebbles, which shone like new threepenny bits, and showed them the path.   They walked all through the night, and at daybreak reached their father's house again.   They knocked at the door, and when the woman opened it she exclaimed : ' You naughty children, what a time you've slept in the wood ! we thought you were never going to come back.'   But the father rejoiced, for his conscience had reproached him for leaving his children behind by themselves.

Not long afterwards there was again great dearth in the land, and the children heard their mother address their father thus in bed one night : 'Everything is eaten up once more ; we have only half a loaf in the house, and when that's done it's all up with us. The children must be got rid of ; we'll lead them deeper into the wood this time, so that they won't be able to find their way out again. There is no other way of saving ourselves.' The man's heart smote him heavily, and he thought : 'Surely it would be better to share the last bite with one's children !' But his wife wouldn't listen to his arguments, and did nothing but scold and reproach him. If a man yields once he's done for, and so, because he had given in the first time, he was forced to do so the second.

But the children were awake, and had heard the conversation. When the old people were asleep Hansel got up, and wanted to go out and pick up pebbles again, as he had done the first time ; but the woman had barred the door, and Hansel couldn't get out. But he consoled his little sister, and said : 'Don't cry, Grettel, and sleep peacefully, for God is sure to help us.'

At early dawn the woman came and made the children get up. They received their bit of bread, but it was even smaller than the time before. On the way to the wood Hansel crumbled it in his pocket, and every few minutes he stood still and dropped a crumb on the ground. 'Hansel, what are you stopping and looking about you for ?' said the father. 'I'm looking back at my little pigeon, which is sitting on the roof waving me a farewell,' answered

Hansel. 'Fool!' said the wife; 'that isn't your pigeon, it's the morning sun glittering on the chimney.'   But Hansel gradually threw all
his crumbs on to the path.   The woman led the children still
deeper into the forest, farther than they had ever been in their lives
before.   Then a big fire was lit again, and the mother said : 'Just sit
down there, children, and if you're tired you can sleep a bit; we're
going into the forest to cut down wood, and in the evening when
we're finished we'll come back to fetch you.'   At midday Grettel
divided her bread with Hansel, for he had strewed his all along
their path.   Then they fell asleep, and evening passed away, but
nobody came to the poor children.   They didn't awake till it was
pitch-dark, and Hansel comforted his sister, saying: 'Only wait,
Grettel, till the moon rises, then we shall see the bread-crumbs I
scattered along the path; they will show us the way back to the
house.'   When the moon appeared they got up, but they found no
crumbs, for the thousands of birds that fly about the woods and
fields had picked them all up.   'Never mind,' said Hansel to Grettel;
'you'll see we'll still find a way out;' but all the same they did not.
They wandered about the whole night, and the next day, from
morning till evening, but they could not find a path out of the wood.
They were very hungry, too, for they had nothing to eat but a few
berries they found growing on the ground.   And at last they were
so tired that their legs refused to carry them any longer, so they
lay down under a tree and fell fast asleep.

On the third morning after they had left their father's house
they set about their wandering again, but only got deeper and
deeper into the wood, and now they felt that if help did not come
to them soon they must perish.   At midday they saw a beautiful little
snow-white bird sitting on a branch, which sang so sweetly that they
stopped still and listened to it.   And when its song was finished
it flapped its wings and flew on in front of them.   They followed it
and came to a little house, on the roof of which it perched; and
when they came quite near they saw that the cottage was made of
bread and roofed with cakes, while the window was made of transparent sugar.   'Now we'll set to,' said Hansel, 'and have a regular
blow-out.[1]   I'll eat a bit of the roof, and you, Grettel, can eat some
of the window, which you'll find a sweet morsel.'   Hansel stretched
up his hand and broke off a little bit of the roof to see what it was
like, and Grettel went to the casement and began to nibble at it.
Thereupon a shrill voice called out from the room inside:

[1] 'He was a vulgar boy !'

'Nibble, nibble, little mouse,
Who's nibbling my house?'

The children answered:

''Tis Heaven's own child,
The tempest wild,'

and went on eating, without putting themselves about. Hansel,
who thoroughly appreciated the roof, tore down a big bit of it, while
Grettel pushed out a whole round window-pane, and sat down the

better to enjoy it. Suddenly the door opened, and an ancient dame
leaning on a staff hobbled out. Hansel and Grettel were so terrified
that they let what they had in their hands fall. But the old woman
shook her head and said: 'Oh, ho! you dear children, who led you
here? Just come in and stay with me, no ill shall befall you.' She
took them both by the hand and led them into the house, and laid
a most sumptuous dinner before them—milk and sugared pancakes,
with apples and nuts. After they had finished, two beautiful little

white beds were prepared for them, and when Hansel and Grettel lay down in them they felt as if they had got into heaven.

The old woman had appeared to be most friendly, but she was really an old witch who had waylaid the children, and had only built the little bread house in order to lure them in. When anyone came into her power she killed, cooked, and ate him, and held a regular feast-day for the occasion. Now witches have red eyes, and cannot see far, but, like beasts, they have a keen sense of smell, and know when human beings pass by. When Hansel and Grettel fell into her hands she laughed maliciously, and said jeeringly : ' I've got them now ; they shan't escape me.' Early in the morning, before the children were awake, she rose up, and when she saw them both sleeping so peacefully, with their round rosy cheeks, she muttered to herself : ' That'll be a dainty bite.' Then she seized Hansel with her bony hand and carried him into a little stable, and barred the door on him ; he might scream as much as he liked, it did him no good. Then she went to Grettel, shook her till she awoke, and cried : ' Get up, you lazy-bones, fetch water and cook something for your brother. When he's fat I'll eat him up.' Grettel began to cry bitterly, ut it was of no use : she had to do what the wicked witch bade her.

So the best food was cooked for poor Hansel, but Grettel got nothing but crab-shells. Every morning the old woman hobbled out to the stable and cried : ' Hansel, put out your finger, that I may feel if you are getting fat.' But Hansel always stretched out a bone, and the old dame, whose eyes were dim, couldn't see it, and thinking always it was Hansel's finger, wondered why he fattened so slowly. When four weeks passed and Hansel still remained thin, she lost patience and determined to wait no longer. ' Hi ! Grettel,' she called to the girl, ' be quick and get some water. Hansel may be fat or thin, I'm going to kill him to-morrow and cook him.' Oh ! how the poor little sister sobbed as she carried the water, and how the tears rolled down her cheeks ! ' Kind heaven help us now ! ' she cried ; ' if only the wild beasts in the wood had eaten us, then at least we should have died together.' ' Just hold your peace,' said the old hag ; ' it won't help you.'

Early in the morning Grettel had to go out and hang up the kettle full of water, and light the fire. ' First we'll bake,' said the old dame ; ' I've heated the oven already and kneaded the dough ' She pushed Grettel out to the oven, from which fiery flames were already issuing. ' Creep in,' said the witch, ' and see if it's properly heated, so that we can shove in the bread.' For when she had got Grettel in she meant to close the oven and let the girl bake, that she might eat her up too. But Grettel perceived her intention, and spoke: 'I don't know how I'm to do it; how do I get in?' 'You silly goose!' said the hag, 'the opening is big enough; see, I could get in myself;' and she crawled towards it, and poked her head into the oven. Then Grettel gave her a shove that sent her right in, shut the iron door, and drew the bolt. Gracious! how she yelled! it was quite horrible; but Grettel fled, and the wretched old woman was left to perish miserably.

Grettel flew straight to Hansel, opened the little stable-door, and cried: 'Hansel, we are free; the old witch is dead.' Then Hansel sprang like a bird out of a cage when the door is opened. How they rejoiced, and fell on each other's necks, and jumped for joy, and kissed one another! And as they had no longer any cause for fear, they went into the old hag's house, and there they found, in every corner of the room, boxes with pearls and precious stones. 'These are even better than pebbles,' said Hansel, and crammed his pockets full of them; and Grettel said: 'I too will bring something home;' and she filled her apron full. 'But now,' said Hansel, 'let's go and get well away from the witches' wood.' When they had wandered about for some hours they came to a big lake. 'We can't get over,' said Hansel; 'I see no bridge of any sort or kind.' 'Yes, and there's no ferry-boat either,' answered Grettel; 'but look, there swims a white duck; if I ask her she'll help us over;' and she called out:

> 'Here are two children, mournful very,
> Seeing neither bridge nor ferry;
> Take us upon your white back,
> And row us over, quack, quack!'

The duck swam towards them, and Hansel got on her back and bade his little sister sit beside him. 'No,' answered Grettel, 'we should be too heavy a load for the duck: she shall carry us across separately.' The good bird did this, and when they were landed safely on the other side, and had gone on for a while, the wood became more and more familiar to them, and at length they saw their father's house in the distance. Then they set off to run, and bounding into the room fell on their father's neck. The man had not passed a happy hour since he left them in the wood, but the woman had died. Grettel shook out her apron so that the pearls and precious stones rolled about the room, and Hansel threw down one handful after the other out of his pocket. Thus all their troubles were ended, and they all lived happily ever afterwards.

My story is done. See! there runs a little mouse; anyone who catches it may make himself a large fur cap out of it.[1]

[1] Grimm.

SNOW-WHITE AND ROSE-RED

A POOR widow once lived in a little cottage with a garden in front of it, in which grew two rose trees, one bearing white roses and the other red. She had two children, who were just like the two rose trees; one was called Snow-white and the other Rose-red, and they were the sweetest and best children in the world, always diligent and always cheerful; but Snow-white was quieter and more gentle than Rose-red. Rose-red loved to run about the fields and meadows, and to pick flowers and catch butterflies; but Snow-white sat at home with her mother and helped her in the household, or read aloud to her when there was no work to do. The two children loved each other so dearly that they always walked about hand-in-hand whenever they went out together, and when Snow-white said: 'We will never desert each other,' Rose-red answered: 'No, not as long as we live;' and the mother added: 'Whatever one gets she shall share with the other.' They often roamed about in the woods gathering berries and no beast offered to hurt them; on the contrary, they came up to them in the most confiding manner; the little hare would eat a cabbage leaf from their hands, the deer grazed beside them, the stag would bound past them merrily, and the birds remained on the branches and sang to them with all their might. No evil ever befell them; if they tarried late in the wood and night overtook them, they lay down together on the moss and slept till morning, and their mother knew they were quite safe, and never felt anxious about them. Once, when they had slept the night in the wood and had been wakened by the morning sun, they perceived a beautiful child in a shining white robe sitting close to their resting-place. The figure got up, looked at them kindly, but said nothing, and vanished into the wood. And when they looked round about them they became aware that they had slept quite close to a precipice, over which they would certainly have fallen had they gone on a few steps further in the darkness. And when they told their mother of their adventure, she said what they had seen must have been the angel that guards good children.

Snow-white and Rose-red kept their mother's cottage so beautifully clean and neat that it was a pleasure to go into it. In summer Rose-red looked after the house, and every morning before her mother awoke she placed a bunch of flowers before the bed, from each tree a rose. In winter Snow-white lit the fire and put on the kettle, which was made of brass, but so beautifully polished that it shone like gold. In the evening when the snowflakes fell their mother said: 'Snow-white, go and close the shutters;' and they drew round the fire, while the mother put on her spectacles and read aloud from a big book, and the two girls listened and sat and span. Beside them on the ground lay a little lamb, and behind them perched a little white dove with its head tucked under its wings.

One evening as they sat thus cosily together someone knocked at the door as though he desired admittance. The mother said: 'Rose-red, open the door quickly; it must be some traveller seeking shelter.' Rose-red hastened to unbar the door, and thought she saw a poor man standing in the darkness outside; but it was no such thing, only a bear, who poked his thick black head through the door. Rose-red screamed aloud and sprang back in terror, the lamb began to bleat, the dove flapped its wings, and Snow-white ran and hid behind her mother's bed. But the bear began to speak, and said: 'Don't be afraid: I won't hurt you. I am half frozen, and only wish to warm myself a little.' 'My poor bear,' said the mother, 'lie down by the fire, only take care you don't burn your fur.' Then she called out: 'Snow-white and Rose-red, come out; the bear will do you no harm: he is a good, honest creature.' So they both came out of their hiding-places, and gradually the lamb and dove drew near too, and they all forgot their fear. The bear asked the children to beat the snow a little out of his fur, and they fetched a brush and scrubbed him till he was dry. Then the beast stretched himself in front of the fire, and growled quite happily and comfortably. The children soon grew quite at their ease with him, and led their helpless guest a fearful life. They tugged his fur with their hands, put their small feet on his back, and rolled him about here and there, or took a hazel wand and beat him with it; and if he growled they only laughed. The bear submitted to everything with the best possible good-nature, only when they went too far he cried: 'Oh! children, spare my life!

Snow-white and Rose-red,
Don't beat your lover dead.'

When it was time to retire for the night, and the others went to bed,
the mother said to the bear: 'You can lie there on the hearth, in
heaven's name; it will be shelter for you from the cold and wet.'
As soon as day dawned the children let him out, and he trotted over
the snow into the wood. From this time on the bear came every
evening at the same hour, and lay down by the hearth and let the
children play what pranks they liked with him; and they got so
accustomed to him that the door was never shut till their black
friend had made his appearance.

When spring came, and all outside was green, the bear said one
morning to Snow-white: 'Now I must go away, and not return
again the whole summer.' 'Where are you going to, dear bear?'
asked Snow-white. 'I must go to the wood and protect my treasure
from the wicked dwarfs. In winter, when the earth is frozen hard,
they are obliged to remain underground, for they can't work their
way through; but now, when the sun has thawed and warmed the
ground, they break through and come up above to spy the land and
steal what they can: what once falls into their hands and into their
caves is not easily brought back to light.' Snow-white was quite
sad over their friend's departure, and when she unbarred the door
for him, the bear, stepping out, caught a piece of his fur in the door-

knocker, and Snow-white thought she caught sight of glittering gold beneath it, but she couldn't be certain of it; and the bear ran hastily away, and soon disappeared behind the trees.

A short time after this the mother sent the children into the wood to collect fagots. They came in their wanderings upon a big tree which lay felled on the ground, and on the trunk among the long grass they noticed something jumping up and down, but what it was they couldn't distinguish. When they approached nearer they perceived a dwarf with a wizened face and a beard a yard

long. The end of the beard was jammed into a cleft of the tree, and the little man sprang about like a dog on a chain, and didn't seem to know what he was to do. He glared at the girls with his fiery red eyes, and screamed out : 'What are you standing there for ? can't you come and help me ? ' 'What were you doing, little man ? ' asked Rose-red. 'You stupid, inquisitive goose ! ' replied the dwarf ; 'I wanted to split the tree, in order to get little chips of wood for our kitchen fire ; those thick logs that serve to make fires for coarse, greedy people like yourselves quite burn up all the little food we

need. I had successfully driven in the wedge, and all was going
well, but the cursed wood was so slippery that it suddenly sprang
out, and the tree closed up so rapidly that I had no time to take
my beautiful white beard out, so here I am stuck fast, and I can't
get away; and you silly, smooth-faced, milk-and-water girls just
stand and laugh! Ugh! what wretches you are!'

The children did all in their power, but they couldn't get the
beard out; it was wedged in far too firmly. 'I will run and fetch
somebody,' said Rose-red. 'Crazy blockheads!' snapped the dwarf;
'what's the good of calling anyone else? you're already two too
many for me. Does nothing better occur to you than that?' 'Don't
be so impatient,' said Snow-white, 'I'll see you get help;' and taking
her scissors out of her pocket she cut the end off his beard. As
soon as the dwarf felt himself free he seized a bag full of gold
which was hidden among the roots of the tree, lifted it up, and muttered aloud: 'Curse these rude wretches, cutting off a piece of my
splendid beard!' With these words he swung the bag over his
back, and disappeared without as much as looking at the children
again.

Shortly after this Snow-white and Rose-red went out to get a
dish of fish. As they approached the stream they saw something
which looked like an enormous grasshopper, springing towards the
water as if it were going to jump in. They ran forward and recognised their old friend the dwarf. 'Where are you going to?' asked
Rose-red; 'you're surely not going to jump into the water?' 'I'm
not such a fool,' screamed the dwarf. 'Don't you see that cursed
fish is trying to drag me in?' The little man had been sitting on the
bank fishing, when unfortunately the wind had entangled his beard
in the line; and when immediately afterwards a big fish bit, the
feeble little creature had no strength to pull it out; the fish had the
upper fin, and dragged the dwarf towards him. He clung on with
all his might to every rush and blade of grass, but it didn't help him
much; he had to follow every movement of the fish, and was in
great danger of being drawn into the water. The girls came up just
at the right moment, held him firm, and did all they could to disen-
tangle his beard from the line; but in vain, beard and line were in a
hopeless muddle. Nothing remained but to produce the scissors
and cut the beard, by which a small part of it was sacrificed.

When the dwarf perceived what they were about he yelled to
them: 'Do you call that manners, you toadstools! to disfigure a
fellow's face? it wasn't enough that you shortened my beard before,

but you must now needs cut off the best bit of it. I can't appear like this before my own people. I wish you'd been at Jericho first.' Then he fetched a sack of pearls that lay among the rushes, and without saying another word he dragged it away and disappeared behind a stone.

It happened that soon after this the mother sent the two girls to the town to buy needles, thread, laces, and ribbons. Their road led over a heath where huge boulders of rock lay scattered here and there. While trudging along they saw a big bird hovering in the air, circling slowly above them, but always descending lower, till at last it settled on a rock not far from them. Immediately afterwards they heard a sharp, piercing cry. They ran forward, and saw with horror that the eagle had pounced on their old friend the dwarf, and was about to carry him off. The tender-hearted children seized a hold of the little man, and struggled so long with the bird that at last he let go his prey. When the dwarf had recovered from the first shock he screamed in his screeching voice : ' Couldn't you have treated me more carefully ? you have torn my thin little coat all to shreds, useless, awkward hussies that you are ! ' Then he took a bag of precious stones and vanished under the rocks into his cave. The girls were accustomed to his ingratitude, and went on their way and did their business in town. On their way home, as they were again passing the heath, they surprised the dwarf pouring out his precious stones on an open space, for he had thought no one would pass by at so late an hour. The evening sun shone on the glittering stones, and they glanced and gleamed so beautifully that the children stood still and gazed on them. ' What are you standing there gaping for ? ' screamed the dwarf, and his ashen-grey face became scarlet with rage. He was about to go off with these angry words when a sudden growl was heard, and a black bear trotted out of the wood. The dwarf jumped up in a great fright, but he hadn't time to reach his place of retreat, for the bear was already close to him. Then he cried in terror : ' Dear Mr. Bear, spare me ! I'll give you all my treasure. Look at those beautiful precious stones lying there. Spare my life ! what pleasure would you get from a poor feeble little fellow like me ? You won't feel me between your teeth. There, lay hold of these two wicked girls, they will be a tender morsel for you, as fat as young quails ; eat them up, for heaven's sake.' But the bear, paying no attention to his words, gave the evil little creature one blow with his paw, and he never moved again.

The girls had run away, but the bear called after them : ' Snow-

white and Rose-red, don't be afraid; wait, and I'll come with you.'
Then they recognised his voice and stood still, and when the bear
was quite close to them his skin suddenly fell off, and a beautiful
man stood beside them, all dressed in gold. ' I am a king's son,' he
said, ' and have been doomed by that unholy little dwarf, who had
stolen my treasure, to roam about the woods as a wild bear till his

death should set me free.   Now he has got his well-merited punishment.'

Snow-white married him, and Rose-red his brother, and they
divided the great treasure the dwarf had collected in nis cave between them.   The old mother lived for many years peacefully with
her children ; and she carried the two rose trees with her, and they
stood in front of her window, and every year they bore the finest
red and white roses.[1]

[1] Grimm.

TOADS AND DIAMONDS

THERE was once upon a time a widow who had two daughters. The eldest was so much like her in the face and humour that whoever looked upon the daughter saw the mother. They were both so disagreeable and so proud that there was no living with them.

The youngest, who was the very picture of her father for courtesy and sweetness of temper, was withal one of the most beautiful girls ever seen. As people naturally love their own likeness, this mother even doted on her eldest daughter, and at the same time had a horrible aversion for the youngest—she made her eat in the kitchen and work continually.

Among other things, this poor child was forced twice a day to draw water above a mile and a-half off the house, and bring home a pitcher full of it. One day, as she was at this fountain, there came to her a poor woman, who begged of her to let her drink.

'Oh! ay, with all my neart, Goody, said this pretty little girl; and rinsing immediately the pitcher, she took up some water from the clearest place of the fountain, and gave it to her, holding up the pitcher all the while, that she might drink the easier.

The good woman having drunk, said to her:

'You are so very pretty, my dear, so good and so mannerly, that I cannot help giving you a gift.' For this was a fairy, who had taken the form of a poor country-woman, to see how far the civility and good manners of this pretty girl would go. 'I will give you for gift,' continued the Fairy, 'that, at every word you speak, there shall come out of your mouth either a flower or a jewel.'

When this pretty girl came home her mother scolded at her for staying so long at the fountain.

'I beg your pardon, mamma,' said the poor girl, 'for not making more haste.'

And in speaking these words there came out of her mouth two roses, two pearls, and two diamonds.

'What is it I see there?' said her mother, quite astonished. 'I think I see pearls and diamonds come out of the girl's mouth! How happens this, child?'

This was the first time she ever called her child.

The poor creature told her frankly all the matter, not without dropping out infinite numbers of diamonds.

'In good faith,' cried the mother, 'I must send my child thither. Come hither, Fanny; look what comes out of thy sister's mouth

when she speaks. Wouldst not thou be glad, my dear, to have the same gift given to thee? Thou hast nothing else to do but go and draw water out of the fountain, and when a certain poor woman asks you to let her drink, to give it her very civilly.'

'It would be a very fine sight indeed,' said this ill-bred minx, 'to see me go draw water.'

'You shall go, hussey!' said the mother; 'and this minute.'

So away she went, but grumbling all the way, taking with her
the best silver tankard in the house.

She was no sooner at the fountain than she saw coming out of
the wood a lady most gloriously dressed, who came up to her, and
asked to drink. This was, you must know, the very fairy who
appeared to her sister, but had now taken the air and dress of a
princess, to see how far this girl's rudeness would go.

'Am I come hither,' said the proud, saucy slut, 'to serve you
with water, pray? I suppose the silver tankard was brought

purely for your ladyship, was it? However, you may drink out of
it, if you have a fancy.'

'You are not over and above mannerly,' answered the Fairy,
without putting herself in a passion. 'Well, then, since you have so
little breeding, and are so disobliging, I give you for gift that at
every word you speak there shall come out of your mouth a snake
or a toad.'

So soon as her mother saw her coming she cried out:

'Well, daughter?'

'Well, mother?' answered the pert hussey, throwing out of her mouth two vipers and two toads.

'Oh! mercy,' cried the mother; 'what is it I see? Oh! it is that wretch her sister who has occasioned all this; but she shall pay for it'; and immediately she ran to beat her. The poor child fled away from her, and went to hide herself in the forest, not far from thence.

The King's son, then on his return from hunting, met her, and seeing her so very pretty, asked her what she did there alone and why she cried.

'Alas! sir, my mamma has turned me out of doors.'

The King's son, who saw five or six pearls and as many diamonds come out of her mouth, desired her to tell him how that happened. She hereupon told him the whole story; and so the King's son fell in love with her, and, considering with himself that such a gift was worth more than any marriage portion, conducted her to the palace of the King his father, and there married her.

As for her sister, she made herself so much hated that her own mother turned her off; and the miserable wretch, having wandered about a good while without finding anybody to take her in, went to a corner of the wood, and there died.[1]

[1] Charles Perrault.

BLUE BEARD

THERE was a man who had fine houses, both in town and country, a deal of silver and gold plate, embroidered furniture, and coaches gilded all over with gold. But this man was so unlucky as to have a blue beard, which made him so frightfully ugly that all the women and girls ran away from him.

One of his neighbours, a lady of quality, had two daughters who were perfect beauties. He desired of her one of them in marriage, leaving to her choice which of the two she would bestow on him. They would neither of them have him, and sent him backwards and forwards from one another, not being able to bear the thoughts of marrying a man who had a blue beard, and what besides gave them disgust and aversion was his having already been married to several wives, and nobody ever knew what became of them.

Blue Beard, to engage their affection, took them, with the lady their mother and three or four ladies of their acquaintance, with other young people of the neighbourhood, to one of his country seats, where they stayed a whole week.

There was nothing then to be seen but parties of pleasure, hunting, fishing, dancing, mirth, and feasting. Nobody went to bed, but all passed the night in rallying and joking with each other. In short, every thing succeeded so well that the youngest daughter began to think the master of the house not to have a beard so very blue, and that he was a mighty civil gentleman.

As soon as they returned home, the marriage was concluded. About a month afterwards, Blue Beard told his wife that he was obliged to take a country journey for six weeks at least, about affairs of very great consequence, desiring her to divert herself in his absence, to send for her friends and acquaintances, to carry them into the country, if she pleased, and to make good cheer wherever she was.

'Here,' said he, 'are the keys of the two great wardrobes,

wherein I have my best furniture ; these are of my silver and gold plate, which is not every day in use ; these open my strong boxes, which hold my money, both gold and silver ; these my caskets of jewels ; and this is the master-key to all my apartments. But for this little one here, it is the key of the closet at the end of the great gallery on the ground floor. Open them all ; go into all and every one of them, except that little closet, which I forbid you, and forbid it in such a manner that, if you happen to open it, there's nothing but what you may expect from my just anger and resentment.'

She promised to observe, very exactly, whatever he had ordered ; when he, after having embraced her, got into his coach and proceeded on his journey.

Her neighbours and good friends did not stay to be sent for by the new married lady, so great was their impatience to see all the rich furniture of her house, not daring to come while her husband was there, because of his blue beard, which frightened them. They ran through all the rooms, closets, and wardrobes, which were all so fine and rich that they seemed to surpass one another.

After that they went up into the two great rooms, where were the best and richest furniture ; they could not sufficiently admire the number and beauty of the tapestry, beds, couches, cabinets, stands, tables, and looking-glasses, in which you might see yourself from head to foot ; some of them were framed with glass, others with silver, plain and gilded, the finest and most magnificent ever were seen.

They ceased not to extol and envy the happiness of their friend, who in the meantime in no way diverted herself in looking upon all these rich things, because of the impatience she had to go and open the closet on the ground floor. She was so much pressed by her curiosity that, without considering that it was very uncivil to leave her company, she went down a little back staircase, and with such excessive haste that she had twice or thrice like to have broken her neck.

Being come to the closet-door, she made a stop for some time, thinking upon her husband's orders, and considering what unhappiness might attend her if she was disobedient ; but the temptation was so strong she could not overcome it. She then took the little key, and opened it, trembling, but could not at first see anything plainly, because the windows were shut. After some moments she began to perceive that the floor was all covered over with clotted blood, on which lay the bodies of several dead women, ranged against the walls. (These were all the wives whom Blue Beard had married and murdered, one after another.) She thought she should have died for fear, and the key, which she pulled out of the lock, fell out of her hand.

After having somewhat recovered

her surprise, she took up the key, locked the door, and went upstairs into her chamber to recover herself; but she could not, so much was she frightened. Having observed that the key of the closet was stained with blood, she tried two or three times to wipe it off, but the blood would not come out; in vain did she wash it, and even rub it with soap and sand, the blood still remained, for the key was magical and she could never make it quite clean; when the blood was gone off from one side, it came again on the other.

Blue Beard returned from his journey the same evening, and said he had received letters upon the road, informing him that the affair he went about was ended to his advantage. His wife did all she could to convince him she was extremely glad of his speedy return.

Next morning he asked her for the keys, which she gave him, but with such a trembling hand that he easily guessed what had happened.

'What!' said he, 'is not the key of my closet among the rest?'

'I must certainly,' said she, 'have left it above upon the table.'

'Fail not,' said Blue Beard, 'to bring it me presently.'

After several goings backwards and forwards she was forced to bring him the key. Blue Beard, having very attentively considered it, said to his wife,

'How comes this blood upon the key?'

'I do not know,' cried the poor woman, paler than death.

'You do not know!' replied Blue Beard. 'I very well know. You were resolved to go into the closet, were you not? Mighty well, madam; you shall go in, and take your place among the ladies you saw there.'

Upon this she threw herself at her husband's feet, and begged his pardon with all the signs of a true repentance, vowing that she would never more be disobedient. She would have melted a rock, so beautiful and sorrowful was she; but Blue Beard had a heart harder than any rock!

'You must die, madam,' said he, 'and that presently.'

'Since I must die,' answered she (looking upon him with her eyes all bathed in tears), 'give me some little time to say my prayers.'

'I give you,' replied Blue Beard, 'half a quarter of an hour, but not one moment more.'

When she was alone she called out to her sister, and said to her:

'Sister Anne' (for that was her name), 'go up, I beg you, upon the top of the tower, and look if my brothers are not coming; they promised me that they would come to-day, and if you see them, give them a sign to make haste.'

Her sister Anne went up upon the top of the tower, and the poor afflicted wife cried out from time to time:

'Anne, sister Anne, do you see anyone coming?'

And sister Anne said:

'I see nothing but the sun, which makes a dust, and the grass, which looks green.'

In the meanwhile Blue Beard, holding a great sabre in his hand, cried out as loud as he could bawl to his wife:

'Come down instantly, or I shall come up to you.'

'One moment longer, if you please,' said his wife; and then she cried out very softly, 'Anne, sister Anne, dost thou see anybody coming?'

And sister Anne answered:

'I see nothing but the sun, which makes a dust, and the grass, which is green.'

'Come down quickly,' cried Blue Beard, 'or I will come up to you.'

'I am coming,' answered his wife; and then she cried, 'Anne, sister Anne, dost thou not see anyone coming?'

'I see,' replied sister Anne, 'a great dust, which comes on this side here.'

'Are they my brothers?'

'Alas! no, my dear sister, I see a flock of sheep.'

'Will you not come down?' cried Blue Beard.

'One moment longer,' said his wife, and then she cried out: 'Anne, sister Anne, dost thou see nobody coming?'

'I see,' said she, 'two horsemen, but they are yet a great way off.'

'God be praised,' replied the poor wife joyfully: 'they are my brothers; I will make them a sign, as well as I can, for them to make haste.'

Then Blue Beard bawled out so loud that he made the whole

house tremble. The distressed wife came down, and threw herself at his feet, all in tears, with her hair about her shoulders.

'This signifies nothing,' says Blue Beard; 'you must die'; then, taking hold of her hair with one hand, and lifting up the sword with the other, he was going to take off her head. The poor lady, turning about to him, and looking at him with dying eyes, desired him to afford her one little moment to recollect herself.

' No, no,' said he, 'recommend thyself to God,' and was just ready to strike . . .

At this very instant there was such a loud knocking at the gate that Blue Beard made a sudden stop. The gate was opened, and presently entered two horsemen, who, drawing their swords, ran directly to Blue Beard. He knew them to be his wife's brothers, one a dragoon, the other a musketeer; so that he ran away immediately to save himself; but the two brothers pursued so close that they overtook him before he could get to the steps of the porch, when they ran their swords through his body and left him dead. The poor wife was almost as dead as her husband, and had not strength enough to rise and welcome her brothers.

Blue Beard had no heirs, and so his wife became mistress of all his estate. She made use of one part of it to marry her sister Anne to a young gentleman who had loved her a long while; another part to buy captains' commissions for her brothers, and the rest to marry herself to a very worthy gentleman, who made her forget the ill time she had passed with Blue Beard.[1]

[1] Charles Perrault.

THE LITTLE GOOD MOUSE

ONCE upon a time there lived a King and Queen who loved each other so much that they were never happy unless they were together. Day after day they went out hunting or fishing; night after night they went to balls or to the opera; they sang, and danced, and ate sugar-plums, and were the gayest of the gay, and all their subjects followed their example so that the kingdom was called the Joyous Land. Now in the next kingdom everything was as different as it could possibly be. The King was sulky and savage, and never enjoyed himself at all. He looked so ugly and cross that all his subjects feared him, and he hated the very sight of a cheerful face; so if he ever caught anyone smiling he had his head cut off that very minute. This kingdom was very appropriately called the Land of Tears. Now when this wicked King heard of the happiness of the Jolly King, he was so jealous that he collected a great army and set out to fight him, and the news of his approach was soon brought to the King and Queen. The Queen, when she heard of it, was frightened out of her wits, and began to cry bitterly. 'Sire,' she said, 'let us collect all our riches and run away as far as ever we can, to the other side of the world.'

But the King answered:

'Fie, madam! I am far too brave for that. It is better to die than to be a coward.'

Then he assembled all his armed men, and after bidding the Queen a tender farewell, he mounted his splendid horse and rode away. When he was lost to sight the Queen could do nothing but weep, and wring her hands, and cry.

'Alas! If the King is killed, what will become of me and of my little daughter?' and she was so sorrowful that she could neither eat nor sleep.

The King sent her a letter every day, but at last, one morning, as she looked out of the palace window, she saw a messenger approaching in hot haste.

'What news, courier? What news?' cried the Queen, and he answered:

'The battle is lost and the King is dead, and in another moment the enemy will be here.'

The poor Queen fell back insensible, and all her ladies carried her to bed, and stood round her weeping and wailing. Then began a tremendous noise and confusion, and they knew that the enemy had arrived, and very soon they heard the King himself stamping about the palace seeking the Queen. Then her ladies put the little Princess into her arms, and covered her up, head and all, in the bedclothes, and ran for their lives, and the poor Queen lay there shaking, and hoping she would not be found. But very soon the wicked King clattered into the room, and in a fury because the Queen would not answer when he called to her, he tore back her silken coverings and tweaked off her lace cap, and when all her lovely hair came tumbling down over her shoulders, he wound it three times round his hand and threw her over his shoulder, where he carried her like a sack of flour.

The poor Queen held her little daughter safe in her arms and shrieked for mercy, but the wicked King only mocked her, and begged her to go on shrieking, as it amused him, and so mounted his great black horse, and rode back to his own country. When he got there he declared that he would have the Queen and the little Princess hanged on the nearest tree; but his courtiers said that seemed a pity, for when the baby grew up she would be a very nice wife for the King's only son.

The King was rather pleased with this idea, and shut the Queen up in the highest room of a tall tower, which was very tiny, and miserably furnished with a table and a very hard bed upon the floor. Then he sent for a fairy who lived near his kingdom, and after receiving her with more politeness than he generally showed, and entertaining her at a sumptuous feast, he took her up to see the Queen. The fairy was so touched by the sight of her misery that when she kissed her hand she whispered:

'Courage, madam! I think I see a way to help you.'

The Queen, a little comforted by these words, received her graciously, and begged her to take pity upon the poor little Princess, who had met with such a sudden reverse of fortune. But the King got very cross when he saw them whispering together, and cried harshly:

'Make an end of these fine speeches, madam. I brought you here to tell me if the child will grow up pretty and fortunate.'

Then the Fairy answered that the Princess would be as pretty, and clever, and well brought up as it was possible to be, and the old King growled to the Queen that it was lucky for her that it was so, as they would certainly have been hanged if it were otherwise. Then he stamped off, taking the Fairy with him, and leaving the poor Queen in tears.

'How can I wish my little daughter to grow up pretty if she is to be married to that horrid little dwarf, the King's son,' she said to herself, 'and yet, if she is ugly we shall both be killed. If I could only hide her away somewhere, so that the cruel King could never find her.'

As the days went on, the Queen and the little Princess grew thinner and thinner, for their hard-hearted gaoler gave them every day only three boiled peas and a tiny morsel of black bread, so they were always terribly hungry. At last, one evening, as the Queen sat at her spinning-wheel—for the King was so avaricious that she was made to work day and night—she saw a tiny, pretty little mouse creep out of a hole, and said to it:

'Alas, little creature! what are you coming to look for here? I only have three peas for my day's provision, so unless you wish to fast you must go elsewhere.'

But the mouse ran hither and thither, and danced and capered so prettily, that at last the Queen gave it her last pea, which she was keeping for her supper, saying: 'Here, little one, eat it up; I have nothing better to offer you, but I give this willingly in return for the amusement I have had from you.'

She had hardly spoken when she saw upon the table a delicious little roast partridge, and two dishes of preserved fruit. 'Truly,' said she, 'a kind action never goes unrewarded;' and she and the little Princess ate their supper with great satisfaction, and then the Queen gave what was left to the little mouse, who danced better than ever afterwards. The next morning came the gaoler with the Queen's allowance of three peas, which he brought in upon a large dish to make them look smaller; but as soon as he set it down the little mouse came and ate up all three, so that when the Queen wanted her dinner there was nothing left for her. Then she was quite provoked, and said:

'What a bad little beast that mouse must be! If it goes on like this I shall be starved.' But when she glanced at the dish again it was covered with all sorts of nice things to eat, and the Queen made a very good dinner, and was gayer than usual over it. But afterwards as she sat at her spinning-wheel she began to consider what would happen if the little Princess did not grow up pretty enough to please the King, and she said to herself:

'Oh! if I could only think of some way of escaping.'

As she spoke she saw the little mouse playing in a corner with some long straws. The Queen took them and began to plait them, saying:

'If only I had straws enough I would make a basket with them, and let my baby down in it from the window to any kind passer-by who would take care of her.'

By the time the straws were all plaited the little mouse had dragged in more and more, until the Queen had plenty to make her basket, and she worked at it day and night, while the little mouse danced for her amusement; and at dinner and supper time the Queen gave it the three peas and the bit of black bread, and always found something good in the dish in their place. She really could not imagine where all the nice things came from. At last one day when the basket was finished, the Queen was look-ing out of the window to see how long a cord she must make to lower it to the bottom of the tower, when she noticed a little old woman who was leaning upon her stick and looking up at her. Presently she said:

'I know your trouble, madam. If you like I will help you.'

'Oh! my dear friend,' said the Queen. 'If you really wish to be of use to me you will come at the time that I will appoint, and I will let down my poor little baby in a basket. If you will take her, and bring her up for me, when I am rich I will reward you splendidly.'

'I don't care about the reward,' said the old woman, 'but there is one thing I should like. You must know that I am very par-ticular about what I eat, and if there is one thing that I fancy above all others, it is a plump, tender little mouse. If there is such a thing in your garret just throw it down to me, and in return I will promise that your little daughter shall be well taken care of.'

The Queen when she heard this began to cry, but made no answer, and the old woman after waiting a few minutes asked her what was the matter.

'Why,' said the Queen, 'there is only one mouse in this garret, and that is such a dear, pretty little thing that I cannot bear to think of its being killed.'

'What!' cried the old woman, in a rage. 'Do you care more for a miserable mouse than for your own baby? Good-bye, madam! I leave you to enjoy its company, and for my own part I thank my stars that I can get plenty of mice without troubling you to give them to me.'

And she hobbled off grumbling and growling. As to the Queen, she was so disappointed that, in spite of finding a better dinner than usual, and seeing the little mouse dancing in its merriest mood, she could do nothing but cry. That night when her baby was fast asleep she packed it into the basket, and wrote on a slip of paper, 'This unhappy little girl is called Delicia!' This she pinned to its robe, and then very sadly she was shutting the basket, when in sprang the little mouse and sat on the baby's pillow.

'Ah! little one,' said the Queen, 'it cost me dear to save your life. How shall I know now whether my Delicia is being taken care of or no? Anyone else would have let the greedy old woman have you, and eat you up, but I could not bear to do it.' Whereupon the Mouse answered:

'Believe me, madam, you will never repent of your kindness.'

The Queen was immensely astonished when the Mouse began to speak, and still more so when she saw its little sharp nose turn to a beautiful face, and its paws to hands and feet; then it suddenly grew tall, and the Queen recognised the Fairy who had come with the wicked King to visit her.

The Fairy smiled at her astonished look, and said:

'I wanted to see if you were faithful and capable of feeling a real friendship for me, for you see we fairies are rich in everything but friends, and those are hard to find.'

'It is not possible that *you* should want for friends, you charming creature,' said the Queen, kissing her.

'Indeed it is so,' the Fairy said. 'For those who are only friendly with me for their own advantage, I do not count at all. But when you cared for the poor little mouse you could not have known there was anything to be gained by it, and to try you further I took the form of the old woman whom you talked to from the window, and then I was convinced that you really loved me.' Then, turning to the little Princess, she kissed her rosy lips three times, saying:

'Dear little one, I promise that you shall be richer than your father, and shall live a hundred years, always pretty and happy, without fear of old age and wrinkles.'

The Queen, quite delighted, thanked the Fairy gratefully, and begged her to take charge of the little Delicia and bring her up as her own daughter. This she agreed to do, and then they shut the basket and lowered it carefully, baby and all, to the ground at the foot of the tower. The Fairy then changed herself back into the form of a mouse, and this delayed her a few seconds, after which she ran nimbly down the straw rope, but only to find when she got to the bottom that the baby had disappeared.

In the greatest terror she ran up again to the Queen, crying :

' All is lost ! my enemy Cancaline has stolen the Princess away. You must know that she is a cruel fairy who hates me, and as she is older than I am and has more power, I can do nothing against her. I know no way of rescuing Delicia from her clutches.'

When the Queen heard this terrible news she was heart-broken, and begged the Fairy to do all she could to get the poor little Princess back again. At this moment in came the gaoler, and when he missed the little Princess he at once told the King, who came in a great fury asking what the Queen had done with her. She answered that a fairy, whose name she did not know, had come and carried her off by force. Upon this the King stamped upon the ground, and cried in a terrible voice :

' You shall be hung ! I always told you you should.' And without another word he dragged the unlucky Queen out into the nearest wood, and climbed up into a tree to look for a branch to which he could hang her. But when he was quite high up, the Fairy, who had made herself invisible and followed them, gave him a sudden push, which made him lose his footing and fall to the ground with a crash and break four of his teeth, and while he was trying to mend them the fairy carried the Queen off in her flying chariot to a beautiful castle, where she was so kind to her that but for the loss of Delicia the Queen would have been perfectly happy. But though the good little mouse did her very utmost, they could not find out where Cancaline had hidden the little Princess.

Thus fifteen years went by, and the Queen had somewhat recovered from her grief, when the news reached her that the son of the wicked King wished to marry the little maiden who kept the turkeys, and that she had refused him ; the wedding-dresses had been made, nevertheless, and the festivities were to be so splendid that all the people for leagues round were flocking in to be present at

them.   The Queen felt quite curious about a little turkey-maiden
who did not wish to be a Queen, so the little mouse conveyed herself to the poultry-yard to find out what she was like.

She found the turkey-maiden sitting upon a big stone, barefooted,
and miserably dressed in an old, coarse linen gown and cap ; the

ground at her feet was all strewn with robes of gold and silver,
ribbons and laces, diamonds and pearls, over which the turkeys were
stalking to and fro, while the King's ugly, disagreeable son stood
opposite her, declaring angrily that if she would not marry him she
should be killed.

The Turkey-maiden answered proudly:

'I never will marry you! you are too ugly and too much like your cruel father. Leave me in peace with my turkeys, which I like far better than all your fine gifts.'

The little mouse watched her with the greatest admiration, for she was as beautiful as the spring; and as soon as the wicked Prince was gone, she took the form of an old peasant woman and said to her:

'Good-day, my pretty one! you have a fine flock of turkeys there.'

The young Turkey-maiden turned her gentle eyes upon the old woman, and answered:

'Yet they wish me to leave them to become a miserable Queen! what is your advice upon the matter?'

'My child,' said the Fairy, 'a crown is a very pretty thing, but you know neither the price nor the weight of it.'

'I know so well that I have refused to wear one,' said the little maiden, 'though I don't know who was my father, or who was my mother, and I have not a friend in the world.'

'You have goodness and beauty, which are of more value than ten kingdoms,' said the wise Fairy. 'But tell me, child, how came you here, and how is it you have neither father, nor mother, nor friend?'

'A Fairy called Cancaline is the cause of my being here,' answered she, 'for while I lived with her I got nothing but blows and harsh words, until at last I could bear it no longer, and ran away from her without knowing where I was going, and as I came through a wood the wicked Prince met me, and offered to give me charge of the poultry-yard. I accepted gladly, not knowing that I should have to see him day by day. And now he wants to marry me, but that I will never consent to.'

Upon hearing this the Fairy became convinced that the little Turkey-maiden was none other than the Princess Delicia.

'What is your name, my little one?' said she.

'I am called Delicia, if it please you,' she answered.

Then the Fairy threw her arms round the Princess's neck, and nearly smothered her with kisses, saying:

'Ah, Delicia! I am a very old friend of yours, and I am truly glad to find you at last; but you might look nicer than you do in that old gown, which is only fit for a kitchen-maid. Take this pretty dress and let us see the difference it will make.'

So Delicia took off the ugly cap, and shook out all her fair shining hair, and bathed her hands and face in clear water from the nearest spring till her cheeks were like roses, and when she was adorned with the diamonds and the splendid robe the Fairy had given her, she looked the most beautiful Princess in the world, and the Fairy with great delight cried:

'Now you look as you ought to look, Delicia: what do you think about it yourself?'

And Delicia answered:

'I feel as if I were the daughter of some great king.'

'And would you be glad if you were?' said the Fairy.

'Indeed I should,' answered she.

'Ah, well,' said the Fairy, 'to-morrow I may have some pleasant news for you.'

So she hurried back to her castle, where the Queen sat busy with her embroidery, and cried:

'Well, madam! will you wager your thimble and your golden needle that I am bringing you the best news you could possibly hear?'

'Alas!' sighed the Queen, 'since the death of the Jolly King and the loss of my Delicia, all the news in the world is not worth a pin to me.

'There, there, don't be melancholy,' said the Fairy. 'I assure you the Princess is quite well, and I have never seen her equal for beauty. She might be a Queen to-morrow if she chose;' and then she told all that had happened, and the Queen first rejoiced over the thought of Delicia's beauty, and then wept at the idea of her being a Turkey-maiden.

'I will not hear of her being made to marry the wicked King's son,' she said. 'Let us go at once and bring her here.'

In the meantime the wicked Prince, who was very angry with Delicia, had sat himself down under a tree, and cried and howled with rage and spite until the King heard him, and cried out from the window:

'What is the matter with you, that you are making all this disturbance?'

The Prince replied:

'It is all because our Turkey-maiden will not love me!'

'Won't love you? eh!' said the King. 'We'll very soon see about that!' So he called his guards and told them to go and fetch Delicia. 'See if I don't make her change her mind pretty soon!' said the wicked King with a chuckle.

Then the guards began to search the poultry-yard, and could find nobody there but Delicia, who, with her splendid dress and her crown of diamonds, looked such a lovely Princess that they hardly dared to speak to her.   But she said to them very politely:

'Pray tell me what you are looking for here?'

'Madam,' they answered, 'we are sent for an insignificant little person called Delicia.'

'Alas!' said she, 'that is my name.   What can you want with me?'

So the guards tied her hands and feet with thick ropes, for fear

she might run away, and brought her to the King, who was waiting with his son.

When he saw her he was very much astonished at her beauty, which would have made anyone less hard-hearted sorry for her. But the wicked King only laughed and mocked at her, and cried: 'Well, little fright, little toad! why don't you love my son, who is far too handsome and too good for you? Make haste and begin to love him this instant, or you shall be tarred and feathered.'

Then the poor little Princess, shaking with terror, went down on her knees, crying:

'Oh, don't tar and feather me, please! It would be so uncomfortable. Let me have two or three days to make up my mind, and then you shall do as you like with me.'

The wicked Prince would have liked very much to see her tarred and feathered, but the King ordered that she should be shut up in a dark dungeon. It was just at this moment that the Queen and the Fairy arrived in the flying chariot, and the Queen was dreadfully distressed at the turn affairs had taken, and said miserably that she was destined to be unfortunate all her days. But the Fairy bade her take courage.

'I'll pay them out yet,' said she, nodding her head with an air of great determination.

That very same night, as soon as the wicked King had gone to bed, the Fairy changed herself into the little mouse, and creeping up on to his pillow nibbled his ear, so that he squealed out quite loudly and turned over on his other side; but that was no good, for the little mouse only set to work and gnawed away at the second ear until it hurt more than the first one.

Then the King cried 'Murder!' and 'Thieves!' and all his guards ran to see what was the matter, but they could find nothing and nobody, for the little mouse had run off to the Prince's room and was serving him in exactly the same way. All night long she ran from one to the other, until at last, driven quite frantic by terror and want of sleep, the King rushed out of the palace crying:

'Help! help! I am pursued by rats.'

The Prince when he heard this got up also, and ran after the King, and they had not gone far when they both fell into the river and were never heard of again.

Then the good Fairy ran to tell the Queen, and they went together to the black dungeon where Delicia was imprisoned. The Fairy touched each door with her wand, and it sprang open instantly, but they had to go through forty before they came to the Princess, who was sitting on the floor looking very dejected. But when the Queen rushed in, and kissed her twenty times in a minute, and laughed, and cried, and told Delicia all her history, the Princess was wild with delight. Then the Fairy showed her all the wonderful dresses and jewels she had brought for her, and said:

'Don't let us waste time; we must go and harangue the people.'

So she walked first, looking very serious and dignified, and wearing a dress the train of which was at least ten ells long. Behind her came the Queen wearing a blue velvet robe embroidered with gold, and a diamond crown that was brighter than the sun itself. Last of all walked Delicia, who was so beautiful that it was nothing short of marvellous.

They proceeded through the streets, returning the salutations of all they met, great or small, and all the people turned and followed them, wondering who these noble ladies could be.

When the audience hall was quite full, the Fairy said to the subjects of the Wicked King that if they would accept Delicia, who was the daughter of the Jolly King, as their Queen, she would undertake to find a suitable husband for her, and would promise that during their reign there should be nothing but rejoicing and merry-making, and all dismal things should be entirely banished. Upon this the people cried with one accord, 'We will, we will! we have been gloomy and miserable too long already.' And they all took hands and danced round the Queen, and Delicia, and the good Fairy, singing : 'Yes, yes; we will, we will!'

Then there were feasts and fireworks in every street in the town, and early the next morning the Fairy, who had been all over the world in the night, brought back with her, in her flying chariot, the most handsome and good-tempered Prince she could find anywhere. He was so charming that Delicia loved him from the moment their eyes met, and as for him, of course he could not help thinking himself the luckiest Prince in the world. The Queen felt that she had really come to the end of her misfortunes at last, and they all lived happily ever after.[1]

[1] *La bonne petite Souris*, par Madame d'Aulnoy.

RAPUNZEL

ONCE upon a time there lived a man and his wife who were very unhappy because they had no children. These good people had a little window at the back of their house, which looked into the most lovely garden, full of all manner of beautiful flowers and vegetables; but the garden was surrounded by a high wall, and no one dared to enter it, for it belonged to a witch of great power, who was feared by the whole world. One day the woman stood at the window overlooking the garden, and saw there a bed full of the finest rampion: the leaves looked so fresh and green that she longed to eat them. The desire grew day by day, and just because she knew she couldn't possibly get any, she pined away and became quite pale and wretched. Then her husband grew alarmed and said:

'What ails you, dear wife?'

'Oh,' she answered, 'if I don't get some rampion to eat out of the garden behind the house, I know I shall die.'

The man, who loved her dearly, thought to himself, 'Come! rather than let your wife die you shall fetch her some rampion, no matter the cost.' So at dusk he climbed over the wall into the witch's garden, and, hastily gathering a handful of rampion leaves, he returned with them to his wife. She made them into a salad, which tasted so good that her longing for the forbidden food was greater than ever. If she were to know any peace of mind, there was nothing for it but that her husband should climb over the garden wall again, and fetch her some more. So at dusk over he got, but when he reached the other side he drew back in terror, for there, standing before him, was the old witch.

'How dare you,' she said, with a wrathful glance, 'climb into my garden and steal my rampion like a common thief? You shall suffer for your foolhardiness.'

'Oh!' he implored, 'pardon my presumption; necessity alone

drove me to the deed. My wife saw your rampion from her window, and conceived such a desire for it that she would certainly have died if her wish had not been gratified.' Then the Witch's anger was a little appeased, and she said :

' If it's as you say, you may take as much rampion away with you as you like, but on one condition only—that you give me the child your wife will shortly bring into the world. All shall go well with it, and I will look after it like a mother.'

The man in his terror agreed to everything she asked, and as soon as the child was born the Witch appeared, and having given it the name of Rapunzel, which is the same as rampion, she carried it off with her.

Rapunzel was the most beautiful child under the sun. When she was twelve years old the Witch shut her up in a tower, in the middle of a great wood, and the tower had neither stairs nor doors, only high up at the very top a small window. When the old Witch wanted to get in she stood underneath and called out :

> ' Rapunzel, Rapunzel,
> Let down your golden hair,'

for Rapunzel had wonderful long hair, and it was as fine as spun gold. Whenever she heard the Witch's voice she unloosed her plaits, and let her hair fall down out of the window about twenty yards below, and the old Witch climbed up by it.

After they had lived like this for a few years, it happened one day that a Prince was riding through the wood and passed by the tower. As he drew near it he heard someone singing so sweetly that he stood still spell-bound, and listened. It was Rapunzel in her loneliness trying to while away the time by letting her sweet voice ring out into the wood. The Prince longed to see the owner of the voice, but he sought in vain for a door in the tower. He rode home, but he was so haunted by the song he had heard that he returned every day to the wood and listened. One day, when he was standing thus behind a tree, he saw the old Witch approach and heard her call out :

> ' Rapunzel, Rapunzel,
> Let down your golden hair.'

Then Rapunzel let down her plaits, and the Witch climbed up by them.

' So that's the staircase, is it ? ' said the Prince, ' Then I too will climb it and try my luck.'

So on the following day, at dusk, he went to the foot of the tower and cried :

> 'Rapunzel, Rapunzel,
> Let down your golden hair,'

and as soon as she had let it down the Prince climbed up.

At first Rapunzel was terribly frightened when a man came in, for she had never seen one before; but the Prince spoke to her so kindly, and told her at once that his heart had been so touched by her singing, that he felt he should know no peace of mind till he had seen her. Very soon Rapunzel forgot her fear, and when he asked her to marry him she consented at once. 'For,' she thought, 'he is young and handsome, and I'll certainly be happier with him than with the old Witch.' So she put her hand in his and said :

'Yes, I will gladly go with you, only how am I to get down out of the tower ? Every time you come to see me you must bring a skein of silk with you, and I will make a ladder of them, and when it is finished I will climb down by it, and you will take me away on your horse.'

They arranged that, till the ladder was ready, he was to come to her every evening, because the old woman was with her during the day. The old Witch, of course, knew nothing of what was going on, till one day Rapunzel, not thinking of what she was about, turned to the Witch and said :

' How is it, good mother, that you are so much harder to pull up than the young Prince ?   He is always with me in a moment.'

' Oh ! you wicked child,' cried the Witch. ' What is this I hear ? I thought I had hidden you safely from the whole world, and in spite of it you have managed to deceive me.'

In her wrath she seized Rapunzel's beautiful hair, wound it round and round her left hand, and then grasping a pair of scissors in her right, snip snap, off it came, and the beautiful plaits lay on the ground. And, worse than this, she was so hard-hearted that she took Rapunzel to a lonely desert place, and there left her to live in loneliness and misery.

But on the evening of the day in which she had driven poor Rapunzel away, the Witch fastened the plaits on to a hook in the window, and when the Prince came and called out :

' Rapunzel, Rapunzel,
Let down your golden hair,'

she let them down, and the Prince climbed up as usual, but instead of his beloved Rapunzel he found the old Witch, who fixed her evil, glittering eyes on him, and cried mockingly :

' Ah, ah ! you thought to find your lady love, but the pretty bird has flown and its song is dumb ; the cat caught it, and will scratch out your eyes too.   Rapunzel is lost to you for ever—you will never see her more.'

The Prince was beside himself with grief, and in his despair he jumped right down from the tower, and, though he escaped with his life, the thorns among which he fell pierced his eyes out.   Then he wandered, blind and miserable, through the wood, eating nothing but roots and berries, and weeping and lamenting the loss of his lovely bride.   So he wandered about for some years, as wretched and unhappy as he could well be, and at last he came to the desert place where Rapunzel was living.   Of a sudden he heard a voice which seemed strangely familiar to him.   He walked eagerly in the direction of the sound, and when he was quite close, Rapunzel recognised him and fell on his neck and wept.   But two of her tears touched his eyes, and in a moment they became quite clear again, and he saw as well as he had ever done.   Then he led her to his kingdom, where they were received and welcomed with great joy, and they lived happily ever after.[1]

[1] Grimm.

THE TRUE HISTORY OF LITTLE GOLDEN-
HOOD

YOU know the tale of poor Little Red Riding hood, that the Wolf deceived and devoured, with her cake, her little butter can, and her Grandmother; well, the true story happened quite differ-ently, as we know now. And first of all the little girl was called and is still called Little Golden-hood; secondly, it was not she, nor the good grand-dame, but the wicked Wolf who was, in the end, caught and devoured.

Only listen.

The story begins something like the tale.

There was once a little peasant girl, pretty and nice as a star in its season. Her real name was Blanchette, but she was more often called Little Golden-hood, on account of a wonderful little cloak with a hood, gold- and fire-coloured, which she always had on. This little hood was given her by her Grandmother, who was so old that she did not know her age; it ought to bring her good luck, for it was made of a ray of sunshine, she said. And as the good old woman was considered something of a witch, everyone thought the little hood rather bewitched too.

And so it was, as you will see.

One day the mother said to the child: 'Let us see, my little Golden-hood, if you know now how to find your way by yourself. You shall take this good piece of cake to your Grandmother for a Sunday treat to-morrow. You will ask her how she is, and come back at once, without stopping to chatter on the way with people you don't know. Do you quite understand?'

'I quite understand,' replied Blanchette gaily. And off she went with the cake, quite proud of her errand.

But the Grandmother lived in another village, and there was a big wood to cross before getting there. At a turn of the road under the trees, suddenly 'Who goes there?'

' Friend Wolf.'

He had seen the child start alone, and the villain was waiting to devour her; when at the same moment he perceived some wood-cutters who might observe him, and he changed his mind. Instead of falling upon Blanchette he came frisking up to her like a good dog.

' 'Tis you! my nice Little Golden-hood,' said he. So the little girl stops to talk with the Wolf, who, for all that, she did not know in the least.

' You know me, then ! ' said she ; ' what is your name ? '

' My name is friend Wolf. And where are you going thus, my pretty one, with your little basket on your arm ? '

' I am going to my Grandmother, to take her a good piece of cake for her Sunday treat to-morrow.'

' And where does she live, your Grandmother ? '

' She lives at the other side of the wood, in the first house in the village, near the windmill, you know.'

' Ah ! yes! I know now,' said the Wolf. ' Well, that's just where I'm going; I shall get there before you, no doubt, with your little bits of legs, and I'll tell her you're coming to see her; then she'll wait for you.'

Thereupon the Wolf cuts across the wood, and in five minutes arrives at the Grandmother's house.

He knocks at the door : toc, toc.

No answer.

He knocks louder.

Nobody.

Then he stands up on end, puts his two fore-paws on the latch and the door opens.

Not a soul in the house.

The old woman had risen early to sell herbs in the town, and she had gone off in such haste that she had left her bed unmade, with her great night-cap on the pillow.

' Good ! ' said the Wolf to himself, ' I know what I'll do.'

He shuts the door, pulls on the Grandmother's night-cap down to his eyes, then he lies down all his length in the bed and draws the curtains.

In the meantime the good Blanchette went quietly on her way, as little girls do, amusing herself here and there by picking Easter daisies, watching the little birds making their nests, and running after the butterflies which fluttered in the sunshine.

At last she arrives at the door.

Knock, knock.

'Who is there?' says the Wolf, softening his rough voice as best he can.

'It's me, Granny, your little Golden-hood. I'm bringing you a big piece of cake for your Sunday treat to-morrow.'

'Press your finger on the latch, then push and the door opens.'

'Why, you've got a cold, Granny,' said she, coming in.

'Ahem! a little, a little . . .' replies the Wolf, pretending to cough. 'Shut the door well, my little lamb. Put your basket on the table, and then take off your frock and come and lie down by me : you shall rest a little.'

The good child undresses, but observe this! She kept her little hood upon her head. When she saw what a figure her Granny cut in bed, the poor little thing was much surprised.

'Oh!' cries she, 'how like you are to friend Wolf, Grandmother!'

'That's on account of my night-cap, child,' replies the Wolf.

'Oh! what hairy arms you've got, Grandmother!'

'All the better to hug you, my child.'

'Oh! what a big tongue you've got, Grandmother!'

'All the better for answering, child.'

'Oh! what a mouthful of great white teeth you have, Grandmother!'

'That's for crunching little children with!' And the Wolf opened his jaws wide to swallow Blanchette.

But she put down her head crying :

'Mamma! Mamma!' and the Wolf only caught her little hood.

Thereupon, oh dear! oh dear! he draws back, crying and shaking his jaw as if he had swallowed red-hot coals.

It was the little fire-coloured hood that had burnt his tongue right down his throat.

The little hood, you see, was one of those magic caps that they used to have in former times, in the stories, for making oneself invisible or invulnerable.

So there was the Wolf with his throat burnt, jumping off the bed and trying to find the door, howling and howling as if all the dogs in the country were at his heels.

Just at this moment the Grandmother arrives, returning from the town with her long sack empty on her shoulder.

'Ah, brigand!' she cries, 'wait a bit!' Quickly she opens her sack wide across the door, and the maddened Wolf springs in head downwards.

It is he now that is caught, swallowed like a letter in the post.

For the brave old dame shuts her sack, so ; and she runs and empties it in the well, where the vagabond, still howling, tumbles in and is drowned.

'Ah, scoundrel ! you thought you would crunch my little grandchild ! Well, to-morrow we will make her a muff of your skin, and

you yourself shall be crunched, for we will give your carcass to the dogs.'

Thereupon the Grandmother hastened to dress poor Blanchette, who was still trembling with fear in the bed.

'Well,' she said to her, 'without my little hood where would you be now, darling ? ' And, to restore heart and legs to the child, she made her eat a good piece of her cake, and drink a good draught of wine, after which she took her by the hand and led her back to the house.

And then, who was it who scolded her when she knew all that had happened?

It was the mother.

But Blanchette promised over and over again that she would never more stop to listen to a Wolf, so that at last the mother forgave her.

And Blanchette, the Little Golden-hood, kept her word. And in fine weather she may still be seen in the fields with her pretty little hood, the colour of the sun.

But to see her you must rise early.[1]

[1] Ch. Marelles.

THE PRINCESS MAYBLOSSOM

ONCE upon a time there lived a King and Queen whose children had all died, first one and then another, until at last only one little daughter remained, and the Queen was at her wits' end to know where to find a really good nurse who would take care of her, and bring her up. A herald was sent who blew a trumpet at every street corner, and commanded all the best nurses to appear before the Queen, that she might choose one for the little Princess. So on the appointed day the whole palace was crowded with nurses, who came from the four corners of the world to offer themselves, until the Queen declared that if she was ever to see the half of them, they must be brought out to her, one by one, as she sat in a shady wood near the palace.

This was accordingly done, and the nurses, after they had made their curtsey to the King and Queen, ranged themselves in a line before her that she might choose. Most of them were fair and fat and charming, but there was one who was dark-skinned and ugly, and spoke a strange language which nobody could understand. The Queen wondered how she dared offer herself, and she was told to go away, as she certainly would not do. Upon which she muttered something and passed on, but hid herself in a hollow tree, from which she could see all that happened. The Queen, without giving her another thought, chose a pretty rosy-faced nurse, but no sooner was her choice made than a snake, which was hidden in the grass, bit that very nurse on her foot, so that she fell down as if dead. The Queen was very much vexed by this accident, but she soon selected another, who was just stepping forward when an eagle flew by and dropped a large tortoise upon her head, which was cracked in pieces like an egg-shell. At this the Queen was much horrified; nevertheless, she chose a third time, but with no better fortune, for the nurse, moving quickly, ran into the branch of a tree and blinded herself with a thorn. Then the Queen in dismay cried that there must be some malignant influence at work, and that she would choose no more that day; and she had just risen to return to the palace when she heard peals of malicious laughter behind her, and turning round saw the ugly stranger whom she had dismissed, who was making very merry over the disasters and mocking everyone, but especially the Queen. This annoyed Her Majesty very much, and she was about to order that she should be arrested, when the witch—for she was a witch—with two blows from a wand summoned a chariot of fire drawn by winged dragons, and was whirled off through the air uttering threats and cries. When the King saw this he cried:

'Alas! now we are ruined indeed, for that was no other than the Fairy Carabosse, who has had a grudge against me ever since I was a boy and put sulphur into her porridge one day for fun.'

Then the Queen began to cry.

'If I had only known who it was,' she said, 'I would have done my best to make friends with her; now I suppose all is lost.'

The King was sorry to have frightened her so much, and proposed that they should go and hold a council as to what was best to be done to avert the misfortunes which Carabosse certainly meant to bring upon the little Princess.

So all the counsellors were summoned to the palace, and when they had shut every door and window, and stuffed up every keyhole that they might not be overheard, they talked the affair over, and decided that every fairy for a thousand leagues round should be invited to the christening of the Princess, and that the time of the ceremony should be kept a profound secret, in case the Fairy Carabosse should take it into her head to attend it.

The Queen and her ladies set to work to prepare presents for the fairies who were invited: for each one a blue velvet cloak, a petticoat of apricot satin, a pair of high-heeled shoes, some sharp needles, and a pair of golden scissors. Of all the fairies the Queen knew, only five were able to come on the day appointed, but they began immediately to bestow gifts upon the Princess. One promised that she should be perfectly beautiful, the second that she should understand anything—no matter what—the first time it was explained to her, the third that she should sing like a nightingale, the fourth that she should succeed in everything she undertook, and the fifth was opening her mouth to speak when a tremendous rumbling was heard in the chimney, and Carabosse, all covered with soot, came rolling down, crying:

'I say that she shall be the unluckiest of the unlucky until she is twenty years old.'

Then the Queen and all the fairies began to beg and beseech her to think better of it, and not be so unkind to the poor little Princess, who had never done her any harm. But the ugly old Fairy only grunted and made no answer. So the last Fairy, who had not yet given her gift, tried to mend matters by promising the Princess a long and happy life after the fatal time was over. At this Carabosse laughed maliciously, and climbed away up the chimney, leaving them all in great consternation, and especially the Queen. However, she entertained the fairies splendidly, and gave them beautiful ribbons, of which they are very fond, in addition to the other presents.

When they were going away the oldest Fairy said that they were of opinion that it would be best to shut the Princess up in some place, with her waiting-women, so that she might not see anyone else until she was twenty years old. So the King had a tower built on purpose. It had no windows, so it was lighted with wax candles, and the only way into it was by an underground passage, which had iron doors only twenty feet apart, and guards were posted everywhere.

The Princess had been named Mayblossom, because she was as fresh and blooming as Spring itself, and she grew up tall and beautiful, and everything she did and said was charming. Every time the King and Queen came to see her they were more delighted with her than before, but though she was weary of the tower, and often begged them to take her away from it, they always refused. The Princess's nurse, who had never left her, sometimes told her about the world outside the tower, and though the Princess had never seen anything for herself, yet she always understood exactly, thanks to the second Fairy's gift. Often the King said to the Queen:

'We were cleverer than Carabosse after all. Our Mayblossom will be happy in spite of her predictions.'

And the Queen laughed until she was tired at the idea of having outwitted the old Fairy. They had caused the Princess's portrait to be painted and sent to all the neighbouring Courts, for in four days she would have completed her twentieth year, and it was time to decide whom she should marry. All the town was rejoicing at the thought of the Princess's approaching freedom, and when the news came that King Merlin was sending his ambassador to ask her in marriage for his son, they were still more delighted. The nurse, who kept the Princess informed of everything that went forward in the town, did not fail to repeat the news that so nearly concerned her, and gave such a description of the splendour in which the ambassador Fanfaronade would enter the town, that the Princess was wild to see the procession for herself.

'What an unhappy creature I am,' she cried, ' to be shut up in this dismal tower as if I had committed some crime ! I have never seen the sun, or the stars, or a horse, or a monkey, or a lion, except in pictures, and though the King and Queen tell me I am to be set free when I am twenty, I believe they only say it to keep me amused, when they never mean to let me out at all.'

And then she began to cry, and her nurse, and the nurse's daughter, and the cradle-rocker, and the nursery-maid, who all loved her dearly, cried too for company, so that nothing could be heard but sobs and sighs. It was a scene of woe. When the Princess saw that they all pitied her she made up her mind to have her own way. So she declared that she would starve herself to death if they did not find some means of letting her see Fanfaronade's grand entry into the town.

'If you really love me,' she said, ' you will manage it, somehow or other, and the King and Queen need never know anything about it.'

Then the nurse and all the others cried harder than ever, and said everything they could think of to turn the Princess from her idea. But the more they said the more determined she was, and at last they consented to make a tiny hole in the tower on the side that looked towards the city gates.

After scratching and scraping all day and all night, they presently made a hole through which they could, with great difficulty, push a very slender needle, and out of this the Princess looked at the day-light for the first time. She was so dazzled and delighted by what she saw, that there she stayed, never taking her eyes away from the peep-hole for a single minute, until presently the ambassador's pro-cession appeared in sight.

At the head of it rode Fanfaronade himself upon a white horse, which pranced and caracoled to the sound of the trumpets. Nothing could have been more splendid than the ambassador's attire. His coat was nearly hidden under an embroidery of pearls and diamonds, his boots were solid gold, and from his helmet floated scarlet plumes. At the sight of him the Princess lost her wits entirely, and deter-mined that Fanfaronade and nobody else would she marry.

'It is quite impossible,' she said, ' that his master should be half as handsome and delightful. I am not ambitious, and having spent all my life in this tedious tower, anything—even a house in the country—will seem a delightful change. I am sure that bread and water shared with Fanfaronade will please me far better than roast chicken and sweetmeats with anybody else.'

And so she went on talk, talk, talking, until her waiting-women wondered where she got it all from. But when they tried to stop her, and represented that her high rank made it perfectly impossible that she should do any such thing, she would not listen, and ordered them to be silent.

As soon as the ambassador arrived at the palace, the Queen started to fetch her daughter.

All the streets were spread with carpets, and the windows were full of ladies who were waiting to see the Princess, and carried baskets of flowers and sweetmeats to shower upon her as she passed.

They had hardly begun to get the Princess ready when a dwarf arrived, mounted upon an elephant. He came from the five fairies, and brought for the Princess a crown, a sceptre, and a robe of golden brocade, with a petticoat marvellously embroidered with butterflies' wings. They also sent a casket of jewels, so splendid that no one had ever seen anything like it before, and the Queen was perfectly dazzled when she opened it. But the Princess scarcely gave a glance to any of these treasures, for she thought of nothing but Fanfaronade. The Dwarf was rewarded with a gold piece, and decorated with so many ribbons that it was hardly possible to see him at all. The Princess sent to each of the fairies a new spinning-wheel with a distaff of cedar wood, and the Queen said she must look through her treasures and find something very charming to send them also.

When the Princess was arrayed in all the gorgeous things the Dwarf had brought, she was more beautiful than ever, and as she walked along the streets the people cried: 'How pretty she is! How pretty she is!'

The procession consisted of the Queen, the Princess, five dozen other princesses her cousins, and ten dozen who came from the neighbouring kingdoms; and as they proceeded at a stately pace the sky began to grow dark, then suddenly the thunder growled, and rain and hail fell in torrents. The Queen put her royal mantle over her head, and all the princesses did the same with their trains.

Mayblossom was just about to follow their example when a terrific croaking, as of an immense army of crows, rooks, ravens, screech-owls, and all birds of ill-omen was heard, and at the same instant a huge owl skimmed up to the Princess, and threw over her a scarf woven of spiders' webs and embroidered with bats' wings. And then peals of mocking laughter rang through the air, and they guessed that this was another of the Fairy Carabosse's unpleasant jokes.

The Queen was terrified at such an evil omen, and tried to pull the black scarf from the Princess's shoulders, but it really seemed as if it must be nailed on, it clung so closely.

'Ah!' cried the Queen, 'can nothing appease this enemy of ours? What good was it that I sent her more than fifty pounds of sweetmeats, and as much again of the best sugar, not to mention two Westphalia hams? She is as angry as ever.'

While she lamented in this way, and everybody was as wet as if they had been dragged through a river, the Princess still thought of nothing but the ambassador, and just at this moment he appeared before her, with the King, and there was a great blowing of trumpets, and all the people shouted louder than ever. Fanfaronade was not generally at a loss for something to say, but when he saw the Princess, she was so much more beautiful and majestic than he had expected that he could only stammer out a few words, and entirely forgot the harangue which he had been learning for months, and knew well enough to have repeated it in his sleep. To gain time to remember at least part of it, he made several low bows to the Princess, who on her side dropped half-a-dozen curtseys without stopping to think, and then said, to relieve his evident embarrassment:

'Sir Ambassador, I am sure that everything you intend to say is charming, since it is you who mean to say it; but let us make haste into the palace, as it is pouring cats and dogs, and the wicked Fairy Carabosse will be amused to see us all stand dripping here. When we are once under shelter we can laugh at her.'

Upon this the Ambassador found his tongue, and replied gallantly that the Fairy had evidently foreseen the flames that would be kindled by the bright eyes of the Princess, and had sent this deluge to extinguish them. Then he offered his hand to conduct the Princess, and she said softly:

'As you could not possibly guess how much I like you, Sir Fanfaronade. I am obliged to tell you plainly that, since I saw you enter the town on your beautiful prancing horse, I have been sorry that you came to speak for another instead of for yourself. So, if you think about it as I do, I will marry you instead of your master. Of course I know you are not a prince, but I shall be just as fond of you as if you were, and we can go and live in some cosy little corner of the world, and be as happy as the days are long.'

The Ambassador thought he must be dreaming, and could hardly believe what the lovely Princess said. He dared not answer, but only squeezed the Princess's hand until he really hurt her little finger, but she did not cry out. When they reached the palace the King kissed his daughter on both cheeks, and said :

'My little lambkin, are you willing to marry the great King Merlin's son, for this Ambassador has come on his behalf to fetch you ? '

'If you please, sire,' said the Princess, dropping a curtsey.

'I consent also,' said the Queen; 'so let the banquet be prepared.'

This was done with all speed, and everybody feasted except Mayblossom and Fanfaronade, who looked at one another and forgot everything else.

After the banquet came a ball, and after that again a ballet, and at last they were all so tired that everyone fell asleep just where he sat. Only the lovers were as wide-awake as mice, and the Princess, seeing that there was nothing to fear, said to Fanfaronade :

'Let us be quick and run away, for we shall never have a better chance than this.'

Then she took the King's dagger, which was in a diamond sheath, and the Queen's neck-handkerchief, and gave her hand to Fanfaronade, who carried a lantern, and they ran out together into the muddy street and down to the sea-shore. Here they got into a little boat in which the poor old boatman was sleeping, and when he woke up and saw the lovely Princess, with all her diamonds and her spiders'-web scarf, he did not know what to think, and obeyed her instantly when she commanded him to set out. They could see neither moon nor stars, but in the Queen's neck-handkerchief there was a carbuncle which glowed like fifty torches. Fanfaronade asked the Princess where she would like to go, but she only answered that she did not care where she went as long as he was with her.

'But, Princess,' said he, 'I dare not take you back to King Merlin's court. He would think hanging too good for me.'

'Oh, in that case,' she answered, 'we had better go to Squirrel Island; it is lonely enough, and too far off for anyone to follow us there.'

So she ordered the old boatman to steer for Squirrel Island.

Meanwhile the day was breaking, and the King and Queen and all the courtiers began to wake up and rub their eyes, and think it was time to finish the preparations for the wedding. And the Queen asked for her neck-handkerchief, that she might look smart.

Then there was a scurrying hither and thither, and a hunting everywhere : they looked into every place, from the wardrobes to the stoves, and the Queen herself ran about from the garret to the cellar, but the handkerchief was nowhere to be found.

By this time the King had missed his dagger, and the search began all over again. They opened boxes and chests of which the keys had been lost for a hundred years, and found numbers of curious things, but not the dagger, and the King tore his beard, and the Queen tore her hair, for the handkerchief and the dagger were the most valuable things in the kingdom.

When the King saw that the search was hopeless he said :

' Never mind, let us make haste and get the wedding over before anything else is lost.' And then he asked where the Princess was. Upon this her nurse came forward and said :

' Sire, I have been seeking her these two hours, but she is nowhere to be found.' This was more than the Queen could bear. She gave a shriek of alarm and fainted away, and they had to pour two barrels of eau-de-cologne over her before she recovered. When she came to herself everybody was looking for the Princess in the greatest terror and confusion, but as she did not appear, the King said to his page :

' Go and find the Ambassador Fanfaronade, who is doubtless asleep in some corner, and tell him the sad news.'

So the page hunted hither and thither, but Fanfaronade was no more to be found than the Princess, the dagger, or the neck-handkerchief !

Then the King summoned his counsellors and his guards, and, accompanied by the Queen, went into his great hall. As he had not had time to prepare his speech beforehand, the King ordered that silence should be kept for three hours, and at the end of that time he spoke as follows :

' Listen, great and small ! My dear daughter Mayblossom is lost : whether she has been stolen away or has simply disappeared I cannot tell. The Queen's neck-handkerchief and my sword, which are worth their weight in gold, are also missing, and, what is worst of all, the Ambassador Fanfaronade is nowhere to be found. I greatly fear that the King, his master, when he receives no tidings from him, will come to seek him among us, and will accuse us of having made mince-meat of him. Perhaps I could bear even that if I had any money, but I assure you that the expenses of the wedding have completely ruined me. Advise me, then, my dear subjects, what had I better do to recover my daughter, Fanfaronade, and the other things.'

This was the most eloquent speech the King had been known to make, and when everybody had done admiring it the Prime Minister made answer:

'Sire, we are all very sorry to see you so sorry. We would give everything we value in the world to take away the cause of your sorrow, but this seems to be another of the tricks of the Fairy Carabosse. The Princess's twenty unlucky years were not quite over, and really, if the truth must be told, I noticed that Fanfaronade and the Princess appeared to admire one another greatly. Perhaps this may give some clue to the mystery of their disappearance.'

Here the Queen interrupted him, saying, 'Take care what you say, sir. Believe me, the Princess Mayblossom was far too well brought up to think of falling in love with an Ambassador.'

At this the nurse came forward, and, falling on her knees, confessed how they had made the little needle-hole in the tower, and how the Princess had declared when she saw the Ambassador that she would marry him and nobody else. Then the Queen was very angry, and gave the nurse, and the cradle-rocker, and the nursery-maid such a scolding that they shook in their shoes. But the Admiral Cocked-Hat interrupted her, crying:

'Let us be off after this good-for-nothing Fanfaronade, for without a doubt he has run away with our Princess.'

Then there was a great clapping of hands, and everybody shouted, 'By all means let us be after him.'

So while some embarked upon the sea, the others ran from kingdom to kingdom beating drums and blowing trumpets, and wherever a crowd collected they cried:

'Whoever wants a beautiful doll, sweetmeats of all kinds, a little pair of scissors, a golden robe, and a satin cap has only to say where Fanfaronade has hidden the Princess Mayblossom.'

But the answer everywhere was, 'You must go farther, we have not seen them.'

However, those who went by sea were more fortunate, for after sailing about for some time they noticed a light before them which burned at night like a great fire. At first they dared not go near it, not knowing what it might be, but by-and-by it remained stationary over Squirrel Island, for, as you have guessed already, the light was the glowing of the carbuncle. The Princess and Fanfaronade on landing upon the island had given the boatman a hundred gold pieces, and made him promise solemnly to tell no one where he had taken them; but the first thing that happened was that, as he rowed away, he got into the midst of the fleet, and before he could escape the Admiral had seen him and sent a boat after him.

When he was searched they found the gold pieces in his pocket, and as they were quite new coins, struck in honour of the Princess's wedding, the Admiral felt certain that the boatman must have been paid by the Princess to aid her in her flight. But he would not answer any questions, and pretended to be deaf and dumb.

Then the Admiral said: ' Oh! deaf and dumb is he? Lash him to the mast and give him a taste of the cat-o'-nine-tails. I don't know anything better than that for curing the deaf and dumb!'

And when the old boatman saw that he was in earnest, he told all he knew about the cavalier and the lady whom he had landed upon Squirrel Island, and the Admiral knew it must be the Princess and Fanfaronade; so he gave the order for the fleet to surround the island.

Meanwhile the Princess Mayblossom, who was by this time terribly sleepy, had found a grassy bank in the shade, and throwing herself down had already fallen into a profound slumber, when Fanfaronade, who happened to be hungry and not sleepy, came and woke her up, saying, very crossly:

' Pray, madam, how long do you mean to stay here? I see nothing to eat, and though you may be very charming, the sight of you does not prevent me from famishing.'

' What! Fanfaronade,' said the Princess, sitting up and rubbing her eyes, ' is it possible that when I am here with you you can want anything else? You ought to be thinking all the time how happy you are.'

' Happy!' cried he; ' say rather unhappy. I wish with all my heart that you were back in your dark tower again.'

' Darling, don't be cross,' said the Princess. ' I will go and see if I can find some wild fruit for you.'

' I wish you might find a wolf to eat you up,' growled Fanfaronade.

The Princess, in great dismay, ran hither and thither all about the wood, tearing her dress, and hurting her pretty white hands with the thorns and brambles, but she could find nothing good to eat, and at last she had to go back sorrowfully to Fanfaronade.

When he saw that she came empty-handed he got up and left her, grumbling to himself.

The next day they searched again, but with no better success.

'Alas!' said the Princess, 'if only I could find something for you to eat, I should not mind being hungry myself.'

'No, I should not mind that either,' answered Fanfaronade.

'Is it possible,' said she, 'that you would not care if I died of hunger? Oh, Fanfaronade, you said you loved me!'

'That was when we were in quite another place and I was not hungry,' said he. 'It makes a great difference in one's ideas to be dying of hunger and thirst on a desert island.'

At this the Princess was dreadfully vexed, and she sat down under a white rose bush and began to cry bitterly.

'Happy roses,' she thought to herself, 'they have only to blossom in the sunshine and be admired, and there is nobody to be unkind to them.' And the tears ran down her cheeks and splashed on to the rose-tree roots. Presently she was surprised to see the whole bush rustling and shaking, and a soft little voice from the prettiest rosebud said:

'Poor Princess! look in the trunk of that tree, and you will find a honeycomb, but don't be foolish enough to share it with Fanfaronade.'

Mayblossom ran to the tree, and sure enough there was the honey. Without losing a moment she ran with it to Fanfaronade, crying gaily:

'See, here is a honeycomb that I have found. I might have eaten it up all by myself, but I had rather share it with you.'

But without looking at her or thanking her he snatched the honeycomb out of her hands and ate it all up—every bit, without offering her a morsel. Indeed, when she humbly asked for some he said mockingly that it was too sweet for her, and would spoil her teeth.

Mayblossom, more downcast than ever, went sadly away and sat down under an oak tree, and her tears and sighs were so piteous that the oak fanned her with his rustling leaves, and said:

'Take courage, pretty Princess, all is not lost yet. Take this pitcher of milk and drink it up, and whatever you do, don't leave a drop for Fanfaronade.'

The Princess, quite astonished, looked round, and saw a big pitcher full of milk, but before she could raise it to her lips the thought of how thirsty Fanfaronade must be, after eating at least fifteen pounds of honey, made her run back to him and say:

'Here is a pitcher of milk; drink some, for you must be thirsty, I am sure; but pray save a little for me, as I am dying of hunger and thirst.'

But he seized the pitcher and drank all it contained at a single draught, and then broke it to atoms on the nearest stone, saying, with a malicious smile: 'As you have not eaten anything you cannot be thirsty.'

'Ah!' cried the Princess, 'I am well punished for disappointing the King and Queen, and running away with this Ambassador, about whom I knew nothing.'

And so saying she wandered away into the thickest part of the wood, and sat down under a thorn tree, where a nightingale was singing. Presently she heard him say: 'Search under the bush, Princess; you will find some sugar, almonds, and some tarts there. But don't be silly enough to offer Fanfaronade any.' And this time the Princess, who was fainting with hunger, took the nightingale's advice, and ate what she found all by herself. But Fanfaronade, seeing that she had found something good, and was not going to share it with him, ran after her in such a fury that she hastily drew out the Queen's carbuncle, which had the property of rendering people invisible if they were in danger, and when she was safely hidden from him she reproached him gently for his unkindness.

Meanwhile Admiral Cocked-Hat had despatched Jack-the-Chatterer-of-the-Straw-Boots, Courier in Ordinary to the Prime Minister, to tell the King that the Princess and the Ambassador had landed on Squirrel Island, but that not knowing the country he had not pursued them, for fear of being captured by concealed enemies. Their Majesties were overjoyed at the news, and the King sent for a great book, each leaf of which was eight ells long. It was the work of a very clever Fairy, and contained a description of the whole earth. He very soon found that Squirrel Island was uninhabited.

'Go,' said he, to Jack-the-Chatterer, 'tell the Admiral from me to land at once. I am surprised at his not having done so sooner.' As soon as this message reached the fleet, every preparation was made for war, and the noise was so great that it reached the ears of the Princess, who at once flew to protect her lover. As he was not very brave he accepted her aid gladly.

'You stand behind me,' said she, 'and I will hold the carbuncle which will make us invisible, and with the King's dagger I can protect you from the enemy.'   So when the soldiers landed they could see nothing, but the Princess touched them one after another with the dagger, and they fell insensible upon the sand, so that at last the Admiral, seeing that there was some enchantment, hastily gave orders for a retreat to be sounded, and got his men back into their boats in great confusion.

Fanfaronade, being once more left with the Princess, began to think that if he could get rid of her, and possess himself of the carbuncle and the dagger, he would be able to make his escape.   So as they walked back over the cliffs he gave the Princess a great push, hoping she would fall into the sea; but she stepped aside so quickly that he only succeeded in overbalancing himself, and over he went, and sank to the bottom of the sea like a lump of lead, and was never heard of any more. While the Princess was still looking after him in horror, her attention was attracted by a rushing noise over her head, and looking up she saw two chariots approaching rapidly from opposite directions.   One was bright and glittering, and drawn by swans and peacocks, while the Fairy who sat in it was beautiful as a sunbeam; but the other was drawn by bats and ravens, and contained a frightful little Dwarf, who was dressed in a snake's skin, and wore a great toad upon her head for a hood.   The

chariots met with a frightful crash in mid-air, and the Princess-
looked on in breathless anxiety while a furious battle took place be

tween the lovely Fairy with her golden lance, and the hideous little
Dwarf and her rusty pike.   But very soon it was evident that the
Beauty had the best of it, and the Dwarf turned her bats' heads and

flickered away in great confusion, while the Fairy came down to where the Princess stood, and said, smiling, 'You see Princess, I have completely routed that malicious old Carabosse. Will you believe it! she actually wanted to claim authority over you for ever, because you came out of the tower four days before the twenty years were ended. However, I think I have settled her pretensions, and I hope you will be very happy and enjoy the freedom I have won for you.'

The Princess thanked her heartily, and then the Fairy despatched one of her peacocks to her palace to bring a gorgeous robe for May-blossom, who certainly needed it, for her own was torn to shreds by the thorns and briars. Another peacock was sent to the Admiral to tell him that he could now land in perfect safety, which he at once did, bringing all his men with him, even to Jack-the-Chatterer, who, happening to pass the spit upon which the Admiral's dinner was roasting, snatched it up and brought it with him.

Admiral Cocked-Hat was immensely surprised when he came upon the golden chariot, and still more so to see two lovely ladies walking under the trees a little farther away. When he reached them, of course he recognised the Princess, and he went down on his knees and kissed her hand quite joyfully. Then she presented him to the Fairy, and told him how Carabosse had been finally routed, and he thanked and congratulated the Fairy, who was most gracious to him. While they were talking she cried suddenly:

'I declare I smell a savoury dinner.'

'Why yes, Madam, here it is,' said Jack-the-Chatterer, holding up the spit, where all the pheasants and partridges were frizzling. 'Will your Highness please to taste any of them?'

'By all means,' said the Fairy, 'especially as the Princess will certainly be glad of a good meal.'

So the Admiral sent back to his ship for everything that was needful, and they feasted merrily under the trees. By the time they had finished the peacock had come back with a robe for the Princess, in which the Fairy arrayed her. It was of green and gold brocade, embroidered with pearls and rubies, and her long golden hair was tied back with strings of diamonds and emeralds, and crowned with flowers. The Fairy made her mount beside her in the golden chariot, and took her on board the Admiral's ship, where she bade her farewell, sending many messages of friendship to the Queen, and bidding the Princess tell her that she was the fifth Fairy who had attended the christening. Then salutes were fired,

the fleet weighed anchor, and very soon they reached the port.
Here the King and Queen were waiting, and they received the
Princess with such joy and kindness that she could not get a word
in edgewise, to say how sorry she was for having run away with
such a very poor spirited Ambassador.   But, after all, it must have
been all Carabosse's fault.   Just at this lucky moment who should
arrive but King Merlin's son, who had become uneasy at not

receiving any news from his Ambassador, and so had started himself with a magnificent escort of a thousand horsemen, and thirty
body-guards in gold and scarlet uniforms, to see what could have
happened.   As he was a hundred times handsomer and braver
than the Ambassador, the Princess found she could like him very
much.   So the wedding was held at once, with so much splendour
and rejoicing that all the previous misfortunes were quite forgotten.[1]

[1] *La Princesse Printanière.*   Par Mme. d'Aulnoy.

JACK AND THE BEANSTALK

JACK SELLS THE COW.

ONCE upon a time there was a poor widow who lived in a little cottage with her only son Jack.

Jack was a giddy, thoughtless boy, but very kind-hearted and affectionate. There had been a hard winter, and after it the poor woman had suffered from fever and ague. Jack did no work as yet, and by degrees they grew dreadfully poor. The widow saw that there was no means of keeping Jack and herself from starvation but by selling her cow; so one morning she said to her son, 'I am too weak to go myself, Jack, so you must take the cow to market for me, and sell her.'

Jack liked going to market to sell the cow very much; but as he was on the way, he met a butcher who had some beautiful beans in his hand. Jack stopped to look at them, and the butcher told the boy that they were of great value, and persuaded the silly lad to sell the cow for these beans.

When he brought them home to his mother instead of the money she expected for her nice cow, she was very vexed and shed many tears, scolding Jack for his folly. He was very sorry, and mother and son went to bed very sadly that night; their last hope seemed gone.

At daybreak Jack rose and went out into the garden.

'At least,' he thought, 'I will sow the wonderful beans. Mother says that they are just common scarlet-runners, and nothing else; but I may as well sow them.'

So he took a piece of stick, and made some holes in the ground, and put in the beans

That day they had very little dinner, and went sadly to bed, knowing that for the next day there would be none and Jack, unable to sleep from grief and vexation, got up at day-dawn and went out into the garden.

What was his amazement to find that the beans had grown up in the night, and climbed up and up till they covered the high cliff that sheltered the cottage, and disappeared above it! The stalks had twined and twisted themselves together till they formed quite a ladder.

'It would be easy to climb it,' thought Jack.

And, having thought of the experiment, he at once resolved to carry it out, for Jack was a good climber. However, after his late mistake about the cow, he thought he had better consult his mother first.

Wonderful Growth of the Beanstalk

So Jack called his mother, and they both gazed in silent wonder at the Beanstalk, which was not only of great height, but was thick enough to bear Jack's weight.

'I wonder where it ends,' said Jack to his mother; 'I think I will climb up and see.'

His mother wished him not to venture up this strange ladder, but Jack coaxed her to give her consent to the attempt, for he was certain there must be something wonderful in the Beanstalk; so at last she yielded to his wishes.

Jack instantly began to climb, and went up and up on the ladder-like bean till everything he had left behind him—the cottage, the village, and even the tall church tower—looked quite little, and still he could not see the top of the Beanstalk.

Jack felt a little tired, and thought for a moment that he would go back again; but he was a very persevering boy, and he knew that the way to succeed in anything is not to give up. So after resting for a moment he went on.

After climbing higher and higher, till he grew afraid to look down for fear he should be giddy, Jack at last reached the top of the Beanstalk, and found himself in a beautiful country, finely wooded, with beautiful meadows covered with sheep. A crystal stream ran through the pastures; not far from the place where he had got off the Beanstalk stood a fine, strong castle.

Jack wondered very much that he had never heard of or seen this castle before; but when he reflected on the subject, he saw that it was as much separated from the village by the perpendicular rock on which it stood as if it were in another land.

While Jack was standing looking at the castle, a very strange-looking woman came out of the wood, and advanced towards him.

She wore a pointed cap of quilted red satin turned up with ermine, her hair streamed loose over her shoulders, and she walked with a staff. Jack took off his cap and made her a bow.

'If you please, ma'am,' said he, 'is this your house ? '

'No,' said the old lady. 'Listen, and I will tell you the story of that castle.

'Once upon a time there was a noble knight, who lived in this castle, which is on the borders of Fairyland. He had a fair and beloved wife and several lovely children : and as his neighbours, the little people, were very friendly towards him, they bestowed on him many excellent and precious gifts.

'Rumour whispered of these treasures; and a monstrous giant, who lived at no great distance, and who was a very wicked being, resolved to obtain possession of them.

'So he bribed a false servant to let him inside the castle, when the knight was in bed and asleep, and he killed him as he lay. Then he went to the part of the castle which was the nursery, and also killed all the poor little ones he found there.

'Happily for her, the lady was not to be found. She had gone with her infant son, who was only two or three months old, to visit her old nurse, who lived in the valley ; and she had been detained all night there by a storm.

'The next morning, as soon as it was light, one of the servants at the castle, who had managed to escape, came to tell the poor lady of the sad fate of her husband and her pretty babes. She could scarcely believe him at first, and was eager at once to go back and share the fate of her dear ones ; but the old nurse, with many tears, besought her to remember that she had still a child, and that it was her duty to preserve her life for the sake of the poor innocent.

'The lady yielded to this reasoning, and consented to remain at her nurse's house as the best place of concealment ; for the servant told her that the giant had vowed, if he could find her, he would kill both her and her baby. Years rolled on. The old nurse died, leaving her cottage and the few articles of furniture it contained to her poor lady, who dwelt in it, working as a peasant for her daily bread. Her spinning-wheel and the milk of a cow, which she had purchased with the little money she had with her, sufficed for the scanty subsistence of herself and her little son. There was a nice little garden attached to the cottage, in which they cultivated peas, beans, and cabbages, and the lady was not ashamed to go out at harvest time, and glean in the fields to supply her little son's wants.

'Jack, that poor lady is your mother. This castle was once your father's, and must again be yours.'

Jack uttered a cry of surprise.

'My mother! oh, madam, what ought I to do? My poor father! My dear mother!'

'Your duty requires you to win it back for your mother. But the task is a very difficult one, and full of peril, Jack. Have you courage to undertake it?'

'I fear nothing when I am doing right,' said Jack.

'Then,' said the lady in the red cap, ' you are one of those who slay giants. You must get into the castle, and if possible possess yourself of a hen that lays golden eggs, and a harp that talks. Remember, all the giant possesses is really yours.' As she ceased speaking, the lady of the red hat suddenly disappeared, and of course Jack knew she was a fairy.

Jack determined at once to attempt the adventure; so he advanced, and blew the horn which hung at the castle portal. The door was opened in a minute or two by a frightful giantess, with one great eye in the middle of her forehead.

As soon as Jack saw her he turned to run away, but she caught him, and dragged him into the castle.

' Ho, ho!' she laughed terribly. ' You didn't expect to see *me* here, that is clear! No, I shan't let you go again. I am weary of my life. I am so overworked, and I don't see why I should not have a page as well as other ladies. And you shall be my boy. You shall clean the knives, and black the boots, and make the fires, and help me generally when the giant is out. When he is at home I must hide you, for he has eaten up all my pages hitherto, and you would be a dainty morsel, my little lad.'

While she spoke she dragged Jack right into the castle. The poor boy was very much frightened, as I am sure you and I would have been in his place. But he remembered that fear disgraces a man; so he struggled to be brave and make the best of things.

' I am quite ready to help you, and do all I can to serve you, madam,' he said, ' only I beg you will be good enough to hide me from your husband, for I should not like to be eaten at all.'

' That's a good boy,' said the Giantess, nodding her head; ' it is lucky for you that you did not scream out when you saw me, as the other boys who have been here did, for if you had done so my husband would have awakened and have eaten you, as he did them,

for breakfast.   Come here, child ; go into my wardrobe : he never
ventures to open *that* ; you will be safe there.'

And she opened a huge wardrobe which stood in the great hall,
and shut him into it.   But the keyhole was so large that it ad-

mitted plenty of air, and he could see everything that took place
through it.   By-and-by he heard a heavy tramp on the stairs, like
the lumbering along of a great cannon, and then a voice like thunder
cried out :

' Fe, fa, fi-fo-fum,
I smell the breath of an Englishman.
Let him be alive or let him be dead,
I'll grind his bones to make my bread.'

' Wife,' cried the Giant, ' there is a man in the castle.   Let me have him for breakfast.'

' You are grown old and stupid,' cried the lady in her loud tones.   ' It is only a nice fresh steak off an elephant, that I have cooked for you, which you smell.   There, sit down and make a good breakfast.'

And she placed a huge dish before him of savoury steaming meat, which greatly pleased him, and made him forget his idea of an Englishman being in the castle.   When he had breakfasted he went out for a walk ; and then the Giantess opened the door, and made Jack come out to help her.   He helped her all day.   She fed him well, and when evening came put him back in the wardrobe.

The Hen that lays Golden Eggs.

The Giant came in to supper.   Jack watched him through the keyhole, and was amazed to see him pick a wolf's bone, and put half a fowl at a time into his capacious mouth.

When the supper was ended he bade his wife bring him his hen that laid the golden eggs.

' It lays as well as it did when it belonged to that paltry knight,' he said ; ' indeed I think the eggs are heavier than ever.'

The Giantess went away, and soon returned with a little brown hen, which she placed on the table before her husband.   ' And now, my dear,' she said, ' I am going for a walk, if you don't want me any longer.'

' Go,' said the Giant ; ' I shall be glad to have a nap by-and-by.'

Then he took up the brown hen and said to her :

' Lay ! ' And she instantly laid a golden egg.

' Lay ! ' said the Giant again.   And she laid another.

' Lay ! ' he repeated the third time.   And again a golden egg lay on the table.

Now Jack was sure this hen was that of which the fairy had spoken.

By-and-by the Giant put the hen down on the floor, and soon after went fast asleep, snoring so loud that it sounded like thunder.

Directly Jack perceived that the Giant was fast asleep, he

pushed open the door of the wardrobe and crept out; very softly he stole across the room, and, picking up the hen, made haste to quit the apartment. He knew the way to the kitchen, the door of which he found was left ajar; he opened it, shut and locked it after him, and flew back to the Beanstalk, which he descended as fast as his feet would move.

When his mother saw him enter the house she wept for joy, for she had feared that the fairies had carried him away, or that the Giant had found him. But Jack put the brown hen down before her, and told her how he had been in the Giant's castle, and all his adventures. She was very glad to see the hen, which would make them rich once more.

The Money Bags.

Jack made another journey up the Beanstalk to the Giant's castle one day while his mother had gone to market; but first he dyed his hair and disguised himself. The old woman did not know him again, and dragged him in as she had done before, to help her to do the work; but she heard her husband coming, and hid him in the wardrobe, not thinking that it was the same boy who had stolen the hen. She bade him stay quite still there, or the Giant would eat him.

Then the Giant came in saying:

' Fe, fa, fi-fo-fum,
I smell the breath of an Englishman.
Let him be alive or let him be dead,
I'll grind his bones to make my bread.'

' Nonsense ! ' said the wife, ' it is only a roasted bullock that I thought would be a tit-bit for your supper; sit down and I will bring it up at once.' The Giant sat down, and soon his wife brought up a roasted bullock on a large dish, and they began their supper. Jack was amazed to see them pick the bones of the bullock as if it had been a lark. As soon as they had finished their meal, the Giantess rose and said :

' Now, my dear, with your leave I am going up to my room to finish the story I am reading. If you want me call for me.'

' First,' answered the Giant, ' bring me my money bags, that I may count my golden pieces before I sleep.' The Giantess obeyed. She went and soon returned with two large bags over her shoulders, which she put down by her husband.

'There,' she said; 'that is all that is left of the knight's money. When you have spent it you must go and take another baron's castle.'

'That he shan't, if I can help it,' thought Jack.

The Giant, when his wife was gone, took out heaps and heaps of golden pieces, and counted them, and put them in piles, till he was tired of the amusement. Then he swept them all back into their bags, and leaning back in his chair fell fast asleep, snoring so loud that no other sound was audible.

Jack stole softly out of the wardrobe, and taking up the bags of money (which were his very own, because the Giant had stolen them from his father), he ran off, and with great difficulty descending the Beanstalk, laid the bags of gold on his mother's table. She had just returned from town, and was crying at not finding Jack.

'There, mother, I have brought you the gold that my father lost.'

'Oh, Jack! you are a very good boy, but I wish you would not risk your precious life in the Giant's castle. Tell me how you came to go there again.'

And Jack told her all about it.

Jack's mother was very glad to get the money, but she did not like him to run any risk for her.

But after a time Jack made up his mind to go again to the Giant's castle.

The Talking Harp.

So he climbed the Beanstalk once more, and blew the horn at the Giant's gate. The Giantess soon opened the door; she was very stupid, and did not know him again, but she stopped a minute before she took him in. She feared another robbery; but Jack's fresh face looked so innocent that she could not resist him, and so she bade him come in, and again hid him away in the wardrobe.

By-and-by the Giant came home, and as soon as he had crossed the threshold he roared out:

'Fe, fa, fi-fo-fum,
I smell the breath of an Englishman.
Let him be alive or let him be dead,
I'll grind his bones to make my bread.'

'You stupid old Giant,' said his wife, 'you only smell a nice sheep, which I have grilled for your dinner.'

And the Giant sat down, and his wife brought up a whole sheep for his dinner.   When he had eaten it all up, he said:

'Now bring me my harp, and I will have a little music while you take your walk.'

The Giantess obeyed, and returned with a beautiful harp.   The framework was all sparkling with diamonds and rubies, and the strings were all of gold.

'This is one of the nicest things I took from the knight,' said the Giant.   'I am very fond of music, and my harp is a faithful servant.'

So he drew the harp towards him, and said:

'Play!'

And the harp played a very soft, sad air.

'Play something merrier!' said the Giant.

And the harp played a merry tune.

'Now play me a lullaby,' roared the Giant; and the harp played a sweet lullaby, to the sound of which its master fell asleep.

Then Jack stole softly out of the wardrobe, and went into the huge kitchen to see if the Giantess had gone out; he found no one there, so he went to the door and opened it softly, for he thought he could not do so with the harp in his hand.

Then he entered the Giant's room and seized the harp and ran away with it; but as he jumped over the threshold the harp called out:

'MASTER! MASTER!'

And the Giant woke up.

With a tremendous roar he sprang from his seat, and in two strides had reached the door.

But Jack was very nimble. He fled like lightning with the harp, talking to it as he went (for he saw it was a fairy), and telling it he was the son of its old master, the knight.

Still the Giant came on so fast that he was quite close to poor Jack, and had stretched out his great hand to catch him. But, luckily, just at that moment he stepped upon a loose stone, stumbled, and fell flat on the ground, where he lay at his full length.

This accident gave Jack time to get on the Beanstalk and hasten down it; but just as he reached their own garden he beheld the Giant descending after him.

'Mother! mother!' cried Jack, 'make haste and give me the axe.'

His mother ran to him with a hatchet in her hand, and Jack with one tremendous blow cut through all the Beanstalks except one.

'Now, mother, stand out of the way!' said he.

THE GIANT BREAKS HIS NECK.

Jack's mother shrank back, and it was well she did so, for just as the Giant took hold of the last branch of the Beanstalk, Jack cut the stem quite through and darted from the spot.

Down came the Giant with a terrible crash, and as he fell on his head, he broke his neck, and lay dead at the feet of the woman he had so much injured.

Before Jack and his mother had recovered from their alarm and agitation, a beautiful lady stood before them.

Jack,' said she, 'you have acted like a brave knight's son, and deserve to have your inheritance restored to you.   Dig a grave and bury the Giant, and then go and kill the Giantess.'

'But,' said Jack, 'I could not kill anyone unless I were fighting with him ; and I could not draw my sword upon a woman. Moreover, the Giantess was very kind to me.'

The Fairy smiled on Jack.

'I am very much pleased with your generous feeling,' she said. 'Nevertheless, return to the castle, and act as you will find needful.'

Jack asked the Fairy if she would show him the way to the castle, as the Beanstalk was now down. She told him that she would drive him there in her chariot, which was drawn by two peacocks. Jack thanked her, and sat down in the chariot with her.

The Fairy drove him a long distance round, till they reached a village which lay at the bottom of the hill. Here they found a number of miserable-looking men assembled. The Fairy stopped her carriage and addressed them :

'My friends,' said she, 'the cruel giant who oppressed you and ate up all your flocks and herds is dead, and this young gentleman was the means of your being delivered from him, and is the son of your kind old master, the knight.'

The men gave a loud cheer at these words, and pressed forward to say that they would serve Jack as faithfully as they had served his father. The Fairy bade them follow her to the castle, and they marched thither in a body, and Jack blew the horn and demanded admittance.

The old Giantess saw them coming from the turret loop-hole. She was very much frightened, for she guessed that something had happened to her husband ; and as she came downstairs very fast she caught her foot in her dress, and fell from the top to the bottom and broke her neck.

When the people outside found that the door was not opened to them, they took crowbars and forced the portal. Nobody was to be seen, but on leaving the hall they found the body of the Giantess at the foot of the stairs.

Thus Jack took possession of the castle. The Fairy went and brought his mother to him, with the hen and the harp. He had the Giantess buried, and endeavoured as much as lay in his power to do right to those whom the Giant had robbed.

Before her departure for fairyland, the Fairy explained to Jack that she had sent the butcher to meet him with the beans, in order to try what sort of lad he was.

If you had looked at the gigantic Beanstalk and only stupidly wondered about it,' she said, 'I should have left you where misfortune had placed you, only restoring her cow to your mother. But you showed an inquiring mind, and great courage and enterprise, therefore you deserve to rise; and when you mounted the Beanstalk you climbed the Ladder of Fortune.'

She then took her leave of Jack and his mother.

SNOWDROP

ONCE upon a time, in the middle of winter when the snow-flakes were falling like feathers on the earth, a Queen sat at a window framed in black ebony and sewed. And as she sewed and gazed out to the white landscape, she pricked her finger with the needle, and three drops of blood fell on the snow outside, and because the red showed out so well against the white she thought to herself:

'Oh! what wouldn't I give to have a child as white as snow, as red as blood, and as black as ebony!'

And her wish was granted, for not long after a little daughter was born to her, with a skin as white as snow, lips and cheeks as red as blood, and hair as black as ebony. They called her Snowdrop, and not long after her birth the Queen died.

After a year the King married again. His new wife was a beautiful woman, but so proud and overbearing that she couldn't stand any rival to her beauty. She possessed a magic mirror, and when she used to stand before it gazing at her own reflection and ask :

'Mirror, mirror, hanging there,
Who in all the land's most fair ? '

it always replied :

'You are most fair, my Lady Queen,
None fairer in the land, I ween.'

Then she was quite happy, for she knew the mirror always spoke the truth.

But Snowdrop was growing prettier and prettier every day, and when she was seven years old she was as beautiful as she could be, and fairer even than the Queen herself. One day when the latter asked her mirror the usual question, it replied :

'My Lady Queen, you are fair, 'tis true,
But Snowdrop is fairer far than you.'

Then the Queen flew into the most awful passion, and turned every shade of green in her jealousy. From this hour she hated poor Snowdrop like poison, and every day her envy, hatred, and

malice grew, for envy and jealousy are like evil weeds which spring up and choke the heart. At last she could endure Snowdrop's presence no longer, and, calling a huntsman to her, she said:

'Take the child out into the wood, and never let me see her face again. You must kill her, and bring me back her lungs and liver, that I may know for certain she is dead.'

The Huntsman did as he was told and led Snowdrop out into the wood, but as he was in the act of drawing out his knife to slay her, she began to cry, and said:

'Oh, dear Huntsman, spare my life, and I will promise to fly forth into the wide wood and never to return home again.'

And because she was so young and pretty the Huntsman had pity on her, and said:

'Well, run along, poor child.' For he thought to himself: 'The wild beasts will soon eat her up.'

And his heart felt lighter because he hadn't had to do the deed himself. And as he turned away a young boar came running past, so he shot it, and brought its lungs and liver home to the Queen as a proof that Snowdrop was really dead. And the wicked woman had them stewed in salt, and ate them up, thinking she had made an end of Snowdrop for ever.

Now when the poor child found herself alone in the big wood the very trees around her seemed to assume strange shapes, and she felt so frightened she didn't know what to do. Then she began to run over the sharp stones, and through the bramble bushes, and the wild beasts ran past her, but they did her no harm. She ran as far as her legs would carry her, and as evening approached she saw a little house, and she stepped inside to rest. Everything was very small in the little house, but cleaner and neater than anything you can imagine. In the middle of the room there stood a little table, covered with a white tablecloth, and seven little plates and forks and spoons and knives and tumblers. Side by side against the wall there were seven little beds, covered with snow-white counterpanes. Snowdrop felt so hungry and so thirsty that she ate a bit of bread and a little porridge from each plate, and drank a drop of wine out of each tumbler. Then feeling tired and sleepy she lay down on one of the beds, but it wasn't comfortable; then she tried all the others in turn, but one was too long, and another too short, and it was only when she got to the seventh that she found one to suit her exactly. So she lay down upon it, said her prayers like a good child, and fell fast asleep.

When it got quite dark the masters of the little house returned. They were seven dwarfs who worked in the mines, right down deep in the heart of the mountain. They lighted their seven little lamps, and as soon as their eyes got accustomed to the glare they saw that someone had been in the room, for all was not in the same order as they had left it.

The first said :

'Who's been sitting on my little chair ? '

The second said :

'Who's been eating my little loaf ? '

The third said :

'Who's been tasting my porridge ? '

The fourth said :

'Who's been eating out of my little plate ?

The fifth said :

'Who's been using my little fork ? '

The sixth said :

'Who's been cutting with my little knife ? '

The seventh said :

Who's been drinking out of my little tumbler ? '

Then the first Dwarf looked round and saw a little hollow in his bed, and he asked again :

'Who's been lying on my bed ? '

The others came running round, and cried when they saw their beds :

'Somebody has lain on ours too.'

But when the seventh came to his bed, he started back in amazement, for there he beheld Snowdrop fast asleep. Then he called the others, who turned their little lamps full on the bed, and when they saw Snowdrop lying there they nearly fell down with surprise.

'Goodness gracious ! ' they cried, 'what a beautiful child ! '

And they were so enchanted by her beauty that they did not wake her, but let her sleep on in the little bed. But the seventh Dwarf slept with his companions one hour in each bed, and in this way he managed to pass the night.

In the morning Snowdrop awoke, but when she saw the seven little Dwarfs she felt very frightened. But they were so friendly, and asked her what her name was in such a kind way, that she replied :

'I am Snowdrop.'

'Why did you come to our house?' continued the Dwarfs.

Then she told them how her stepmother had wished her put to death, and how the Huntsman had spared her life, and how she had run the whole day till she had come to their little house. The Dwarfs, when they had heard her sad story, asked her:

'Will you stay and keep house for us, cook, make the beds, do the washing, sew and knit? and if you give satisfaction and keep everything neat and clean, you shall want for nothing.'

'Yes,' answered Snowdrop, 'I will gladly do all you ask.'

And so she took up her abode with them. Every morning the Dwarfs went into the mountain to dig for gold, and in the evening, when they returned home, Snowdrop always had their supper ready for them. But during the day the girl was left quite alone, so the good Dwarfs warned her, saying:

'Beware of your step-mother. She will soon find out you are here, and whatever you do don't let anyone into the house.'

Now the Queen, after she thought she had eaten Snowdrop's lungs and liver, never dreamed but that she was once more the most beautiful woman in the world; so stepping before her mirror one day she said:

> 'Mirror, mirror, hanging there,
> Who in all the land's most fair?'

and the mirror replied:

> 'My Lady Queen, you are fair, 'tis true,
> But Snowdrop is fairer far than you.
> Snowdrop, who dwells with the seven little men,
> Is as fair as you, as fair again.'

When the Queen heard these words she was nearly struck dumb with horror, for the mirror always spoke the truth, and she knew now that the Huntsman must have deceived her, and that Snowdrop was still alive. She pondered day and night how she might destroy her, for as long as she felt she had a rival in the land her jealous heart left her no rest. At last she hit upon a plan. She stained her face and dressed herself up as an old peddler wife, so that she was quite unrecognisable. In this guise she went over the seven hills till she came to the house of the seven Dwarfs. There she knocked at the door, calling out at the same time:

'Fine wares to sell, fine wares to sell!'

Snowdrop peeped out of the window, and called out:

'Good-day, mother, what have you to sell?'

'Good wares, fine wares,' she answered; 'laces of every shade and description,' and she held one up that was made of some gay coloured silk.

'Surely I can let the honest woman in,' thought Snowdrop; so she unbarred the door and bought the pretty lace.

'Good gracious! child,' said the old woman, 'what a figure you've got. Come! I'll lace you up properly for once.'

Snowdrop, suspecting no evil, stood before her and let her lace her bodice up, but the old woman laced her so quickly and so tightly that it took Snowdrop's breath away, and she fell down dead.

'Now you are no longer the fairest,' said the wicked old woman, and then she hastened away.

In the evening the seven Dwarfs came home, and you may think what a fright they got when they saw their dear Snowdrop lying on the floor, as still and motionless as a dead person. They lifted her up tenderly, and when they saw how tightly laced she was they cut the lace in two, and she began to breathe a little and gradually came back to life. When the Dwarfs heard what had happened, they said:

'Depend upon it, the old peddler wife was none other than the old Queen. In future you must be sure to let no one in, if we are not at home.'

As soon as the wicked old Queen got home she went straight to her mirror, and said:

'Mirror, mirror, hanging there,
Who in all the land's most fair?'

and the mirror answered as before:

'My Lady Queen, you are fair, 'tis true,
But Snowdrop is fairer far than you.
Snowdrop, who dwells with the seven little men,
Is as fair as you, as fair again.'

When she heard this she became as pale as death, because she saw at once that Snowdrop must be alive again.

'This time,' she said to herself, 'I will think of something that will make an end of her once and for all.'

And by the witchcraft which she understood so well she made a poisonous comb; then she dressed herself up and assumed the form of another old woman. So she went over the seven hills till she reached the house of the seven Dwarfs, and knocking at the door she called out:

'Fine wares for sale.'

Snowdrop looked out of the window and said:

'You must go away, for I may not let anyone in.'

'But surely you are not forbidden to look out?' said the old woman, and she held up the poisonous comb for her to see.

It pleased the girl so much that she let herself be taken in, and opened the door. When they had settled their bargain the old woman said:

'Now I'll comb your hair properly for you, for once in the way.'

Poor Snowdrop thought no evil, but hardly had the comb touched her hair than the poison worked and she fell down unconscious.

'Now, my fine lady, you're really done for this time,' said the wicked woman, and she made her way home as fast as she could.

Fortunately it was now near evening, and the seven Dwarfs returned home. When they saw Snowdrop lying dead on the ground, they at once suspected that her wicked step-mother had been at work again; so they searched till they found the poisonous comb, and the moment they pulled it out of her head Snowdrop came to herself again, and told them what had happened. Then they warned her once more to be on her guard, and to open the door to no one.

As soon as the Queen got home she went straight to her mirror, and asked:

> 'Mirror, mirror, hanging there,
> Who in all the land's most fair?'

and it replied as before:

> 'My Lady Queen, you are fair, 'tis true,
> But Snowdrop is fairer far than you.
> Snowdrop, who dwells with the seven little men,
> Is as fair as you, as fair again.'

When she heard these words she literally trembled and shook with rage.

'Snowdrop shall die,' she cried; 'yes, though it cost me my own life.'

Then she went to a little secret chamber, which no one knew of but herself, and there she made a poisonous apple. Outwardly it looked beautiful, white with red cheeks, so that everyone who saw it longed to eat it, but anyone who might do so would certainly die on the spot. When the apple was quite finished she stained her face and dressed herself up as a peasant, and so she went over the seven hills to the seven Dwarfs'. She knocked at the door, as usual, but Snowdrop put her head out of the window and called out:

'I may not let anyone in, the seven Dwarfs have forbidden me to do so.'

'Are you afraid of being poisoned?' asked the old woman. 'See, I will cut this apple in half. I'll eat the white cheek and you can eat the red.'

But the apple was so cunningly made that only the red cheek was poisonous. Snowdrop longed to eat the tempting fruit, and when she saw that the peasant woman was eating it herself, she couldn't resist the temptation any longer, and stretching out her hand she took the poisonous half. But hardly had the first bite passed her lips than she fell down dead on the ground. Then the eyes of the cruel Queen sparkled with glee, and laughing aloud she cried:

'As white as snow, as red as blood, and as black as ebony, this time the Dwarfs won't be able to bring you back to life.'

When she got home she asked the mirror:

> 'Mirror, mirror, hanging there,
> Who in all the land's most fair?'

and this time it replied:

> 'You are most fair, my Lady Queen,
> None fairer in the land, I ween.'

Then her jealous heart was at rest—at least, as much at rest as a jealous heart can ever be.

When the little Dwarfs came home in the evening they found Snowdrop lying on the ground, and she neither breathed nor stirred. They lifted her up, and looked round everywhere to see if they could find anything poisonous about. They unlaced her bodice, combed her hair, washed her with water and wine, but all in vain; the child was dead and remained dead. Then they placed her on a bier, and all the seven Dwarfs sat round it, weeping and sobbing for three whole days. At last they made up their minds to bury her, but she looked as blooming as a living being, and her cheeks were still such a lovely colour, that they said:

'We can't hide her away in the black ground.'

So they had a coffin made of transparent glass, and they laid her in it, and wrote on the lid in golden letters that she was a royal Princess. Then they put the coffin on the top of the mountain, and one of the Dwarfs always remained beside it and kept watch over it.

And the very birds of the air came and bewailed Snowdrop's death, first an owl, and then a raven, and last of all a little dove.

Snowdrop lay a long time in the coffin, and she always looked the same, just as if she were fast asleep, and she remained as white as snow, as red as blood, and her hair as black as ebony.

Now it happened one day that a Prince came to the wood and passed by the Dwarfs' house. He saw the coffin on the hill, with the beautiful Snowdrop inside it, and when he had read what was written on it in golden letters, he said to the Dwarf:

'Give me the coffin. I'll give you whatever you like for it.'

But the Dwarf said: 'No; we wouldn't part with it for all the gold in the world.'

Well, then,' he replied, 'give it to me, because I can't live with-

out Snowdrop. I will cherish and love it as my dearest possession.'

He spoke so sadly that the good Dwarfs had pity on him, and gave him the coffin, and the Prince made his servants bear it away on their shoulders. Now it happened that as they were going down the hill they stumbled over a bush, and jolted the coffin so violently that the poisonous bit of apple Snowdrop had swallowed fell out of her throat. She gradually opened her eyes, lifted up the lid of the coffin, and sat up alive and well.

'Oh! dear me, where am I?' she cried.

The Prince answered joyfully, 'You are with me,' and he told her all that had happened, adding, 'I love you better than anyone in the whole wide world. Will you come with me to my father's palace and be my wife?'

Snowdrop consented, and went with him, and the marriage was celebrated with great pomp and splendour.

Now Snowdrop's wicked step-mother was one of the guests invited to the wedding feast. When she had dressed herself very gorgeously for the occasion, she went to the mirror, and said:

'Mirror, mirror, hanging there,
　Who in all the land's most fair?'

and the mirror answered:

> ' My Lady Queen, you are fair, 'tis true,
> But Snowdrop is fairer far than you.'

When the wicked woman heard these words she uttered a curse, and was beside herself with rage and mortification. At first she didn't want to go to the wedding at all, but at the same time she felt she would never be happy till she had seen the young Queen. As she entered Snowdrop recognised her, and nearly fainted with fear ; but red-hot iron shoes had been prepared for the wicked old Queen, and she was made to get into them and dance till she fell down dead.[1]

[1] Grimm.

SYLVAIN AND JOCOSA

ONCE upon a time there lived in the same village two children, one called Sylvain and the other Jocosa, who were both remarkable for beauty and intelligence. It happened that their parents were not on terms of friendship with one another, on account of some old quarrel, which had, however, taken place so long ago, that they had quite forgotten what it was all about, and only kept up the feud from force of habit. Sylvain and Jocosa for their parts were far from sharing this enmity, and indeed were never happy when apart. Day after day they fed their flocks of sheep together, and spent the long sunshiny hours in playing, or resting upon some shady bank. It happened one day that the Fairy of the Meadows passed by and saw them, and was so much attracted by their pretty faces and gentle manners that she took them under her protection, and the older they grew the dearer they became to her. At first she showed her interest by leaving in their favourite haunts many little gifts such as they delighted to offer one to the other, for they loved each other so much that their first thought was always, 'What will Jocosa like?' or, 'What will please Sylvain?' And the Fairy took a great delight in their innocent enjoyment of the cakes and sweetmeats she gave them nearly every day. When they were grown up she resolved to make herself known to them, and chose a time when they were sheltering from the noonday sun in the deep shade of a flowery hedgerow. They were startled at first by the sudden apparition of a tall and slender lady, dressed all in green, and crowned with a garland of flowers. But when she spoke to them sweetly, and told them how she had always loved them, and that it was she who had given them all the pretty things which it had so surprised them to find, they thanked her gratefully, and took pleasure in answering the questions she put to them. When she presently bade them farewell, she told them never to tell anyone else that they had

seen her. 'You will often see me again,' added she, 'and I shall
be with you frequently, even when you do not see me.' So saying she
vanished, leaving them in a state of great wonder and excitement.
After this she came often, and taught them numbers of things, and

showed them many of the marvels of her beautiful kingdom, and
at last one day she said to them, 'You know that I have always
been kind to you; now I think it is time you did something for me
in your turn. You both remember the fountain I call my favourite?
Promise me that every morning before the sun rises you will go to

it and clear away every stone that impedes its course, and every dead leaf or broken twig that sullies its clear waters. I shall take it as a proof of your gratitude to me if you neither forget nor delay this duty, and I promise that so long as the sun's earliest rays find my favourite spring the clearest and sweetest in all my meadows, you two shall not be parted from one another.'

Sylvain and Jocosa willingly undertook this service, and indeed felt that it was but a very small thing in return for all that the fairy had given and promised to them. So for a long time the fountain was tended with the most scrupulous care, and was the clearest and prettiest in all the country round. But one morning in the spring, long before the sun rose, they were hastening towards it from opposite directions, when, tempted by the beauty of the myriads of gay flowers which grew thickly on all sides, they paused each to gather some for the other.

'I will make Sylvain a garland,' said Jocosa, and ' How pretty Jocosa will look in this crown ! ' thought Sylvain.

Hither and thither they strayed, led ever farther and farther, for the brightest flowers seemed always just beyond them, until at last they were startled by the first bright rays of the rising sun. With one accord they turned and ran towards the fountain, reaching it at the same moment, though from opposite sides. But what was their horror to see its usually tranquil waters seething and bubbling, and even as they looked down rushed a mighty stream, which entirely engulfed it, and Sylvain and Jocosa found themselves parted by a wide and swiftly-rushing river. All this had happened with such rapidity that they had only time to utter a cry, and each to hold up to the other the flowers they had gathered ; but this was explanation enough. Twenty times did Sylvain throw himself into the turbulent waters, hoping to be able to swim to the other side, but each time an irresistible force drove him back upon the bank he had just quitted, while, as for Jocosa, she even essayed to cross the flood upon a tree which came floating down torn up by the roots, but her efforts were equally useless. Then with heavy hearts they set out to follow the course of the stream, which had now grown so wide that it was only with difficulty they could distinguish each other. Night and day, over mountains and through valleys, in cold or in heat, they struggled on, enduring fatigue and hunger and every hardship, and consoled only by the hope of meeting once more—until three years had passed, and at last they stood upon the cliffs where the river flowed into the mighty sea.

And now they seemed farther apart than ever, and in despair they tried once more to throw themselves into the foaming waves. But the Fairy of the Meadows, who had really never ceased to watch over them, did not intend that they should be drowned at last, so she hastily waved her wand, and immediately they found themselves standing side by side upon the golden sand. You may imagine their joy and delight when they realised that their weary struggle was ended, and their utter contentment as they clasped each other by the hand. They had so much to say that they hardly knew where to begin, but they agreed in blaming themselves bitterly for the negligence which had caused all their trouble; and when she heard this the Fairy immediately appeared to them. They threw themselves at her feet and implored her forgiveness, which she granted freely, and promised at the same time that now their punishment was ended she would always befriend them. Then she sent for her chariot of green rushes, ornamented with May dew-drops, which she particularly valued and always collected with great care; and ordered her six short-tailed moles to carry them all back to the well-known pastures, which they did in a remarkably short time; and Sylvain and Jocosa were overjoyed to see their dearly-loved home once more after all their toilful wanderings. The Fairy, who had set her mind upon securing their happiness, had in their absence quite made up the quarrel between their parents, and gained their consent to the marriage of the faithful lovers; and now she conducted them to the most charming little cottage that can be imagined, close to the fountain, which had once more resumed its peaceful aspect, and flowed gently down into the little brook which enclosed the garden and orchard and pasture which belonged to the cottage. Indeed, nothing more could have been thought of, either for Sylvain and Jocosa or for their flocks; and their delight satisfied even the Fairy who had planned it all to please them. When they had explored and admired until they were tired they sat down to rest under the rose-covered porch, and the Fairy said that to pass the time until the wedding guests whom she had invited could arrive she would tell them a story. This is it:

THE YELLOW BIRD

Once upon a time a Fairy, who had somehow or other got into mischief, was condemned by the High Court of Fairyland to live for several years under the form of some creature, and at the

moment of resuming her natural appearance once again to make
the fortune of two men. It was left to her to choose what form
she would take, and because she loved yellow she transformed herself into a lovely bird with shining golden feathers such as no one
had ever seen before. When the time of her punishment was at

an end the beautiful yellow bird flew to Bagdad, and let herself be
caught by a Fowler at the precise moment when Badi-al-Zaman
was walking up and down outside his magnificent summer palace.
This Badi-al-Zaman—whose name means 'Wonder-of-the-World'
—was looked upon in Bagdad as the most fortunate creature under
the sun, because of his vast wealth. But really, what with anxiety

about his riches and being weary of everything, and always desiring something he had not, he never knew a moment's real happiness. Even now he had come out of his palace, which was large and splendid enough for fifty kings, weary and cross because he could find nothing new to amuse him. The Fowler thought that this would be a favourable opportunity for offering him the marvellous bird, which he felt certain he would buy the instant he saw it. And he was not mistaken, for when Badi-al-Zaman took the lovely prisoner into his own hands, he saw written under its right wing the words, ' He who eats my head will become a king,' and under its left wing, ' He who eats my heart will find a hundred gold pieces under his pillow every morning.' In spite of all his wealth he at once began to desire the promised gold, and the bargain was soon completed. Then the difficulty arose as to how the bird was to be cooked; for among all his army of servants not one could Badi-al-Zaman trust. At last he asked the Fowler if he were married, and on hearing that he was he bade him take the bird home with him and tell his wife to cook it.

' Perhaps,' said he, ' this will give me an appetite, which I have not had for many a long day, and if so your wife shall have a hundred pieces of silver.'

The Fowler with great joy ran home to his wife, who speedily made a savoury stew of the Yellow Bird. But when Badi-al-Zaman reached the cottage and began eagerly to search in the dish for its head and its heart he could not find either of them, and turned to the Fowler's wife in a furious rage. She was so terrified that she fell upon her knees before him and confessed that her two children had come in just before he arrived, and had so teased her for some of the dish she was preparing that she had presently given the head to one and the heart to the other, since these morsels are not generally much esteemed; and Badi-al-Zaman rushed from the cottage vowing vengeance against the whole family. The wrath of a rich man is generally to be feared, so the Fowler and his wife resolved to send their children out of harm's way; but the wife, to console her husband, confided to him that she had purposely given them the head and heart of the bird because she had been able to read what was written under its wings. So, believing that their children's fortunes were made, they embraced them and sent them forth, bidding them get as far away as possible, to take different roads, and to send news of their welfare. For themselves, they remained hidden and disguised in the town, which was really rather clever of them ; but very soon afterwards Badi-al-Zaman died of vexation and annoyance at the loss of the promised treasure, and then they went back to their cottage to wait for news of their children.　The younger, who had eaten the heart of the Yellow Bird, very soon found out what it had done for him, for each morning when he awoke he found a purse containing a hundred gold pieces under his pillow.　But, as all poor people may remember for their consolation, nothing in the world causes so much trouble or requires so much care as a great treasure.　Consequently, the Fowler's son, who spent with reckless profusion and was supposed to be possessed of a great hoard of gold, was before very long attacked by robbers, and in trying to defend himself was so badly wounded that he died.

The elder brother, who had eaten the Yellow Bird's head, travelled a long way without meeting with any particular adventure, until at last he reached a large city in Asia, which was all in an uproar over the choosing of a new Emir.　All the principal citizens had formed themselves into two parties, and it was not until after a prolonged squabble that they agreed that the person to whom the most singular thing happened should be Emir.　Our young traveller entered the town at this juncture, with his agreeable face and jaunty air, and all at once felt something alight upon his head, which proved to be a snow-white pigeon.　Thereupon all the people began to stare, and to run after him, so that he presently reached the palace with the pigeon upon his head and all the inhabitants of the city at his heels, and before he knew where he was they made him Emir, to his great astonishment.

As there is nothing more agreeable than to command, and nothing to which people get accustomed more quickly, the young Emir soon felt quite at his ease in his new position ; but this did not prevent him from making every kind of mistake, and so mis- governing the kingdom that at last the whole city rose in revolt and deprived him at once of his authority and his life—a punish- ment which he richly deserved, for in the days of his prosperity he disowned the Fowler and his wife, and allowed them to die in poverty.

' I have told you this story, my dear Sylvain and Jocosa,' added the Fairy, ' to prove to you that this little cottage and all that belongs to it is a gift more likely to bring you happiness and con- tentment than many things that would at first seem grander and more desirable.　If you will faithfully promise me to till your fields and feed your flocks, and will keep your word better than you did before, I will see that you never lack anything that is really for your good.

Sylvain and Jocosa gave their faithful promise, and as they kept it they always enjoyed peace and prosperity. The Fairy had asked all their friends and neighbours to their wedding, which took place at once with great festivities and rejoicings, and they lived to a good old age, always loving one another with all their hearts.

By the Comte de Caylus.

FAIRY GIFTS

IT generally happens that people's surroundings reflect more or
less accurately their minds and dispositions, so perhaps that is
why the Flower Fairy lived in a lovely palace, with the most
delightful garden you can imagine, full of flowers, and trees, and
fountains, and fish-ponds, and everything nice. For the Fairy
herself was so kind and charming that everybody loved her, and all
the young princes and princesses who formed her court, were as
happy as the day was long, simply because they were near her.
They came to her when they were quite tiny, and never left her
until they were grown up and had to go away into the great world ;
and when that time came she gave to each whatever gift he asked
of her. But it is chiefly of the Princess Sylvia that you are going
to hear now. The Fairy loved her with all her heart, for she was
at once original and gentle, and she had nearly reached the age at
which the gifts were generally bestowed. However, the Fairy had
a great wish to know how the other princesses who had grown up
and left her, were prospering, and before the time came for Sylvia
to go herself, she resolved to send her to some of them. So one
day her chariot. drawn by butterflies, was made ready, and the
Fairy said : ' Sylvia, I am going to send you to the court of Iris ;
she will receive you with pleasure for my sake as well as for your
own. In two months you may come back to me again, and I shall
expect you to tell me what you think of her.'

Sylvia was very unwilling to go away, but as the Fairy wished
it she said nothing—only when the two months were over she
stepped joyfully into the butterfly chariot, and could not get back
quickly enough to the Flower-Fairy, who, for her part, was equally
delighted to see her again.

' Now, child,' said she, ' tell me what impression you have
received.'

'You sent me, madam,' answered Sylvia, 'to the Court of
Iris, on whom you had bestowed the gift of beauty. She never tells
anyone, however, that it was your gift, though she often speaks of
your kindness in general. It seemed to me that her loveliness,
which fairly dazzled me at first, had absolutely deprived her of the
use of any of her other gifts or graces. In allowing herself to be
seen, she appeared to think that she was doing all that could possibly be required of her. But, unfortunately, while I was still with
her she became seriously ill, and though she presently recovered, her

beauty is entirely gone, so that she hates the very sight of herself,
and is in despair. She entreated me to tell you what had happened,
and to beg you, in pity, to give her beauty back to her. And,
indeed, she does need it terribly, for all the things in her that were
tolerable, and even agreeable, when she was so pretty, seem quite
different now she is ugly, and it is so long since she thought of
using her mind or her natural cleverness, that I really don't think
she has any left now. She is quite aware of all this herself, so you
may imagine how unhappy she is, and how earnestly she begs for
your aid.'

'You have told me what I wanted to know,' cried the Fairy, 'but alas! I cannot help her; my gifts can be given but once.'

Some time passed in all the usual delights of the Flower-Fairy's palace, and then she sent for Sylvia again, and told her she was to stay for a little while with the Princess Daphne, and accordingly the butterflies whisked her off, and set her down in quite a strange kingdom. But she had only been there a very little time before a wandering butterfly brought a message from her to the Fairy, begging that she might be sent for as soon as possible, and before very long she was allowed to return.

'Ah! madam,' cried she, 'what a place you sent me to that time!'

'Why, what was the matter?' asked the Fairy. 'Daphne was one of the princesses who asked for the gift of eloquence, if I remember rightly.'

'And very ill the gift of eloquence becomes a woman,' replied Sylvia, with an air of conviction. 'It is true that she speaks well, and her expressions are well chosen; but then she never leaves off talking, and though at first one may be amused, one ends by being wearied to death. Above all things she loves any assembly for settling the affairs of her kingdom, for on those occasions she can talk and talk without fear of interruption; but, even then, the moment it is over she is ready to begin again about anything or nothing, as the case may be. Oh! how glad I was to come away I cannot tell you.

The Fairy smiled at Sylvia's unfeigned disgust at her late experience; but after allowing her a little time to recover she sent her to the Court of the Princess Cynthia, where she left her for three months. At the end of that time Sylvia came back to her with all the joy and contentment that one feels at being once more beside a dear friend. The Fairy, as usual, was anxious to hear what she thought of Cynthia, who had always been amiable, and to whom she had given the gift of pleasing.

'I thought at first,' said Sylvia, 'that she must be the happiest Princess in the world; she had a thousand lovers who vied with one another in their efforts to please and gratify her. Indeed, I had nearly decided that I would ask a similar gift.'

'Have you altered your mind, then?' interrupted the Fairy.

'Yes, indeed, madam,' replied Sylvia; 'and I will tell you why. The longer I stayed the more I saw that Cynthia was not really happy. In her desire to please everyone she ceased to be sincere, and degenerated into a mere coquette; and even her lovers felt that the charms and fascinations which were exercised upon all who approached her without distinction were valueless, so that in the end they ceased to care for them, and went away disdainfully.'

'I am pleased with you, child,' said the Fairy; 'enjoy yourself here for awhile and presently you shall go to Phyllida.'

Sylvia was glad to have leisure to think, for she could not make up her mind at all what she should ask for herself, and the time was drawing very near. However, before very long the Fairy sent her to Phyllida, and waited for her report with unabated interest.

'I reached her court safely,' said Sylvia, 'and she received me with much kindness, and immediately began to exercise upon me that brilliant wit which you had bestowed upon her. I confess that I was fascinated by it, and for a week thought that nothing could be more desirable ; the time passed like magic, so great was the charm of her society. But I ended by ceasing to covet that gift more than any of the others I have seen, for, like the gift of pleasing, it cannot really give satisfaction. By degrees I wearied of what had so delighted me at first, especially as I perceived more and more plainly that it is impossible to be constantly smart and amusing without being frequently ill-natured, and too apt to turn all things, even the most serious, into mere occasions for a brilliant jest.'

The Fairy in her heart agreed with Sylvia's conclusions, and felt pleased with herself for having brought her up so well.

But now the time was come for Sylvia to receive her gift, and all her companions were assembled ; the Fairy stood in the midst and in the usual manner asked what she would take with her into the great world.

Sylvia paused for a moment, and then answered: 'A quiet spirit.' And the Fairy granted her request.

This lovely gift makes life a constant happiness to its possessor, and to all who are brought into contact with her. She has all the beauty of gentleness and contentment in her sweet face; and if at times it seems less lovely through some chance grief or disquietude, the hardest thing that one ever hears said is :

'Sylvia's dear face is pale to-day. It grieves one to see her so.'

And when, on the contrary, she is gay and joyful, the sunshine of her presence rejoices all who have the happiness of being near her.

By the Comte de Caylus.

HEART OF ICE

ONCE upon a time there lived a King and Queen who were foolish beyond all telling, but nevertheless they were vastly fond of one another. It is true that certain spiteful people were heard to say that this was only one proof the more of their exceeding foolishness, but of course you will understand that these were not their own courtiers, since, after all, they *were* a King and Queen, and up to this time all things had prospered with them. For in those days the one thing to be thought of in governing a kingdom was to keep well with all the Fairies and Enchanters, and on no account to stint them of the cakes, the ells of ribbon, and similar trifles which were their due, and, above all things, when there was a christening, to remember to invite every single one, good, bad, or indifferent, to the ceremony. Now, the foolish Queen had one little son who was just going to be christened, and for several months she had been hard at work preparing an enormous list of the names of those who were to be invited, but she quite forgot that it would take nearly as long to read it over as it had taken to write it out. So, when the moment of the christening arrived the King —to whom the task had been entrusted—had barely reached the end of the second page and his tongue was tripping with fatigue and haste as he repeated the usual formula : 'I conjure and pray you, Fairy so-and-so'—or 'Enchanter such-a-one '—' to honour me with a visit, and graciously bestow your gifts upon my son.'

To make matters worse, word was brought to him that the Fairies asked on the first page had already arrived and were waiting impatiently in the Great Hall, and grumbling that nobody was there to receive them. Thereupon he gave up the list in despair and hurried to greet those whom he had succeeded in asking, imploring their goodwill so humbly that most of them were touched, and promised that they would do his son no harm. But there happened to be among them a Fairy from a far country about whom they knew nothing, though her name had been written on the first page of the list. This Fairy was annoyed that after having taken the trouble to come so quickly, there had been no one to receive her, or help her to alight from the great ostrich on which she had travelled from her distant home, and now she began to mutter to herself in the most alarming way.

'Oh! prate away,' said she, 'your son will never be anything to boast of. Say what you will, he will be nothing but a Mannikin——'

No doubt she would have gone on longer in this strain, and given the unhappy little Prince half-a-dozen undesirable gifts, if it had not been for the good Fairy Genesta, who held the kingdom under her special protection, and who luckily hurried in just in time to prevent further mischief. When she had by compliments and entreaties pacified the unknown Fairy, and persuaded her to say no more, she gave the King a hint that now was the time to distribute the presents, after which ceremony they all took their departure, excepting the Fairy Genesta, who then went to see the Queen, and said to her:

'A nice mess you seem to have made of this business, madam. Why did you not condescend to consult me? But foolish people like you always think they can do without help or advice, and I observe that, in spite of all my goodness to you, you had not even the civility to invite me!'

'Ah! dear madam,' cried the King, throwing himself at her feet; 'did I ever have time to get as far as your name? See where I put in this mark when I abandoned the hopeless undertaking which I had but just begun!'

'There! there!' said the Fairy, 'I am not offended. I don't allow myself to be put out by trifles like that with people I really am fond of. But now about your son: I have saved him from a great many disagreeable things, but you must let me take him away and take care of him, and you will not see him again until he is all covered with fur!'

At these mysterious words the King and Queen burst into tears, for they lived in such a hot climate themselves that how or why the Prince should come to be covered with fur they could not imagine, and thought it must portend some great misfortune to him.

However, Genesta told them not to disquiet themselves.

'If I left him to you to bring up,' said she, 'you would be certain to make him as foolish as yourselves. I do not even intend to

let him know that he is your son. As for you, you had better give your minds to governing your kingdom properly.' So saying, she opened the window, and catching up the little Prince, cradle and all, she glided away in the air as if she were skating upon ice, leaving the King and Queen in the greatest affliction. They consulted everyone who came near them as to what the Fairy could possibly have meant by saying that when they saw their son again he would be covered with fur. But nobody could offer any solution of the mystery, only they all seemed to agree that it must be something frightful, and the King and Queen made themselves more miserable than ever, and wandered about their palace in a way to make anyone pity them. Meantime the Fairy had carried off the little Prince to her own castle, and placed him under the care of a young peasant woman, whom she bewitched so as to make her think that this new baby was one of her own children. So the Prince grew up healthy and strong, leading the simple life of a young peasant, for the Fairy thought that he could have no better training ; only as he grew older she kept him more and more with herself, that his mind might be cultivated and exercised as well as his body. But her care did not cease there : she resolved that he should be tried by hardships and disappointments and the knowledge of his fellow-men ; for indeed she knew the Prince would need every advantage that she could give him, since, though he increased in years, he did not increase in height, but remained the tiniest of Princes. However, in spite of this he was exceedingly active and well formed, and altogether so handsome and agreeable that the smallness of his stature was of no real consequence. The Prince was perfectly aware that he was called by the ridiculous name of ' Mannikin,' but he consoled himself by vowing that, happen what might, he would make it illustrious.

In order to carry out her plans for his welfare the Fairy now began to send Prince Mannikin the most wonderful dreams of adventure by sea and land, and of these adventures he himself was always the hero. Sometimes he rescued a lovely Princess from some terrible danger, again he earned a kingdom by some brave deed, until at last he longed to go away and seek his fortune in a far country where his humble birth would not prevent his gaining honour and riches by his courage, and it was with a heart full of ambitious projects that he rode one day into a great city not far from the Fairy's castle. As he had set out intending to hunt in the surrounding forest he was quite simply dressed, and carried only a bow and arrows and a light spear ; but even thus arrayed he looked graceful and distinguished. As he entered the city he saw that the inhabitants were all racing with one accord

towards the market-place, and he also turned his horse in the same
direction, curious to know what was going forward. When he reached
the spot he found that certain foreigners of strange and outlandish
appearance were about to make a proclamation to the assembled
citizens, and he hastily pushed his way into the crowd until he was
near enough to hear the words of the venerable old man who was
their spokesman :

'Let the whole world know that he who can reach the summit
of the Ice Mountain shall receive as his reward, not only the
incomparable Sabella, fairest of the fair, but also all the realms
of which she is Queen ! ' 'Here,' continued the old man after he
had made this proclamation—' here is the list of all those Princes
who, struck by the beauty of the Princess, have perished in the
attempt to win her ; and here is the list of those who have just
entered upon the high emprise.'

Prince Mannikin was seized with a violent desire to inscribe his
name among the others, but the remembrance of his dependent
position and his lack of wealth held him back. But while he hesitated the old man, with many respectful ceremonies, unveiled a
portrait of the lovely Sabella, which was carried by some of the
attendants, and after one glance at it the Prince delayed no longer,
but, rushing forward, demanded permission to add his name to the
list. When they saw his tiny stature and simple attire the
strangers looked at each other doubtfully, not knowing whether to
accept or refuse him. But the Prince said haughtily :

'Give me the paper that I may sign it,' and they obeyed.
What between admiration for the Princess and annoyance at the
hesitation shown by her ambassadors the Prince was too much
agitated to choose any other name than the one by which he was
always known. But when, after all the grand titles of the other
Princes, he simply wrote ' Mannikin,' the ambassadors broke into
shouts of laughter.

'Miserable wretches ! ' cried the Prince ; ' but for the presence of
that lovely portrait I would cut off your heads.'

But he suddenly remembered that, after all, it *was* a funny
name, and that he had not yet had time to make it famous ; so he
was calm, and enquired the way to the Princess Sabella's country.

Though his heart did not fail him in the least, still he felt there
were many difficulties before him, and he resolved to set out at
once, without even taking leave of the Fairy, for fear she might try
to stop him. Everybody in the town who knew him made great

fun of the idea of Mannikin's undertaking such an expedition, and it even came to the ears of the foolish King and Queen, who laughed over it more than any of the others, without having an idea that the presumptuous Mannikin was their only son!

Meantime the Prince was travelling on, though the direction he had received for his journey were none of the clearest.

'Four hundred leagues north of Mount Caucasus you will receive your orders and instructions for the conquest of the Ice Mountain.'

Fine marching orders, those, for a man starting from a country near where Japan is nowadays!

However, he fared eastward, avoiding all towns, lest the people should laugh at his name, for, you see, he was not a very experienced traveller, and had not yet learned to enjoy a joke even if it were against himself. At night he slept in the woods, and at first he lived upon wild fruits; but the Fairy, who was keeping a benevolent eye upon him, thought that it would never do to let him be half-starved in that way, so she took to feeding him with all sorts of good things while he was asleep, and the Prince wondered very much that when he was awake he never felt hungry! True to her plan the Fairy sent him various adventures to prove his courage, and he came successfully through them all, only in his last fight with a furious monster rather like a tiger he had the ill luck to lose his horse. However, nothing daunted, he struggled on on foot, and at last reached a seaport. Here he found a boat sailing for the coast which he desired to reach, and, having just enough money to pay his passage, he went on board and they started. But after some days a fearful storm came on, which completely wrecked the little ship, and the Prince only saved his life by swimming a long, long way to the only land that was in sight, and which proved to be a desert island. Here he lived by fishing and hunting, always hoping that the good Fairy would presently rescue him. One day, as he was looking sadly out to sea, he became aware of a curious-looking boat which was drifting slowly towards the shore, and which presently ran into a little creek and there stuck fast in the sand. Prince Mannikin rushed down eagerly to examine it, and saw with amazement that the masts and spars were all branched, and covered thickly with leaves until it looked like a little wood. Thinking from the stillness that there could be no one on board, the Prince pushed aside the branches and sprang over the side, and found himself surrounded by the crew, who lay motionless as dead men and in a most deplorable condition. They, too, had become almost like trees, and were growing to the deck, or to the masts, or to the sides of the vessel, or to whatever they had happened to be touching when the enchantment fell upon them. Mannikin was struck with pity for their miserable plight, and set to work with might and main to release them. With the sharp point of one of his arrows he gently detached their hands and feet from the wood which held them fast, and carried them on shore, one after another, where he rubbed their rigid limbs, and bathed them with infusions of various herbs with such success, that, after a few days, they recovered perfectly and were as fit to manage a boat as ever. You may be sure that the good Fairy Genesta had something to do with this marvellous cure, and she also put it into the Prince's head to rub the boat itself with the same magic herbs, which cleared it entirely, and not before it was time, for, at the rate at which it was growing before, it would very soon have become a forest! The gratitude of the sailors was extreme, and they willingly promised to land the Prince upon

any coast he pleased; but, when he questioned them about the extraordinary thing that had happened to them and to their ship, they could in no way explain it, except that they said that, as they were passing along a thickly wooded coast, a sudden gust of wind had reached them from the land and enveloped them in a dense cloud of dust, after which everything in the boat that was not metal had sprouted and blossomed, as the Prince had seen, and that they themselves had grown gradually numb and heavy, and had finally

lost all consciousness. Prince Mannikin was deeply interested in
this curious story, and collected a quantity of the dust from the
bottom of the boat, which he carefully preserved, thinking that its
strange property might one day stand him in good stead.

Then they joyfully left the desert island, and after a long and
prosperous voyage over calm seas they at length came in sight of
land, and resolved to go on shore, not only to take in a fresh stock
of water and provisions, but also to find out, if possible, where they
were and in what direction to proceed.

As they neared the coast they wondered if this could be another
uninhabited land, for no human beings could be distinguished. and
yet that something was stirring became evident, for in the dust-
clouds that moved near the ground small dark forms were dimly
visible. These appeared to be assembling at the exact spot where
they were preparing to run ashore, and what was their surprise to
find they were nothing more nor less than large and beautiful
spaniels, some mounted as sentries, others grouped in companies
and regiments, all eagerly watching their disembarkation. When
they found that Prince Mannikin, instead of saying, ' Shoot them,'
as they had feared, said ' Hi. good dog ! ' in a thoroughly friendly
and ingratiating way, they crowded round him with a great
wagging of tails and giving of paws, and very soon made him
understand that they wanted him to leave his men with the boat
and follow them. The Prince was so curious to know more about
them that he agreed willingly ; so, after arranging with the sailors
to wait for him fifteen days, and then, if he had not come back,
to go on their way without him, he set out with his new friends.
Their way lay inland, and Mannikin noticed with great surprise
that the fields were well cultivated and that the carts and ploughs
were drawn by horses or oxen, just as they might have been in any
other country, and when they passed any village the cottages were
trim and pretty, and an air of prosperity was everywhere. At one
of the villages a dainty little repast was set before the Prince, and
while he was eating, a chariot was brought, drawn by two splendid
horses, which were driven with great skill by a large spaniel. In
this carriage he continued his journey very comfortably, passing
many similar equipages upon the road, and being always most
courteously saluted by the spaniels who occupied them. At last
they drove rapidly into a large town, which Prince Mannikin had
no doubt was the capital of the kingdom. News of his approach
had evidently been received, for all the inhabitants were at their

doors and windows, and all the little spaniels had climbed upon the wall and gates to see him arrive. The Prince was delighted with the hearty welcome they gave him, and looked round him with the deepest interest. After passing through a few wide streets, well paved, and adorned with avenues of fine trees, they drove into the courtyard of a grand palace, which was full of spaniels who were evidently soldiers. 'The King's body-guard,' thought the Prince to himself as he returned their salutations, and then the carriage stopped, and he was shown into the presence of the King, who lay upon a rich Persian carpet surrounded by several little spaniels, who were occupied in chasing away the flies lest they should disturb his Majesty. He was the most beautiful of all spaniels, with a look of sadness in his large eyes, which, however, quite disappeared as he sprang up to welcome Prince Mannikin with every demonstration of delight; after which he made a sign to his courtiers, who came one by one to pay their respects to the visitor. The Prince thought that he would find himself puzzled as to how he should carry on a conversation, but as soon as he and the King were once more left alone, a Secretary of State was sent for, who wrote from his Majesty's dictation a most polite speech, in which he regretted much that they were unable to converse, except in writing, the language of dogs being difficult to understand. As for the writing, it had remained the same as the Prince's own.

Mannikin thereupon wrote a suitable reply, and then begged the King to satisfy his curiosity about all the strange things he had seen and heard since his landing. This appeared to awaken sad recollections in the King's mind, but he informed the Prince that he was called King Bayard, and that a Fairy, whose kingdom was next his own, had fallen violently in love with him, and had done all she could to persuade him to marry her; but that he could not do so, as he himself was the devoted lover of the Queen of the Spice Islands. Finally, the Fairy, furious at the indifference with which her love was treated, had reduced him to the state in which the Prince found him, leaving him unchanged in mind, but deprived of the power of speech; and, not content with wreaking her vengeance upon the King alone, she had condemned all his subjects to a similar fate, saying:

'Bark, and run upon four feet, until the time comes when virtue shall be rewarded by love and fortune.'

Which, as the poor King remarked, was very much the same thing as if she had said, 'Remain a spaniel for ever and ever.'

Prince Mannikin was quite of the same opinion ; nevertheless he said what we should all have said in the same circumstances :

'Your Majesty must have patience.'

He was indeed deeply sorry for poor King Bayard, and said all the consoling things he could think of, promising to aid him with all his might if there was anything to be done. In short they became firm friends, and the King proudly displayed to Mannikin the portrait of the Queen of the Spice Islands, and he quite agreed that it was worth while to go through anything for the sake of a creature so lovely. Prince Mannikin in his turn told his own history, and the great undertaking upon which he had set out, and King Bayard was able to give him some valuable instructions as to which would be the best way for him to proceed, and then they went together to the place where the boat had been left. The sailors were delighted to see the Prince again, though they had known that he was safe, and when they had taken on board all the supplies which the King had sent for them, they started once more. The King and Prince parted with much regret, and the former insisted that Mannikin should take with him one of his own pages, named Mousta, who was charged to attend to him everywhere, and serve him faithfully, which he promised to do.

The wind being favourable they were soon out of hearing of the general howl of regret from the whole army, which had been given by order of the King, as a great compliment, and it was not long before the land was entirely lost to view. They met with no further adventures worth speaking of, and presently found themselves within two leagues of the harbour for which they were making. The Prince, however, thought it would suit him better to land where he was, so as to avoid the town, since he had no money left and was very doubtful as to what he should do next. So the sailors set him and Mousta on shore, and then went back sorrowfully to their ship, while the Prince and his attendant walked off in what looked to them the most promising direction. They soon reached a lovely green meadow on the border of a wood, which seemed to them so pleasant after their long voyage that they sat down to rest in the shade and amused themselves by watching the gambols and antics of a pretty tiny monkey in the trees close by. The Prince presently became so fascinated by it that he sprang up and tried to catch it, but it eluded his grasp and kept just out of arm's reach, until it had made him promise to follow wherever it led him, and then it sprang upon his shoulder and whispered in his ear :

' We have no money, my poor Mannikin, and we are altogether badly off, and at a loss to know what to do next.'

' Yes, indeed,' answered the Prince ruefully, ' and I have nothing to give you, no sugar or biscuits, or anything that you like, my pretty one.'

' Since you are so thoughtful for me, and so patient about your own affairs,' said the little monkey, ' I will show you the way to the Golden Rock, only you must leave Mousta to wait for you here.'

Prince Mannikin agreed willingly, and then the little monkey sprang from his shoulder to the nearest tree, and began to run through the wood from branch to branch, crying, ' Follow me.'

This the Prince did not find quite so easy, but the little monkey waited for him and showed him the easiest places, until presently the wood grew thinner and they came out into a little clear grassy space at the foot of a mountain, in the midst of which stood a single rock, about ten feet high. When they were quite close to it the little monkey said:

' This stone looks pretty hard, but give it a blow with your spear and let us see what will happen.'

So the Prince took his spear and gave the rock a vigorous dig, which split off several pieces, and showed that, though the surface was thinly coated with stone, inside it was one solid mass of pure gold.

Thereupon the little monkey said, laughing at his astonishment :

' I make you a present of what you have broken off; take as much of it as you think proper.'

The Prince thanked her gratefully, and picked up one of the smallest of the lumps of gold ; as he did so the little monkey was suddenly transformed into a tall and gracious lady, who said to him :

' If you are always as kind and persevering and easily contented as you are now you may hope to accomplish the most difficult tasks ; go on your way and have no fear that you will be troubled any more for lack of gold, for that little piece which you modestly chose shall never grow less, use it as much as you will. But that you may see the danger you have escaped by your moderation, come with me.' So saying she led him back into the wood by a different path, and he saw that it was full of men and women; their faces were pale and haggard, and they ran hither and thither seeking madly upon the ground, or in the air, starting at every sound, pushing and trampling upon one another in their frantic eagerness to find the way to the Golden Rock.

'You see how they toil,' said the Fairy; 'but it is all of no avail: they will end by dying of despair, as hundreds have done before them.'

As soon as they had got back to the place where they had left Mousta the Fairy disappeared, and the Prince and his faithful Squire, who had greeted him with every demonstration of joy, took the nearest way to the city. Here they stayed several days, while the Prince provided himself with horses and attendants, and made many enquiries about the Princess Sabella, and the way to her kingdom, which was still so far away that he could hear but little, and that of the vaguest description, but when he presently reached Mount Caucasus it was quite a different matter. Here they seemed to talk of nothing but the Princess Sabella, and strangers from all parts of the world were travelling towards her father's Court.

The Prince heard plenty of assurances as to her beauty and her riches, but he also heard of the immense number of his rivals and their power. One brought an army at his back, another had vast treasures, a third was as handsome and accomplished as it was possible to be; while, as to poor Mannikin, he had nothing but his determination to succeed, his faithful spaniel, and his ridiculous name—which last was hardly likely to help him, but as he could not alter it he wisely determined not to think of it any more. After journeying for two whole months they came at last to Trelintin, the capital of the Princess Sabella's kingdom, and here he heard dismal stories about the Ice Mountain, and how none of those who had attempted to climb it had ever come back. He heard also the story of King Farda-Kinbras, Sabella's father. It appeared that he, being a rich and powerful monarch, had married a lovely Princess named Birbantine, and they were as happy as the day was long—so happy that as they were out sledging one day they were foolish enough to defy fate to spoil their happiness.

'We shall see about that,' grumbled an old hag who sat by the wayside blowing her fingers to keep them warm. The King thereupon was very angry, and wanted to punish the woman; but the Queen prevented him, saying:

GORGONZOLA FLIES OFF ON HER DRAGON

'Alas! sire, do not let us make bad worse; no doubt this is a Fairy!'

'You are right there,' said the old woman, and immediately she stood up, and as they gazed at her in horror she grew gigantic and terrible, her staff turned to a fiery dragon with outstretched wings, her ragged cloak to a golden mantle, and her wooden shoes to two bundles of rockets. 'You are right there, and you will see what will come of your fine goings on, and remember the Fairy Gorgonzola!' So saying she mounted the dragon and flew off, the rockets shooting in all directions and leaving long trails of sparks.

In vain did Farda-Kinbras and Birbantine beg her to return, and endeavour by their humble apologies to pacify her; she never so much as looked at them, and was very soon out of sight, leaving them a prey to all kinds of dismal forebodings. Very soon after this the Queen had a little daughter, who was the most beautiful creature ever seen; all the Fairies of the North were invited to her christening, and warned against the malicious Gorgonzola. She also was invited, but she neither came to the banquet nor received her present; but as soon as all the others were seated at table, after bestowing their gifts upon the little Princess, she stole into the Palace, disguised as a black cat, and hid herself under the cradle until the nurses and the cradle-rockers had all turned their backs, and then she sprang out, and in an instant had stolen the little Princess's heart and made her escape, only being chased by a few dogs and scullions on her way across the courtyard. Once outside she mounted her chariot and flew straight away to the North Pole, where she shut up her stolen treasure on the summit of the Ice Mountain, and surrounded it with so many difficulties that she felt quite easy about its remaining there as long as the Princess lived, and then she went home, chuckling at her success. As to the other Fairies, they went home after the banquet without discovering that anything was amiss, and so the King and Queen were quite happy. Sabella grew prettier day by day. She learnt everything a Princess ought to know without the slightest trouble, and yet something always seemed lacking to make her perfectly charming. She had an exquisite voice, but whether her songs were grave or gay it did not matter, she did not seem to know what they meant; and everyone who heard her said:

'She certainly sings perfectly; but there is no tenderness, no heart in her voice.' Poor Sabella! how could there be when her heart was far away on the Ice Mountains? And it was just the same with all the other things that she did. As time went on, in spite of the admiration of the whole Court and the blind fondness of the King and Queen, it became more and more evident that something was fatally wrong: for those who love no one cannot long be loved; and at last the King called a general assembly, and invited the Fairies to attend, that they might, if possible, find out what was the matter. After explaining their grief as well as he could, he ended by begging them to see the Princess for themselves. 'It is certain,' said he, 'that something is wrong—*what* it is I don't know how to tell you, but in some way your work is imperfect.'

They all assured him that, so far as they knew, everything had been done for the Princess, and they had forgotten nothing that they could bestow on so good a neighbour as the King had been to them. After this they went to see Sabella; but they had no sooner entered her presence than they cried out with one accord:

'Oh! horror!—she has no heart!'

On hearing this frightful announcement, the King and Queen gave a cry of despair, and entreated the Fairies to find some remedy for such an unheard-of misfortune. Thereupon the eldest Fairy consulted her Book of Magic, which she always carried about with her, hung to her girdle by a thick silver chain, and there she found out at once that it was Gorgonzola who had stolen the Princess's heart, and also discovered what the wicked old Fairy had done with it.

'What shall we do? What shall we do?' cried the King and Queen in one breath.

'You must certainly suffer much annoyance from seeing and loving Sabella, who is nothing but a beautiful image,' replied the Fairy, 'and this must go on for a long time; but I think I see that, in the end, she will once more regain her heart. My advice is that you shall at once cause her portrait to be sent all over the world, and promise her hand and all her possessions to the Prince who is successful in reaching her heart. Her beauty alone is sufficient to engage all the Princes of the world in the quest.'

This was accordingly done, and Prince Mannikin heard that already five hundred Princes had perished in the snow and ice, not to mention their squires and pages, and that more continued to arrive daily, eager to try their fortune. After some consideration he determined to present himself at Court; but his arrival made no stir, as his retinue was as inconsiderable as his stature, and the

splendour of his rivals was great enough to throw even Farda-
Kinbras himself into the shade.   However, he paid his respects to

the King very gracefully, and asked permission to kiss the hand
of the Princess in the usual manner; but when he said he was

called ' Mannikin,' the King could hardly repress a smile, and the Princes who stood by openly shouted with laughter.

Turning to the King, Prince Mannikin said with great dignity :

' Pray laugh if it pleases your Majesty, I am glad that it is in my power to afford you any amusement ; but I am not a plaything for these gentlemen, and I must beg them to dismiss any ideas of that kind from their minds at once,' and with that he turned upon the one who had laughed the loudest and proudly challenged him to a single combat. This Prince, who was called Fadasse, accepted the challenge very scornfully, mocking at Mannikin, whom he felt sure had no chance against himself; but the meeting was arranged for the next day. When Prince Mannikin quitted the King's presence he was conducted to the audience hall of the Princess Sabella. The sight of so much beauty and magnificence almost took his breath away for an instant, but, recovering himself with an effort, he said :

' Lovely Princess, irresistibly drawn by the beauty of your portrait, I come from the other end of the world to offer my services to you. My devotion knows no bounds, but my absurd name has already involved me in a quarrel with one of your courtiers. To-morrow I am to fight this ugly, overgrown Prince, and I beg you to honour the combat with your presence, and prove to the world that there is nothing in a name, and that you deign to accept Mannikin as your knight.'

When it came to this the Princess could not help being amused, for, though she had no heart, she was not without humour. However, she answered graciously that she accepted with pleasure, which encouraged the Prince to entreat further that she would not show any favour to his adversary.

' Alas !' said she, ' I favour none of these foolish people, who weary me with their sentiment and their folly. I do very well as I am, and yet from one year's end to another they talk of nothing but delivering me from some imaginary affliction. Not a word do I understand of all their pratings about love, and who knows what dull things besides, which, I declare to you, I cannot even remember.'

Mannikin was quick enough to gather from this speech that to amuse and interest the Princess would be a far surer way of gaining her favour than to add himself to the list of those who continually teased her about that mysterious thing called ' love ' which she was so incapable of comprehending. So he began to talk of his rivals, and found in each of them something to make merry

over, in which diversion the Princess joined him heartily, and so well
did he succeed in his attempt to amuse her that before very long
she declared that of all the people at Court he was the one to whom
she preferred to talk.

The following day, at the time appointed for the combat, when
the King, the Queen, and the Princess had taken their places, and
the whole Court and the whole town were assembled to see the
show, Prince Fadasse rode into the lists magnificently armed and
accoutred, followed by twenty-four squires and a hundred men-at-
arms, each one leading a splendid horse, while Prince Mannikin
entered from the other side armed only with his spear and followed

by the faithful Mousta.   The contrast between the two champions
was so great that there was a shout of laughter from the whole
assembly ; but when at the sounding of a trumpet the combatants
rushed upon each other, and Mannikin, eluding the blow aimed at
him, succeeded in thrusting Prince Fadasse from his horse and
pinning him to the sand with his spear, it changed to a murmur of
admiration.

So soon as he had him at his mercy, however, Mannikin, turning
to the Princess, assured her that he had no desire to kill anyone
who called himself her courtier, and then he bade the furious and
humiliated Fadasse rise and thank the Princess to whom he owed

his life. Then, amid the sounding of the trumpets and the shout-ings of the people, he and Mousta retired gravely from the lists.

The King soon sent for him to congratulate him upon his success, and to offer him a lodging in the Palace, which he joyfully accepted. While the Princess expressed a wish to have Mousta brought to her, and, when the Prince sent for him, she was so delighted with his courtly manners and his marvellous intelligence that she entreated Mannikin to give him to her for her own. The Prince consented with alacrity, not only out of politeness, but because he foresaw that to have a faithful friend always near the Princess might some day be of great service to him. All these events made Prince Mannikin a person of much more consequence at the Court. Very soon after, there arrived upon the frontier the Ambassador of a very powerful King, who sent to Farda-Kinbras the following letter, at the same time demanding permission to enter the capital in state to receive the answer :

' I, Brandatimor, to Farda-Kinbras send greeting. If I had before this time seen the portrait of your beautiful daughter Sabella I should not have permitted all these adventurers and petty Princes to be dancing attendance and getting themselves frozen with the absurd idea of meriting her hand. For myself I am not afraid of any rivals, and, now I have declared my intention of marrying your daughter, no doubt they will at once withdraw their preten-sions. My Ambassador has orders, therefore, to make arrange-ments for the Princess to come and be married to me without delay —for I attach no importance at all to the farrago of nonsense which you have caused to be published all over the world about this Ice Mountain. If the Princess really has no heart, be assured that I shall not concern myself about it, since, if anybody can help her to discover one, it is myself. My worthy father-in-law, farewell ! '

The reading of this letter embarrassed and displeased Farda-Kinbras and Birbantine immensely, while the Princess was furious at the insolence of the demand. They all three resolved that its contents must be kept a profound secret until they could decide what reply should be sent, but Mousta contrived to send word of all that had passed to Prince Mannikin. He was naturally alarmed and indignant, and, after thinking it over a little, he begged an audience of the Princess, and led the conversation so cunningly up to the subject that was uppermost in her thoughts, as well as his own, that she presently told him all about the matter and asked his advice as to what it would be best to do. This was exactly what he had not been able to decide for himself; however, he replied that he should advise her to gain a little time by promising her answer after the grand entry of the Ambassador, and this was accordingly done.

The Ambassador did not at all like being put off after that fashion, but he was obliged to be content, and only said very arrogantly that so soon as his equipages arrived, as he expected they would do very shortly, he would give all the people of the city, and the stranger Princes with whom it was inundated, an idea of the power and the magnificence of his master. Mannikin, in despair, resolved that he would for once beg the assistance of the kind Fairy Genesta. He often thought of her and always with gratitude, but from the moment of his setting out he had determined to seek her aid only on the greatest occasions. That very night, when he had fallen asleep quite worn out with thinking over all the difficulties of the situation, he dreamed that the Fairy stood beside him, and said :

' Mannikin, you have done very well so far ; continue to please me and you shall always find good friends when you need them most. As for this affair with the Ambassador, you can assure Sabella that she may look forward tranquilly to his triumphal entry, since it will all turn out well for her in the end.'

The Prince tried to throw himself at her feet to thank her, but woke to find it was all a dream ; nevertheless he took fresh courage, and went next day to see the Princess, to whom he gave many mysterious assurances that all would yet be well. He even went so far as to ask her if she would not be very grateful to anyone who would rid her of the insolent Brandatimor. To which she replied that her gratitude would know no bounds. Then he wanted to know what would be her best wish for the person who was lucky enough to accomplish it. To which she said that she would wish them to be as insensible to the folly called 'love' as she was herself!

This was indeed a crushing speech to make to such a devoted lover as Prince Mannikin, but he concealed the pain it caused him with great courage.

And now the Ambassador sent to say that on the very next day he would come in state to receive his answer, and from the earliest dawn the inhabitants were astir, to secure the best places for the grand sight ; but the good Fairy Genesta was providing them an amount of amusement they were far from expecting, for she so

enchanted the eyes of all the spectators that when the Ambassador's gorgeous procession appeared, the splendid uniforms seemed
to them miserable rags that a beggar would have been ashamed to
wear, the prancing horses appeared as wretched skeletons hardly able
to drag one leg after the other, while their trappings, which really
sparkled with gold and jewels, looked like old sheepskins that
would not have been good enough for a plough horse. The pages
resembled the ugliest sweeps. The trumpets gave no more sound
than whistles made of onion-stalks, or combs wrapped in paper ;
while the train of fifty carriages looked no better than fifty donkey

carts. In the last of these sat the Ambassador with the haughty
and scornful air which he considered becoming in the represen-
tative of so powerful a monarch : for this was the crowning point
of the absurdity of the whole procession, that all who took part in
it wore the expression of vanity and self-satisfaction and pride in
their own appearance and all their surroundings which they
believed their splendour amply justified.

The laughter and howls of derision from the whole crowd rose
ever louder and louder as the extraordinary cortège advanced, and
at last reached the ears of the King as he waited in the audience

hall, and before the procession reached the palace he had been
informed of its nature, and, supposing that it must be intended as
an insult, he ordered the gates to be closed. You may imagine the
fury of the Ambassador when, after all his pomp and pride, the King
absolutely and unaccountably refused to receive him. He raved
wildly both against King and people, and the cortège retired in
great confusion, jeered at and pelted with stones and mud by the
enraged crowd. It is needless to say that he left the country as
fast as horses could carry him, but not before he had declared
war, with the most terrible menaces, threatening to devastate the
country with fire and sword.

Some days after this disastrous embassy King Bayard sent
couriers to Prince Mannikin with a most friendly letter, offering
his services in any difficulty, and enquiring with the deepest interest
how he fared.

Mannikin at once replied, relating all that had happened since
they parted, not forgetting to mention the event which had just
involved Farda-Kinbras and Brandatimor in this deadly quarrel,
and he ended by entreating his faithful friend to despatch a few
thousands of his veteran spaniels to his assistance.

Neither the King, the Queen, nor the Princess could in the least
understand the amazing conduct of Brandatimor's Ambassador;
nevertheless the preparations for the war went forward briskly and
all the Princes who had not gone on towards the Ice Mountain
offered their services, at the same time demanding all the best
appointments in the King's army. Mannikin was one of the first
to volunteer, but he only asked to go as aide-de-camp to the Com-
mander-in chief, who was a gallant soldier and celebrated for his
victories. As soon as the army could be got together it
was marched to the frontier, where it met the opposing force
headed by Brandatimor himself, who was full of fury, determined
to avenge the insult to his Ambassador and to possess himself of
the Princess Sabella. All the army of Farda-Kinbras could do,
being so heavily outnumbered, was to act upon the defensive, and
before long Mannikin won the esteem of the officers for his ability,
and of the soldiers for his courage, and care for their welfare, and
in all the skirmishes which he conducted he had the good fortune
to vanquish the enemy.

At last Brandatimor engaged the whole army in a terrific
conflict, and though the troops of Farda-Kinbras fought with
desperate courage, their general was killed, and they were defeated

and forced to retreat with immense loss. Mannikin did wonders, and half-a-dozen times turned the retreating forces and beat back the enemy; and he afterwards collected troops enough to keep them in check until, the severe winter setting in, put an end to hostilities for a while.

He then returned to the Court, where consternation reigned. The King was in despair at the death of his trusty general, and ended by imploring Mannikin to take the command of the army, and his counsel was followed in all the affairs of the Court. He followed up his former plan of amusing the Princess, and on no account reminding her of that tedious thing called 'love,' so that she was always glad to see him, and the winter slipped by gaily for both of them.

The Prince was all the while secretly making plans for the next campaign; he received private intelligence of the arrival of a strong reinforcement of Spaniels, to whom he sent orders to post themselves along the frontier without attracting attention, and as soon as he possibly could he held a consultation with their Commander, who was an old and experienced warrior. Following his advice, he decided to have a pitched battle as soon as the enemy advanced, and this Brandatimor lost not a moment in doing, as he was perfectly persuaded that he was now going to make an end of the war and utterly vanquish Farda-Kinbras. But no sooner had he given the order to charge than the Spaniels, who had mingled with his troops unperceived, leaped each upon the horse nearest to him, and not only threw the whole squadron into confusion by the terror they caused, but, springing at the throats of the riders, unhorsed many of them by the suddenness of their attack; then turning the horses to the rear, they spread consternation everywhere, and made it easy for Prince Mannikin to gain a complete victory. He met Brandatimor in single combat, and succeeded in taking him prisoner; but he did not live to reach the Court, to which Mannikin had sent him: his pride killed him at the thought of appearing before Sabella under these altered circumstances. In the meantime Prince Fadasse and all the others who had remained behind were setting out with all speed for the conquest of the Ice Mountain, being afraid that Prince Mannikin might prove as successful in that as he seemed to be in everything else, and when Mannikin returned he heard of it with great annoyance. True he had been serving the Princess, but she only admired and praised him for his gallant deeds, and seemed no whit nearer bestowing on him the

love he so ardently desired, and all the comfort Mousta could give
him on the subject was that at least she loved no one else, and
with that he had to content himself.　But he determined that, come
what might, he would delay no longer, but attempt the great undertaking for which he had come so far.　When he went to take leave
of the King and Queen they entreated him not to go, as they had
just heard that Prince Fadasse, and all who accompanied him, had
perished in the snow ; but he persisted in his resolve.　As for
Sabella, she gave him her hand to kiss with precisely the same
gracious indifference as she had given it to him the first time
they met.　It happened that this farewell took place before the

whole Court, and so great a favourite had Prince Mannikin become
that they were all indignant at the coldness with which the Princess
treated him.

Finally the King said to him :

'Prince, you have constantly refused all the gifts which, in my
gratitude for your invaluable services, I have offered to you, but I
wish the Princess to present you with her cloak of marten's fur,
and *that* I hope you will not reject !'　Now this was a splendid fur
mantle which the Princess was very fond of wearing, not so much
because she felt cold, as that its richness set off to perfection the
delicate tints of her complexion and the brilliant gold of her hair.

However, she took it off, and with graceful politeness begged Prince Mannikin to accept it, which you may be sure he was charmed to do, and, taking only this and a little bundle of all kinds of wood, and accompanied only by two spaniels out of the fifty who had stayed with him when the war was ended, he set forth, receiving many tokens of love and favour from the people in every town he passed through. At the last little village he left his horse behind him, to begin his toilful march through the snow, which extended, blank and terrible, in every direction as far as the eye could see. Here he had appointed to meet the other forty-eight spaniels, who received him joyfully, and assured him that, happen what might, they would follow and serve him faithfully. And so they started, full of heart and hope. At first there was a slight track, difficult, but not impossible to follow; but this was soon lost, and the Pole Star was their only guide. When the time came to call a halt, the Prince, who had after much consideration decided on his plan of action, caused a few twigs from the faggot he had brought with him to be planted in the snow, and then he sprinkled over them a pinch of the magic powder he had collected from the enchanted boat. To his great joy they instantly began to sprout and grow, and in a marvellously short time the camp was surrounded by a perfect grove of trees of all sorts, which blossomed and bore ripe fruit, so that all their wants were easily supplied, and they were able to make huge fires to warm themselves. The Prince then sent out several spaniels to reconnoitre, and they had the good luck to discover a horse laden with provisions stuck fast in the snow. They at once fetched their comrades, and brought the spoil triumphantly into the camp, and, as it consisted principally of biscuits, not a spaniel among them went supperless to sleep. In this way they journeyed by day and encamped safely at night, always remembering to take on a few branches to provide them with food and shelter. They passed by the way armies of those who had set out upon the perilous enterprise, who stood frozen stiffly, without sense or motion; but Prince Mannikin strictly forbade that any attempt should be made to thaw them. So they went on and on for more than three months, and day by day the Ice Mountain, which they had seen for a long time, grew clearer, until at last they stood close to it, and shuddered at its height and steepness. But by patience and perseverance they crept up foot by foot, aided by their fires of magic wood, without which they must have perished in the intense cold, until presently they stood at the gates of the magnificent Ice Palace which crowned the mountain, where, in deadly silence and icy sleep, lay the heart of Sabella. Now the difficulty became immense, for if they maintained enough heat to keep themselves alive they were in danger every moment of melting the blocks of solid ice of which

the palace was entirely built, and bringing the whole structure down upon their heads; but cautiously and quickly they traversed courtyards and halls, until they found themselves at the foot of a vast throne, where, upon a cushion of snow, lay an enormous and brilliantly sparkling diamond, which contained the heart of the lovely Princess Sabella. Upon the lowest step of the throne was inscribed in icy letters, 'Whosoever thou art who by courage and virtue canst win the heart of Sabella enjoy peacefully the good fortune which thou hast richly deserved.'

Prince Mannikin bounded forward, and had just strength left to grasp the precious diamond which contained all he coveted in the world before he fell insensible upon the snowy cushion. But his good spaniels lost no time in rushing to the rescue, and between them they bore him hastily from the hall, and not a moment too soon, for all around them they heard the clang of the falling blocks of ice as the Fairy Palace slowly collapsed under the unwonted heat. Not until they reached the foot of the mountain did they pause to restore the Prince to consciousness, and then his joy to find himself the possessor of Sabella's heart knew no bounds.

With all speed they began to retrace their steps, but this time the happy Prince could not bear the sight of his defeated and disappointed rivals, whose frozen forms lined his triumphant way. He gave orders to his spaniels to spare no pains to restore them to life, and so successful were they that day by day his train increased, so that by the time he got back to the little village where he had left his horse he was escorted by five hundred sovereign Princes, and knights and squires without number, and he was so courteous and unassuming that they all followed him willingly, anxious to do him honour. But then he was so happy and blissful himself that he found it easy to be at peace with all the world. It was not long before he met the faithful Mousta, who was coming at the top of his speed hoping to meet the Prince, that he might tell him of the sudden and wonderful change that had come over the Princess, who had become gentle and thoughtful and had talked to him of nothing but Prince Mannikin, of the hardships she feared he might be suffering, and of her anxiety for him, and all this with a hundred tender expressions which put the finishing stroke to the Prince's delight. Then came a courier bearing the congratulations of the King and Queen, who had just heard of his successful return, and there was even a graceful compliment from Sabella herself. The Prince sent Mousta back to her, and he was welcomed with joy, for was he not her lover's present?

At last the travellers reached the capital, and were received with regal magnificence. Farda-Kinbras and Birbantine embraced Prince Mannikin, declaring that they regarded him as their heir and the future husband of the Princess, to which he replied that they did him too much honour. And then he was admitted into the presence of the Princess, who for the first time in her life blushed as he kissed her hand, and could not find a word to say. But the Prince, throwing himself on his knees beside her, held out the splendid diamond, saying:

'Madam, this treasure is yours, since none of the dangers and difficulties I have gone through have been sufficient to make me deserve it.'

'Ah! Prince,' said she, 'if I take it, it is only that I may give it back to you, since truly it belongs to you already.'

At this moment in came the King and Queen, and interrupted them by asking all the questions imaginable, and not infrequently the same over and over again. It seems that there is always one thing that is sure to be said about an event by everybody, and Prince Mannikin found that the question which he was asked by more than a thousand people on this particular occasion was:

'And didn't you find it very cold?'

The King had come to request Prince Mannikin and the Princess to follow him to the Council Chamber, which they did, not knowing that he meant to present the Prince to all the nobles assembled there as his son-in-law and successor. But when Mannikin perceived his intention, he begged permission to speak first, and told his whole story, even to the fact that he believed himself to be a peasant's son. Scarcely had he finished speaking when the sky grew black, the thunder growled, and the lightning flashed, and in the blaze of light the good Fairy Genesta suddenly appeared. Turning to Prince Mannikin, she said:

'I am satisfied with you, since you have shown not only courage but a good heart.' Then she addressed King Farda-Kinbras, and informed him of the real history of the Prince, and how she had determined to give him the education she knew would be best for a man who was to command others. 'You have already found the advantage of having a faithful friend,' she added to the Prince, 'and now you will have the pleasure of seeing King Bayard and his subjects regain their natural forms as a reward for his kindness to you.'

Just then arrived a chariot drawn by eagles, which proved to contain the foolish King and Queen, who embraced their long-lost son with great joy, and were greatly struck with the fact that they did indeed find him covered with fur! While they were caressing Sabella and wringing her hands (which is a favourite form of endearment with foolish people) chariots were seen approaching from all points of the compass, containing numbers of Fairies.

'Sire,' said Genesta to Farda-Kinbras, 'I have taken the liberty of appointing your Court as a meeting-place for all the Fairies who could spare the time to come; and I hope you can arrange to hold the great ball, which we have once in a hundred years, on this occasion.'

The King having suitably acknowledged the honour done him, was next reconciled to Gorgonzola, and they two presently opened the ball together. The Fairy Marsontine restored their natural forms to King Bayard and all his subjects, and he appeared once more as handsome a king as you could wish to see. One of the Fairies immediately despatched her chariot for the Queen of the Spice Islands, and their wedding took place at the same time as that of Prince Mannikin and the lovely and gracious Sabella. They lived happily ever afterwards, and their vast kingdoms were presently divided between their children.

The Prince, out of grateful remembrance of the Princess Sabella's first gift to him, bestowed the right of bearing her name upon the most beautiful of the martens, and that is why they are called *sables* to this day.

Comte de Caylus.

THE ENCHANTED RING

ONCE upon a time there lived a young man named Rosimond, who was as good and handsome as his elder brother Bramintho was ugly and wicked. Their mother detested her eldest son, and had only eyes for the youngest. This excited Bramintho's jealousy, and he invented a horrible story in order to ruin his brother. He told his father that Rosimond was in the habit of visiting a neighbour who was an enemy of the family, and betraying to him all that went on in the house, and was plotting with him to poison their father.

The father flew into a rage, and flogged his son till the blood came. Then he threw him into prison and kept him for three days without food, and after that he turned him out of the house, and threatened to kill him if he ever came back. The mother was miserable, and did nothing but weep, but she dared not say anything.

The youth left his home with tears in his eyes, not knowing where to go, and wandered about for many hours till he came to a thick wood. Night overtook him at the foot of a great rock, and he fell asleep on a bank of moss, lulled by the music of a little brook.

It was dawn when he woke, and he saw before him a beautiful woman seated on a grey horse, with trappings of gold, who looked as if she were preparing for the hunt.

'Have you seen a stag and some deerhounds go by?' she asked.

'No, madam,' he replied.

Then she added, 'You look unhappy; is there anything the matter? Take this ring, which will make you the happiest and most powerful of men, provided you never make a bad use of it. If you turn the diamond inside, you will become invisible. If you turn it outside, you will become visible again. If you place it on your little finger, you will take the shape of the King's son, followed by a splendid court. If you put it on your fourth finger, you will take your own shape.'

Then the young man understood that it was a Fairy who was speaking to him, and when she had finished she plunged into the woods. The youth was very impatient to try the ring, and returned home immediately. He found that the Fairy had spoken the truth, and that he could see and hear everything, while he himself was

unseen. It lay with him to revenge himself, if he chose, on his brother, without the slightest danger to himself, and he told no one but his mother of all the strange things that had befallen him. He afterwards put the enchanted ring on his little finger, and appeared as the King's son, followed by a hundred fine horses, and a guard of officers all richly dressed.

His father was much surprised to see the King's son in his quiet little house, and he felt rather embarrassed, not knowing what

was the proper way to behave on such a grand occasion. Then
Rosimond asked him how many sons he had.

'Two,' replied he.

'I wish to see them,' said Rosimond. 'Send for them at once.
I desire to take them both to Court, in order to make their fortunes.'

The father hesitated, then answered: 'Here is the eldest, whom
I have the honour to present to your Highness.'

'But where is the youngest? I wish to see him too,' persisted
Rosimond.

'He is not here,' said the father. 'I had to punish him for a
fault, and he has run away.'

Then Rosimond replied, 'You should have shown him what
was right, but not have punished him. However, let the elder
come with me, and as for you, follow these two guards, who will
escort you to a place that I will point out to them.'

Then the two guards led off the father, and the Fairy of whom
you have heard found him in the forest, and beat him with a golden
birch rod, and cast him into a cave that was very deep and dark,
where he lay enchanted. 'Lie there,' she said, 'till your son comes
to take you out again.'

Meanwhile the son went to the King's palace, and arrived just
when the real prince was absent. He had sailed away to make
war on a distant island, but the winds had been contrary, and he
had been shipwrecked on unknown shores, and taken captive by a
savage people. Rosimond made his appearance at Court in the
character of the Prince, whom everyone wept for as lost, and told
them that he had been rescued when at the point of death by some
merchants. His return was the signal for great public rejoicings,
and the King was so overcome that he became quite speechless,
and did nothing but embrace his son. The Queen was even more
delighted, and fêtes were ordered over the whole kingdom.

One day the false Prince said to his real brother, 'Bramintho,
you know that I brought you here from your native village in order
to make your fortune; but I have found out that you are a liar,
and that by your deceit you have been the cause of all the troubles
of your brother Rosimond. He is in hiding here, and I desire that
you shall speak to him, and listen to his reproaches.'

Bramintho trembled at these words, and, flinging himself at the
Prince's feet, confessed his crime.

'That is not enough,' said Rosimond. 'It is to your brother that you must confess, and I desire that you shall ask his forgiveness. He will be very generous if he grants it, and it will be more than you deserve. He is in my ante-room, where you shall see him at once. I myself will retire into another apartment, so as to leave you alone with him.'

Bramintho entered, as he was told, into the ante-room. Then Rosimond changed the ring, and passed into the room by another door.

Bramintho was filled with shame as soon as he saw his brother's face. He implored his pardon, and promised to atone for all his faults. Rosimond embraced him with tears, and at once forgave him, adding, 'I am in great favour with the King. It rests with me to have your head cut off, or to condemn you to pass the remainder of your life in prison; but I desire to be as good to you as you have been wicked to me.' Bramintho, confused and ashamed, listened to his words without daring to lift his eyes or to remind Rosimond that he was his brother. After this, Rosimond gave out that he was going to make a secret voyage, to marry a Princess who lived in a neighbouring kingdom; but in reality he only went to see his mother, whom he told all that had happened at the Court, giving her at the same time some money that she needed, for the King allowed him to take exactly what he liked, though he was always careful not to abuse this permission. Just then a furious war broke out between the King his master and the Sovereign of the adjoining country, who was a bad man and one that never kept his word. Rosimond went straight to the palace of the wicked King, and by means of his ring was able to be present at all the councils, and learnt all their schemes, so that he was able to forestall them and bring them to naught. He took the command of the army which was brought against the wicked King, and defeated him in a glorious battle, so that peace was at once concluded on conditions that were just to everyone.

Henceforth the King's one idea was to marry the young man to a Princess who was the heiress to a neighbouring kingdom, and, besides that, was as lovely as the day. But one morning, while Rosimond was hunting in the forest where for the first time he had seen the Fairy, his benefactress suddenly appeared before him. 'Take heed,' she said to him in severe tones, 'that you do not marry anybody who believes you to be a Prince. You must never deceive anyone. The real Prince, whom the whole nation thinks you are, will have to succeed his father, for that is just and right. Go and seek him in some distant island, and I will send winds that will swell your sails and bring you to him. Hasten to render this service to your master, although it is against your own ambition, and prepare, like an honest man, to return to your natural state. If you do not do this, you will become wicked and unhappy, and I will abandon you to all your former troubles.'

Rosimond took these wise counsels to heart. He gave out that he had undertaken a secret mission to a neighbouring state, and embarked on board a vessel, the winds carrying him straight to the island where the Fairy had told him he would find the real Prince. This unfortunate youth had been taken captive by a savage people, who had kept him to guard their sheep. Rosimond, becoming invisible, went to seek him amongst the pastures, where he kept his flock, and, covering him with his mantle, he delivered him out of the hands of his cruel masters, and bore him back to the ship. Other winds sent by the Fairy swelled the sails, and together the two young men entered the King's presence.

Rosimond spoke first and said, ' You have believed me to be your son. I am not he, but I have brought him back to you.' The King, filled with astonishment, turned to his real son and asked, ' Was it not you, my son, who conquered my enemies and won such a glorious peace ? Or is it true that you have been shipwrecked and taken captive, and that Rosimond has set you free ? '

' Yes, my father,' replied the Prince. ' It is he who sought me out in my captivity and set me free, and to him I owe the happiness of seeing you once more. It was he, not I, who gained the victory.'

The King could hardly believe his ears ; but Rosimond, turning the ring, appeared before him in the likeness of the Prince, and the King gazed distractedly at the two youths who seemed both to be his son. Then he offered Rosimond immense rewards for his services, which were refused, and the only favour the young man would accept was that one of his posts at Court should be conferred on his brother Bramintho. For he feared for himself the changes of fortune, the envy of mankind and his own weakness. His desire was to go back to his mother and his native village, and to spend his time in cultivating the land.

One day, when he was wandering through the woods, he met the Fairy, who showed him the cavern where his father was imprisoned, and told him what words he must use in order to set him free. He repeated them joyfully, for he had always longed to bring the old man back and to make his last days happy. Rosimond thus became the benefactor of all his family, and had the pleasure of doing good to those who had wished to do him evil. As for the Court, to whom he had rendered such services, all he asked was the freedom to live far from its corruption ; and, to crown all, fearing that if he kept the ring he might be tempted to use it in order to regain his lost place in the world, he made up his mind to restore it to the Fairy. For many days he sought her up and down the woods and at last he found her. 'I want to give you back,' he said, holding out the ring, 'a gift as dangerous as it is powerful, and which I fear to use wrongfully. I shall never feel safe till I have made it impossible for me to leave my solitude and to satisfy my passions.'

While Rosimond was seeking to give back the ring to the Fairy, Bramintho, who had failed to learn any lessons from experience, gave way to all his desires, and tried to persuade the Prince, lately become King, to ill-treat Rosimond. But the Fairy, who knew all about everything, said to Rosimond, when he was imploring her to accept the ring :

'Your wicked brother is doing his best to poison the mind of the King towards you, and to ruin you. He deserves to be punished, and he must die; and in order that he may destroy himself, I shall give the ring to him.'

Rosimond wept at these words, and then asked :

'What do you mean by giving him the ring as a punishment ? He will only use it to persecute everyone, and to become master.'

'The same things,' answered the Fairy, 'are often a healing medicine to one person and a deadly poison to another. Prosperity is the source of all evil to a naturally wicked man. If you wish to punish a scoundrel, the first thing to do is to give him power. You will see that with this rope he will soon hang himself.'

Having said this, she disappeared, and went straight to the Palace, where she showed herself to Bramintho under the disguise of an old woman covered with rags. She at once addressed him in these words :

'I have taken this ring from the hands of your brother, to whom I had lent it, and by its help he covered himself with glory. I now give it to you, and be careful what you do with it.'

Bramintho replied with a laugh :

'I shall certainly not imitate my brother, who was foolish enough to bring back the Prince instead of reigning in his place,' and he was as good as his word. The only use he made of the ring was to find out family secrets and betray them, to commit murders and every sort of wickedness, and to gain wealth for him-

self unlawfully. All these crimes, which could be traced to nobody, filled the people with astonishment. The King, seeing so many affairs, public and private, exposed, was at first as puzzled as anyone, till Bramintho's wonderful prosperity and amazing insolence made him suspect that the enchanted ring had become his property. In order to find out the truth he bribed a stranger just arrived at Court, one of a nation with whom the King was always at war, and arranged that he was to steal in the night to Bramintho and to offer him untold honours and rewards if he would betray the State secrets.

Bramintho promised everything, and accepted at once the first payment of his crime, boasting that he had a ring which rendered him invisible, and that by means of it he could penetrate into the most private places. But his triumph was short. Next day he was seized by order of the King, and his ring was taken from him. He was searched, and on him were found papers which proved his crimes; and, though Rosimond himself came back to the Court to entreat his pardon, it was refused. So Bramintho was put to death, and the ring had been even more fatal to him than it had been useful in the hands of his brother.

To console Rosimond for the fate of Bramintho, the King gave him back the enchanted ring, as a pearl without price. The unhappy Rosimond did not look upon it in the same light, and the first thing he did on his return home was to seek the Fairy in the woods.

'Here,' he said, 'is your ring. My brother's experience has made me understand many things that I did not know before. Keep it, it has only led to his destruction. Ah! without it he would be alive now, and my father and mother would not in their old age be bowed to the earth with shame and grief! Perhaps he might have been wise and happy if he had never had the chance of gratifying his wishes! Oh! how dangerous it is to have more power than the rest of the world! Take back your ring, and as ill fortune seems to follow all on whom you bestow it, I will implore you, as a favour to myself, that you will never give it to anyone who is dear to me.'

Fénelon.

THE GOLDEN MERMAID

A POWERFUL king had, among many other treasures, a wonderful tree in his garden, which bore every year beautiful golden apples. But the King was never able to enjoy his treasure, for he might watch and guard them as he liked, as soon as they began to get ripe they were always stolen. At last, in despair, he sent for his three sons, and said to the two eldest, 'Get yourselves ready for a journey. Take gold and silver with you, and a large retinue of servants, as beseems two noble princes, and go through the

world till you find out who it is that steals my golden apples, and, if possible, bring the thief to me that I may punish him as he deserves.' His sons were delighted at this proposal, for they had long wished to see something of the world, so they got ready for their journey with all haste, bade their father farewell, and left the town.

The youngest Prince was much disappointed that he too was not sent out on his travels; but his father wouldn't hear of his going, for he had always been looked upon as the stupid one of the family, and the King was afraid of something happening to him. But the Prince begged and implored so long, that at last his father consented to let him go, and furnished him with gold and silver as he had done his brothers. But he gave him the most wretched horse in his stable, because the foolish youth hadn't asked for a better. So he too set out on his journey to secure the thief, amid the jeers and laughter of the whole court and town.

His path led him first through a wood, and he hadn't gone very far when he met a lean-looking wolf who stood still as he approached. The Prince asked him if he were hungry, and when the wolf said he was, he got down from his horse and said, 'If you are really as you say and look, you may take my horse and eat it.'

The wolf didn't wait to have the offer repeated, but set to work, and soon made an end of the poor beast. When the Prince saw how different the wolf looked when he had finished his meal, he said to him, ' Now, my friend, since you have eaten up my horse, and I have such a long way to go, that, with the best will in the world, I couldn't manage it on foot, the least you can do for me is to act as my horse and to take me on your back.'

' Most certainly,' said the wolf, and, letting the Prince mount him, he trotted gaily through the wood. After they had gone a little way he turned round and asked his rider where he wanted to go to, and the Prince proceeded to tell him the whole story of the golden apples that had been stolen out of the King's garden, and how his other two brothers had set forth with many followers to find the thief. When he had finished his story, the wolf, who was in reality no wolf but a mighty magician, said he thought he could tell him who the thief was, and could help him to secure him. ' There lives,' he said, ' in a neighbouring country, a mighty emperor who has a beautiful golden bird in a cage, and this is the creature who steals the golden apples, but it flies so fast that it is impossible to catch it at its theft. You must slip into the Emperor's palace by night and steal the bird with the cage ; but be very careful not to touch the walls as you go out.'

The following night the Prince stole into the Emperor's palace, and found the bird in its cage as the wolf had told him he would. He took hold of it carefully, but in spite of all his caution he touched the wall in trying to pass by some sleeping watchmen. They awoke at once, and, seizing him, beat him and put him into chains. Next day he was led before the Emperor, who at once condemned him to death and to be thrown into a dark dungeon till the day of his execution arrived.

The wolf, who, of course, knew by his magic arts all that had happened to the Prince, turned himself at once into a mighty monarch with a large train of followers, and proceeded to the Court of the Emperor, where he was received with every show of honour. The Emperor and he conversed on many subjects, and, among other things, the stranger asked his host if he had many slaves. The Emperor told him he had more than he knew what to do with, and that a new one had been captured that very night for trying to steal his magic bird, but that as he had already more than enough to feed and support, he was going to have this last captive hanged next morning.

'He must have been a most daring thief,' said the King, 'to try and steal the magic bird, for depend upon it the creature must have been well guarded. I would really like to see this bold rascal.' 'By all means,' said the Emperor; and he himself led his guest down to the dungeon where the unfortunate Prince was kept prisoner. When the Emperor stepped out of the cell with the King, the latter turned to him and said, 'Most mighty Emperor, I have been much disappointed. I had thought to find a powerful robber, and instead of that I have seen the most miserable creature I can imagine. Hanging is far too good for him. If I had to sentence him I should make him perform some very difficult task, under pain of death. If he did it so much the better for you, and if he didn't, matters would just be as they are now and he could still be hanged.' 'Your counsel,' said the Emperor, 'is excellent, and, as it happens, I've got the very thing for him to do. My nearest neighbour, who is also a mighty Emperor, possesses a golden horse which he guards most carefully. The prisoner shall be told to steal this horse and bring it to me.'

The Prince was then let out of his dungeon, and told his life would be spared if he succeeded in bringing the golden horse to the Emperor. He did not feel very elated at this announcement, for he did not know how in the world he was to set about the task, and he started on his way weeping bitterly, and wondering what had made him leave his father's house and kingdom. But before he had gone far his friend the wolf stood before him and said, 'Dear Prince, why are you so cast down? It is true you didn't succeed in catching the bird; but don't let that discourage you, for this time you will be all the more careful, and will doubtless catch the horse.'

With these and like words the wolf comforted the Prince, and
warned him specially not to touch the wall or let the horse touch
it as he led it out, or he would fail in the same way as he had
done with the bird.

After a somewhat lengthy journey the Prince and the wolf

came to the kingdom ruled over by the Emperor who possessed the
golden horse. One evening late they reached the capital, and the
wolf advised the Prince to set to work at once, before their presence
in the city had aroused the watchfulness of the guards. They

slipped unnoticed into the Emperor's stables and into the very place where there were the most guards, for there the wolf rightly surmised they would find the horse. When they came to a certain inner door the wolf told the Prince to remain outside, while he went in. In a short time he returned and said, ' My dear Prince, the horse is most securely watched, but I have bewitched all the guards, and if you will only be careful not to touch the wall yourself, or let the horse touch it as you go out, there is no danger and the game is yours. The Prince, who had made up his mind to be more than cautious this time, went cheerfully to work. He found all the guards fast asleep, and, slipping into the horse's stall, he seized it by the bridle and led it out; but, unfortunately, before they had got quite clear of the stables a gadfly stung the horse and caused it to switch its tail, whereby it touched the wall. In a moment all the guards awoke, seized the Prince and beat him mercilessly with their horse-whips, after which they bound him with chains, and flung him into a dungeon. Next morning they brought him before the Emperor, who treated him exactly as the King with the golden bird had done, and commanded him to be beheaded on the following day.

When the wolf-magician saw that the Prince had failed this time too, he transformed himself again into a mighty king, and proceeded with an even more gorgeous retinue than the first time to the Court of the Emperor. He was courteously received and entertained, and once more after dinner he led the conversation on to the subject of slaves, and in the course of it again requested to be allowed to see the bold robber who had dared to break into the Emperor's stable to steal his most valuable possession. The Emperor consented, and all happened exactly as it had done at the court of the Emperor with the golden bird; the prisoner's life was to be spared only on condition that within three days he should obtain possession of the golden mermaid, whom hitherto no mortal had ever approached.

Very depressed by his dangerous and difficult task, the Prince left his gloomy prison; but, to his great joy, he met his friend the wolf before he had gone many miles on his journey. The cunning creature pretended he knew nothing of what had happened to the Prince, and asked him how he had fared with the horse. The Prince told him all about his misadventure, and the condition on which the Emperor had promised to spare his life. Then the wolf reminded him that he had twice got him out of prison, and that if

he would only trust in him, and do exactly as he told him, he
would certainly succeed in this last undertaking. Thereupon they
bent their steps towards the sea, which stretched out before them,
as far as their eyes could see, all the waves dancing and glittering
in the bright sunshine. ' Now,' continued the wolf, ' I am going to
turn myself into a boat full of the most beautiful silken merchandise,
and you must jump boldly into the boat, and steer with my tail in
your hand right out into the open sea. You will soon come upon
the golden mermaid. Whatever you do, don't follow her if she calls
you, but on the contrary say to her, " The buyer comes to the
seller, not the seller to the buyer." After which you must steer
towards the land, and she will follow you, for she won't be able to
resist the beautiful wares you have on board your ship.'

The Prince promised faithfully to do all he had been told,
whereupon the wolf changed himself into a ship full of most exquisite silks, of every shade and colour imaginable. The astonished
Prince stepped into the boat, and, holding the wolf's tail in his hand,
he steered boldly out into the open sea, where the sun was gilding
the blue waves with its golden rays. Soon he saw the golden
mermaid swimming near the ship, beckoning and calling to him to
follow her; but, mindful of the wolf's warning, he told her in a loud
voice that if she wished to buy anything she must come to him.
With these words he turned his magic ship round and steered
back towards the land. The mermaid called out to him to stand
still, but he refused to listen to her and never paused till he reached
the sand of the shore. Here he stopped and waited for the mermaid,
who had swum after him. When she drew near the boat he saw
that she was far more beautiful than any mortal he had ever beheld. She swam round the ship for some time, and then swung
herself gracefully on board, in order to examine the beautiful silken
stuffs more closely. Then the Prince seized her in his arms, and
kissing her tenderly on the cheeks and lips, he told her she was his
for ever ; at the same moment the boat turned into a wolf again,
which so terrified the mermaid that she clung to the Prince for
protection.

So the golden mermaid was successfully caught, and she soon
felt quite happy in her new life when she saw she had nothing to
fear either from the Prince or the wolf—she rode on the back of
the latter, and the Prince rode behind her. When they reached the
country ruled over by the Emperor with the golden horse, the Prince
jumped down, and, helping the mermaid to alight, he led her before

the Emperor. At the sight of the beautiful mermaid and of the grim wolf, who stuck close to the Prince this time, the guards all made respectful obeisance, and soon the three stood before his Imperial Majesty. When the Emperor heard from the Prince how he had gained possession of his fair prize, he at once recognised that he had been helped by some magic art, and on the spot gave up all claim to the beautiful mermaid. 'Dear youth,' he said, 'forgive me for my shameful conduct to you, and, as a sign that you pardon me, accept the golden horse as a present. I acknowledge your power to be greater even than I can understand, for you have succeeded in gaining possession of the golden mermaid, whom hitherto no mortal has ever been able to approach.' Then they all sat down to a huge feast, and the Prince had to relate his adventures all over again, to the wonder and astonishment of the whole company.

But the Prince was wearying now to return to his own kingdom, so as soon as the feast was over he took farewell of the Emperor, and set out on his homeward way. He lifted the mermaid on to the golden horse, and swung himself up behind her—and so they rode on merrily, with the wolf trotting behind, till they came to the country of the Emperor with the golden bird. The renown of the Prince and his adventure had gone before him, and the Emperor sat on his throne awaiting the arrival of the Prince and his companions. When the three rode into the courtyard of the palace, they were surprised and delighted to find everything festively illuminated and decorated for their reception. When the Prince and the golden mermaid, with the wolf behind them, mounted the steps of the palace, the Emperor came forward to meet them, and led them to the throne room. At the same moment a servant appeared with the golden bird in its golden cage, and the Emperor begged the Prince to accept it with his love, and to forgive him the indignity he had suffered at his hands. Then the Emperor bent low before the beautiful mermaid, and, offering her his arm, he led her into dinner, closely followed by the Prince and her friend the wolf; the latter seating himself at table, not the least embarrassed that no one had invited him to do so.

As soon as the sumptuous meal was over, the Prince and his mermaid took leave of the Emperor, and, seating themselves on the golden horse, continued their homeward journey. On the way the wolf turned to the Prince and said, 'Dear friends, I must now bid you farewell, but I leave you under such happy circumstances that

I cannot feel our parting to be a sad one.' The Prince was very unhappy when he heard these words, and begged the wolf to stay with them always; but this the good creature refused to do, though he thanked the Prince kindly for his invitation, and called out as he disappeared into the thicket, 'Should any evil befall you, dear Prince, at any time, you may rely on my friendship and gratitude.' These were the wolf's parting words, and the Prince could not restrain his tears when he saw his friend vanishing in the distance; but one glance at his beloved mermaid soon cheered him up again, and they continued on their journey merrily.

The news of his son's adventures had already reached his father's Court, and everyone was more than astonished at the success of the once despised Prince. His elder brothers, who had in vain gone in pursuit of the thief of the golden apples, were furious over their younger brother's good fortune, and plotted and planned how they were to kill him. They hid themselves in the wood through which the Prince had to pass on his way to the palace, and there fell on him, and, having beaten him to death, they carried off the golden horse and the golden bird. But nothing they could do would persuade the golden mermaid to go with them or move from the spot, for ever since she had left the sea, she had so attached herself to her Prince that she asked nothing else than to live or die with him.

For many weeks the poor mermaid sat and watched over the dead body of her lover, weeping salt tears over his loss, when suddenly one day their old friend the wolf appeared and said, 'Cover the Prince's body with all the leaves and flowers you can find in the wood.' The maiden did as he told her, and then the wolf breathed over the flowery grave, and, lo and behold! the Prince lay there sleeping as peacefully as a child. 'Now you may wake him if you like,' said the wolf, and the mermaid bent over him and gently kissed the wounds his brothers had made on his forehead, and the Prince awoke, and you may imagine how delighted he was to find his beautiful mermaid beside him, though he felt a little depressed when he thought of the loss of the golden bird and the golden horse. After a time the wolf, who had likewise fallen on the Prince's neck, advised them to continue their journey, and once more the Prince and his lovely bride mounted on the faithful beast's back.

The King's joy was great when he embraced his youngest son, for he had long since despaired of his return. He received the wolf and the beautiful golden mermaid most cordially too, and the Prince was made to tell his adventures all over from the beginning. The poor old father grew very sad when he heard of the shameful conduct of his elder sons, and had them called before him. They turned as white as death when they saw their brother, whom they thought they had murdered, standing beside them alive and well, and so startled were they that when the King asked them why they had behaved so wickedly to their brother they could think of no lie, but confessed at once that they had slain the young Prince in order

to obtain possession of the golden horse and the golden bird. Their father's wrath knew no bounds, and he ordered them both to be banished, but he could not do enough to honour his youngest son, and his marriage with the beautiful mermaid was celebrated with much pomp and magnificence. When the festivities were over, the wolf bade them all farewell, and returned once more to his life in the woods, much to the regret of the old King and the young Prince and his bride.

And so ended the adventures of the Prince with his friend the wolf.

Grimm.

THE WHITE SNAKE

NOT very long ago there lived a King, the fame of whose wisdom was spread far and wide. Nothing appeared to be unknown to him, and it really seemed as if tidings of the most secret matters must be borne to him by the winds. He had one very peculiar habit. Every day, after the dinner table had been cleared, and everyone had retired, a confidential servant brought in a dish. It was covered, and neither the servant nor anyone else had any idea what was on it, for the King never removed the cover or partook of the dish, till he was quite alone.

This went on for some time till, one day, the servant who removed the dish was so overcome with curiosity, that he could not resist carrying it off to his own room. After carefully locking the door, he lifted the cover, and there he saw a white snake lying on the dish. On seeing it he could not restrain his desire to taste it, so he cut off a small piece and put it in his mouth.

Hardly had it touched his tongue than he heard a strange sort of whispering of tiny voices outside his window. He stepped to the casement to listen, and found that the sound proceeded from the sparrows, who were talking together and telling each other all they had seen in the fields and woods. The piece of the white snake which he had eaten had enabled him to understand the language of animals.

Now on this particular day, it so happened that the Queen lost her favourite ring, and suspicion fell on the confidential servant who had access to all parts of the palace. The King sent for him, and threatened him angrily, saying that if he had not found the thief by the next day, he should himself be taken up and tried.

It was useless to assert his innocence; he was dismissed without ceremony. In his agitation and distress, he went down to the yard to think over what he could do in this trouble. Here were a number of ducks resting near a little stream, and pluming themselves with their bills, whilst they kept up an animated conversation amongst themselves. The servant stood still listening to them. They were talking of where they had been waddling about all the morning, and of the good food they had found, but one of them remarked rather sadly, 'There's something lying very heavy

on my stomach, for in my haste I've swallowed a ring, which was lying just under the Queen's window.'

No sooner did the servant hear this than he seized the duck by the neck, carried it off to the kitchen, and said to the cook, 'Suppose you kill this duck; you see she's nice and fat.'

'Yes, indeed,' said the cook, weighing the duck in his hand, 'she certainly has spared no pains to stuff herself well, and must have been waiting for the spit for some time.' So he chopped off her head, and when she was opened there was the Queen's ring in her stomach.

It was easy enough now for the servant to prove his innocence, and the King, feeling he had done him an injustice, and anxious to make some amends, desired him to ask any favour he chose, and promised to give him the highest post at Court he could wish for.

The servant, however, declined everything, and only begged for a horse and some money to enable him to travel, as he was anxious to see something of the world.

When his request was granted, he set off on his journey, and in the course of it he one day came to a large pond, on the edge of which he noticed three fishes which had got entangled in the reeds and were gasping for water. Though fish are generally supposed to be quite mute, he heard them grieving aloud at the prospect of dying in this wretched manner. Having a very kind heart he dismounted and soon set the prisoners free, and in the water once more. They flapped with joy, and stretching up their heads cried to him : ' We will remember, and reward you for saving us.'

He rode further, and after a while he thought he heard a voice in the sand under his feet. He paused to listen, and heard the King of the Ants complaining : ' If only men with their awkward beasts would keep clear of us ! That stupid horse is crushing my people mercilessly to death with his great hoofs.' The servant at once turned into a side path, and the Ant-King called after him, ' We'll remember and reward you.'

The road next led through a wood, where he saw a father and a mother raven standing by their nest and throwing out their young : ' Away with you, you young rascals ! ' they cried, ' we can't feed you any longer. You are quite big enough to support yourselves now.' The poor little birds lay on the ground flapping and beating their wings, and shrieked, ' We poor helpless children, feed ourselves indeed ! Why, we can't even fly yet ; what can we do but die of hunger ? ' Then the kind youth dismounted, drew his sword, and killing his horse left it there as food for the young ravens. They hopped up, satisfied their hunger, and piped : ' We'll remember, and reward you ! '

He was now obliged to trust to his own legs, and after walking a long way he reached a big town. Here he found a great crowd and much commotion in the streets, and a herald rode about announcing, ' The King's daughter seeks a husband, but whoever would woo her must first execute a difficult task, and if he does not succeed he must be content to forfeit his life.' Many had risked their lives, but in vain. When the youth saw the King's daughter, he was so dazzled by her beauty, that he forgot all idea of danger, and went to the King to announce himself a suitor.

On this he was led out to a large lake, and a gold ring was thrown into it before his eyes. The King desired him to dive after it, adding, ' If you return without it you will be thrown back into the lake time after time, till you are drowned in its depths.'

Everyone felt sorry for the handsome young fellow, and left him alone on the shore. There he stood thinking and wondering what he could do, when all of a sudden he saw three fishes swimming along, and recognised them as the very same whose lives he had saved. The middle fish held a mussel in its mouth, which it laid at the young man's feet, and when he picked it up and opened it, there was the golden ring inside.

Full of delight he brought it to the King's daughter, expecting to receive his promised reward. The haughty Princess, however, on hearing that he was not her equal by birth despised him, and exacted the fulfilment of a second task.

She went into the garden, and with her own hands she strewed ten sacks full of millet all over the grass. ' He must pick all that up to-morrow morning before sunrise,' she said ; ' not a grain must be lost.'

The youth sat down in the garden and wondered how it would be possible for him to accomplish such a task, but he could think of no expedient, and sat there sadly expecting to meet his death at daybreak.

But when the first rays of the rising sun fell on the garden, he saw the ten sacks all completely filled, standing there in a row, and not a single grain missing. The Ant-King, with his thousands and thousands of followers, had come during the night, and the grateful creatures had industriously gathered all the millet together and put it in the sacks.

The King's daughter came down to the garden herself, and saw to her amazement that her suitor had accomplished the task she had given him. But even now she could not bend her proud heart, and she said, ' Though he has executed these two tasks, yet he shall not be my husband till he brings me an apple from the tree of life.'

The young man did not even know where the tree of life grew, but he set off, determined to walk as far as his legs would carry him, though he had no hope of ever finding it.

After journeying through three different kingdoms he reached a wood one night, and lying down under a tree prepared to go to sleep there.   Suddenly he heard a sound in the boughs, and a golden apple fell right into his hand.   At the same moment three ravens flew down to him, perched on his knee and said, ' We are the three young ravens whom you saved from starvation.   When we grew

up and heard you were searching for the golden apple, we flew far away over the seas to the end of the world, where the tree of life grows, and fetched the golden apple for you.'

Full of joy the young man started on his way back and brought the golden apple to the lovely Princess, whose objections were now entirely silenced. They divided the apple of life and ate it together, and her heart grew full of love for him, so they lived together to a great age in undisturbed happiness.

Grimm

THE LITTLE SOLDIER

I

ONCE upon a time there was a little soldier who had just come back from the war. He was a brave little fellow, but he had lost neither arms nor legs in battle. Still, the fighting was ended and the army disbanded, so he had to return to the village where he was born.

Now the soldier's name was really John, but for some reason or other his friends always called him the Kinglet; why, no one ever knew, but so it was.

As he had no father or mother to welcome him home, he did not hurry himself, but went quietly along, his knapsack on his back and his sword by his side, when suddenly one evening he was seized with a wish to light his pipe. He felt for his match-box to strike a light, but to his great disgust he found he had lost it.

He had only gone about a stone's throw after making this discovery when he noticed a light shining through the trees. He went towards it, and perceived before him an old castle, with the door standing open.

The little soldier entered the courtyard, and, peeping through a window, saw a large fire blazing at the end of a low hall. He put his pipe in his pocket and knocked gently, saying politely:

'Would you give me a light?'

But he got no answer.

After waiting for a moment John knocked again, this time more loudly. There was still no reply.

He raised the latch and entered; the hall was empty.

The little soldier made straight for the fireplace, seized the tongs, and was stooping down to look for a nice red hot coal with which to light his pipe, when clic! something went, like a spring giving way, and in the very midst of the flames an enormous serpent reared itself up close to his face.

And what was more strange still, this serpent had the head of a woman.

At such an unexpected sight many men would have turned and run for their lives; but the little soldier, though he *was* so small,

had a true soldier's heart. He only made one step backwards, and grasped the hilt of his sword.

'Don't unsheath it,' said the serpent. 'I have been waiting for you, as it is you who must deliver me.'

'Who are you?'

'My name is Ludovine, and I am the daughter of the King of

the Low Countries. Deliver me, and I will marry you and make you happy for ever after.'

Now, some people might not have liked the notion of being made happy by a serpent with the head of a woman, but the Kinglet had no such fears. And, besides, he felt the fascination of Ludovine's eyes, which looked at him as a snake looks at a little bird. They were beautiful green eyes, not round like those of a cat, but long and almond-shaped, and they shone with a strange light, and the golden hair which floated round them seemed all the brighter for their lustre. The face had the beauty of an angel, though the body was only that of a serpent.

'What must I do?' asked the Kinglet.

'Open that door. You will find yourself in a gallery with a room at the end just like this. Cross that, and you will see a closet, out of which you must take a tunic, and bring it back to me.'

The little soldier boldly prepared to do as he was told. He crossed the gallery in safety, but when he reached the room he saw by the light of the stars eight hands on a level with his face, which threatened to strike him. And, turn his eyes which way he would, he could discover no bodies belonging to them.

He lowered his head and rushed forward amidst a storm of blows, which he returned with his fists. When he got to the closet, he opened it, took down the tunic, and brought it to the first room.

'Here it is,' he panted, rather out of breath.

'Clic!' once more the flames parted. Ludovine was a woman down to her waist. She took the tunic and put it on.

It was a magnificent tunic of orange velvet, embroidered in pearls, but the pearls were not so white as her own neck.

'That is not all,' she said. 'Go to the gallery, take the staircase which is on the left, and in the second room on the first story you will find another closet with my skirt. Bring this to me.'

The Kinglet did as he was told, but in entering the room he saw, instead of merely hands, eight arms, each holding an enormous stick. He instantly unsheathed his sword and cut his way through with such vigour that he hardly received a scratch.

He brought back the skirt, which was made of silk as blue as the skies of Spain.

'Here it is,' said John, as the serpent appeared. She was now a woman as far as her knees.

'I only want my shoes and stockings now,' she said. 'Go and get them from the closet which is on the second story.'

The little soldier departed, and found himself in the presence of eight goblins armed with hammers, and flames darting from their eyes. This time he stopped short at the threshold. 'My sword is no use,' he thought to himself; 'these wretches will break it like glass, and if I can't think of anything else, I am a dead man.' At this moment his eyes fell on the door, which was made of oak, thick and heavy. He wrenched it off its hinges and held it over his head, and then went straight at the goblins, whom he crushed beneath it. After that he took the shoes and stockings out of the closet and brought them to Ludovine, who, directly she had put them on, became a woman all over.

When she was quite dressed in her white silk stockings and little blue slippers dotted over with carbuncles, she said to her deliverer, 'Now you must go away, and never come back here, whatever happens. Here is a purse with two hundred ducats. Sleep to-night at the inn which is at the edge of the wood, and awake early in the morning: for at nine o'clock I shall pass the door, and shall take you up in my carriage.' 'Why shouldn't we go now?' asked the little soldier. 'Because the time has not yet come,' said the Princess. 'But first you may drink my health in this glass of wine,' and as she spoke she filled a crystal goblet with a liquid that looked like melted gold.

John drank, then lit his pipe and went out.

II

When he arrived at the inn he ordered supper, but no sooner had he sat down to eat it than he felt that he was going sound asleep.

'I must be more tired than I thought,' he said to himself, and, after telling them to be sure to wake him next morning at eight o'clock, he went to bed.

All night long he slept like a dead man. At eight o'clock they came to wake him, and at half-past, and a quarter of an hour later, but it was no use; and at last they decided to leave him in peace.

The clocks were striking twelve when John awoke. He sprang out of bed, and, scarcely waiting to dress himself, hastened to ask if anyone had been to inquire for him.

'There came a lovely princess,' replied the landlady, 'in a coach of gold. She left you this bouquet, and a message to say that she would pass this way to-morrow morning at eight o'clock.'

The little soldier cursed his sleep, but tried to console himself by looking at his bouquet, which was of *immortelles*.

'It is the flower of remembrance,' thought he, forgetting that it is also the flower of the dead.

When the night came, he slept with one eye open, and jumped up twenty times an hour. When the birds began to sing he could lie still no longer, and climbed out of his window into the branches of one of the great lime-trees that stood before the door. There he

sat, dreamily gazing at his bouquet till he ended by going fast asleep.

Once asleep, nothing was able to wake him; neither the brightness of the sun, nor the songs of the birds, nor the noise of Ludovine's golden coach, nor the cries of the landlady who sought him in every place she could think of.

As the clock struck twelve he woke, and his heart sank as he came down out of his tree and saw them laying the table for dinner.

'Did the Princess come?' he asked.

'Yes, indeed, she did. She left this flower-coloured scarf for you; said she would pass by to-morrow at seven o'clock, but it would be the last time.'

'I must have been bewitched,' thought the little soldier. Then he took the scarf, which had a strange kind of scent, and tied it round his left arm, thinking all the while that the best way to keep awake was not to go to bed at all. So he paid his bill, and bought a horse with the money that remained, and when the evening came he mounted his horse and stood in front of the inn door. determined to stay there all night.

Every now and then he stooped to smell the sweet perfume of the scarf round his arm; and gradually he smelt it so often that at last his head sank on to the horse's neck, and he and his horse snored in company.

When the Princess arrived, they shook him, and beat him, and screamed at him, but it was all no good. Neither man nor horse woke till the coach was seen vanishing away in the distance.

Then John put spurs to his horse, calling with all his might 'Stop! stop!' But the coach drove on as before, and though the little soldier rode after it for a day and a night, he never got one step nearer.

Thus they left many villages and towns behind them, till they came to the sea itself. Here John thought that at last the coach must stop, but, wonder of wonders! it went straight on, and rolled over the water as easily as it had done over the land. John's horse, which had carried him so well, sank down from fatigue, and the little soldier sat sadly on the shore, watching the coach which was fast disappearing on the horizon.

III

However, he soon plucked up his spirits again, and walked along the beach to try and find a boat in which he could sail after the Princess. But no boat was there, and at last, tired and hungry, he sat down to rest on the steps of a fisherman's hut.

In the hut was a young girl who was mending a net. She invited John to come in, and set before him some wine and fried fish, and John ate and drank and felt comforted, and he told his adventures to the little fisher-girl. But though she was very pretty, with a skin as white as a gull's breast, for which her neighbours gave her the name of the Seagull, he did not think about her at all, for he was dreaming of the green eyes of the Princess.

When he had finished his tale, she was filled with pity and said:

'Last week, when I was fishing, my net suddenly grew very heavy, and when I drew it in I found a great copper vase, fastened with lead. I brought it home and placed it on the fire. When the lead had melted a little, I opened the vase with my knife and drew out a mantle of red cloth and a purse containing fifty crowns. That is the mantle, covering my bed, and I have kept the money for my marriage-portion. But take it and go to the nearest sea-port, where you will find a ship sailing for the Low Countries, and when you become King you will bring me back my fifty crowns.'

And the Kinglet answered: 'When I am King of the Low Countries, I will make you lady-in-waiting to the Queen, for you are as good as you are beautiful. So farewell,' said he, and as the Sea-gull went back to her fishing he rolled himself in the mantle and threw himself down on a heap of dried grass, thinking of the strange things that had befallen him, till he suddenly exclaimed:

'Oh, how I wish I was in the capital of the Low Countries!'

IV

In one moment the little soldier found himself standing before a splendid palace. He rubbed his eyes and pinched himself, and when he was quite sure he was not dreaming he said to a man who was smoking his pipe before the door, 'Where am I?'

'Where are you? Can't you see? Before the King's palace, of course.'

'What King?'

'Why the King of the Low Countries!' replied the man, laughing and supposing that he was mad.

Was there ever anything so strange? But as John was an honest fellow, he was troubled at the thought that the Seagull would think he had stolen her mantle and purse. And he began to wonder how he could restore them to her the soonest. Then he remembered that the mantle had some hidden charm that enabled the bearer to transport himself at will from place to place, and in order to make sure of this he wished himself in the best inn of the town. In an instant he was there.

Enchanted with this discovery, he ordered supper, and as it was too late to visit the King that night he went to bed.

The next day, when he got up, he saw that all the houses were wreathed with flowers and covered with flags, and all the church bells were ringing. The little soldier inquired the meaning of all this noise, and was told that the Princess Ludovine, the King's beautiful daughter, had been found, and was about to make her triumphal entry. ' That will just suit me,' thought the Kinglet ; ' I will stand at the door and see if she knows me.'

He had scarcely time to dress himself when the golden coach of Ludovine went by. She had a crown of gold upon her head, and the King and Queen sat by her side. By accident her eyes fell upon the little soldier, and she grew pale and turned away her head.

' Didn't she know me ? ' the little soldier asked himself, ' or was she angry because I missed our meetings ? ' and he followed the crowd till he got to the palace. When the royal party entered he told the guards that it was he who had delivered the Princess, and wished to speak to the King. But the more he talked the more they believed him mad and refused to let him pass.

The little soldier was furious. He felt that he needed his pipe to calm him, and he entered a tavern and ordered a pint of beer. ' It is this miserable soldier's helmet,' said he to himself. ' If I had only money enough I could look as splendid as the lords of the Court ; but what is the good of thinking of that when I have only the remains of the Seagull's fifty crowns ? '

He took out his purse to see what was left, and he found that there were still fifty crowns.

' The Seagull must have miscounted,' thought he, and he paid for his beer. Then he counted his money again, and there were still fifty crowns. He took away five and counted a third time, but there were still fifty. He emptied the purse altogether and then shut it ; when he opened it the fifty crowns were still there !

Then a plan came into his head, and he determined to go at once to the Court tailor and coachbuilder.

He ordered the tailor to make him a mantle and vest of blue velvet embroidered with pearls, and the coachbuilder to make him a golden coach like the coach of the Princess Ludovine. If the tailor and the coachbuilder were quick he promised to pay them double.

A few days later the little soldier was driven through the city in his coach drawn by six white horses, and with four lacqueys richly dressed standing behind. Inside sat John, clad in blue velvet, with a bouquet of immortelles in his hand and a scarf bound round his arm. He drove twice round the city, throwing money to the right and left, and the third time, as he passed under the palace windows, he saw Ludovine lift a corner of the curtain and peep out.

V

The next day no one talked of anything but the rich lord who had distributed money as he drove along. The talk even reached the Court, and the Queen, who was very curious, had a great desire to see the wonderful Prince.

'Very well,' said the King; 'let him be asked to come and play cards with me.'

This time the Kinglet was not late for his appointment.

The King sent for the cards and they sat down to play. They

had six games, and John always lost. The stake was fifty crowns, and each time he emptied his purse, which was full the next instant.

The sixth time the King exclaimed, 'It is amazing!'

The Queen cried, 'It is astonishing!'

The Princess said, 'It is bewildering!'

'Not so bewildering,' replied the little soldier, 'as your change into a serpent.'

'Hush!' interrupted the King, who did not like the subject.

'I only spoke of it,' said John, 'because you see in me the man who delivered the Princess from the goblins and whom she promised to marry.'

'Is that true?' asked the King of the Princess.

'Quite true,' answered Ludovine. 'But I told my deliverer to be ready to go with me when I passed by with my coach. I passed three times, but he slept so soundly that no one could wake him.'

'What is your name?' said the King, 'and who are you?'

'My name is John. I am a soldier, and my father is a boatman.'

'You are not a fit husband for my daughter. Still, if you will give us your purse, you shall have her for your wife.'

'My purse does not belong to me, and I cannot give it away.'

'But you can lend it to me till our wedding-day,' said the Princess with one of those glances the little soldier never could resist.

'And when will that be?'

'At Easter,' said the monarch.

'Or in a blue moon!' murmured the Princess; but the Kinglet did not hear her and let her take his purse.

Next evening he presented himself at the palace to play picquet with the King and to make his court to the Princess. But he was told that the King had gone into the country to receive his rents. He returned the following day, and had the same answer. Then he asked to see the Queen, but she had a headache. When this had happened five or six times, he began to understand that they were making fun of him.

'That is not the way for a King to behave,' thought John. 'Old scoundrel!' and then suddenly he remembered his red cloak.

'Ah, what an idiot I am!' said he. 'Of course I can get in whenever I like with the help of this.'

That evening he was in front of the palace, wrapped in his red cloak.

On the first story one window was lighted, and John saw on the curtains the shadow of the Princess.

'I wish myself in the room of the Princess Ludovine,' said he, and in a second he was there.

The King's daughter was sitting before a table counting the money that she emptied from the inexhaustible purse.

'Eight hundred and fifty, nine hundred, nine hundred and fifty——'

'A thousand,' finished John. 'Good evening everybody!'

The Princess jumped and gave a little cry. '*You* here ! What business have you to do it ?   Leave at once, or I shall call——'

'I have come,' said the Kinglet, 'to remind you of your promise. The day after to-morrow is Easter Day, and it is high time to think of our marriage.'

Ludovine burst out into a fit of laughter. 'Our marriage ! Have you really been foolish enough to believe that the daughter of the King of the Low Countries would ever marry the son of a boatman ? '

'Then give me back the purse,' said John.

'Never,' said the Princess, and put it calmly in her pocket.

'As you like,' said the little soldier. 'He laughs best who laughs the last; ' and he took the Princess in his arms. 'I wish,' he cried, 'that we were at the ends of the earth ; ' and in one second he was there, still clasping the Princess tightly in his arms.

'Ouf,' said John, laying her gently at the foot of a tree. 'I never took such a long journey before. What do you say, madam ? ' The Princess understood that it was no time for jesting, and did not answer.   Besides she was still feeling giddy from her rapid flight, and had not yet collected her senses.

VI

The King of the Low Countries was not a very scrupulous person, and his daughter took after him. This was why she had been changed into a serpent. It had been prophesied that she should be delivered by a little soldier, and that she must marry him, unless he failed to appear at the meeting-place three times running. The cunning Princess then laid her plans accordingly.

The wine that she had given to John in the castle of the goblins, the bouquet of immortelles, and the scarf, all had the power of producing sleep like death. And we know how they had acted on John.

However, even in this critical moment, Ludovine did not lose her head.

'I thought you were simply a street vagabond,' said she, in her most coaxing voice ; 'and I find you are more powerful than any king. Here is your purse. Have you got my scarf and my bouquet ? '

'Here they are,' said the Kinglet, delighted with this change of tone, and he drew them from his bosom. Ludovine fastened one in his button-hole and the other round his arm. 'Now,' she said, 'you are my lord and master, and I will marry you at your good pleasure.'

'You are kinder than I thought,' said John; 'and you shall never be unhappy, for I love you.'

'Then, my little husband, tell me how you managed to carry me so quickly to the ends of the world.'

The little soldier scratched his head. 'Does she really mean to marry me,' he thought to himself, 'or is she only trying to deceive me again?'

But Ludovine repeated, 'Won't you tell me?' in such a tender voice he did not know how to resist her.

'After all,' he said to himself, 'what does it matter telling her the secret, as long as I don't give her the cloak.'

And he told her the virtue of the red mantle.

'Oh dear, how tired I am!' sighed Ludovine. 'Don't you think we had better take a nap? And then we can talk over our plans.'

She stretched herself on the grass, and the Kinglet did the same. He laid his head on his left arm, round which the scarf was tied, and was soon fast asleep.

Ludovine was watching him out of one eye, and no sooner did she hear him snore than she unfastened the mantle, drew it gently from under him and wrapped it round her, took the purse from his pocket, and put it in hers, and said: 'I wish I was back in my own room.' In another moment she was there.

VII

Who felt foolish but John, when he awoke, twenty-four hours after, and found himself without purse, without mantle, and without Princess? He tore his hair, he beat his breast, he trampled on the bouquet, and tore the scarf of the traitress to atoms.

Besides this he was very hungry, and he had nothing to eat.

He thought of all the wonderful things his grandmother had told him when he was a child, but none of them helped him now. He was in despair, when suddenly he looked up and saw that the tree under which he had been sleeping was a superb plum, covered with fruit as yellow as gold.

'Here goes for the plums,' he said to himself, 'all is fair in war.'

He climbed the tree and began to eat steadily. But he had hardly swallowed two plums when, to his horror, he felt as if something was growing on his forehead. He put up his hand and found that he had two horns!

He leapt down from the tree and rushed to a stream that flowed close by. Alas! there was no escape : two charming little horns, that would not have disgraced the head of a goat.

Then his courage failed him.

'As if it was not enough,' said he, 'that a woman should trick me, but the devil must mix himself up in it and lend me his horns. What a pretty figure I should cut if I went back into the world!'

But as he was still hungry, and the mischief was done, he climbed boldly up another tree, and plucked two plums of a lovely green colour. No sooner had he swallowed two than the horns disappeared. The little soldier was enchanted, though greatly surprised, and came to the conclusion that it was no good to despair too quickly. When he had done eating an idea suddenly occurred to him.

'Perhaps,' thought he, 'these pretty little plums may help me to recover my purse, my cloak, and my heart from the hands of this wicked Princess. She has the eyes of a deer already ; let her have the horns of one. If I can manage to set her up with a pair, I will bet any money that I shall cease to want her for my wife. A horned maiden is by no means lovely to look at.' So he plaited a basket out of the long willows, and placed in it carefully both sorts of plums. Then he walked bravely on for many days, having no food but the berries by the wayside, and was in great danger from wild beasts and savage men. But he feared nothing, except that his plums should decay, and this never happened.

At last he came to a civilised country, and with the sale of some jewels that he had about him on the evening of his flight he took passage on board a vessel for the Low Countries. So, at the end of a year and a day, he arrived at the capital of the kingdom.

VIII

The next day he put on a false beard and the dress of a date merchant, and, taking a little table, he placed himself before the door of the church.

He spread carefully out on a fine white cloth his Mirabelle plums, which looked for all the world as if they had been freshly gathered, and when he saw the Princess coming out of church he began to call out in a feigned voice : 'Fine plums! lovely plums!'

'How much are they?' said the Princess.

'Fifty crowns each.'

'Fifty crowns! But what is there so very precious about them? Do they give one wit, or will they increase one's beauty?'

'They could not increase what is perfect already, fair Princess, but still they might add something.'

Rolling stones gather no moss, but they sometimes gain polish; and the months which John had spent in roaming about the world had not been wasted. Such a neatly turned compliment flattered Ludovine.

'What will they add?' she smilingly asked.

'You will see, fair Princess, when you taste them. It will be a surprise for you.'

Ludovine's curiosity was roused. She drew out the purse and shook out as many little heaps of fifty crowns as there were plums in the basket. The little soldier was seized with a wild desire to snatch the purse from her and proclaim her a thief, but he managed to control himself.

His plums all sold, he shut up shop, took off his disguise, changed his inn, and kept quiet, waiting to see what would happen.

No sooner had she reached her room than the Princess exclaimed, 'Now let us see what these fine plums can add to my beauty,' and throwing off her hood, she picked up a couple and ate them.

Imagine with what surprise and horror she felt all of a sudden that something was growing out of her forehead. She flew to her mirror and uttered a piercing cry.

'Horns! so that was what he promised me! Let someone find the plum-seller at once and bring him to me! Let his nose and ears be cut off! Let him be flayed alive, or burnt at a slow fire and his ashes scattered to the winds! Oh, I shall die of shame and despair!'

Her women ran at the sound of her screams, and tried to wrench off the horns, but it was of no use, and they only gave her a violent headache.

The King then sent round a herald to proclaim that he would give the hand of the Princess to anyone who would rid her of her strange ornaments. So all the doctors and sorcerers and surgeons in the Low Countries and the neighbouring kingdoms thronged to the palace, each with a remedy of his own. But it was all no good, and the Princess suffered so much from their remedies that the

THE PRINCESS DRINKS THE PHIAL TO TAKE AWAY THE HORNS

King was obliged to send out a second proclamation that anyone who undertook to cure the Princess, and who failed to do it, should be hanged up to the nearest tree.

But the prize was too great for any proclamation to put a stop to the efforts of the crowd of suitors, and that year the orchards of the Low Countries all bore a harvest of dead men.

IX

The King had given orders that they should seek high and low for the plum-seller, but in spite of all their pains, he was nowhere to be found.

When the little soldier discovered that their patience was worn out, he pressed the juice of the green Queen Claude plums into a small phial, bought a doctor's robe, put on a wig and spectacles, and presented himself before the King of the Low Countries. He gave himself out as a famous physician who had come from distant lands, and he promised that he would cure the Princess if only he might be left alone with her.

'Another madman determined to be hanged,' said the King. 'Very well, do as he asks; one should refuse nothing to a man with a rope round his neck.'

As soon as the little soldier was in the presence of the Princess he poured some drops of the liquid into a glass. The Princess had scarcely tasted it, when the tip of the horns disappeared.

'They would have disappeared completely,' said the pretended doctor, 'if there did not exist something to counteract the effect. It is only possible to cure people whose souls are as clean as the palm of my hand. Are you sure you have not committed some little sin? Examine yourself well.'

Ludovine had no need to think over it long, but she was torn in pieces between the shame of a humiliating confession, and the desire to be unhorned. At last she made answer with downcast eyes,

'I have stolen a leather purse from a little soldier.'

'Give it to me. The remedy will not act till I hold the purse in my hands.'

It cost Ludovine a great pang to give up the purse, but she remembered that riches would not benefit her if she was still to keep the horns.

With a sigh, she handed the purse to the doctor, who poured

more of the liquid into the glass, and when the Princess had drunk it, she found that the horns had diminished by one half.

' You must really have another little sin on your conscience. Did you steal nothing from this soldier but his purse ? '

' I also stole from him his cloak.'

' Give it me.'

' Here it is.'

This time Ludovine thought to herself that when once the horns had departed, she would call her attendants and take the things from the doctor by force.

She was greatly pleased with this idea, when suddenly the pretended physician wrapped himself in the cloak, flung away the wig and spectacles, and showed to the traitress the face of the Little Soldier.

She stood before him dumb with fright.

' I might,' said John, ' have left you horned to the end of your days, but I am a good fellow and I once loved you, and besides—you are too like the devil to have any need of his horns.'

X

John had wished himself in the house of the Seagull. Now the Seagull was seated at the window, mending her net, and from time to time her eyes wandered to the sea as if she was expecting someone. At the noise made by the little soldier, she looked up and blushed.

' So it is you ! ' she said. ' How did you get here ? ' And then she added in a low voice, ' And have you married your Princess ? '

Then John told her all his adventures, and when he had finished, he restored to her the purse and the mantle.

' What can I do with them ? ' said she. ' You have proved to me that happiness does not lie in the possession of treasures.'

' It lies in work and in the love of an honest women,' replied the little soldier, who noticed for the first time what pretty eyes she had. ' Dear Seagull, will you have me for a husband ? ' and he held out his hand.

' Yes, I will,' answered the fisher maiden, blushing very red, ' but only on condition that we seal up the purse and the mantle in the copper vessel and throw them into the sea.'

And this they did.

Charles Deulin.

THE SIX SWANS

A KING was once hunting in a great wood, and he hunted the game so eagerly that none of his courtiers could follow him. When evening came on he stood still and looked round him, and he saw that he had quite lost himself. He sought a way out, but could find none. Then he saw an old woman with a shaking head coming towards him; but she was a witch.

'Good woman,' he said to her, 'can you not show me the way out of the wood?'

'Oh, certainly, Sir King,' she replied, 'I can quite well do that, but on one condition, which if you do not fulfil you will never get out of the wood, and will die of hunger.'

'What is the condition?' asked the King.

'I have a daughter,' said the old woman, 'who is so beautiful that she has not her equal in the world, and is well fitted to be your wife; if you will make her lady-queen I will show you the way out of the wood.'

The King in his anguish of mind consented, and the old woman led him to her little house where her daughter was sitting by the fire. She received the King as if she were expecting him, and he saw that she was certainly very beautiful; but she did not please him, and he could not look at her without a secret feeling of horror. As soon as he had lifted the maiden on to his horse the old woman showed him the way, and the King reached his palace, where the wedding was celebrated.

The King had already been married once, and had by his first wife seven children, six boys and one girl, whom he loved more than anything in the world. And now, because he was afraid that their stepmother might not treat them well and might do them harm, he put them in a lonely castle that stood in the middle of a wood. It lay so hidden, and the way to it was so hard to find, that he himself could not have found it out had not a **wise-woman** given him a reel of thread which possessed a marvellous property : when he threw it before him it unwound itself and showed him the way. But the King went so often to his dear children that the Queen was offended at his absence. She grew curious, and wanted to know what he had to do quite alone in the wood. She gave his servants a great deal of money, and they betrayed the secret to her, and also told her of the reel which alone could point out the way. She had no rest now till she had found out where the King guarded the reel, and then she made some little white shirts, and, as she had learnt from her witch-mother, sewed an enchantment in each of them.

And when the King had ridden off she took the little shirts and went into the wood, and the reel showed her the way. The children, who saw someone coming in the distance, thought it was their dear father coming to them, and sprang to meet him very joyfully. Then she threw over each one a little shirt, which when it had touched their bodies changed them into swans, and they flew away over the forest. The Queen went home quite satisfied, and thought she had got rid of her step-children ; but the girl had not run to meet her with her brothers, and she knew nothing of her.

The next day the King came to visit his children, but he found no one but the girl.

' Where are your brothers ? ' asked the King.

' Alas ! dear father,' she answered, ' they have gone away and left me all alone.' And she told him that looking out of her little window she had seen her brothers flying over the wood in the shape of swans, and she showed him the feathers which they had let fall in the yard, and which she had collected. The King mourned, but he did not think that the Queen had done the wicked deed, and as he was afraid the maiden would also be taken from him, he wanted to take her with him. But she was afraid of the stepmother, and begged the King to let her stay just one night more in the castle in the wood. The poor maiden thought, ' My home is no longer here ; I will go and seek my brothers.' And when night came she fled away into the forest. She ran all through the night and the next day, till she could go no farther for weariness. Then she saw a little hut, went in, and found a room with six little beds. She was afraid to lie down on one, so she crept under one of them, lay on the hard floor, and was going to spend the night there. But when the sun had set she heard a noise, and saw six swans flying in at the window. They stood on the floor and blew at one another, and blew all their feathers off, and their swan-skin came off like a shirt. Then the maiden recognised her brothers, and overjoyed she crept out from under the bed. Her brothers were not less delighted than she to see their little sister again, but their joy did not last long.

'You cannot stay here,' they said to her. 'This is a den of robbers; if they were to come here and find you they would kill you.'

'Could you not protect me?' asked the little sister.

'No,' they answered, 'for we can only lay aside our swan skins for a quarter of an hour every evening. For this time we regain our human forms, but then we are changed into swans again.'

Then the little sister cried and said, 'Can you not be freed?'

'Oh, no,' they said, 'the conditions are too hard. You must not speak or laugh for six years, and must make in that time six shirts for us out of star-flowers. If a single word comes out of your mouth, all your labour is vain.' And when the brothers had said this the quarter of an hour came to an end, and they flew away out of the window as swans.

But the maiden had determined to free her brothers even if it should cost her her life. She left the hut, went into the forest, climbed a tree, and spent the night there. The next morning she went out, collected star-flowers, and began to sew. She could speak to no one, and she had no wish to laugh, so she sat there, looking only at her work.

When she had lived there some time, it happened that the King of the country was hunting in the forest, and his hunters came to the tree on which the maiden sat. They called to her and said 'Who are you?'

But she gave no answer.

'Come down to us,' they said, 'we will do you no harm.'

But she shook her head silently. As they pressed her further with questions, she threw them the golden chain from her neck. But they did not leave off, and she threw them her girdle, and when this was no use, her garters, and then her dress. The huntsmen would not leave her alone, but climbed the tree, lifted the maiden down, and led her to the King. The King asked, 'Who are you? What are you doing up that tree?'

But she answered nothing.

He asked her in all the languages he knew, but she remained

as dumb as a fish. Because she was so beautiful, however, the King's heart was touched, and he was seized with a great love for her. He wrapped her up in his cloak, placed her before him on his horse, and brought her to his castle. There he had her dressed in rich clothes, and her beauty shone out as bright as day, but not a word could be drawn from her. He set her at table by his side, and her modest ways and behaviour pleased him so much that he said, ' I will marry this maiden and none other in the world,' and after some days he married her. But the King had a wicked mother who was displeased with the marriage, and said wicked things of the young Queen. ' Who knows who this girl is ? ' she said; ' she cannot speak, and is not worthy of a king.'

After a year, when the Queen had her first child, the old mother took it away from her. Then she went to the King and said that the Queen had killed it. The King would not believe it, and would not allow any harm to be done her. But she sat quietly

' And then her dress '

sewing at the shirts and troubling herself about nothing. The next time she had a child the wicked mother did the same thing, but the King could not make up his mind to believe her. He said, ' She is too sweet and good to do such a thing as that. If she were not dumb and could defend herself, her innocence would be proved.' But when the third child was taken away, and the Queen was again accused, and could not utter a word in her own defence, the King was obliged to give her over to the law, which decreed that she must be burnt to death. When the day came on which the sentence was to be executed, it was the last day of the six years in which she must not speak or laugh, and now she had freed her dear brothers from the power of the enchantment. The six shirts were done; there was only the left sleeve wanting to the last.

When she was led to the stake, she laid the shirts on her arm, and as she stood on the pile and the fire was about to be lighted, she looked around her and saw six swans flying through the air. Then she knew that her release was at hand and her heart danced for joy. The swans fluttered round her, and hovered low so that she could throw the shirts over them. When they had touched them the swan-skins fell off, and her brothers stood before her living, well and beautiful. Only the youngest had a swan's wing instead of his left arm. They embraced and kissed each other, and the Queen went to the King, who was standing by in great astonishment, and began to speak to him, saying, 'Dearest husband, now I can speak and tell you openly that I am innocent and have been falsely accused.'

She told him of the old woman's deceit, and how she had taken the three children away and hidden them. Then they were fetched, to the great joy of the King, and the wicked mother came to no good end.

But the King and the Queen with their six brothers lived many years in happiness and peace.

The Six Brothers Changed
Into Swans By Their
Stepmother.

THE DONKEY CABBAGE

THERE was once a young Hunter who went boldly into the forest. He had a merry and light heart, and as he went whistling along there came an ugly old woman, who said to him, 'Good-day, dear hunter! You are very merry and contented, but I suffer hunger and thirst, so give me a trifle.' The Hunter was sorry for the poor old woman, and he felt in his pocket and gave her all he could spare. He was going on then, but the old woman stopped him and said, 'Listen, dear hunter, to what I say. Because of your kind heart I will make you a present. Go on your way, and in a short time you will come to a tree on which sit nine birds who have a cloak in their claws and are quarrelling over it. Then take aim with your gun and shoot in the middle of them; they will let the cloak fall, but one of the birds will be hit and will drop down dead. Take the cloak with you; it is a wishing-cloak, and when you throw it on your shoulders you have only to wish yourself at a certain place, and in the twinkling of an eye you are there. Take the heart out of the dead bird and swallow it whole, and early every morning when you get up you will find a gold piece under your pillow.'

The Hunter thanked the wise woman, and thought to himself 'These are splendid things she has promised me, if only they come to pass!' So he walked on about a hundred yards, and then he heard above him in the branches such a screaming and chirping that he looked up, and there he saw a heap of birds tearing a cloth with their beaks and feet, shrieking, tugging, and fighting, as if each wanted it for himself. 'Well,' said the Hunter, 'this is wonderful! It is just as the old woman said'; and he took his gun on his shoulder, pulled the trigger, and shot into the midst of them, so that their feathers flew about. Then the flock took flight with much screaming, but one fell dead, and the cloak fluttered down. Then the Hunter did as the old woman had told him: he cut open the bird, found its heart, swallowed it, and took the cloak home with him. The next morning when he awoke he remembered the promise, and wanted to see if it had come true. But when he lifted up his pillow, there sparkled the gold piece, and the next morning he found another, and so on every time he got up. He collected a heap of gold, but at last he thought to himself, 'What good is all my gold to me if I stay at home? I will travel and look a bit about me in the world.' So he took leave of his parents, slung his hunting knapsack and his gun round him, and journeyed into the world.

It happened that one day he went through a thick wood, and when he came to the end of it there lay in the plain before him a large castle. At one of the windows in it stood an old woman with a most beautiful maiden by her side, looking out. But the old woman was a witch, and she said to the girl, 'There comes one out of the wood who has a wonderful treasure in his body which we must manage to possess ourselves of, darling daughter; we have more right to it than he. He has a bird's heart in him, and so every morning there lies a gold piece under his pillow.'

She told her how they could get hold of it, and how she was to coax it from him, and at last threatened her angrily, saying, 'And if you do not obey me, you shall repent it!'

When the Hunter came nearer he saw the maiden, and said to himself, 'I have travelled so far now that I will rest, and turn into this beautiful castle; money I have in plenty.' But the real reason was that he had caught sight of the lovely face.

He went into the house, and was kindly received and hospitably entertained. It was not long before he was so much in love with the witch-maiden that he thought of nothing else, and only looked in her eyes, and whatever she wanted, that he gladly did. Then the old witch said, 'Now we must have the bird-heart; he will not feel when it is gone.' She prepared a drink, and when it was ready she poured it in a goblet and gave it to the maiden, who had to hand it to the hunter.

'Drink to me now, my dearest,' she said. Then he took the goblet, and when he had swallowed the drink the bird-heart came out of his mouth. The maiden had to get hold of it secretly and then swallow it herself, for the old witch wanted to have it. Thenceforward he found no more gold under his pillow, and it lay under the maiden's; but he was so much in love and so much bewitched that he thought of nothing except spending all his time with the maiden.

Then the old witch said, 'We have the bird-heart, but we must also get the wishing-cloak from him.'

The maiden answered, 'We will leave him that; he has already lost his wealth!'

The old witch grew angry, and said, 'Such a cloak is a wonderful thing, it is seldom to be had in the world, and have it I must

THE MAIDEN OBTAINS THE BIRD-HEART

and will.' She beat the maiden, and said that if she did not obey it would go ill with her.

So she did her mother's bidding, and, standing one day by the window, she looked away into the far distance as if she were very sad.

'Why are you standing there looking so sad?' asked the Hunter.

'Alas, my love,' she replied, 'over there lies the granite mountain where the costly precious stones grow. I have a great longing
to go there, so that when I think of it I am very sad. For who
can fetch them? Only the birds who fly; a man, never.'

'If you have no other trouble,' said the Hunter, 'that one I can
easily remove from your heart.'

So he wrapped her round in his cloak and wished themselves to
the granite mountain, and in an instant there they were, sitting on
it! The precious stones sparkled so brightly on all sides that it
was a pleasure to see them, and they collected the most beautiful
and costly together. But now the old witch had through her
witchcraft caused the Hunter's eyes to become heavy.

He said to the maiden, 'We will sit down for a little while and
rest; I am so tired that I can hardly stand on my feet.'

So they sat down, and he laid his head on her lap and fell
asleep. As soon as he was sound asleep she unfastened the cloak
from his shoulders, threw it on her own, left the granite and stones,
and wished herself home again.

But when the Hunter had finished his sleep and awoke, he
found that his love had betrayed him and left him alone on the
wild mountain. 'Oh,' said he, 'why is faithlessness so great in
the world?' and he sat down in sorrow and trouble, not knowing
what to do.

But the mountain belonged to fierce and huge giants, who lived
on it and traded there, and he had not sat long before he saw three
of them striding towards him. So he lay down as if he had fallen
into a deep sleep.

The giants came up, and the first pushed him with his foot, and
said, 'What sort of an earthworm is that?'

The second said, 'Crush him dead.'

But the third said contemptuously, 'It is not worth the trouble!
Let him live; he cannot remain here, and if he goes higher up the
mountain the clouds will take him and carry him off.'

Talking thus they went away. But the Hunter had listened to
their talk, and as soon as they had gone he rose and climbed to
the summit. When he had sat there a little while a cloud swept
by, and, seizing him, carried him away. It travelled for a time in
the sky, and then it sank down and hovered over a large vegetable
garden surrounded by walls, so that he came safely to the ground
amidst cabbages and vegetables. The Hunter then looked about
him, saying, 'If only I had something to eat! I am so hungry,

and it will go badly with me in the future, for I see here not an
apple or pear or fruit of any kind—nothing but vegetables everywhere.'   At last he thought, ' At a pinch I can eat a salad ; it does
not taste particularly nice, but it will refresh me.'   So he looked
about for a good head and ate it, but no sooner had he swallowed
a couple of mouthfuls than he felt very strange, and found himself
wonderfully changed.   Four legs began to grow on him, a thick
head, and two long ears, and he saw with horror that he had
changed into a donkey.   But as he was still very hungry and this

The hunter is transformed into a donkey

juicy salad tasted very good to his present nature, he went on
eating with a still greater appetite.   At last he got hold of another
kind of cabbage, but scarcely had swallowed it when he felt another
change, and he once more regained his human form.

The Hunter now lay down and slept off his weariness.   When
he awoke the next morning he broke off a head of the bad and a head
of the good cabbage, thinking, ' This will help me to regain my
own, and to punish faithlessness.'   Then he put the heads in his
pockets, climbed the wall, and started off to seek the castle of his

love. When he had wandered about for a couple of days he found it quite easily. He then browned his face quickly, so that his own mother would not have known him, and went into the castle, where he begged for a lodging.

'I am so tired,' he said, 'I can go no farther.'

The witch asked, 'Countryman, who are you, and what is your business?'

He answered, 'I am a messenger of the King, and have been sent to seek the finest salad that grows under the sun. I have been so lucky as to find it, and am bringing it with me; but the heat of the sun is so great that the tender cabbage threatens to grow soft, and I do not know if I shall be able to bring it any farther.'

When the old witch heard of the fine salad she wanted to eat it, and said, 'Dear countryman, just let me taste the wonderful salad.'

'Why not?' he answered; 'I have brought two heads with me, and will give you one.'

So saying, he opened his sack and gave her the bad one. The witch suspected no evil, and her mouth watered to taste the new dish, so that she went into the kitchen to prepare it herself. When it was ready she could not wait till it was served at the table, but she immediately took a couple of leaves and put them in her mouth. No sooner, however, had she swallowed them than she lost human form, and ran into the courtyard in the shape of a donkey.

Now the servant came into the kitchen, and when she saw the salad standing there ready cooked she was about to carry it up, but on the way, according to her old habit, she tasted it and ate a couple of leaves. Immediately the charm worked, and she became a donkey, and ran out to join the old witch, and the dish with the salad in it fell to the ground. In the meantime, the messenger was sitting with the lovely maiden, and as no one came with the salad, and she wanted very much to taste it, she said, 'I don't know where the salad is.'

Then thought the Hunter, 'The cabbage must have already begun to work.' And he said, 'I will go to the kitchen and fetch it myself.'

When he came there he saw the two donkeys running about in the courtyard, but the salad was lying on the ground.

'That's all right,' said he; 'two have had their share!' And lifting the remaining leaves up, he laid them on the dish and brought them to the maiden.

'I am bringing you the delicious food my own self,' he said, 'so that you need not wait any longer.'

Then she ate, and, as the others had done, she at once lost her human form, and ran as a donkey into the yard.

When the Hunter had washed his face, so that the changed ones might know him, he went into the yard, saying, 'Now you shall receive a reward for your faithlessness.'

He tied them all three with a rope, and drove them away till he came to a mill. He knocked at the window, and the miller put his head out and asked what he wanted.

'I have three tiresome animals,' he answered, 'which I don't want to keep any longer. If you will take them, give them food and

stabling, and do as I tell you with them, I will pay you as much as you want.'

The miller replied, 'Why not? What shall I do with them?'

Then the Hunter said that to the old donkey, which was the witch, three beatings and one meal; to the younger one, which was the servant, one beating and three meals; and to the youngest one, which was the maiden, no beating and three meals; for he could not find it in his heart to let the maiden be beaten.

Then he went back into the castle, and he found there all that he wanted. After a couple of days the miller came and said that he must tell him that the old donkey which was to have three beatings and only one meal had died. 'The two others,' he added, ' are certainly not dead, and get their three meals every day, but they are so sad that they cannot last much longer.'

Then the Hunter took pity on them, laid aside his anger, and told the miller to drive them back again. And when they came he gave them some of the good cabbage to eat, so that they became human again. Then the beautiful maiden fell on her knees before him, saying, ' Oh, my dearest, forgive me the ill I have done you! My mother compelled me to do it; it was against my will, for I love you dearly. Your wishing-cloak is hanging in a cupboard, and as for the bird-heart I will make a drink and give it back to you.'

But he changed his mind, and said, ' Keep it; it makes no dif-ference, for I will take you to be my own dear true wife.'

And the wedding was celebrated, and they lived happy together till death.

FAIRER-THAN-A-FAIRY

ONCE there lived a King who had no children for many years after his marriage. At length heaven granted him a daughter of such remarkable beauty that he could think of no name so appropriate for her as 'Fairer-than-a-Fairy.'

It never occurred to the good-natured monarch that such a name was certain to call down the hatred and jealousy of the fairies in a body on the child, but this was what happened. No sooner had they heard of this presumptuous name than they resolved to gain possession of her who bore it, and either to torment her cruelly, or at least to conceal her from the eyes of all men.

The eldest of their tribe was entrusted to carry out their revenge. This Fairy was named Lagree; she was so old that she only had one eye and one tooth left, and even these poor remains she had to keep all night in a strengthening liquid. She was also so spiteful that she gladly devoted all her time to carrying out all the mean or ill-natured tricks of the whole body of fairies.

With her large experience, added to her native spite, she found but little difficulty in carrying off Fairer-than-a-Fairy. The poor child, who was only seven years old, nearly died of fear on finding herself in the power of this hideous creature. However, when after an hour's journey underground she found herself in a splendid palace with lovely gardens, she felt a little reassured, and was further cheered when she discovered that her pet cat and dog had followed her.

The old Fairy led her to a pretty room which she said should be hers, at the same time giving her the strictest orders never to let out the fire which was burning brightly in the grate. She then gave two glass bottles into the Princess's charge, desiring her to take the greatest care of them, and having enforced her orders with the most awful threats in case of disobedience, she vanished, leaving the little girl at liberty to explore the palace and grounds and a good deal relieved at having only two apparently easy tasks set her.

Several years passed, during which time the Princess grew accustomed to her lonely life, obeyed the Fairy's orders, and by degrees forgot all about the court of the King her father.

One day, whilst passing near a fountain in the garden, she noticed that the sun's rays fell on the water in such a manner as to produce a brilliant rainbow. She stood still to admire it, when, to her great surprise, she heard a voice addressing her which seemed

LAGREE gives the 2 bottles to FAIRERTHANAFAIRY.

to come from the centre of its rays. The voice was that of a young man, and its sweetness of tone and the agreeable things it uttered, led one to infer that its owner must be equally charming; but this had to be a mere matter of fancy, for no one was visible.

The beautiful Rainbow informed Fairer-than-a-Fairy that he was young, the son of a powerful king, and that the Fairy, Lagree, who owed his parents a grudge, had revenged herself by depriving him of his natural shape for some years; that she had imprisoned him in the palace, where he had found his confinement hard to bear for some time, but now, he owned, he no longer sighed for freedom since he had seen and learned to love Fairer-than-a-Fairy.

He added many other tender speeches to this declaration, and the Princess, to whom such remarks were a new experience, could not help feeling pleased and touched by his attentions.

The Prince could only appear or speak under the form of a Rainbow, and it was therefore necessary that the sun should shine on water so as to enable the rays to form themselves.

Fairer-than-a-Fairy lost no moment in which she could meet her lover, and they enjoyed many long and interesting interviews. One day, however, their conversation became so absorbing and time passed so quickly that the Princess forgot to attend to the fire, and it went out. Lagree, on her return, soon found out the neglect, and seemed only too pleased to have the opportunity of showing her spite to her lovely prisoner. She ordered Fairer-than-a-Fairy to start next day at dawn to ask Locrinos for fire with which to re-light the one she had allowed to go out.

Now this Locrinos was a cruel monster who devoured everyone he came across, and especially enjoyed a chance of catching and eating any young girls. Our heroine obeyed with great sweetness, and without having been able to take leave of her lover she set off to go to Locrinos as to certain death. As she was crossing a wood a bird sang to her to pick up a shining pebble which she would find in a fountain close by, and to use it when needed. She took the bird's advice, and in due time arrived at the house of Locrinos. Luckily she only found his wife at home, who was much struck by the Princess's youth and beauty and sweet gentle manners, and still further impressed by the present of the shining pebble.

She readily let Fairer-than-a-Fairy have the fire, and in return for the stone she gave her another, which, she said, might prove useful some day. Then she sent her away without doing her any harm.

Lagree was as much surprised as displeased at the happy result of this expedition, and Fairer-than-a-Fairy waited anxiously for an opportunity of meeting Prince Rainbow and telling him her adventures. She found, however, that he had already been told all about them by a Fairy who protected him, and to whom he was related.

The dread of fresh dangers to his beloved Princess made him devise some more convenient way of meeting than by the garden fountain, and Fairer-than-a-Fairy carried out his plan daily with entire success. Every morning she placed a large basin full of water on her window-sill, and as soon as the sun's rays fell on the water the Rainbow appeared as clearly as it had ever done in the fountain. By this means they were able to meet without losing sight of the fire or of the two bottles in which the old Fairy kept her eye and her tooth at night, and for some time the lovers enjoyed every hour of sunshine together.

One day Prince Rainbow appeared in the depths of woe. He had just heard that he was to be banished from this lovely spot, but he had no idea where he was to go. The poor young couple were in despair, and only parted with the last ray of sunshine, and in hopes of meeting next morning. Alas! next day was dark and gloomy, and it was only late in the afternoon that the sun broke through the clouds for a few minutes.

Fairer-than-a-Fairy eagerly ran to the window, but in her haste she upset the basin, and spilt all the water with which she had carefully filled it overnight. No other water was at hand except that in the two bottles. It was the only chance of seeing her lover before they were separated, and she did not hesitate to break the bottle and pour their contents into the basin, when the Rainbow appeared at once. Their farewells were full of tenderness; the Prince made the most ardent and sincere protestations, and promised to neglect nothing which might help to deliver his dear Fairer-than-a-Fairy from her captivity, and implored her to consent to their marriage as soon as they should both be free. The Princess, on her side, vowed to have no other husband, and declared herself willing to brave death itself in order to rejoin him.

They were not allowed much time for their adieus; the Rainbow vanished, and the Princess, resolved to run all risks, started off at once, taking nothing with her but her dog, her cat, a sprig of myrtle, and the stone which the wife of Locrinos gave her.

When Lagree became aware of her prisoner's flight she was furious, and set off at full speed in pursuit. She overtook her just as the poor girl, overcome by fatigue, had lain down to rest in a cave which the stone had formed itself into to shelter her. The little dog who was watching her mistress promptly flew at Lagree and bit her so severely that she stumbled against a corner of the cave and broke off her only tooth. Before she had recovered from the pain and rage this caused her, the Princess had time to escape, and was some way on her road. Fear gave her strength for some time, but at last she could go no further, and sank down to rest. As she did so, the sprig of myrtle she carried touched the ground, and immediately a green and shady bower sprang up round her, in which she hoped to sleep in peace.

But Lagree had not given up her pursuit, and arrived just as Fairer-than-a-Fairy had fallen fast asleep. This time she made

sure of catching her victim, but the cat spied her out, and, springing from one of the boughs of the arbour she flew at Lagree's face and tore out her only eye, thus delivering the Princess for ever from her persecutor.

One might have thought that all would now be well, but no sooner had Lagree been put to flight than our heroine was overwhelmed with hunger and thirst. She felt as though she should certainly expire, and it was with some difficulty that she dragged herself as far as a pretty little green and white house, which stood at no great distance. Here she was received by a beautiful lady dressed in green and white to match the house, which apparently belonged to her, and of which she seemed the only inhabitant.

She greeted the fainting Princess most kindly, gave her an excellent supper, and after a long night's rest in a delightful bed told her that after many troubles she should finally attain her desire.

As the green and white lady took leave of the Princess she gave her a nut, desiring her only to open it in the most urgent need.

After a long and tiring journey Fairer-than-a-Fairy was once more received in a house, and by a lady exactly like the one she had quitted. Here again she received a present with the same injunctions, but instead of a nut this lady gave her a golden pomegranate. The mournful Princess had to continue her weary way and after many troubles and hardships she again found rest and shelter in a third house exactly similar to the two others.

These houses belonged to three sisters, all endowed with fairy gifts, and all so alike in mind and person that they wished their houses and garments to be equally alike. Their occupation consisted in helping those in misfortune, and they were as gentle and benevolent as Lagree had been cruel and spiteful.

The third Fairy comforted the poor traveller, begged her not to lose heart, and assured her that her troubles should be rewarded. She accompanied her advice by the gift of a crystal smelling-bottle, with strict orders only to open it in case of urgent need. Fairer-than-a-Fairy thanked her warmly, and resumed her way cheered by pleasant thoughts.

After a time her road led through a wood, full of soft airs and sweet odours, and before she had gone a hundred yards she saw a wonderful silver Castle suspended by strong silver chains to four of the largest trees. It was so perfectly hung that a gentle breeze rocked it sufficiently to send you pleasantly to sleep.

Fairer-than-a-Fairy felt a strong desire to enter this Castle, but besides being hung a little above the ground there seemed to be neither doors nor windows. She had no doubt (though really I cannot think why) that the moment had come in which to use the

nut which had been given her. She opened it, and out came a
diminutive hall porter at whose belt hung a tiny chain, at the end
of which was a golden key half as long as the smallest pin you
ever saw.

The Princess climbed up one of the silver chains, holding in her
hand the little porter who, in spite of his minute size, opened a
secret door with his golden key and let her in. She entered a
magnificent room which appeared to occupy the entire Castle, and
which was lighted by gold and jewelled stars in the ceiling. In
the midst of this room stood a couch, draped with curtains of all
the colours of the rainbow, and suspended by golden cords so that
it swayed with the Castle in a manner which rocked its occupant
delightfully to sleep.

On this elegant couch lay Prince Rainbow, looking more beautiful
than ever, and sunk in profound slumber, in which he had been
held ever since his disappearance.

Fairer-than-a-Fairy, who now saw him for the first time in his
real shape, hardly dared to gaze at him, fearing lest his appearance
might not be in keeping with the voice and language which had
won her heart. At the same time she could not help feeling rather
hurt at the apparent indifference with which she was received.

She related all the dangers and difficulties she had gone through,
and though she repeated the story twenty times in a loud clear voice,
the Prince slept on and took no heed. She then had recourse to
the golden pomegranate, and on opening it found that all the seeds
were as many little violins which flew up in the vaulted roof and
at once began playing melodiously.

The Prince was not completely roused, but he opened his eyes
a little and looked all the handsomer.

Impatient at not being recognised, Fairer-than-a-Fairy now
drew out her third present, and on opening the crystal scent-bottle
a little syren flew out, who silenced the violins and then sang close
to the Prince's ear the story of all his lady love had suffered in her
search for him. She added some gentle reproaches to her tale, but
before she had got far he was wide awake, and transported with joy
threw himself at the Princess's feet. At the same moment the
walls of the room expanded and opened out, revealing a golden
throne covered with jewels. A magnificent Court now began
to assemble, and at the same time several elegant carriages filled
with ladies in magnificent dresses drove up. In the first and most
splendid of these carriages sat Prince Rainbow's mother. She

fondly embraced her son, after which she informed him that his father had been dead for some years, that the anger of the Fairies was at length appeased, and that he might return in peace to reign over his people, who were longing for his presence.

The Court received the new King with joyful acclamations which would have delighted him at any other time, but all his thoughts were full of Fairer-than-a-Fairy. He was just about to present her to his mother and the Court, feeling sure that her charms would win all hearts, when the three green and white sisters appeared.

They declared the secret of Fairer-than-a-Fairy's royal birth, and the Queen taking the two lovers in her carriage set off with them for the capital of the kingdom.

Here they were received with tumultuous joy. The wedding was celebrated without delay, and succeeding years diminished neither the virtues, beauty, nor the mutual affection of King Rainbow and his Queen, Fairer-than-a-Fairy.

IN THE LAND OF SOULS

F̵AR away, in North America, where the Red Indians dwell
there lived a long time ago a beautiful maiden, who was
lovelier than any other girl in the whole tribe. Many of the young
braves sought her in marriage, but she would listen to one only—
a handsome chief, who had taken her fancy some years before.
So they were to be married, and great rejoicings were made, and
the two looked forward to a long life of happiness together, when
the very night before the wedding feast a sudden illness seized the
girl, and, without a word to her friends who were weeping round
her, she passed silently away.

The heart of her lover had been set upon her, and the thought
of her remained with him night and day. He put aside his bow,
and went neither to fight nor to hunt, but from sunrise to sunset he
sat by the place where she was laid, thinking of his happiness that
was buried there. At last, after many days, a light seemed to
come to him out of the darkness. He remembered having heard
from the old, old people of the tribe, that there was a path that
led to the Land of Souls—that if you sought carefully you could
find it.

So the next morning he got up early, and put some food in his
pouch and slung an extra skin over his shoulders, for he knew not
how long his journey would take, nor what sort of country he
would have to go through. Only one thing he knew, that if the
path was there, he would find it. At first he was puzzled, as there
seemed no reason he should go in one direction more than another.
Then all at once he thought he had heard one of the old men say
that the Land of Souls lay to the south, and so, filled with new
hope and courage, he set his face southwards. For many, many
miles the country looked the same as it did round his own home.
The forests, the hills, and the rivers all seemed exactly like the ones

¹ From the Red Indian.

he had left. The only thing that was different was the snow, which had lain thick upon the hills and trees when he started, but grew less and less the farther he went south, till it disappeared altogether. Soon the trees put forth their buds, and flowers sprang up under his feet, and instead of thick clouds there was blue sky over his head, and everywhere the birds were singing. Then he knew that he was in the right road.

The thought that he should soon behold his lost bride made his heart beat for joy, and he sped along lightly and swiftly. Now his way led through a dark wood, and then over some steep cliffs, and on the top of these he found a hut or wigwam. An old man clothed in skins, and holding a staff in his hand, stood in the doorway; and he said to the young chief who was beginning to tell his story, 'I was waiting for you, wherefore you have come I know. It is but a short while since she whom you seek was here. Rest in my hut, as she also rested, and I will tell you what you ask, and whither you should go.'

On hearing these words, the young man entered the hut, but his heart was too eager within him to suffer him to rest, and when he arose, the old man rose too, and stood with him at the door. 'Look,' he said, 'at the water which lies far out yonder, and the plains which stretch beyond. That is the Land of Souls, but no man enters it without leaving his body behind him. So, lay down your body here; your bow and arrows, your skin and your dog. They shall be kept for you safely.'

Then he turned away, and the young chief, light as air, seemed hardly to touch the ground; and as he flew along the scents grew sweeter and the flowers more beautiful, while the animals rubbed their noses against him, instead of hiding as he approached, and birds circled round him, and fishes lifted up their heads and looked as he went by. Very soon he noticed with wonder, that neither rocks nor trees barred his path. He passed through them without knowing it, for indeed, they were not rocks and trees at all, but only the souls of them; for this was the Land of Shadows.

So he went on with winged feet till he came to the shores of a great lake, with a lovely island in the middle of it; while on the bank of the lake was a canoe of glittering stone, and in the canoe were two shining paddles.

The chief jumped straight into the canoe, and seizing the paddles pushed off from the shore, when to his joy and wonder he saw following him in another canoe exactly like his own the maiden

for whose sake he had made this long journey.   But they could not
touch each other, for between them rolled great waves, which looked
as if they would sink the boats, yet never did.   And the young man
and the maiden shrank with fear, for down in the depths of the
water they saw the bones of those who had died before, and in the
waves themselves men and women were struggling, and but few
passed over.   Only the children had no fear, and reached the other
side in safety.   Still, though the chief and the young girl quailed in
terror at these horrible sights and sounds, no harm came to them,
for their lives had been free from evil, and the Master of Life had
said that no evil should happen unto them.   So they reached unhurt
the shore of the Happy Island, and wandered through the flowery
fields and by the banks of rushing streams, and they knew not
hunger nor thirst; neither cold nor heat.   The air fed them and
the sun warmed them, and they forgot the dead, for they saw no
graves, and the young man's thoughts turned not to wars, neither
to the hunting of animals.   And gladly would these two have walked
thus for ever, but in the murmur of the wind he heard the Master
of Life saying to him, 'Return whither you came, for I have work
for you to do, and your people need you, and for many years you
shall rule over them.   At the gate my messenger awaits you, and
you shall take again your body which you left behind, and he will
show you what you are to do.   Listen to him, and have patience,
and in time to come you shall rejoin her whom you must now leave,
for she is accepted, and will remain ever young and beautiful, as
when I called her hence from the Land of Snows.'

THE DRAGON OF THE NORTH [1]

VERY long ago, as old people have told me, there lived a **terrible** monster, who came out of the North, and laid waste whole tracts of country, devouring both men and beasts; and this monster was so destructive that it was feared that unless help came no living creature would be left on the face of the earth. It had a body like an ox, and legs like a frog, two short fore-legs, and two long ones behind, and besides that it had a tail like a serpent, ten fathoms in length. When it moved it jumped like a frog, and with every spring it covered half a mile of ground. Fortunately its habit was to remain for several years in the same place, and not to move on till the whole neighbourhood was eaten up. Nothing could hunt it, because its whole body was covered with scales, which were harder than stone or metal; its two great eyes shone by night, and even by day, like the brightest lamps, and anyone who had the ill luck to look into those eyes became as it were bewitched, and was obliged to rush of his own accord into the monster's jaws. In this way the Dragon was able to feed upon both men and beasts without the least trouble to itself, as it needed not to move from the spot where it was lying. All the neighbouring kings had offered rich rewards to anyone who should be able to destroy the monster, either by force or enchantment, and many had tried their luck, but all had miserably failed. Once a great forest in which the Dragon lay had been set on fire; the forest was burnt down, but the fire did not do the monster the least harm. However, there was a tradition amongst the wise men of the country that the Dragon might be overcome by one who possessed King Solomon's signet-ring, upon which a secret writing was engraved. This inscription would enable anyone who was wise enough to interpret it to find out how the Dragon could be destroyed. Only no one knew where the ring was hidden, nor was there any sorcerer

[1] 'Der Norlands Drache,' from *Esthnische Mährchen*. Kreutzwald.

or learned man to be found who would be able to explain the inscription.

At last a young man, with a good heart and plenty of courage, set out to search for the ring. He took his way towards the sunrising, because he knew that all the wisdom of old time comes from the East. After some years he met with a famous Eastern magician, and asked for his advice in the matter. The magician answered :

' Mortal men have but little wisdom, and can give you no help, but the birds of the air would be better guides to you if you could learn their language. I can help you to understand it if you will stay with me a few days.

The youth thankfully accepted the magician's offer, and said, ' I cannot now offer you any reward for your kindness, but should my undertaking succeed your trouble shall be richly repaid.'

Then the magician brewed a powerful potion out of nine sorts of herbs which he had gathered himself all alone by moonlight, and he gave the youth nine spoonfuls of it daily for three days, which made him able to understand the language of birds.

At parting the magician said to him, ' If you ever find Solomon's ring and get possession of it, then come back to me, that I may explain the inscription on the ring to you, for there is no one else in the world who can do this.'

From that time the youth never felt lonely as he walked along; he always had company, because he understood the language of birds; and in this way he learned many things which mere human knowledge could never have taught him. But time went on, and he heard nothing about the ring. It happened one evening, when he was hot and tired with walking, and had sat down under a tree in a forest to eat his supper, that he saw two gaily-plumaged birds, that were strange to him, sitting at the top of the tree talking to one another about him. The first bird said :

' I know that wandering fool under the tree there, who has come so far without finding what he seeks. He is trying to find King Solomon's lost ring.'

The other bird answered, ' He will have to seek help from the *Witch-maiden*,[1] who will doubtless be able to put him on the right track. If she has not got the ring herself, she knows well enough who has it.'

' But where is he to find the Witch-maiden ? ' said the first

[1] Höllenmädchen.

bird. ' She has no settled dwelling, but is here to-day and gone to-morrow. He might as well try to catch the wind.'

The other replied, ' I do not know, certainly, where she is at present, but in three nights from now she will come to the spring to wash her face, as she does every month when the moon is full, in order that she may never grow old nor wrinkled, but may always keep the bloom of youth.'

' Well,' said the first bird, ' the spring is not far from here. Shall we go and see how it is she does it ? '

' Willingly, if you like,' said the other.

The youth immediately resolved to follow the birds to the spring, only two things made him uneasy : first, lest he might be asleep when the birds went, and secondly, lest he might lose sight of them, since he had not wings to carry him along so swiftly. He was too tired to keep awake all night, yet his anxiety prevented him from sleeping soundly, and when with the earliest dawn he looked up to the tree-top, he was glad to see his feathered companions still asleep with their heads under their wings. He ate his breakfast, and waited until the birds should start, but they did not leave the place all day. They hopped about from one tree to another looking for food, all day long until the evening, when they went back to their old perch to sleep. The next day the same thing happened, but on the third morning one bird said to the other, ' To-day we must go to the spring to see the Witch-maiden wash her face.' They remained on the tree till noon ; then they flew away and went towards the south. The young man's heart beat with anxiety lest he should lose sight of his guides, but he managed to keep the birds in view until they again perched upon a tree. The young man ran after them until he was quite exhausted and out of breath, and after three short rests the birds at length reached a small open space in the forest, on the edge of which they placed themselves on the top of a high tree. When the youth had overtaken them, he saw that there was a clear spring in the middle of the space. He sat down at the foot of the tree upon which the birds were perched, and listened attentively to what they were saying to each other.

' The sun is not down yet,' said the first bird ; ' we must wait yet awhile till the moon rises and the maiden comes to the spring. Do you think she will see that young man sitting under the tree ? '

Nothing is likely to escape her eyes, certainly not a young man, said the other bird. ' Will the youth have the sense not to let himself be caught in her toils ? '

'We will wait,' said the first bird, 'and see how they get on together.'

The evening light had quite faded, and the full moon was already shining down upon the forest, when the young man heard a slight rustling sound. After a few moments there came out of the forest a maiden, gliding over the grass so lightly that her feet seemed scarcely to touch the ground, and stood beside the spring. The youth could not turn away his eyes from the maiden, for he had never in his life seen a woman so beautiful. Without seeming to notice anything, she went to the spring, looked up to the full moon, then knelt down and bathed her face nine times, then looked up to the moon again and walked nine times round the well, and as she walked she sang this song:

> 'Full-faced moon with light unshaded,
> Let my beauty ne'er be faded.
> Never let my cheek grow pale!
> While the moon is waning nightly,
> May the maiden bloom more brightly,
> May her freshness never fail!'

Then she dried her face with her long hair, and was about to go away, when her eye suddenly fell upon the spot where the young man was sitting, and she turned towards the tree. The youth rose and stood waiting. Then the maiden said, 'You ought to have a heavy punishment because you have presumed to watch my secret doings in the moonlight. But I will forgive you this time, because you are a stranger and knew no better. But you must tell me truly who you are and how you came to this place, where no mortal has ever set foot before.'

The youth answered humbly: 'Forgive me, beautiful maiden, if I have unintentionally offended you. I chanced to come here after long wandering, and found a good place to sleep under this tree. At your coming I did not know what to do, but stayed where I was, because I thought my silent watching could not offend you.'

The maiden answered kindly, 'Come and spend this night with us. You will sleep better on a pillow than on damp moss.' The youth hesitated for a little, but presently he heard the birds saying from the top of the tree, 'Go where she calls you, but take care to give no blood, or you will sell your soul.' So the youth went with her, and soon they reached a beautiful garden, where

THE WITCH-MAIDEN SEES THE YOUNG MAN UNDER A TREE

stood a splendid house, which glittered in the moonlight as if it
was all built out of gold and silver. When the youth entered he
found many splendid chambers, each one finer than the last.
Hundreds of tapers burnt upon golden candlesticks, and shed a
light like the brightest day. At length they reached a chamber
where a table was spread with the most costly dishes. At the
table were placed two chairs, one of silver, the other of gold. The
maiden seated herself upon the golden chair, and offered the silver
one to her companion. They were served by maidens dressed in
white, whose feet made no sound as they moved about, and not a
word was spoken during the meal. Afterwards the youth and the
Witch-maiden conversed pleasantly together, until a woman, dressed
in red, came in to remind them that it was bedtime. The youth
was now shown into another room, containing a silken bed with
down cushions, where he slept delightfully, yet he seemed to hear
a voice near his bed which repeated to him, ' Remember to give no
blood ! '

The next morning the maiden asked him whether he would not
like to stay with her always in this beautiful place, and as he did
not answer immediately, she continued : ' You see how I always
remain young and beautiful, and I am under no one's orders, but
can do just what I like, so that I have never thought of marrying
before. But from the moment I saw you I took a fancy to you, so
if you agree, we might be married and might live together like
princes, because I have great riches.'

The youth could not but be tempted with the beautiful maiden's
offer, but he remembered how the birds had called her the witch,
and their warning always sounded in his ears. Therefore he answered cautiously, ' Do not be angry, dear maiden, if I do not decide
immediately on this important matter. Give me a few days to
consider before we come to an understanding.'

' Why not ? ' answered the maiden. ' Take some weeks to consider if you like, and take counsel with your own heart.' And to
make the time pass pleasantly, she took the youth over every part
of her beautiful dwelling, and showed him all her splendid treasures.
But these treasures were all produced by enchantment, for the
maiden could make anything she wished appear by the help of
King Solomon's signet ring; only none of these things remained
fixed ; they passed away like the wind without leaving a trace behind. But the youth did not know this; he thought they were all
real.

One day the maiden took him into a secret chamber, where a little gold box was standing on a silver table. Pointing to the box, she said, ' Here is my greatest treasure, whose like is not to be found in the whole world. It is a precious gold ring. When you marry me, I will give you this ring as a marriage gift, and it will make you the happiest of mortal men. But in order that our love may last for ever, you must give me for the ring three drops of blood from the little finger of your left hand.'

When the youth heard these words a cold shudder ran over him, for he remembered that his soul was at stake. He was cunning enough, however, to conceal his feelings and to make no direct answer, but he only asked the maiden, as if carelessly, what was remarkable about the ring ?

She answered, ' No mortal is able entirely to understand the power of this ring, because no one thoroughly understands the secret signs engraved upon it. But even with my half-knowledge I can work great wonders. If I put the ring upon the little finger of my left hand, then I can fly like a bird through the air wherever I wish to go. If I put it on the third finger of my left hand I am invisible, and I can see everything that passes around me, though no one can see me. If I put the ring upon the middle finger of my left hand, then neither fire nor water nor any sharp weapon can hurt me. If I put it on the forefinger of my left hand, then I can with its help produce whatever I wish. I can in a single moment build houses or anything I desire. Finally, as long as I wear the ring on the thumb of my left hand, that hand is so strong that it can break down rocks and walls. Besides these, the ring has other secret signs which, as I said, no one can understand. No doubt it contains secrets of great importance. The ring formerly belonged to King Solomon, the wisest of kings, during whose reign the wisest men lived. But it is not known whether this ring was ever made by mortal hands : it is supposed that an angel gave it to the wise King.'

When the youth heard all this he determined to try and get possession of the ring, though he did not quite believe in all its wonderful gifts. He wished the maiden would let him have it in his hand, but he did not quite like to ask her to do so, and after a while she put it back into the box. A few days after they were again speaking of the magic ring, and the youth said, ' I do not think it possible that the ring can have all the power you say it has.'

Then the maiden opened the box and took the ring out, and it glittered as she held it like the clearest sunbeam. She put it on the middle finger of her left hand, and told the youth to take a knife and try as hard as he could to cut her with it, for he would not be able to hurt her. He was unwilling at first, but the maiden insisted. Then he tried, at first only in play, and then seriously, to strike her with the knife, but an invisible wall of iron seemed to be between them, and the maiden stood before him laughing and un-hurt. Then she put the ring on her third finger, and in an instant she had vanished from his eyes. Presently she was beside him again laughing, and holding the ring between her fingers.

'Do let me try,' said the youth, 'whether I can do these won-derful things.'

The maiden, suspecting no treachery, gave him the magic ring.

The youth pretended to have forgotten what to do, and asked what finger he must put the ring on so that no sharp weapon could hurt him?'

'Oh, the middle finger of your left hand,' the maiden answered, laughing.

She took the knife and tried to strike the youth, and he even tried to cut himself with it, but found it impossible. Then he asked the maiden to show him how to split stones and rocks with the help of the ring. So she led him into a courtyard where stood a great boulder-stone. 'Now,' she said, 'put the ring upon the thumb of your left hand, and you will see how strong that hand has be-come. The youth did so, and found to his astonishment that with a single blow of his fist the stone flew into a thousand pieces. Then the youth bethought him that he who does not use his luck when he has it is a fool, and that this was a chance which once lost might never return. So while they stood laughing at the shattered stone he placed the ring, as if in play, upon the third finger of his left hand.

'Now,' said the maiden, 'you are invisible to me until you take the ring off again.'

But the youth had no mind to do that; on the contrary, he went farther off, then put the ring on the little finger of his left hand, and soared into the air like a bird.

When the maiden saw him flying away she thought at first that he was still in play, and cried, 'Come back, friend, for now you see I have told you the truth.' But the young man never came back.

Then the maiden saw she was deceived, and bitterly repented that she had ever trusted him with the ring.

The young man never halted in his flight until he reached the dwelling of the wise magician who had taught him the speech of birds. The magician was delighted to find that his search had been successful, and at once set to work to interpret the secret signs engraved upon the ring, but it took him seven weeks to make them out clearly. Then he gave the youth the following instructions how to overcome the Dragon of the North : 'You must have an iron horse cast, which must have little wheels under each foot. You must also be armed with a spear two fathoms long, which you will be able to wield by means of the magic ring upon your left thumb. The spear must be as thick in the middle as a large tree, and both its ends must be sharp. In the middle of the spear you must have two strong chains ten fathoms in length. As soon as the Dragon has made himself fast to the spear, which you must thrust through his jaws, you must spring quickly from the iron horse and fasten the ends of the chains firmly to the ground with iron stakes, so that he cannot get away from them. After two or three days the monster's strength will be so far exhausted that you will be able to come near him. Then you can put Solomon's ring upon your left thumb and give him the finishing stroke, but keep the ring on your third finger until you have come close to him, so that the monster cannot see you, else he might strike you dead with his long tail. But when all is done, take care you do not lose the ring, and that no one takes it from you by cunning.'

The young man thanked the magician for his directions, and promised, should they succeed, to reward him. But the magician answered, ' I have profited so much by the wisdom the ring has taught me that I desire no other reward.' Then they parted, and the youth quickly flew home through the air. After remaining in his own home for some weeks, he heard people say that the terrible Dragon of the North was not far off, and might shortly be expected in the country. The King announced publicly that he would give his daughter in marriage, as well as a large part of his kingdom, to whosoever should free the country from the monster. The youth then went to the King and told him that he had good hopes of subduing the Dragon, if the King would grant him all he desired for the purpose. The King willingly agreed, and the iron horse, the great spear, and the chains were all prepared as the youth requested. When all was ready, it was found that the iron horse was so heavy that a hundred men could not move it from the spot, so the youth found there was nothing for it but to move it with his cwn strength by means of the magic ring. The Dragon was now so near that in a couple of springs he would be over the frontier. The youth now began to consider how he should act, for if he had

The youth secures the dragon

to push the iron horse from behind he could not ride upon it as the sorcerer had said he must. But a raven unexpectedly gave him this advice : ' Ride upon the horse, and push the spear against the ground, as if you were pushing off a boat from the land.' The youth did so, and found that in this way he could easily move forwards. The Dragon had his monstrous jaws wide open, all ready for his expected prey. A few paces nearer, and man and horse would have been swallowed up by them! The youth trembled with horror, and his blood ran cold, yet he did not lose his courage; but, holding the iron spear upright in his hand, he brought it down with all his might right through the monster's lower jaw. Then quick as lightning he sprang from his horse before the Dragon had time to shut his mouth. A fearful clap like thunder, which could be heard for miles around, now warned him that the Dragon's jaws had closed upon the spear. When the youth turned round he saw the point of the spear sticking up high above the Dragon's upper jaw, and knew that the other end must be fastened firmly to the ground; but the Dragon had got his teeth fixed in the iron horse, which was now useless. The youth now hastened to fasten down the chains to the ground by means of the enormous iron pegs which he had provided. The death struggle of the monster lasted three days and three nights; in his writhing he beat his tail so violently against the ground, that at ten miles' distance the earth trembled as if with an earthquake. When he at length lost power to move his tail, the youth with the help of the ring took up a stone which twenty ordinary men could not have moved, and beat the Dragon so hard about the head with it that very soon the monster lay lifeless before him.

You can fancy how great was the rejoicing when the news was spread abroad that the terrible monster was dead. His conqueror was received into the city with as much pomp as if he had been the mightiest of kings. The old King did not need to urge his daughter to marry the slayer of the Dragon; he found her already willing to bestow her hand upon this hero, who had done all alone what whole armies had tried in vain to do. In a few days a magnificent wedding was celebrated, at which the rejoicings lasted four whole weeks, for all the neighbouring kings had met together to thank the man who had freed the world from their common enemy. But everyone forgot amid the general joy that they ought to have buried the Dragon's monstrous body, for it began now to have such a bad smell that no one could live in the neighbourhood, and before long the whole air was poisoned, and a pestilence broke out which destroyed many hundreds of people. In this distress, the King's son-in-law resolved to seek help once more from the Eastern magician, to whom he at once travelled through the air like a bird by the help of the ring. But there is a proverb which says that ill-gotten gains never prosper, and the Prince found that the stolen ring brought him ill-luck after all. The Witch-maiden had never rested night nor day until she had found out where the ring was. As soon as she had discovered by means of magical arts that the Prince in the form of a bird was on his way to the Eastern magician, she changed herself into an eagle and watched in the air until the bird she was waiting for came in sight, for she knew him at once by the ring which was hung round his neck by a ribbon. Then the eagle pounced upon the bird, and the moment she seized him in her talons she tore the ring from his neck before the man in bird's shape had time to prevent her. Then the eagle flew down to the earth with her prey, and the two stood face to face once more in human form.

' Now, villain, you are in my power ! ' cried the Witch-maiden. 'I favoured you with my love, and you repaid me with treachery and theft. You stole my most precious jewel from me, and do you expect to live happily as the King's son-in-law ? Now the tables are turned ; you are in my power, and I will be revenged on you for your crimes.'

' Forgive me ! forgive me ! ' cried the Prince ; ' I know too well how deeply I have wronged you, and most heartily do I repent it.'

The maiden answered, ' Your prayers and your repentance come too late, and if I were to spare you everyone would think me a fool. You have doubly wronged me ; first you scorned my love, and then you stole my ring, and you must bear the punishment.'

With these words she put the ring upon her left thumb, lifted the young man with one hand, and walked away with him under her arm. This time she did not take him to a splendid palace, but to a deep cave in a rock, where there were chains hanging from the wall. The maiden now chained the young man's hands and feet so that he could not escape ; then she said in an angry voice, ' Here you shall remain chained up until you die. I will bring you every day enough food to prevent you dying of hunger, but you need never hope for freedom any more.' With these words she left him.

The old King and his daughter waited anxiously for many weeks for the Prince's return, but no news of him arrived. The King's daughter often dreamed that her husband was going through some great suffering ; she therefore begged her father to summon all the enchanters and magicians, that they might try to find out where the Prince was and how he could be set free. But the magicians, with all their arts, could find out nothing, except that he was still living and undergoing great suffering; but none could tell where he was to be found. At last a celebrated magician from Finland was brought before the King, who had found out that the King's son-in-law was imprisoned in the East, not by men, but by some more powerful being. The King now sent messengers to the East to look for his son-in-law, and they by good luck met with the old magician who had interpreted the signs on King Solomon's ring, and thus was possessed of more wisdom than anyone else in the world. The magician soon found out what he wished to know, and pointed out the place where the Prince was imprisoned, but said : ' He is kept there by enchantment, and cannot be set free without my help. I will therefore go with you myself.'

So they all set out, guided by birds, and after some days came to the cave where the unfortunate Prince had been chained up for nearly seven years. He recognised the magician immediately, but the old man did not know him, he had grown so thin. However, he undid the chains by the help of magic, and took care of the Prince until he recovered and became strong enough to travel. When he reached home he found that the old King had died that morning, so that he was now raised to the throne. And now after his long suffering came prosperity, which lasted to the end of his life; but he never got back the magic ring, nor has it ever again been seen by mortal eyes.

Now, if *you* had been the Prince, would you not rather have stayed with the pretty witch-maiden ?

HOW SIX MEN TRAVELLED THROUGH THE WIDE WORLD

THERE was once upon a time a man who understood all sorts of arts ; he served in the war, and bore himself bravely and well : but when the war was over, he got his discharge, and set out on his travels with three farthings of his pay in his pocket. 'Wait,' he said ; 'that does not please me ; only let me find the right people, and the King shall yet give me all the treasures of his kingdom.' He strode angrily into the forest, and there he saw a man standing who had uprooted six trees as if they were straws. He said to him, 'Will you be my servant and travel with me ? '

'Yes,' he answered ; ' but first of all I will take this little bundle of sticks home to my mother,' and he took one of the trees and wound it round the other five, raised the bundle on his shoulders and bore it off. Then he came back and went with his master, who said, 'We two ought to be able to travel through the wide world !' And when they had gone a little way they came upon a hunter, who was on his knees, his gun on his shoulder, aiming at something. The master said to him, ' Hunter, what are you aiming at ? '

He answered, 'Two miles from this place sits a fly on a branch of an oak ; I want to shoot out its left eye.'

'Oh, go with me,' said the man ; 'if we three are together we shall easily travel through the wide world.'

The hunter agreed and went with him, and they came to seven windmills whose sails were going round quite fast, and yet there was not a breath of wind, nor was a leaf moving. The man said, ' I don't know what is turning those windmills ; there is not the slightest breeze blowing.' So he walked on with his servants, and when they had gone two miles they saw a man sitting on a tree, holding one of his nostrils and blowing out of the other.

' Fellow, what are you puffing at up there ? ' asked the man.

He replied, ' Two miles from this place are standing seven windmills ; see, I am blowing to drive them round.'

' Oh, go with me,' said the man ; ' if we four are together we shall easily travel through the wide world.'

So the blower got down and went with him, and after a time they saw a man who was standing on one leg, and had unstrapped the other and laid it near him.   Then said the master, ' You have made yourself very comfortable to rest ! '

' I am a runner,' answered he ; 'and so that I shall not go too quickly, I have unstrapped one leg ; when I run with two legs, I go faster than a bird flies.'

' Oh, go with me ; if we five are together, we shall easily travel through the wide world.'   So he went with him, and, not long afterwards, they met a man who wore a little hat, but he had it slouched over one ear.

' Manners, manners ! ' said the master to him ; ' don't hang your hat over one ear ; you look like a madman ! '

' I dare not,' said the other, ' for if I were to put my hat on straight, there would come such a frost that the very birds in the sky would freeze and fall dead on the earth.'

' Oh, go with me,' said the master ; ' if we six are together, we shall easily travel through the wide world.

Now the Six came to a town in which the King had proclaimed that whoever should run with his daughter in a race, and win, should become her husband ; but if he lost, he must lose his head.   This was reported to the man who declared he would compete, ' but,' he said, ' I shall let my servant run for me.'

The King replied, ' Then both your heads must be staked, and your head and his must be guaranteed for the winner.'

When this was agreed upon and settled, the man strapped on the runner's other leg, saying to him, ' Now be nimble, and see that we win ! '   It was arranged that whoever should first bring water out of a stream a long way off, should be the victor.   Then the runner got a pitcher, and the King's daughter another, and they began to run at the same time ; but in a moment, when the King's daughter was only just a little way off, no spectator could see the runner, and it seemed as if the wind had whistled past.   In a short time he reached the stream, filled his pitcher with water, and turned round again.   But, half way home, a great drowsiness came over him ; he put down his pitcher, lay down, and fell asleep.   He had, however. put a horse's skull which was lying on the ground, for his pillow, so that he should not be too comfortable and might soon wake up.

In the meantime the King's daughter, who could also run well, as well as an ordinary man could, reached the stream, and hastened back with her pitcher full of water. When she saw the runner lying there asleep, she was delighted, and said, ' My enemy is given into my hands! ' She emptied his pitcher and ran on.

Everything now would have been lost, if by good luck the hunter had not been standing on the castle tower and had seen everything with his sharp eyes.

·MY·ENEMY·IS·GIVEN·INTO·MY·HANDS·

' Ah,' said he, ' the King's daughter shall not overreach us;' and, loading his gun, he shot so cleverly, that he shot away the horse's skull from under the runner's head, without its hurting him. Then the runner awoke, jumped up, and saw that his pitcher was empty and the King's daughter far ahead. But he did not lose courage, and ran back to the stream with his pitcher, filled it once more with water, and was home ten minutes before the King's daughter arrived.

' Look,' said he, ' I have only just exercised my legs; that was nothing of a run.'

But the King was angry, and his daughter even more so, that she should be carried away by a common, discharged soldier. They consulted together how they could destroy both him and his companions.

'Then,' said the King to her, 'I have found a way. Don't be frightened ; they shall not come home again.' He said to them, 'You must now make merry together, and eat and drink,' and he led them into a room which had a floor of iron ; the doors were also of iron, and the windows were barred with iron. In the room was a table spread with delicious food. The King said to them, 'Go in and enjoy yourselves,' and as soon as they were inside he had the doors shut and bolted. Then he made the cook come, and ordered him to keep up a large fire under the room until the iron was red-hot. The cook did so, and the Six sitting round the table felt it grow very warm, and they thought this was because of their good fare ; but when the heat became still greater and they wanted to go out, but found the doors and windows fastened, then they knew that the King meant them harm and was trying to suffocate them.

'But he shall not succeed,' cried he of the little hat, 'I will make a frost come which shall make the fire ashamed and die out ! ' So he put his hat on straight, and at once there came such a frost that all the heat disappeared and the food on the dishes began to freeze. When a couple of hours had passed, and the King thought they must be quite dead from the heat, he had the doors opened and went in himself to see.

But when the doors were opened, there stood all Six, alive and well, saying they were glad they could come out to warm themselves, for the great cold in the room had frozen all the food hard in the dishes. Then the King went angrily to the cook, and scolded him, and asked him why he had not done what he was told.

But the cook answered, 'There is heat enough there; see for yourself.' Then the King saw a huge fire burning under the iron room, and understood that he could do no harm to the Six in this way. The King now began again to think how he could free himself from his unwelcome guests. He commanded the master to come before him, and said, 'If you will take gold, and give up your right to my daughter, you shall have as much as you like.'

'Oh, yes, your Majesty,' answered he, 'give me as much as my servant can carry, and I will give up your daughter.'

The King was delighted, and the man said, 'I will come and fetch it in fourteen days.'

Then he called all the tailors
in the kingdom together, and
made them sit down for fourteen
days sewing at a sack. When it
was finished, he made the strong
man who had uprooted the trees
take the sack on his shoulder and
go with him to the King. Then
the King said, 'What a powerful
fellow that is, carrying that bale
of linen as large as a house on

his shoulder!' and he was much frightened, and thought 'What a lot of gold he will make away with!' Then he had a ton of gold brought, which sixteen of the strongest men had to carry; but the strong man seized it with one hand, put it in the sack, saying, 'Why don't you bring me more? That scarcely covers the bottom!' Then the King had to send again and again to fetch his treasures, which the strong man shoved into the sack, and the sack was only half full.

'Bring more,' he cried, 'these crumbs don't fill it.' So seven thousand waggons of the gold of the whole kingdom were driven up; these the strong man shoved into the sack, oxen and all.

'I will no longer be particular,' he said, 'and will take what comes, so that the sack shall be full.'

When everything was put in and there was not yet enough, he said, 'I will make an end of this; it is easy to fasten a sack when it is not full.' Then he threw it on his back and went with his companions.

Now, when the King saw how a single man was carrying away the wealth of the whole country he was very angry, and made his cavalry mount and pursue the Six, and bring back the strong man with the sack. Two regiments soon overtook them, and called to them, 'You are prisoners! lay down the sack of gold or you shall be cut down.'

'What do you say?' said the blower, 'we are prisoners? Before that, you shall dance in the air!' And he held one nostril and blew with the other at the two regiments; they were separated and blown away in the blue sky over the mountains, one this way, and the other that. A sergeant-major cried for mercy, saying he had nine wounds, and was a brave fellow, and did not deserve this disgrace. So the blower let him off, and he came down without hurt. Then he said to him, 'Now go home to the King, and say that if he sends any more cavalry I will blow them all into the air.'

When the King received the message, he said, 'Let the fellows go; they are bewitched.' Then the Six brought the treasure home, shared it among themselves, and lived contentedly till the end of their days.

THUMBELINA

THERE was once a woman who wanted to have quite a tiny, little child, but she did not know where to get one from. So one day she went to an old Witch and said to her: 'I should so much like to have a tiny, little child; can you tell me where I can get one?'

'Oh, we have just got one ready!' said the Witch. 'Here is a barley-corn for you, but it's not the kind the farmer sows in his field, or feeds the cocks and hens with, I can tell you. Put it in a flower-pot, and then you will see something happen.'

'Oh, thank you!' said the woman, and gave the Witch a shilling, for that was what it cost. Then she went home and planted the barley-corn; immediately there grew out of it a large and beautiful flower, which looked like a tulip, but the petals were tightly closed as if it were still only a bud.

'What a beautiful flower!' exclaimed the woman, and she kissed the red and yellow petals; but as she kissed them the flower burst open. It was a real tulip, such as one can see any day; but in the middle of the blossom, on the green velvety petals, sat a little girl, quite tiny, trim, and pretty. She was scarcely half a thumb in height; so they called her Thumbelina. An elegant polished walnut-shell served Thumbelina as a cradle, the blue petals of a violet were her mattress, and a rose-leaf her coverlid. There she lay at night, but in the day-time she used to play about on the table: here the woman had put a bowl, surrounded by a ring of flowers, with their stalks in water, in the middle of which floated a great tulip pedal, and on this Thumbelina sat, and sailed from one side of the bowl to the other, rowing herself with two white horse-hairs for oars. It was such a pretty sight! She could sing, too, with a voice more soft and sweet than had ever been heard before.

One night, when she was lying in her pretty little bed, an old toad crept in through a broken pane in the window. She was very ugly, clumsy, and clammy; she hopped on to the table where Thumbelina lay asleep under the red rose-leaf.

'This would make a beautiful wife for my son,' said the toad, taking up the walnut-shell, with Thumbelina inside, and hopping with it through the window into the garden.

There flowed a great wide stream, with slippery and marshy banks; here the toad lived with her son. Ugh! how ugly and clammy he was, just like his mother! 'Croak, croak, croak!' was all he could say when he saw the pretty little girl in the walnut-shell.

CROAK CROAK CROAK was all he could say.

'Don't talk so loud, or you'll wake her,' said the old toad. 'She might escape us even now; she is as light as a feather. We will put her at once on a broad water-lily leaf in the stream. That will be quite an island for her; she is so small and light. She can't run away from us there, whilst we are preparing the guest-chamber under the marsh where she shall live.'

Outside in the brook grew many water-lilies, with broad green leaves, which looked as if they were swimming about on the water. The leaf farthest away was the largest, and to this the old toad swam with Thumbelina in her walnut-shell.

The tiny Thumbelina woke up very early in the morning, and

when she saw where she was she began to cry bitterly; for on
every side of the great green leaf was water, and she could not get
to the land.

The old toad was down under the marsh, decorating her room
with rushes and yellow marigold leaves, to make it very grand for
her new daughter-in-law; then she swam out with her ugly son to
the leaf where Thumbelina lay. She wanted to fetch the pretty
cradle to put it into her room before Thumbelina herself came there.
The old toad bowed low in the water before her, and said: 'Here
is my son; you shall marry him, and live in great magnificence
down under the marsh.'

Thumbelina rides on the waterlily leaf

'Croak, croak, croak!' was all that the son could say. Then
they took the neat little cradle and swam away with it; but
Thumbelina sat alone on the great green leaf and wept, for she did
not want to live with the clammy toad, or marry her ugly son.
The little fishes swimming about under the water had seen the toad
quite plainly, and heard what she had said; so they put up their
heads to see the little girl. When they saw her, they thought her
so pretty that they were very sorry she should go down with the
ugly toad to live. No; that must not happen. They assembled in
the water round the green stalk which supported the leaf on which
she was sitting, and nibbled the stem in two. Away floated the leaf

down the stream, bearing Thumbelina far beyond the reach of the toad.

On she sailed past several towns, and the little birds sitting in the bushes saw her, and sang, 'What a pretty little girl!' The leaf floated farther and farther away; thus Thumbelina left her native land.

A beautiful little white butterfly fluttered above her, and at last settled on the leaf. Thumbelina pleased him, and she, too, was delighted, for now the toads could not reach her, and it was so beautiful where she was travelling; the sun shone on the water and made it sparkle like the brightest silver. She took off her sash, and tied one end round the butterfly; the other end she fastened to the leaf, so that now it glided along with her faster than ever.

A great cockchafer came flying past; he caught sight of Thumbelina, and in a moment had put his arms round her slender waist, and had flown off with her to a tree. The green leaf floated away down the stream, and the butterfly with it, for he was fastened to the leaf and could not get loose from it. Oh, dear! how terrified poor little Thumbelina was when the cockchafer flew off with her to the tree! But she was especially distressed on the beautiful white butterfly's account, as she had tied him fast, so that if he could not get away he must starve to death. But the cockchafer did not trouble himself about that; he sat down with her on a large green leaf, gave her the honey out of the flowers to eat, and told her that she was very pretty, although she wasn't in the least like a cock chafer. Later on, all the other cockchafers who lived in the same tree came to pay calls; they examined Thumbelina closely, and remarked, 'Why, she has only two legs! How very miserable!'

'She has no feelers!' cried another.

'How ugly she is!' said all the lady chafers—and yet Thumbelina was really very pretty.

The cockchafer who had stolen her knew this very well; but when he heard all the ladies saying she was ugly, he began to think so too, and would not keep her; she might go wherever she liked. So he flew down from the tree with her and put her on a daisy. There she sat and wept, because she was so ugly that the cockchafer would have nothing to do with her; and yet she was the most beautiful creature imaginable, so soft and delicate, like the loveliest rose-leaf.

The whole summer poor little Thumbelina lived alone in the great wood. She plaited a bed for herself of blades of grass, and hung it up under a clover-leaf, so that she was protected from the rain; she gathered honey from the flowers for food, and drank the dew on the leaves every morning. Thus the summer and autumn passed, but then came winter—the long, cold winter. All the birds who had sung so sweetly about her had flown away; the trees shed their leaves, the flowers died; the great clover-leaf under which she had lived curled up, and nothing remained of it but the withered stalk. She was terribly cold, for her clothes were ragged, and she herself was so small and thin. Poor little Thumbelina! she would surely be frozen to death. It began to snow, and every snow-flake that fell on her was to her as a whole shovelful thrown on one of us, for we are so big, and she was only an inch high. She wrapt herself round in a dead leaf, but it was torn in the middle and gave her no warmth; she was trembling with cold.

Just outside the wood where she was now living lay a great corn-field. But the corn had been gone a long time; only the dry, bare stubble was left standing in the frozen ground. This made a forest for her to wander about in. All at once she came across the door of a field-mouse, who had a little hole under a corn-stalk. There the mouse lived warm and snug, with a store-room full of corn, a splendid kitchen and dining-room. Poor little Thumbelina went up to the door and begged for a little piece of barley, for she had not had anything to eat for the last two days.

'Poor little creature!' said the field-mouse, for she was a kind-hearted old thing at the bottom. 'Come into my warm room and have some dinner with me.'

As Thumbelina pleased her, she said: 'As far as I am concerned you may spend the winter with me; but you must keep my room clean and tidy, and tell me stories, for I like that very much.'

And Thumbelina did all that the kind old field-mouse asked, and did it remarkably well too.

'Now I am expecting a visitor,' said the field-mouse; 'my neighbour comes to call on me once a week. He is in better circumstances than I am, has great, big rooms, and wears a fine black-velvet coat. If you could only marry him, you would be well provided for. But he is blind. You must tell him all the prettiest stories you know.'

But Thumbelina did not trouble her head about him, for he was only a mole. He came and paid them a visit in his black-velvet coat.

'He is so rich and so accomplished,' the field-mouse told her.

His house is twenty times larger than mine; he possesses **great** knowledge, but he cannot bear the sun and the beautiful flowers, and speaks slightingly of them, for he has never seen them.'

Thumbelina had to sing to him, so she sang 'Lady-bird, lady-bird, fly away home!' and other songs so prettily that the mole fell in love with her; but he did not say anything, he was a very cautious man. A short time before he had dug a long passage through the ground from his own house to that of his neighbour; in this he gave the field-mouse and Thumbelina permission to walk as often as they liked. But he begged them not to be afraid of the dead bird that lay in the passage: it was a real bird with beak and feathers, and must have died a little time ago, and now laid buried just where he had made his tunnel. The mole took a piece of rotten wood in his mouth, for that glows like fire in the dark, and went in front, lighting them through the long dark passage. When they came to the place where the dead bird lay, the mole put his broad nose against the ceiling and pushed a hole through, so that the day-light could shine down. In the middle of the path lay a dead swal-low, his pretty wings pressed close to his sides, his claws and head drawn under his feathers; the poor bird had evidently died of cold. Thumbelina was very sorry, for she was very fond of all little birds; they had sung and twittered so beautifully to her all through the summer. But the mole kicked him with his bandy legs and said:

'Now he can't sing any more! It must be very miserable to be a little bird! I'm thankful that none of my little children are; birds always starve in winter.'

'Yes, you speak like a sensible man,' said the field-mouse. 'What has a bird, in spite of all his singing, in the winter-time? He must starve and freeze, and that must be very pleasant for him, I must say!'

Thumbelina did not say anything; but when the other two had passed on she bent down to the bird, brushed aside the feathers from his head, and kissed his closed eyes gently. 'Perhaps it was he that sang to me so prettily in the summer,' she thought. 'How much pleasure he did give me, dear little bird!'

The mole closed up the hole again which let in the light, and then escorted the ladies home. But Thumbelina could not sleep that night; so she got out of bed, and plaited a great big blanket of straw, and carried it off, and spread it over the dead bird, and piled upon it thistle-down as soft as cotton-wool, which she had found in the field-mouse's room, so that the poor little thing should lie warmly buried.

'Farewell, pretty little bird!' she said. 'Farewell, and thank you for your beautiful songs in the summer, when the trees were green, and the sun shone down warmly on us!' Then she laid her head against the bird's heart. But the bird was not dead : he had been frozen, but now that she had warmed him, he was coming to life again.

In autumn the swallows fly away to foreign lands; but there are some who are late in starting, and then they get so cold that they drop down as if dead, and the snow comes and covers them over.

Thumbelina trembled, she was so frightened; for the bird was

Thumbelina brings thistledown for the Swallow

very large in comparison with herself—only an inch high. But she took courage, piled up the down more closely over the poor swallow, fetched her own coverlid and laid it over his head.

Next night she crept out again to him. There he was alive, but very weak ; he could only open his eyes for a moment and look at Thumbelina, who was standing in front of him with a piece of rotten wood in her hand, for she had no other lantern.

'Thank you, pretty little child!' said the swallow to her. 'I am so beautifully warm! Soon I shall regain my strength, and then I shall be able to fly out again into the warm sunshine.'

'Oh!' she said, 'it is very cold outside; it is snowing and freezing! stay in your warm bed; I will take care of you!'

Then she brought him water in a petal, which he drank, after

which he related to her how he had torn one of his wings on a
bramble, so that he could not fly as fast as the other swallows, who
had flown far away to warmer lands. So at last he had dropped
down exhausted, and then he could remember no more. The
whole winter he remained down there, and Thumbelina looked
after him and nursed him tenderly. Neither the mole nor the
field-mouse learnt anything of this, for they could not bear the
poor swallow.

When the spring came, and the sun warmed the earth again,
the swallow said farewell to Thumbelina, who opened the hole in
the roof for him which the mole had made. The sun shone
brightly down upon her, and the swallow asked her if she would go
with him; she could sit upon his back. Thumbelina wanted very
much to fly far away into the green wood, but she knew that the
old field-mouse would be sad if she ran away. 'No, I mustn't
come!' she said.

'Farewell, dear good little girl!' said the swallow, and flew off
into the sunshine. Thumbelina gazed after him with the tears
standing in her eyes, for she was very fond of the swallow.

'Tweet, tweet!' sang the bird, and flew into the green wood.
Thumbelina was very unhappy. She was not allowed to go out
into the warm sunshine. The corn which had been sowed in the
field over the field-mouse's home grew up high into the air, and
made a thick forest for the poor little girl, who was only an inch
high.

'Now you are to be a bride, Thumbelina!' said the field-mouse,
'for our neighbour has proposed for you! What a piece of fortune
for a poor child like you! Now you must set to work at your linen
for your dowry, for nothing must be lacking if you are to become
the wife of our neighbour, the mole!'

Thumbelina had to spin all day long, and every evening the
mole visited her, and told her that when the summer was over the
sun would not shine so hot; now it was burning the earth as hard
as a stone. Yes, when the summer had passed, they would keep
the wedding.

But she was not at all pleased about it, for she did not like the
stupid mole. Every morning when the sun was rising, and every
evening when it was setting, she would steal out of the house-door,
and when the breeze parted the ears of corn so that she could see
the blue sky through them, she thought how bright and beautiful it
must be outside, and longed to see her dear swallow again. But

he never came; no doubt he had flown away far into the great green wood.

By the autumn Thumbelina had finished the dowry.

'In four weeks you will be married!' said the field-mouse: 'don't be obstinate, or I shall bite you with my sharp white teeth! You will get a fine husband! The King himself has not such a velvet coat. His store-room and cellar are full, and you should be thankful for that.'

Well, the wedding-day arrived. The mole had come to fetch Thumbelina to live with him deep down under the ground, never to

Thumbelina has to spin

come out into the warm sun again, for that was what he didn't like. The poor little girl was very sad; for now she must say good-bye to the beautiful sun.

'Farewell, bright sun!' she cried, stretching out her arms towards it, and taking another step outside the house; for now the corn had been reaped, and only the dry stubble was left standing. 'Farewell, farewell!' she said, and put her arms round a little red flower that grew there. 'Give my love to the dear swallow when you see him!'

'Tweet, tweet!' sounded in her ear all at once. She looked up. There was the swallow flying past! As soon as he saw Thumbelina, he was very glad. She told him how unwilling she was to marry the ugly mole, as then she had to live underground where the sun never shone, and she could not help bursting into tears.

'The cold winter is coming now,' said the swallow. 'I must fly away to warmer lands : will you come with me ? You can sit on my back, and we will fly far away from the ugly mole and his dark house, over the mountains, to the warm countries where the sun shines more brightly than here, where it is always summer, and there are always beautiful flowers. Do come with me, dear little Thumbelina, who saved my life when I lay frozen in the dark tunnel !'

'Yes, I will go with you,' said Thumbelina, and got on the swallow's back, with her feet on one of his outstretched wings. Up he flew into the air, over woods and seas, over the great mountains where the snow is always lying. And if she was cold she crept under his warm feathers, only keeping her little head out to admire all the beautiful things in the world beneath. At last they came to warm lands ; there the sun was brighter, the sky seemed twice as high, and in the hedges hung the finest green and purple grapes ; in the woods grew oranges and lemons : the air was scented with myrtle and mint, and on the roads were pretty little children running about and playing with great gorgeous butterflies. But the swallow flew on farther, and it became more and more beautiful. Under the most splendid green trees besides a blue lake stood a glittering white-marble castle. Vines hung about the high pillars ; there were many swallows' nests, and in one of these lived the swallow who was carrying Thumbelina.

'Here is my house !' said he. 'But it won't do for you to live with me ; I am not tidy enough to please you. Find a home for yourself in one of the lovely flowers that grow down there ; now I will set you down, and you can do whatever you like.'

'That will be splendid !' said she, clapping her little hands.

There lay a great white marble column which had fallen to the ground and broken into three pieces, but between these grew the most beautiful white flowers. The swallow flew down with Thumbelina, and set her upon one of the broad leaves. But there, to her astonishment, she found a tiny little man sitting in the middle of the flower, as white and transparent as if he were made of glass ; he had the prettiest golden crown on his head, and the most beautiful wings on his shoulders ; he himself was no bigger than Thumbelina. He was the spirit of the flower. In each blossom there dwelt a tiny man or woman: but this one was the King over the others.

'How handsome he is!' whispered Thumbelina to the swallow.

The little Prince was very much frightened at the swallow, for in comparison with one so tiny as himself he seemed a giant. But when he saw Thumbelina, he was delighted, for she was the most beautiful girl he had ever seen. So he took his golden crown from

WE WILL CALL YOU MAYBLOSSOM

off his head and put it on hers, asking her her name, and if she would be his wife, and then she would be Queen of all the flowers. Yes! he was a different kind of husband to the son of the toad and the mole with the black-velvet coat. So she said 'Yes' to the noble Prince. And out of each flower came a lady and gentleman, each so tiny and pretty that it was a pleasure to see them. Each brought Thumbelina a present, but the best of all was a beautiful pair of wings which were fastened on to her back, and now she too could fly from flower to flower. They all wished her joy, and the swallow sat above in his nest and sang the wedding march, and that he did as well as he could; but he was sad, because he was very fond of Thumbelina and did not want to be separated from her.

'You shall not be called Thumbelina!' said the spirit of the flower to her; 'that is an ugly name, and you are much too pretty for that. We will call you May Blossom.'

'Farewell, farewell!' said the little swallow with a heavy heart, and flew away to farther lands, far, far away, right back to Denmark. There he had a little nest above a window, where his wife lived, who can tell fairy-stories. 'Tweet, tweet!' he sang to her. And that is the way we learnt the whole story.

THE NIGHTINGALE

IN China, as I daresay you know, the Emperor is a Chinaman, and all his courtiers are also Chinamen. The story I am going to tell you happened many years ago, but it is worth while for you to listen to it, before it is forgotten.

The Emperor's Palace was the most splendid in the world, all made of priceless porcelain, but so brittle and delicate that you had to take great care how you touched it. In the garden were the most beautiful flowers, and on the loveliest of them were tied silver bells which tinkled, so that if you passed you could not help looking at the flowers. Everything in the Emperor's garden was admirably arranged with a view to effect; and the garden was so large that even the gardener himself did not know where it ended. If you ever got beyond it, you came to a stately forest with great trees and deep lakes in it. The forest sloped down to the sea, which was a clear blue. Large ships could sail under the boughs of the trees, and in these trees there lived a Nightingale. She sang so beautifully that even the poor fisherman who had so much to do stood and listened when he came at night to cast his nets. ' How beautiful it is !' he said ; but he had to attend to his work, and forgot about the bird. But when she sang the next night and the fisherman came there again, he said the same thing, ' How beautiful it is !'

From all the countries round came travellers to the Emperor's town, who were astonished at the Palace and the garden. But when they heard the Nightingale they all said, ' This is the finest thing after all !'

The travellers told all about it when they went home, and learned scholars wrote many books upon the town, the Palace, and the garden. But they did not forget the Nightingale ; she was praised the most, and all the poets composed splendid verses on the Nightingale in the forest by the deep sea.

The books were circulated throughout the world, and some of them reached the Emperor. He sat in his golden chair, and read and read. He nodded his head every moment, for he liked reading the brilliant accounts of the town, the Palace, and the garden. 'But the Nightingale is better than all,' he saw written.

'What is that?' said the Emperor. 'I don't know anything about the Nightingale! Is there such a bird in my empire, and so near as in my garden? I have never heard it! Fancy reading for the first time about it in a book!'

And he called his First Lord to him. He was so proud that if anyone of lower rank than his own ventured to speak to him or ask him anything, he would say nothing but 'P!' and that does not mean anything.

'Here is a most remarkable bird which is called a Nightingale!' said the Emperor. 'They say it is the most glorious thing in my kingdom. Why has no one ever said anything to me about it?'

'I have never before heard it mentioned!' said the First Lord. 'I will look for it and find it!'

But where was it to be found? The First Lord ran up and down stairs, through the halls and corridors; but none of those he met had ever heard of the Nightingale. And the First Lord ran again to the Emperor, and told him that it must be an invention on the part of those who had written the books.

'Your Imperial Majesty cannot really believe all that is written! There are some inventions called the Black Art!'

'But the book in which I read this,' said the Emperor, 'is sent me by His Great Majesty the Emperor of Japan; so it cannot be untrue, and I will hear the Nightingale! She must be here this evening! She has my gracious permission to appear, and if she does not, the whole Court shall be trampled under foot after supper!'

'Tsing pe!' said the First Lord; and he ran up and down stairs, through the halls and corridors, and half the Court ran with him, for they did not want to be trampled under foot. Everyone was asking after the wonderful Nightingale which all the world knew of, except those at Court.

At last they met a poor little girl in the kitchen, who said, 'Oh! I know the Nightingale well. How she sings! I have permission to carry the scraps over from the Court meals to my poor sick mother, and when I am going home at night, tired and weary, and rest for a little in the wood, then I hear the Nightingale singing!

It brings tears to my eyes, and I feel as if my mother were kissing me!'

'Little kitchenmaid!' said the First Lord, 'I will give you a place in the kitchen, and you shall have leave to see the Emperor at

THE KITCHENMAID LISTENS TO THE NIGHTINGALE

dinner, if you can lead us to the Nightingale, for she is invited to come to Court this evening.'

And so they all went into the wood where the Nightingale was wont to sing, and half the Court went too.

When they were on the way there they heard a cow mooing.

'Oh!' said the Courtiers, 'now we have found her! What a wonderful power for such a small beast to have! I am sure we have heard her before!'

'No; that is a cow mooing!' said the little kitchenmaid. 'We are still a long way off!'

Then the frogs began to croak in the marsh. 'Splendid!' said the Chinese chaplain. 'Now we hear her; it sounds like a little church-bell!'

'No, no; those are frogs!' said the little kitchenmaid. 'But I think we shall soon hear her now!'

Then the Nightingale began to sing.

'There she is!' cried the little girl. 'Listen! She is sitting there!' And she pointed to a little dark-grey bird up in the branches.

'Is it possible!' said the First Lord. 'I should never have thought it! How ordinary she looks! She must surely have lost her feathers because she sees so many distinguished men round her!'

'Little Nightingale,' called out the little kitchenmaid, 'our Gracious Emperor wants you to sing before him!'

'With the greatest of pleasure!' said the Nightingale; and she sang so gloriously that it was a pleasure to listen.

'It sounds like glass bells!' said the First Lord. 'And look how her little throat works! It is wonderful that we have never heard her before! She will be a great success at Court.'

'Shall I sing once more for the Emperor?' asked the Nightingale, thinking that the Emperor was there.

'My esteemed little Nightingale,' said the First Lord, 'I have the great pleasure to invite you to Court this evening, where His Gracious Imperial Highness will be enchanted with your charming song!'

'It sounds best in the green wood,' said the Nightingale; but still, she came gladly when she heard that the Emperor wished it. At the Palace everything was splendidly prepared. The porcelain walls and floors glittered in the light of many thousand gold lamps; the most gorgeous flowers which tinkled out well were placed in the corridors. There was such a hurrying and draught that all the bells jingled so much that one could not hear oneself speak. In the centre of the great hall where the Emperor sat was a golden perch, on which the Nightingale sat. The whole Court was there, and the little kitchenmaid was allowed to stand behind the door, now that she was a Court-cook. Everyone was dressed in his best, and everyone was looking towards the little grey bird to whom the Emperor nodded.

The Nightingale sang so gloriously that the tears came into the Emperor's eyes and ran down his cheeks. Then the Nightingale sang even more beautifully; it went straight to all hearts. The

The Present from
the Emperor of Japan

Emperor was so delighted that he said she should wear his gold slipper round her neck. But the Nightingale thanked him, and said she had had enough reward already. 'I have seen tears in the Emperor's eyes—that is a great reward. An Emperor's tears have such power!' Then she sang again with her gloriously sweet voice.

'That is the most charming coquetry I have ever seen!' said

all the ladies round. And they all took to holding water in their mouths that they might gurgle whenever anyone spoke to them. Then they thought themselves nightingales. Yes, the lackeys and chambermaids announced that they were pleased; which means a great deal, for they are the most difficult people of all to satisfy. In short, the Nightingale was a real success.

She had to stay at Court now; she had her own cage, and permission to walk out twice in the day and once at night.

She was given twelve servants, who each held a silken string which was fastened round her leg. There was little pleasure in flying about like this.

The whole town was talking about the wonderful bird, and when two people met each other one would say 'Nightin,' and the other 'Gale,' and then they would both sigh and understand one another. Yes, and eleven grocer's children were called after her, but not one of them could sing a note.

One day the Emperor received a large parcel on which was written 'The Nightingale.'

'Here is another new book about our famous bird!' said the Emperor.

But it was not a book, but a little mechanical toy, which lay in a box—an artificial nightingale which was like the real one, only that it was set all over with diamonds, rubies, and sapphires. When it was wound up, it could sing the piece the real bird sang, and moved its tail up and down, and glittered with silver and gold. Round its neck was a little collar on which was written, 'The Nightingale of the Emperor of Japan is nothing compared to that of the Emperor of China.'

'This is magnificent!' they all said, and the man who had brought the clockwork bird received on the spot the title of 'Bringer of the Imperial First Nightingale.'

'Now they must sing together; what a duet we shall have!'

And so they sang together, but their voices did not blend, for the real Nightingale sang in her way and the clockwork bird sang waltzes.

'It is not its fault!' said the bandmaster; 'it keeps very good time and is quite after my style!'

Then the artificial bird had to sing alone. It gave just as much pleasure as the real one, and then it was so much prettier to look at; it sparkled like bracelets and necklaces. Three-and-thirty times it sang the same piece without being tired. People would like to have heard it again, but the Emperor thought that the living Nightingale should sing now—but where was she ? No one had noticed that she had flown out of the open window away to her green woods.

'What *shall* we do ! ' said the Emperor.

And all the Court scolded, and said that the Nightingale was very ungrateful. 'But we have still the best bird ! ' they said ; and the artificial bird had to sing again, and that was the thirty-fourth time they had heard the same piece. But they did not yet know it by heart ; it was much too difficult. And the bandmaster praised the bird tremendously ; yes, he assured them it was better than a real nightingale, not only because of its beautiful plumage and diamonds, but inside as well. 'For see, my Lords and Ladies and your Imperial Majesty, with the real Nightingale one can never tell what will come out, but all is known about the artificial bird ! You can explain it, you can open it and show people where the waltzes lie, how they go, and how one follows the other ! '

'That's just what we think ! ' said everyone ; and the bandmaster received permission to show the bird to the people the next Sunday. They should hear it sing, commanded the Emperor. And they heard it, and they were as pleased as if they had been intoxicated with tea, after the Chinese fashion, and they all said 'Oh ! ' and held up their forefingers and nodded time. But the poor fishermen who had heard the real Nightingale said : 'This one sings well enough, the tunes glide out ; but there is something wanting— I don't know what ! '

The real Nightingale was banished from the kingdom.

The artificial bird was put on silken cushions by the Emperor's bed, all the presents which it received, gold and precious stones, lay round it, and it was given the title of Imperial Night-singer, First from the left. For the Emperor counted that side as the more distinguished, being the side on which the heart is ; the Emperor's heart is also on the left.

And the bandmaster wrote a work of twenty-five volumes about the artificial bird. It was so learned, long, and so full of the hardest Chinese words that everyone said they had read it and understood it ; for once they had been very stupid about a book, and had been trampled under foot in consequence. So a whole year passed. The Emperor, the Court, and all the Chinese knew every note of the artificial bird's song by heart. But they liked it all the better for this ; they could even sing with it, and they did. The street boys sang 'Tra-la-la-la-la,' and the Emperor sang too sometimes. It was indeed delightful.

But one evening, when the artificial bird was singing its best, and the Emperor lay in bed listening to it, something in the bird went crack. Something snapped! Whir-r-r! all the wheels ran down and then the music ceased. The Emperor sprang up, and had his physician summoned, but what could *he* do! Then the clockmaker came, and, after a great deal of talking and examining, he put the bird somewhat in order, but he said that it must be very seldom used as the works were nearly worn out, and it was impossible to put in new ones. Here was a calamity! Only once a year was the artificial bird allowed to sing, and even that was almost too much for it. But then the bandmaster made a little speech full of hard words, saying that it was just as good as before. And so, of course, it *was* just as good as before. So five years passed, and then a great sorrow came to the nation. The Chinese look upon their Emperor as everything, and now he was ill, and not likely to live it was said.

Already a new Emperor had been chosen, and the people stood outside in the street and asked the First Lord how the old Emperor was. 'P!' said he, and shook his head.

Cold and pale lay the Emperor in his splendid great bed; the whole Court believed him dead, and one after the other left him to pay their respects to the new Emperor. Everywhere in the halls and corridors cloth was laid down so that no footstep could be heard, and everything was still—very, very still. And nothing came to break the silence.

The Emperor longed for something to come and relieve the monotony of this deathlike stillness. If only someone would speak to him! If only someone would sing to him. Music would carry his thoughts away, and would break the spell lying on him. The moon was streaming in at the open window; but that, too, was silent, quite silent.

'Music! music!' cried the Emperor. 'You little bright golden bird, sing! do sing! I gave you gold and jewels; I have hung my gold slipper round your neck with my own hand—sing! do sing!' But the bird was silent. There was no one to wind it up, and so it could not sing. And all was silent, so terribly silent!

All at once there came in at the window the most glorious burst of song. It was the little living Nightingale, who, sitting outside on a bough, had heard the need of her Emperor and had come to sing

to him of comfort and hope.   And as she sang the blood flowed
quicker and quicker in the Emperor's weak limbs, and life began to
return.

'Thank you, thank you!' said the Emperor.   'You divine little
bird!   I know you.   I chased you from my kingdom, and you
have given me life again! How can I reward you?'

'You have done that already!' said the Nightingale.   'I brought
tears to your eyes the first time I sang.   I shall never forget that.
They are jewels that rejoice a singer's heart.   But now sleep and
get strong again; I will sing you a lullaby.'   And the Emperor fell
into a deep, calm sleep as she sang.

The true Nightingale sings to the Emperor

The sun was shining through the window when he awoke, strong
and well.   None of his servants had come back yet, for they thought
he was dead.   But the Nightingale sat and sang to him.

'You must always stay with me!' said the Emperor.   'You
shall sing whenever you like, and I will break the artificial bird
into a thousand pieces.'

'Don't do that!' said the Nightingale.   'He did his work as
long as he could.   Keep him as you have done!   I cannot build my
nest in the Palace and live here; but let me come whenever I like.
I will sit in the evening on the bough outside the window, and I will
sing you something that will make you feel happy and grateful.
I will sing of joy, and of sorrow; I will sing of the evil and the

good which lies hidden from you. The little singing-bird flies all around, to the poor fisherman's hut, to the farmer's cottage, to all those who are far away from you and your Court. I love your heart more than your crown, though that has about it a brightness as of something holy. Now I will sing to you again; but you must promise me one thing——'

'Anything!' said the Emperor, standing up in his Imperial robes, which he had himself put on, and fastening on his sword richly embossed with gold.

'One thing I beg of you! Don't tell anyone that you have a little bird who tells you everything. It will be much better not to!' Then the Nightingale flew away.

The servants came in to look at their dead Emperor.

The Emperor said, 'Good-morning!'

THE TINDER-BOX

A SOLDIER came marching along the high road—left, right! left, right! He had his knapsack on his back and a sword by his side, for he had been to the wars and was now returning home.

An old Witch met him on the road. She was very ugly to look at : her under-lip hung down to her breast.

'Good evening, Soldier!' she said. 'What a fine sword and knapsack you have! You are something like a soldier! You ought to have as much money as you would like to carry!'

'Thank you, old Witch,' said the Soldier.

'Do you see that great tree there?' said the Witch, pointing to a tree beside them. 'It is hollow within. You must climb up to the top, and then you will see a hole through which you can let yourself down into the tree. I will tie a rope round your waist, so that I may be able to pull you up again when you call.'

'What shall I do down there?' asked the Soldier.

'Get money!' answered the Witch. 'Listen! When you reach the bottom of the tree you will find yourself in a large hall; it is light there, for there are more than three hundred lamps burning. Then you will see three doors, which you can open—the keys are in the locks. If you go into the first room, you will see a great chest in the middle of the floor with a dog sitting upon it; he has eyes as large as saucers, but you needn't trouble about him. I will give you my blue-check apron, which you must spread out on the floor, and then go back quickly and fetch the dog and set him upon it; open the chest and take as much money as you like. It is copper there. If you would rather have silver, you must go into the next room, where there is a dog with eyes as large as mill-wheels. But don't take any notice of him; just set him upon my apron, and help yourself to the money. If you prefer gold, you can get that too, if you go into the third room, and as much as you like to carry. But the dog that guards the chest there has eyes as large as the Round Tower at Copenhagen! He is a savage dog, I can tell you; but you needn't be afraid of him either. Only, put him on my apron and he won't touch you, and you can take out of the chest as much gold as you like!'

'Come, this is not bad!' said the Soldier. 'But what am I to give you, old Witch; for surely you are not going to do this for nothing?'

'Yes, I am!' replied the Witch. 'Not a single farthing will I take! For me you shall bring nothing but an old tinder-box which my grandmother forgot last time she was down there.'

'Well, tie the rope round my waist!' said the Soldier.

'Here it is,' said the Witch, 'and here is my blue-check apron.'

Then the Soldier climbed up the tree, let himself down through the hole, and found himself standing, as the Witch had said, underground in the large hall, where the three hundred lamps were burning.

Well, he opened the first door. Ugh! there sat the dog with eyes as big as saucers glaring at him.

'You are a fine fellow!' said the Soldier, and put him on the Witch's apron, took as much copper as his pockets could hold; then he shut the chest, put the dog on it again, and went into the second room. Sure enough there sat the dog with eyes as large as mill-wheels.

'You had better not look at me so hard!' said the Soldier. 'Your eyes will come out of their sockets!'

And then he set the dog on the apron. When he saw all the silver in the chest, he threw away the copper he had taken, and filled his pockets and knapsack with nothing but silver.

Then he went into the third room. Horrors! the dog there had two eyes, each as large as the Round Tower at Copenhagen, spinning round in his head like wheels.

'Good evening!' said the Soldier and saluted, for he had never seen a dog like this before. But when he had examined him more closely, he thought to himself: 'Now then, I've had enough of this!' and put him down on the floor, and opened the chest. Heavens! what a heap of gold there was! With all that he could buy up the whole town, and all the sugar pigs, all the tin soldiers, whips and rocking-horses in the whole world. Now he threw away all the silver with which he had filled his pockets and knapsack, and filled them with gold instead—yes, all his pockets, his knapsack, cap and boots even, so that he could hardly walk. Now he was rich indeed. He put the dog back **upon** the chest, shut the door, and then called up through the tree:

'Now pull me up again, old Witch!'

'Have you got the tinder-box also?' asked the Witch.

'Botheration!' said the Soldier, 'I had clean forgotten it!' And then he went back and fetched it.

The Witch pulled him up, and there he stood again on the high **road**, with pockets, knapsack, cap and boots filled with gold.

The Soldier fills his Knapsack with Money

'What do you want to do with the tinder-box?' asked the Soldier.

'That doesn't matter to you,' replied the Witch. 'You have got your money, give me my tinder-box.'

'We'll see!' said the Soldier. 'Tell me at once what you want to do with it, or I will draw my sword, and cut off your head!'

'No!' screamed the Witch.

The Soldier immediately cut off her head. That was the end **of** her! But he tied up all his gold in her apron, slung it like a bundle over his shoulder, put the tinder-box in his pocket, and set out towards the town.

It was a splendid town ! He turned into the finest inn, ordered the best chamber and his favourite dinner ; for now that he had so much money he was really rich.

It certainly occurred to the servant who had to clean his boots that they were astonishingly old boots for such a rich lord. But that was because he had not yet bought new ones ; next day he appeared in respectable boots and fine clothes. Now, instead of a common soldier he had become a noble lord, and the people told him about all the grand doings of the town and the King, and what a beautiful Princess his daughter was.

' How can one get to see her ? ' asked the Soldier.

' She is never to be seen at all ! ' they told him ; ' she lives in a great copper castle, surrounded by many walls and towers ! No one except the King may go in or out, for it is prophesied that she will marry a common soldier, and the King cannot submit to that.'

' I should very much like to see her,' thought the Soldier ; but he could not get permission.

Now he lived very gaily, went to the theatre, drove in the King's garden, and gave the poor a great deal of money, which was very nice of him ; he had experienced in former times how hard it is not to have a farthing in the world. Now he was rich, wore fine clothes, and made many friends, who all said that he was an excellent man, a real nobleman. And the Soldier liked that. But as he was always spending money, and never made any more, at last the day came when he had nothing left but two shillings, and he had to leave the beautiful rooms in which he had been living, and go into a little attic under the roof, and clean his own boots, and mend them with a darning-needle. None of his friends came to visit him there, for there were too many stairs to climb.

It was a dark evening, and he could not even buy a light. But all at once it flashed across him that there was a little end of tinder in the tinder-box, which he had taken from the hollow tree into which the Witch had helped him down. He found the box with the tinder in it ; but just as he was kindling a light, and had struck a spark out of the tinder-box, the door burst open, and the dog with eyes as large as saucers, which he had seen down in the tree, stood before him and said :

' What does my lord command ? '

' What's the meaning of this ? ' exclaimed the Soldier. ' This is

a pretty kind of tinder-box, if I can get whatever I want like this
Get me money!' he cried to the dog, and hey, presto! he was off
and back again, holding a great purse full of money in his mouth.

Now the Soldier knew what a capital tinder-box this was. If he
rubbed once, the dog that sat on the chest of copper appeared; if
he rubbed twice, there came the dog that watched over the silver
chest; and if he rubbed three times, the one that guarded the gold
appeared. Now, the Soldier went down again to his beautiful
rooms, and appeared once more in splendid clothes. All his friends
immediately recognised him again, and paid him great court.

One day he thought to himself: 'It is very strange that no one

The DOG BRings in The Princess

can get to see the Princess. They all say she is very pretty, but
what's the use of that if she has to sit for ever in the great copper
castle with all the towers? Can I not manage to see her somehow?
Where is my tinder-box?' and so he struck a spark, and, presto!
there came the dog with eyes as large as saucers.

'It is the middle of the night, I know,' said the Soldier; 'but I
should very much like to see the Princess for a moment.'

The dog was already outside the door, and before the Soldier
could look round, in he came with the Princess. She was lying
asleep on the dog's back, and was so beautiful that anyone could
see she was a real Princess. The Soldier really could not refrain

from kissing her—he was such a thorough Soldier. Then the dog ran back with the Princess. But when it was morning, and the King and Queen were drinking tea, the Princess said that the night before she had had such a strange dream about a dog and a Soldier : she had ridden on the dog's back, and the Soldier had kissed her.

'That is certainly a fine story,' said the Queen. But the next night one of the ladies-in-waiting was to watch at the Princess's bed, to see if it was only a dream, or if it had actually happened.

The Soldier had an overpowering longing to see the Princess again, and so the dog came in the middle of the night and fetched her, running as fast as he could. But the lady-in-waiting slipped on indiarubber shoes and followed them. When she saw them disappear into a large house, she thought to herself: 'Now I know where it is ; ' and made a great cross on the door with a piece of chalk. Then she went home and lay down, and the dog came back also, with the Princess. But when he saw that a cross had been made on the door of the house where the Soldier lived, he took a piece of chalk also, and made crosses on all the doors in the town ; and that was very clever, for now the lady-in-waiting could not find the right house, as there were crosses on all the doors.

Early next morning the King, Queen, ladies-in-waiting, and officers came out to see where the Princess had been.

'There it is ! ' said the King, when he saw the first door with a cross on it.

'No, there it is, my dear ! ' said the Queen, when she likewise saw a door with a cross.

'But here is one, and there is another ! ' they all exclaimed ; wherever they looked there was a cross on the door. Then they realised that the sign would not help them at all.

But the Queen was an extremely clever woman, who could do a great deal more than just drive in a coach. She took her great golden scissors, cut up a piece of silk, and made a pretty little bag of it. This she filled with the finest buckwheat grains, and tied it round the Princess' neck ; this done, she cut a little hole in the bag, so that the grains would strew the whole road wherever the Princess went.

In the night the dog came again, took the Princess on his back and ran away with her to the Soldier, who was very much in love with her, and would have liked to have been a Prince, so that he might have had her for his wife.

The dog did not notice how the grains were strewn right from the castle to the Soldier's window, where he ran up the wall with the Princess.

In the morning the King and the Queen saw plainly where

' He was skipping along so merrily '

their daughter had been, and they took the Soldier and put him into prison.

There he sat. Oh, how dark and dull it was there! And they told him: 'To-morrow you are to be hanged.' Hearing that did not exactly cheer him, and he had left his tinder-box in the inn.

Next morning he could see through the iron grating in front of his little window how the people were hurrying out of the town to see him hanged. He heard the drums and saw the soldiers marching; all the people were running to and fro. Just below his window was a shoemaker's apprentice, with leather apron and shoes; he was skipping along so merrily that one of his shoes flew off and fell against the wall, just where the Soldier was sitting peeping through the iron grating.

'Oh, shoemaker's boy, you needn't be in such a hurry!' said the Soldier to him. 'There's nothing going on till I arrive. But if you will run back to the house where I lived, and fetch me my tinder-box, I will give you four shillings. But you must put your best foot foremost.'

The shoemaker's boy was very willing to earn four shillings, and fetched the tinder-box, gave it to the Soldier, and—yes—now you shall hear.

Outside the town a great scaffold had been erected, and all round were standing the soldiers, and hundreds of thousands of people. The King and Queen were sitting on a magnificent throne opposite the judges and the whole council.

The Soldier was already standing on the top of the ladder; but when they wanted to put the rope round his neck, he said that the fulfilment of one innocent request was always granted to a poor criminal before he underwent his punishment. He would so much like to smoke a small pipe of tobacco; it would be his last pipe in this world.

The King could not refuse him this, and so he took out his tinder-box, and rubbed it once, twice, three times. And lo, and behold! there stood all three dogs—the one with eyes as large as saucers, the second with eyes as large as mill-wheels, and the third with eyes each as large as the Round Tower of Copenhagen.

'Help me now, so that I may not be hanged!' cried the Soldier. And thereupon the dogs fell upon the judges and the whole council, seized some by the legs, others by the nose, and threw them so high into the air that they fell and were smashed into pieces.

'I won't stand this!' said the King; but the largest dog seized him too, and the Queen as well, and threw them up after the others. This frightened the soldiers, and all the people cried: 'Good Soldier, you shall be our King, and marry the beautiful Princess!'

Then they put the Soldier into the King's coach, and the three dogs danced in front, crying 'Hurrah!' And the boys whistled and the soldiers presented arms.

The Princess came out of the copper castle, and became Queen; and that pleased her very much.

The wedding festivities lasted for eight days, and the dogs sat at table and made eyes at everyone.

THE SNOW-QUEEN [1]

THERE was once a dreadfully wicked hobgoblin. One
day he was in capital spirits because he had made a
looking-glass which reflected everything that was good
and beautiful in such a way that it dwindled almost to
nothing, but anything that was bad and ugly stood out
very clearly and looked much worse. The most beautiful
landscapes looked like boiled spinach, and the best
people looked repulsive or seemed to stand on their heads
with no bodies; their faces were so changed that they
could not be recognised, and if anyone had a freckle you
might be sure it would be spread over the nose and
mouth.

That was the best part of it, said the hobgoblin.

But one day the looking-glass was dropped, and it
broke into a million-billion and more pieces.

And now came the greatest misfortune of all, for each
of the pieces was hardly as large as a grain of sand, and
they flew about all over the world, and if anyone had a
bit in his eye there it stayed, and then he would see
everything awry, or else could only see the bad sides of
a case. For every tiny splinter of the glass possessed
the same power that the whole glass had.

Some people got a splinter in their hearts, and that
was dreadful, for then it began to turn into a lump of ice.

The hobgoblin laughed till his sides ached, but still
the tiny bits of glass flew about.

[1] Translated from the German of Hans Andersen by Miss Alma
Alleyne.

And now we will hear all about it.

In a large town, where there were so many people and houses that there was not room enough for everybody to

The Hobgoblin laughed till his sides ached

have gardens, lived two poor children. They were not brother and sister, but they loved each other just as much as if they were. Their parents lived opposite one another in two attics, and out on the leads they had put two boxes filled with flowers. There were sweet peas in it, and two rose trees, which grew beautifully, and in summer the two children were allowed to take their little chairs and sit out under the roses. Then they had splendid games.

In the winter they could not do this, but then they put hot pennies against the frozen window-panes, and made round holes to look at each other through.

His name was Kay, and hers was Gerda.

Outside it was snowing fast.

'Those are the white bees swarming,' said the old grandmother.

'Have they also a queen bee?' asked the little boy, for he knew that the real bees have one.

'To be sure,' said the grandmother. 'She flies wherever they swarm the thickest. She is larger than any of them, and never stays upon the earth, but flies again up into the black clouds. Often at midnight she flies through the streets, and peeps in at all the windows, and then they freeze in such pretty patterns and look like flowers.'

'Yes, we have seen that,' said both children; they knew that it was true.

'Can the Snow-queen come in here?' asked the little girl.

'Just let her!' cried the boy, 'I would put her on the stove, and melt her!'

But the grandmother stroked his hair, and told some more stories.

In the evening, when little Kay was going to bed, he jumped on the chair by the window, and looked through the little hole. A few snow-flakes were falling outside, and one of them, the largest, lay on the edge of one of the window-boxes. The snow-flake grew larger and larger till it took the form of a maiden, dressed in finest white gauze.

THE SNOW QUEEN APPEARS TO LITTLE KAY

She was so beautiful and dainty, but all of ice, hard bright ice.

Still she was alive; her eyes glittered like two clear stars, but there was no rest or peace in them. She nodded at the window, and beckoned with her hand. The little boy was frightened, and sprang down from the chair. It seemed as if a great white bird had flown past the window.

The next day there was a harder frost than before.

Then came the spring, and then the summer, when the roses grew and smelt more beautifully than ever.

Kay and Gerda were looking at one of their picture-books—the clock in the great church-tower had just struck five, when Kay exclaimed, 'Oh! something has stung my heart, and I've got something in my eye!'

The little girl threw her arms round his neck; he winked hard with both his eyes; no, she could see nothing in them.

'I think it is gone now," said he; but it had not gone. It was one of the tiny splinters of the glass of the magic mirror which we have heard about, that turned everything great and good reflected in it small and ugly. And poor Kay had also a splinter in his heart, and it began to change into a lump of ice. It did not hurt him at all, but the splinter was there all the same.

'Why are you crying?' he asked; 'it makes you look so ugly! There's nothing the matter with me. 'Just look! that rose is all slug-eaten, and this one is stunted! What ugly roses they are!'

And he began to pull them to pieces.

'Kay, what *are* you doing?' cried the little girl.

And when he saw how frightened she was, he pulled off another rose, and ran in at his window away from dear little Gerda.

When she came later on with the picture book, he said that it was only fit for babies, and when his grandmother told them stories, he was always interrupting with, 'But—' and then he would get behind her and put on her spectacles, and speak just as she did. This he did very well, and everybody laughed. Very soon he could imitate the way all the people in the street walked and talked.

His games were now quite different. On a winter's day he would take a burning glass and hold it out on his blue coat and let the snow-flakes fall on it.

'Look in the glass, Gerda! Just see how regular they are! They are much more interesting than real flowers. Each is perfect; they are all made according to rule. If only they did not melt!'

One morning Kay came out with his warm gloves on, and his little sledge hung over his shoulder. He shouted to Gerda, 'I am going to the market-place to play with the other boys,' and away he went.

In the market-place the boldest boys used often to fasten their sledges to the carts of the farmers, and then they got a good ride.

When they were in the middle of their games there drove into the square a large sledge, all white, and in it sat a figure dressed in a rough white fur pelisse with a white fur cap on.

The sledge drove twice round the square, and Kay fastened his little sledge behind it and drove off. It went quicker and quicker into the next street. The driver turned round, and nodded to Kay in a friendly way as if they had known each other before. Every time that Kay tried to unfasten his sledge the driver nodded again, and Kay sat still once more. Then they drove out of the town, and the snow began to fall so thickly that the little boy could not see his hand before him, and on and on they went. He quickly unfastened the cord to get loose from the big sledge, but it was of no use; his little sledge hung on fast, and it went on like the wind.

Then he cried out, but nobody heard him. He was dreadfully frightened.

The snowflakes grew larger and larger till they looked like great white birds. All at once they flew aside, the large sledge stood still, and the figure who was driving stood up. The fur cloak and cap were all of snow. It was a lady, tall and slim, and glittering. It was the Snow-queen.

'We have come at a good rate,' she said; 'but you are almost frozen. Creep in under my cloak.'

And she set him close to her in the sledge and drew the cloak over him. He felt as though he were sinking into a snow-drift.

'Are you cold now?' she asked, and kissed his forehead. The kiss was cold as ice and reached down to his heart, which was already half a lump of ice.

'My sledge! Don't forget my sledge!' He thought of that first, and it was fastened to one of the white birds who flew behind with the sledge on its back.

The Snow-queen kissed Kay again, and then he forgot all about little Gerda, his grandmother, and everybody at home.

'Now I must not kiss you any more,' she said, 'or else I should kiss you to death.'

Then away they flew over forests and lakes, over sea and land. Round them whistled the cold wind, the wolves howled, and the snow hissed; over them flew the black shrieking crows. But high up the moon shone large and bright, and thus Kay passed the long winter night. In the day he slept at the Snow-queen's feet.

But what happened to little Gerda when Kay did not come back?

What had become of him? Nobody knew. The other boys told how they had seen him fasten his sledge on to a large one which had driven out of the town gate.

Gerda cried a great deal. The winter was long and dark to her.

Then the spring came with warm sunshine. 'I will go and look for Kay,' said Gerda.

· THE · SNOW · QUEEN · TAKES · KAY · IN · HER · SLEDGE ·

So she went down to the river and got into a little boat that was there. Presently the stream began to carry it away.

'Perhaps the river will take me to Kay,' thought Gerda. She glided down, past trees and fields, till she came to a large cherry garden, in which stood a little house with strange red and blue windows and a straw roof. Before the door stood two wooden soldiers, who were shouldering arms.

Gerda called to them, but they naturally did not answer. The river carried the boat on to the land.

Gerda called out still louder, and there came out of the house a very old woman. She leant upon a crutch, and she wore a large sun-hat which was painted with the most beautiful flowers.

'You poor little girl!' said the old woman.

And then she stepped into the water, brought the boat in close with her crutch, and lifted little Gerda out.

'And now come and tell me who you are, and how you came here,' she said.

Then Gerda told her everything, and asked her if she had seen Kay. But she said he had not passed that way yet, but he would soon come.

She told Gerda not to be sad, and that she should stay with her and take of the cherry trees and flowers, which were better than any picture-book, as they could each tell a story.

She then took Gerda's hand and led her into the little house and shut the door.

The windows were very high, and the panes were red, blue, and yellow, so that the light came through in curious colours. On the table were the most delicious cherries, and the old woman let Gerda eat as many as she liked, while she combed her hair with a gold comb as she ate.

The beautiful sunny hair rippled and shone round the dear little face, which was so soft and sweet. 'I have always longed to have a dear little girl just like you, and you shall see how happy we will be together.'

And as she combed Gerda's hair, Gerda thought less and less about Kay, for the old woman was a witch, but not a wicked witch, for she only enchanted now and then to amuse herself, and she did want to keep little Gerda very much.

So she went into the garden and waved her stick over all the rose bushes and blossoms and all; they sank down into the black earth, and no one could see where they had been.

The old woman was afraid that if Gerda saw the roses she would begin to think about her own, and then would remember Kay and run away.

Then she led Gerda out into the garden. How glorious it was, and what lovely scents filled the air! All the flowers you can think of blossomed there all the year round.

Gerda jumped for joy and played there till the sun set behind the tall cherry trees, and then she slept in a beautiful bed with red silk pillows filled with violets, and she slept soundly and dreamed as a queen does on her wedding day.

The next day she played again with the flowers in the warm sunshine, and so many days passed by. Gerda knew every flower, but although there were so many, it seemed to her as if *one* were not there, though she could not remember which.

She was looking one day at the old woman's sun-hat which had the painted flowers on it, and there she saw a rose.

The witch had forgotten to make that vanish when she had made the other roses disappear under the earth. It is so difficult to think of everything.

'Why, there are no roses here!' cried Gerda, and she hunted amongst all the flowers, but not one was to be found. Then she sat down and cried, but her tears fell just on the spot where a rose bush had sunk, and when her warm tears watered the earth, the bush came up in full bloom just as it had been before. Gerda kissed the roses and thought of the lovely roses at home, and with them came the thought of little Kay.

'Oh, what have I been doing!' said the little girl. 'I wanted to look for Kay.'

She ran to the end of the garden. The gate was shut, but she pushed against the rusty lock so that it came open.

She ran out with her little bare feet. No one came after her. At last she could not run any longer, and she sat down on a large stone. When she looked round she saw that the summer was over; it was late autumn. It had not changed in the beautiful garden, where were sunshine and flowers all the year round.

'Oh, dear, how late I have made myself!' said Gerda. 'It's autumn already! I cannot rest!' And she sprang up to run on.

Oh, how tired and sore her little feet grew, and it became colder and colder.

She had to rest again, and there on the snow in front of her was a large crow.

It had been looking at her for some time, and it nodded its head and said, 'Caw! caw! good day.' Then it asked the little girl why she was alone in the world. She told the crow her story, and asked if he had seen Kay.

The crow nodded very thoughtfully and said, 'It might be! It *might* be!'

'What! Do you think you have?' cried the little girl, and she almost squeezed the crow to death as she kissed him.

'Gently, gently!' said the crow. 'I think—I know —I think—it might be little Kay, but now he has forgotten you for the princess!'

'Does he live with a princess?' asked Gerda.

'Yes, listen,' said the crow.

Then he told all he knew.

'In the kingdom in which we are now sitting lives a princess who is dreadfully clever. She has read all the newspapers in the world and has forgotten them again. She is as clever as that. The other day she came to the throne, and that is not so pleasant as people think. Then she began to say, " Why should I not marry ? " But she wanted a husband who could answer when he was spoken to, not one who would stand up stiffly and look respectable—that would be too dull.

'When she told all the Court ladies, they were delighted. You can believe every word I say,' said the crow. ' I have a tame sweetheart in the palace, and she tells me everything.'

Of course his sweetheart was a crow.

'The newspapers came out next morning with a border of hearts round it, and the princess's monogram on it, and inside you could read that every good-looking young man might come into the palace and speak to the princess, and whoever should speak loud enough to be heard would be well fed and looked after, and the one who spoke best should become the princess's husband. Indeed,' said the crow, ' you can quite believe me. It is as true as that I am sitting here.

'Young men came in streams, and there was such a crowding and a mixing together ! But nothing came of it on the first nor on the second day. They could all speak quite well when they were in the street, but as soon as they came inside the palace door, and saw the guards in silver, and upstairs the footmen in gold, and the great hall all lighted up, then their wits left them ! And when they stood in front of the throne where the princess was sitting, then they could not think of anything to say except to repeat the last word she had spoken, and she did not much care to hear that again. It seemed as if they were walking in their sleep until they came out into the street again, when they could speak once more. There was a row stretching from the gate of the town up to the castle.

'They were hungry and thirsty, but in the palace they did not even get a glass of water.

'A few of the cleverest had brought some slices of bread and butter with them, but they did not share them with their neighbour, for they thought, "If he looks hungry, the princess will not take him!"'

'But what about Kay?' asked Gerda. 'When did he come? Was he in the crowd?'

'Wait a bit; we are coming to him! On the third day a little figure came without horse or carriage and walked jauntily up to the palace. His eyes shone as yours do; he had lovely curling hair, but quite poor clothes.'

'That was Kay!' cried Gerda with delight. 'Oh, then I have found him!' and she clapped her hands.

'He had a little bundle on his back,' said the crow.

'No, it must have been his skates, for he went away with his skates!'

'Very likely,' said the crow, 'I did not see for certain. But I know this from my sweetheart, that when he came to the palace door and saw the royal guards in silver, and on the stairs the footmen in gold, he was not the least bit put out. He nodded to them, saying, "It must be rather dull standing on the stairs; I would rather go inside!"

'The halls blazed with lights; councillors and ambass-adors were walking about in noiseless shoes carrying gold dishes. It was enough to make one nervous! His boots creaked dreadfully loud, but he was not frightened.'

'That *must* be Kay!' said Gerda. 'I know he had new boots on; I have heard them creaking in his grandmother's room!'

'They *did* creak, certainly!' said the crow. 'And, not one bit afraid, up he went to the princess, who was sitting on a large pearl as round as a spinning wheel. All the ladies-in-waiting were standing round, each with their attendants, and the lords-in-waiting with *their* attendants. The nearer they stood to the door the prouder they were.'

'HE HAD NOT COME TO WOO' HE SAID ·

'It must have been dreadful!' said little Gerda. 'And Kay did win the princess?'

'I heard from my tame sweetheart that he was merry and quick-witted; he had not come to woo, he said, but to listen to the princess's wisdom. And the end of it was that they fell in love with each other.'

'Oh, yes; that was Kay!' said Gerda. 'He was so clever; he could do sums with fractions. Oh, do lead me to the palace!'

'That's easily said!' answered the crow, 'but how are we to manage that? I must talk it over with my tame sweetheart. She may be able to advise us, for I must tell you that a little girl like you could never get permission to enter it.'

'Yes, I will get it!' said Gerda. 'When Kay hears that I am there he will come out at once and fetch me!'

'Wait for me by the railings,' said the crow, and he nodded his head and flew away.

It was late in the evening when he came back.

'Caw, caw!' he said, 'I am to give you her love, and here is a little roll for you. She took it out of the kitchen; there's plenty there, and you must be hungry. You cannot come into the palace. The guards in silver and the footmen in gold would not allow it. But don't cry! You shall get in all right. My sweetheart knows a little back-stairs which leads to the sleeping-room, and she knows where to find the key.'

They went into the garden, and when the lights in the palace were put out one after the other, the crow led Gerda to a back-door.

Oh, how Gerda's heart beat with anxiety and longing! It seemed as if she were going to do something wrong, but she only wanted to know if it were little Kay. Yes, it must be he! She remembered so well his clever eyes, his curly hair. She could see him smiling as he did when they were at home under the rose trees! He would be so pleased to see her, and to hear how they all were at home.

Now they were on the stairs; a little lamp was burning, and on the landing stood the tame crow. She put her head on one side and looked at Gerda, who bowed as her grandmother had taught her.

'My betrothed has told me many nice things about

you, my dear young lady,' she said. 'Will you take the lamp while I go in front? We go this way so as to meet no one.'

Through beautiful rooms they came to the sleeping-room. In the middle of it, hung on a thick rod of gold, were two beds, shaped like lilies, one all white, in which lay the princess, and the other red, in which Gerda hoped to find Kay. She pushed aside the curtain, and saw a brown neck. Oh, it *was* Kay! She called his name out loud, holding the lamp towards him.

He woke up, turned his head and—it was *not* Kay!

It was only his neck that was like Kay's, but he was young and handsome. The princess sat up in her lily-bed and asked who was there.

Then Gerda cried, and told her story and all that the crows had done.

'You poor child!' said the prince and princess, and they praised the crows, and said that they were not angry with them, but that they must not do it again. Now they should have a reward.

'Would you like to fly away free?' said the princess, 'or will you have a permanent place as court crows with what you can get in the kitchen?'

And both crows bowed and asked for a permanent appointment, for they thought of their old age.

And they put Gerda to bed, and she folded her hands, thinking, as she fell asleep, 'How good people and animals are to me!'

The next day she was dressed from head to foot in silk and satin. They wanted her to stay on in the palace, but she begged for a little carriage and a horse, and a pair of shoes so that she might go out again into the world to look for Kay.

They gave her a muff as well as some shoes; she was warmly dressed, and when she was ready, there in front of the door stood a coach of pure gold, with a coachman, footmen and postilions with gold crowns on.

The prince and princess helped her into the carriage and wished her good luck.

The wild crow who was now married drove with her for the first three miles ; the other crow could not come because she had a bad headache.

'Good-bye, good-bye !' called the prince and princess ; and little Gerda cried, and the crow cried.

When he said good-bye, he flew on to a tree and waved with his black wings as long as the carriage, which shone like the sun, was in sight.

They came at last to a dark wood, but the coach lit it up like a torch.   When the robbers saw it, they rushed out, exclaiming 'Gold ! gold !'

They seized the horses, killed the coachman, footmen and postilions, and dragged Gerda out of the carriage.

'She is plump and tender !   I will eat her !' said the old robber-queen, and she drew her long knife, which glittered horribly.

'You shall not kill her !' cried her little daughter. 'She shall play with me.   She shall give me her muff and her beautiful dress, and she shall sleep in my bed.'

The little robber-girl was as big as Gerda, but was stronger, broader, with dark hair and black eyes.   She threw her arms round Gerda and said, 'They shall not kill you, so long as you are not naughty.   Aren't you a princess ?'

'No,' said Gerda, and she told all that had happened to her, and how dearly she loved little Kay.

The robber-girl looked at her very seriously, and nodded her head, saying, 'They shall not kill you, even if you are naughty, for then I will kill you myself !'

And she dried Gerda's eyes, and stuck both her hands in the beautiful warm muff.

The little robber-girl took Gerda to a corner of the robbers' camp where she slept.

All round were more than a hundred wood-pigeons

which seemed to be asleep, but they moved a little when the two girls came up.

There was also, near by, a reindeer which the robber-girl teased by tickling it with her long sharp knife.

Gerda lay awake for some time.

'Coo, coo!' said the wood-pigeons. 'We have seen little Kay. A white bird carried his sledge; he was sitting in the Snow-queen's carriage which drove over the forest when our little ones were in the nest. She breathed on them, and all except we two died. Coo, coo!'

'What are you saying over there?' cried Gerda. 'Where was the Snow-queen going to? Do you know at all?'

'She was probably travelling to Lapland, where there is always ice and snow. Ask the reindeer.'

'There is capital ice and snow there!' said the reindeer. 'One can jump about there in the great sparkling valleys. There the Snow-queen has her summer palace, but her best palace is up by the North Pole, on the island called Spitzbergen.'

'O Kay, my little Kay!' sobbed Gerda.

'You must lie still!' said the little robber-girl, 'or else I shall stick my knife into you!'

In the morning Gerda told her all that the wood-pigeons had said. She nodded. 'Do you know where Lapland is?' she asked the reindeer.

'Who should know better than I?' said the beast, and his eyes sparkled. 'I was born and bred there on the snow-fields.'

'Listen!' said the robber-girl to Gerda; 'you see that all the robbers have gone; only my mother is left, and she will fall asleep in the afternoon—then I will do something for you!'

When her mother had fallen asleep, the robber-girl went up to the reindeer and said, 'I am going to set you free so that you can run to Lapland. But you must go quickly and carry this little girl to the Snow-queen's palace, where her playfellow is. You must have heard all that she told about it, for she spoke loud enough!'

The reindeer sprang high for joy. The robber-girl lifted little Gerda up, and had the foresight to tie her on firmly, and even gave her a little pillow for a saddle. 'You must have your fur boots,' she said, 'for it will be cold; but I shall keep your muff, for it is so cosy! But, so that you may not freeze, here are my mother's great fur gloves; they will come up to your elbows. Creep into them!'

And Gerda cried for joy.

'Don't make such faces!' said the little robber-girl. 'You must look very happy. And here are two loaves and a sausage; now you won't be hungry!'

They were tied to the reindeer, the little robber-girl opened the door, made all the big dogs come away, cut through the halter with her sharp knife, and said to the reindeer, 'Run now! But take great care of the little girl.'

And Gerda stretched out her hands with the large fur gloves towards the little robber-girl and said, 'Good-bye!'

Then the reindeer flew over the ground, through the great forest, as fast as he could.

The wolves howled, the ravens screamed, the sky seemed on fire.

'Those are my dear old northern lights,' said the reindeer; 'see how they shine!'

And then he ran faster still, day and night.

The loaves were eaten, and the sausage also, and then they came to Lapland.

They stopped by a wretched little house; the roof almost touched the ground, and the door was so low that you had to creep in and out.

There was no one in the house except an old Lapland woman who was cooking fish over an oil-lamp. The reindeer told Gerda's whole history, but first he told his

The Robber-girl sends Gerda off on the Reindeer.

own, for that seemed to him much more important, and Gerda was so cold that she could not speak.

'Ah, you poor creatures!' said the Lapland woman; 'you have still further to go! You must go over a hundred miles into Finland, for there the Snow-queen lives, and every night she burns Bengal lights. I will write some words on a dried stock-fish, for I have no paper, and you must give it to the Finland woman, for she can give you better advice than I can.'

And when Gerda was warmed and had had something to eat and drink, the Lapland woman wrote on a dried stock-fish, and begged Gerda to take care of it, tied Gerda securely on the reindeer's back, and away they went again.

The whole night was ablaze with northern lights, and then they came to Finland and knocked at the Finland woman's chimney, for door she had none.

Inside it was so hot that the Finland woman wore very few clothes; she loosened Gerda's clothes and drew off her fur gloves and boots. She laid a piece of ice on the reindeer's head, and then read what was written on the stock-fish. She read it over three times till she knew it by heart, and then put the fish in the saucepan, for she never wasted anything.

Then the reindeer told his story, and afterwards little Gerda's, and the Finland woman blinked her eyes but said nothing.

'You are very clever,' said the reindeer, 'I know. Cannot you give the little girl a drink so that she may have the strength of twelve men and overcome the Snow-queen?'

'The strength of twelve men!' said the Finland woman; '*that* would not help much. Little Kay is with the Snow-queen, and he likes everything there very much and thinks it the best place in the world. But that is because he has a splinter of glass in his heart and a bit in his eye. If these do not come out, he will never be free, and the Snow-queen will keep her power over him.'

'But cannot you give little Gerda something so that she can have power over her?'

'I can give her no greater power than she has already; don't you see how great it is? Don't you see how men and beasts must help her when she wanders into the wide world with her bare feet? She is powerful already, because she is a dear little innocent child. If she cannot by herself conquer the Snow-queen and take away the glass splinters from little Kay, *we* cannot help her! The Snow-queen's garden begins two miles from here. You can carry the little maiden so far; put her down by the large bush with red berries growing in the snow. Then you must come back here as fast as you can.'

Then the Finland woman lifted little Gerda on the reindeer and away he sped.

'Oh, I have left my gloves and boots behind!' cried Gerda. She missed them in the piercing cold, but the reindeer did not dare to stop. On he ran till he came to the bush with red berries. Then he set Gerda down and kissed her mouth, and great big tears ran down his cheeks, and then he ran back. There stood poor Gerda without shoes or gloves in the middle of the bitter cold of Finland.

She ran on as fast as she could. A regiment of gigantic snowflakes came against her, but they melted when they touched her, and she went on with fresh courage.

And now we must see what Kay was doing. He was not thinking of Gerda, and never dreamt that she was standing outside the palace.

The walls of the palace were built of driven snow, and the doors and windows of piercing winds.

There were more than a hundred halls in it all of frozen snow. The largest was several miles long; the bright Northern lights lit them up, and very large and empty and cold and glittering they were! In the middle of the great hall was a frozen lake which had cracked in a thousand pieces; each piece was exactly like the other. Here the Snow-queen used to sit when she was at home.

Little Kay was almost blue and black with cold, but he did not feel it, for she had kissed away his feelings and his heart was a lump of ice.

He was pulling about some sharp, flat pieces of ice, and trying to fit one into the other. He thought each was most beautiful, but that was because of the splinter of glass in his eye. He fitted them into a great many shapes, but he wanted to make them spell the word 'Love.' The Snow-queen had said, 'If you can spell out that word you shall be your own master. I will give you the whole world and a new pair of skates.'

But he could not do it.

'Now I must fly to warmer countries,' said the Snow-queen. 'I must go and powder my black kettles!' (This was what she called Mount Etna and Mount Vesuvius.) 'It does the lemons and grapes good.'

And off she flew, and Kay sat alone in the great hall trying to do his puzzle.

He sat so still that you would have thought he was frozen.

Then it happened that little Gerda stepped into the hall. The biting cold winds became quiet as if they had fallen asleep when she appeared in the great, empty, freezing hall.

She caught sight of Kay; she recognised him, ran and put her arms round his neck, crying, 'Kay! dear little Kay! I have found you at last!'

But he sat quite still and cold. Then Gerda wept hot tears which fell on his neck and thawed his heart and swept away the bit of the looking-glass. He looked at her and then he burst into tears. He cried so much that the glass splinter swam out of his eye; then he knew

her, and cried out, 'Gerda! dear little Gerda! Where
have you been so long? and where have I been?'

And he looked round him.

'How cold it is here! How wide and empty!' and
he threw himself on Gerda, and she laughed and wept

for joy. It was such a happy time that the pieces of ice
even danced round them for joy, and when they were
tired and lay down again they formed themselves into
the letters that the Snow-queen had said he must spell
in order to become his own master and have the whole
world and a new pair of skates.

And Gerda kissed his cheeks and they grew rosy; she kissed his eyes and they sparkled like hers; she kissed his hands and feet and he became warm and glowing. The Snow-queen might come home now; his release— the word 'Love'—stood written in sparkling ice.

They took each other's hands and wandered out of the great palace; they talked about the grandmother and the roses on the leads, and wherever they came the winds hushed and the sun came out. When they reached the bush with red berries there stood the reindeer waiting for them.

He carried Kay and Gerda first to the Finland woman, who warmed them in her hot room and gave them advice for their journey home.

Then they went to the Lapland woman, who gave them new clothes and mended their sleigh. The reindeer ran with them till they came to the green fields fresh with the spring green. Here he said good-bye.

They came to the forest, which was bursting into bud, and out of it came a splendid horse which Gerda knew; it was one which had drawn the gold coach ridden by a young girl with a red cap on and pistols in her belt. It was the little robber girl who was tired of being at home and wanted to go out into the world. She and Gerda knew each other at once.

'You are a nice fellow!' she said to Kay. 'I should like to know if you deserve to be run after all over the world!'

But Gerda patted her cheeks and asked after the prince and princess.

'They are travelling about,' said the robber girl.

'And the crow?' asked Gerda.

'Oh, the crow is dead!' answered the robber girl. 'His tame sweetheart is a widow and hops about with a bit of black crape round her leg. She makes a great fuss, but it's all nonsense. But tell me what happened to you, and how you caught him.'

And Kay and Gerda told her all.

'Dear, dear!' said the robber girl, shook both their hands, and promised that if she came to their town she would come and see them. Then she rode on.

But Gerda and Kay went home hand in hand. There they found the grandmother and everything just as it had been, but when they went through the doorway they found they were grown-up.

There were the roses on the leads; it was summer. warm, glorious summer.

THE WATER OF LIFE[1]

THREE brothers and one sister lived together in a small cottage, and they loved one another dearly. One day the eldest brother, who had never done anything but amuse himself from sunrise to sunset, said to the rest, ' Let us all work hard, and perhaps we shall grow rich, and be able to build ourselves a palace.'

And his brothers and sister answered joyfully, ' Yes, we will all work ! '

So they fell to working with all their might, till at last they became rich, and were able to build themselves a beautiful palace ; and everyone came from miles round to see its wonders, and to say how splendid it was. No one thought of finding any faults, till at length an old woman, who had been walking through the rooms with a crowd of people, suddenly exclaimed, ' Yes, it is a splendid palace, but there is still something it needs ! '

' And what may that be ? '

' A church.'

When they heard this the brothers set to work again to earn some more money, and when they had got enough they set about building a church, which should be as large and beautiful as the palace itself.

And after the church was finished greater numbers of people than ever flocked to see the palace and the church and vast gardens and magnificent halls.

[1] *Cuentos Populars Catalans*, per lo Dr. D. Francisco de S. Maspous y Labros. Barcelona, 1885.

But one day, as the brothers were as usual doing the honours to their guests, an old man turned to them and said, ' Yes, it is all most beautiful, but there is still something it needs ! '

' And what may that be ? '

' A pitcher of the water of life, a branch of the tree the smell of whose flowers gives eternal beauty, and the talking bird.'

' And where am I to find all those ? '

' Go to the mountain that is far off yonder, and you will find what you seek.'

After the old man had bowed politely and taken farewell of them the eldest brother said to the rest, ' I will go in search of the water of life, and the talking bird, and the tree of beauty.'

'But suppose some evil thing befalls you ? ' asked his sister. 'How shall we know ? '

' You are right,' he replied ; ' I had not thought of that ! '

Then they followed the old man, and said to him, ' My eldest brother wishes to seek for the water of life, and the tree of beauty, and the talking bird, that you tell him are needful to make our palace perfect. But how shall we know if any evil thing befall him ? '

So the old man took them a knife, and gave it to them, saying, ' Keep this carefully, and as long as the blade is bright all is well ; but if the blade is bloody, then know that evil has befallen him.'

The brothers thanked him, and departed, and went straight to the palace, where they found the young man making ready to set out for the mountain where the treasures he longed for lay hid.

And he walked, and he walked, and he walked, till he had gone a great way, and there he met a giant.

' Can you tell me how much further I have still to go before I reach that mountain yonder ? '

' And why do you wish to go there ? '

'I am seeking the water of life, the talking bird, and a branch of the tree of beauty.'

'Many have passed by seeking those treasures, but none have ever come back; and you will never come back either, unless you mark my words. Follow this path, and when you reach the mountain you will find it covered with stones. Do not stop to look at them, but keep on your way. As you go you will hear scoffs and laughs behind you; it will be the stones that mock. Do not heed them; above all, do not turn round. If you do you will become as one of them. Walk straight on till you get to the top, and then take all you wish for.'

The young man thanked him for his counsel, and walked, and walked, and walked, till he reached the mountain. And as he climbed he heard behind him scoffs and jeers, but he kept his ears steadily closed to them. At last the noise grew so loud that he lost patience, and he stooped to pick up a stone to hurl into the midst of the clamour, when suddenly his arm seemed to stiffen, and the next moment he was a stone himself!

That day his sister, who thought her brother's steps were long in returning, took out the knife and found the blade was red as blood. Then she cried out to her brothers that something terrible had come to pass.

'I will go and find him,' said the second. And he went.

And he walked, and he walked, and he walked, till he met the giant, and asked him if he had seen a young man travelling towards the mountain.

And the giant answered, 'Yes, I have seen him pass, but I have not seen him come back. The spell must have worked upon him.'

'Then what can I do to disenchant him, and find the water of life, the talking bird, and a branch of the tree of beauty?'

'Follow this path, and when you reach the mountain you will find it covered with stones. Do not stop to look

at them, but climb steadily on. Above all, heed not the
laughs and scoffs that will arise on all sides, and never
turn round. And when you reach the top you can then
take all you desire.'

The young man thanked him for his counsel, and set
out for the mountain. But no sooner did he reach it
than loud jests and gibes broke out on every side, and
almost deafened him. For some time he let them rail,
and pushed boldly on, till he had passed the place which
his brother had gained; then suddenly he thought that
among the scoffing sounds he heard his brother's voice.
He stopped and looked back; and another stone was
added to the number.

Meanwhile the sister left at home was counting the
days when her two brothers should return to her. The
time seemed long, and it would be hard to say how often
she took out the knife and looked at its polished blade
to make sure that this one at least was still safe. The
blade was always bright and clear; each time she looked
she had the happiness of knowing that all was well, till
one evening, tired and anxious, as she frequently was
at the end of the day, she took it from its drawer, and
behold! the blade was red with blood. Her cry of horror
brought her youngest brother to her, and, unable to speak,
she held out the knife!

'I will go,' he said.

So he walked, and he walked, and he walked, until he
met the giant, and he asked, 'Have two young men,
making for yonder mountain, passed this way?'

And the giant answered, 'Yes, they have passed by,
but they never came back, and by this I know that the
spell has fallen upon them.'

'Then what must I do to free them, and to get the
water of life, and the talking bird, and the branch of the
tree of beauty?'

'Go to the mountain, which you will find so thickly
covered with stones that you will hardly be able to place

your feet, and walk straight forward, turning neither to
the right hand nor to the left, and paying no heed to the
laughs and scoffs which will follow you, till you reach
the top, and then you may take all that you desire.'

The young man thanked the giant for his counsel,
and set forth to the mountain. And when he began to
climb there burst forth all around him a storm of scoffs
and jeers; but he thought of the giant's words, and looked
neither to the right hand nor to the left, till the mountain
top lay straight before him. A moment now and he
would have gained it, when, through the groans and yells,
he heard his brothers' voices. He turned, and there was
one stone the more.

And all this while his sister was pacing up and down
the palace, hardly letting the knife out of her hand, and
dreading what she knew she would see, and what she *did*
see. The blade grew red before her eyes, and she said,
'Now it is my turn.'

So she walked, and she walked, and she walked till
she came to the giant, and prayed him to tell her if he
had seen three young men pass that way seeking the
distant mountain.

'I have seen them pass, but they have never returned,
and by this I know that the spell has fallen upon them.'

'And what must I do to set them free, and to find the
water of life, and the talking bird, and a branch of the
tree of beauty?'

'You must go to that mountain, which is so full of
stones that your feet will hardly find a place to tread, and
as you climb you will hear a noise as if all the stones in
the world were mocking you; but pay no heed to anything you may hear, and, once you gain the top, you have
gained everything.'

The girl thanked him for his counsel, and set out for
the mountain; and scarcely had she gone a few steps
upwards when cries and screams broke forth around her,
and she felt as if each stone she trod on was a living

thing. But she remembered the words of the giant, and knew not what had befallen her brothers, and kept her face steadily towards the mountain top, which grew nearer and nearer every moment. But as she mounted the clamour increased sevenfold: high above them all rang the voices of her three brothers. But the girl took no heed, and at last her feet stood upon the top.

HOW THE SISTER FETCHED THE WATER OF LIFE

Then she looked round, and saw, lying in a hollow, the pool of the water of life. And she took the brazen pitcher that she had brought with her, and filled it to the brim. By the side of the pool stood the tree of beauty, with the talking bird on one of its boughs; and she caught the bird, and placed it in a cage, and broke off one of the branches.

After that she turned, and went joyfully down the hill again, carrying her treasures, but her long climb had tired her out, and the brazen pitcher was very heavy, and as she walked a few drops of the water spilt on the stones, and as it touched them they changed into young men and maidens, crowding about her to give thanks for their deliverance.

So she learnt by this how the evil spell might be broken, and she carefully sprinkled every stone till there was not one left—only a great company of youths and girls who followed her down the mountain.

When they arrived at the palace she did not lose a moment in planting the branch of the tree of beauty and watering it with the water of life. And the branch shot up into a tree, and was heavy with flowers, and the talking bird nestled in its branches.

Now the fame of these wonders was noised abroad, and the people flocked in great numbers to see the three marvels, and the maiden who had won them ; and among the sightseers came the king's son, who would not go till everything was shown him, and till he had heard how it had all happened. And the prince admired the strangeness and beauty of the treasures in the palace, but more than all he admired the beauty and courage of the maiden who had brought them there. So he went home and told his parents, and gained their consent to wed her for his wife.

Then the marriage was celebrated in the church adjoining the palace. Then the bridegroom took her to his own home, where they lived happy for ever after.

THE PRINCESS IN THE CHEST[1]

THERE were once a king and a queen who lived in a beautiful castle, and had a large, and fair, and rich, and happy land to rule over. From the very first they loved each other greatly, and lived very happily together, but they had no heir.

They had been married for seven years, but had neither son nor daughter, and that was a great grief to both of them. More than once it happened that when the king was in a bad temper, he let it out on the poor queen, and said that here they were now, getting old, and neither they nor the kingdom had an heir, and it was all her fault. This was hard to listen to, and she went and cried and vexed herself.

Finally, the king said to her one day, 'This can't be borne any longer. I go about childless, and it's your fault. I am going on a journey and shall be away for a year. If you have a child when I come back again, all will be well, and I shall love you beyond all measure, and never more say an angry word to you. But if the nest is just as empty when I come home, then I must part with you.'

After the king had set out on his journey, the queen went about in her loneliness, and sorrowed and vexed herself more than ever. At last her maid said to her one day, 'I think that some help could be found, if your majesty would seek it.' Then she told about a wise old woman in that country, who had helped many in troubles

[1] Translated from the Danish.

of the same kind, and could no doubt help the queen as well, if she would send for her. The queen did so, and the wise woman came, and to her she confided her sorrow, that she was childless, and the king and his kingdom had no heir.

The wise woman knew help for this. ' Out in the king's garden,' said she, ' under the great oak that stands on the left hand, just as one goes out from the castle, is a little bush, rather brown than green, with hairy leaves and long spikes. On that bush there are just at this moment three buds. If your majesty goes out there alone, fasting, before sunrise, and takes the middle one of the three buds, and eats it, then in six months you will bring a princess into the world. As soon as she is born, she must have a nurse, whom I shall provide, and this nurse must live with the child in a secluded part of the palace; no other person must visit the child; neither the king nor the queen must see it until it is fourteen years old, for that would cause great sorrow and misfortune.'

The queen rewarded the old woman richly, and next morning, before the sun rose, she was down in the garden, found at once the little bush with the three buds, plucked the middle one and ate it. It was sweet to taste, but afterwards was as bitter as gall. Six months after this, she brought into the world a little girl. There was a nurse in readiness, whom the wise woman had provided, and preparations were made for her living with the child, quite alone, in a secluded wing of the castle, looking out on the pleasure-park. The queen did as the wise woman had told her; she gave up the child immediately, and the nurse took it and lived with it there.

When the king came home and heard that a daughter had been born to him, he was of course very pleased and happy, and wanted to see her at once.

The queen had then to tell him this much of the story, that it had been foretold that it would cause great

sorrow and misfortune if either he or she got a sight of
the child until it had completed its fourteenth year.

This was a long time to wait. The king longed so
much to get a sight of his daughter, and the queen no less
than he, but she knew that it was not like other children,
for it could speak immediately after it was born, and was

The Queen eats the Magic bud

as wise as older folk. This the nurse had told her, for
with her the queen had a talk now and again, but there
was no one else who had ever seen the princess. The
queen had also seen what the wise woman could do, so
she insisted strongly that her warning should be obeyed.
The king often lost his patience, and was determined to
see his daughter, but the queen always put him off the

idea, and so things went on, until the very day before
the princess completed her fourteenth year.

The king and the queen were out in the garden then,
and the king said, 'Now I *can't* and I *won't* wait any
longer. I *must* see my daughter *at once*. A few hours,
more or less, can't make any difference.'

The queen begged him to have patience till the
morning. When they had waited so long, they could
surely wait a single day more. But the king was quite
unreasonable. 'No nonsense,' said he; 'she is just as
much mine as yours, and I *will* see her,' and with that
he went straight up to her room.

He burst the door open, and pushed aside the nurse,
who tried to stop him, and there he saw his daughter.
She was the loveliest young princess, red and white, like
milk and blood, with clear blue eyes and golden hair,
but right in the middle of her forehead there was a little
tuft of brown hair.

The princess went to meet her father, fell on his neck
and kissed him, but with that she said, ' O father, father !
what have you done now? to-morrow I must die, and
you must choose one of three things : either the land
must be smitten by the black pestilence, or you must
have a long and bloody war, or you must, as soon as I
am dead, lay me in a plain wooden chest, and set it in
the church, and for a whole year place a sentinel beside
it every night.'

The king was frightened indeed, and thought she was
raving, but in order to please her, he said, ' Well, of these
three things I shall choose the last; if you die, I shall
lay you at once in a plain wooden chest, and have it set
in the church, and every night I shall place a sentinel
beside it. But you shall not die, even if you are ill now.'

He immediately summoned all the best doctors in
the country, and they came with all their prescriptions
and their medicine bottles, but next day the princess was
stiff and cold in death. All the doctors could certify to

that, and they all put their names to this and appended their seals, and then they had done all they could.

The king kept his promise. The princess's body was lain the same day in a plain wooden chest, and set in the chapel of the castle, and on that night and every night after it, a sentinel was posted in the church, to keep watch over the chest.

The first morning when they came to let the sentinel out, there was no sentinel there. They thought he had just got frightened and run away, and next evening a new one was posted in the church. In the morning he was also gone. So it went every night. When they came in the morning to let the sentinel out, there was no one there, and it was impossible to discover which way he had gone if he had run away. And what should they run away for, every one of them, so that nothing more was ever heard or seen of them, from the hour that they were set on guard beside the princess's chest?

It became now a general belief that the princess's ghost walked, and ate up all those who were to guard her chest, and very soon there was no one left who would be placed on this duty, and the king's soldiers deserted the service, before their turn came to be her bodyguard. The king then promised a large reward to the soldier who would volunteer for the post. This did for some time, as there were found a few reckless fellows, who wished to earn this good payment. But they never got it, for in the morning they too had disappeared like the rest.

So it had gone on for something like a whole year; every night a sentinel had been placed beside the chest, either by compulsion or of his own free will, but not a single one of the sentinels was to be seen, either on the following day or any time thereafter. And so it had also gone with one, on the night before a certain day, when a merry young smith came wandering to the town where the king's castle stood. It was the capital of the country, and people of every kind came to it to get work. This smith, whose name was Christian, had come for that same purpose. There was no work for him in the place he belonged to, and he wanted now to seek a place in the capital.

There he entered an inn where he sat down in the public room, and got something to eat. Some under-officers were sitting there, who were out to try to get some one enlisted to stand sentry. They had to go in this way, day after day, and hitherto they had always succeeded in finding one or other reckless fellow. But on this day they had, as yet, found no one. It was too well known how all the sentinels disappeared, who were set on that post, and all that they had got hold of had refused with thanks. These sat down beside Christian, and ordered drinks, and drank along with him. Now Christian was a merry fellow who liked good company; he could both drink and sing, and talk and boast as well, when he got a little drop in his head. He told these under-officers that he was one of that kind of folk who never are afraid of anything. Then he was just the kind of man they liked, said they, and he might easily earn a good penny, before he was a day older, for the king paid a hundred dollars to anyone who would stand as sentinel in the church all night, beside his daughter's chest.

Christian was not afraid of *that—he* wasn't afraid of anything, so they drank another bottle of wine on this, and Christian went with them up to the colonel, where he was put into uniform, with musket, and all the rest, and was then shut up in the church, to stand as sentinel that night.

It was eight o'clock when he took up his post, and for the first hour he was quite proud of his courage; during the second hour he was well pleased with the large reward that he would get, but in the third hour, when it was getting near eleven, the effects of the wine passed off, and he began to get uncomfortable, for he had heard about this post; that no one had ever escaped alive from it, so far as was known. But neither did anyone know what had become of all the sentinels. The thought of this ran in his head so much, after the wine was out of it, that he searched about everywhere for a way of escape, and finally, at eleven o'clock, he found a little postern in the steeple which was not locked, and out at this he crept, intending to run away.

At the same moment as he put his foot outside the church door, he saw standing before him a little man, who said, 'Good evening, Christian, where are *you* going?'

With that he felt as if he were rooted to the spot and could not move.

'Nowhere,' said he.

'Oh, yes,' said the little man, 'You were just about to run away, but you have taken upon you to stand sentinel in the church to-night, and there you must stay.'

Christian said, very humbly, that he dared not, and therefore wanted to get away, and begged to be let go.

'No,' said the little one, 'you must remain at your post, but I shall give you a piece of good advice; you shall go up into the pulpit, and remain standing there. You need never mind what you see or hear, it will not be able to do you any harm, if you remain in your place until you hear the lid of the chest slam down again behind the dead : then all danger is past, and you can go about the church, wherever you please.'

The little man then pushed him in at the door again, and locked it after him. Christian made haste to get up into the pulpit, and stood there, without noticing anything, until the clock struck twelve. Then the lid of the princess's chest sprang up, and out of it there came something like the princess, dressed as you see in the picture. It shrieked and howled, 'Sentry, where are you? Sentry, where are you? If you don't come, you shall get the most cruel death anyone has ever got.'

It went all round the church, and when it finally caught sight of the smith, up in the pulpit, it came rushing thither and mounted the steps.   But it could not get up the whole way, and for all that it stretched and strained, it could not touch Christian, who meanwhile stood and trembled up in the pulpit.   When the clock struck one, the appearance had to go back into the chest again, and Christian heard the lid slam after it.   After this there was dead silence in the church.   He lay down where he was and fell asleep, and did not awake before it was bright daylight, and he heard steps outside, and the noise of the key being put into the lock.   Then he came down from the pulpit, and stood with his musket in front of the princess's chest.

It was the colonel himself who came with the patrol, and he was not a little surprised when he found the recruit safe and sound.   He wanted to have a report, but Christian would give him none, so he took him straight up to the king, and announced for the first time that here was the sentinel who had stood guard in the church over-night.   The king immediately got out of bed, and laid the hundred dollars for him on the table, and then wanted to question him.   'Have you seen anything?' said he.   'Have you seen my daughter?'   'I have stood at my post,' said the young smith, 'and that is quite enough; I undertook nothing more.'   He was not sure whether he dared tell what he had seen and heard, and besides he was also a little conceited because he had done what no other man had been able to do, or had had courage for. The king professed to be quite satisfied, and asked him whether he would engage himself to stand on guard again the following night.   'No, thank you,' said Christian, 'I will have no more of that!'

'As you please,' said the king, 'you have behaved like a brave fellow, and now you shall have your breakfast. You must be needing something to strengthen you after *that* turn.'

The king had breakfast laid for him, and sat down at
the table with him in person ; he kept constantly filling
his glass for him and praising him, and drinking his
health.   Christian needed no pressing, but did full justice
both to the food and drink, and not least to the latter.
Finally he grew bold, and said that if the king would give
him two hundred dollars for it, he was his man to stand
sentry next night as well.

When this was arranged, Christian bade him ' Good-
day,' and went down among the guards, and then out
into the town along with other soldiers and under-officers.
He had his pocket full of money, and treated them, and
drank with them and boasted and made game of the
good-for-nothings who were afraid to stand on guard,
because they were frightened that the dead princess
would eat them.   See whether she had eaten *him !*   So
the day passed in mirth and glee, but when eight o'clock
came, Christian was again shut up in the church, all
alone.

Before he had been there two hours, he got tired of it,
and thought only of getting away.   He found a little door
behind the altar which was not locked, and at ten o'clock
he slipped out at it, and took to his heels and made for
the beach.   He had got half-way thither, when all at once
the same little man stood in front of him and said, ' Good
evening, Christian, where are *you* going ? ' ' I've leave to go
where I please,' said the smith, but at the same time he
noticed that he could not move a foot.   ' No, you have
undertaken to keep guard to-night as well,' said the little
man, ' and you must attend to that.'   He then took hold of
him, and, however unwilling he was, Christian had to go
with him right back to the same little door that he had
crept out at.   When they got there, the little man said to
him, ' Go in front of the altar now, and take in your hand
the book that is lying there.   There you shall stay till you
hear the lid of the chest slam down over the dead.   In
that way you will come to no harm.'

With that, the little man shoved him in at the door, and locked it. Christian then immediately went in front of the altar, and took the book in his hand, and stood thus until the clock struck twelve, and the appearance sprang out of the chest. 'Sentry, where are you? Sentry, where are you?' it shrieked, and then rushed to the pulpit, and right up into it. But there was no one there that night. Then it howled and shrieked again,

> My father has set no sentry in,
> War and Pest this night begin.

At the same moment, it noticed the smith standing in front of the altar, and came rushing towards him. 'Are you there?' it screamed; 'now I'll catch you.' But it could not come up over the step in front of the altar, and there it continued to howl, and scream, and threaten, until the clock struck one, when it had to go into the chest again, and Christian heard the lid slam above it. That night, however, it had not the same appearance as on the previous one; it was less ugly.

When all was quiet in the church, the smith lay down before the altar and slept calmly till the following morning, when the colonel came to fetch him. He was taken up to the king again, and things went as on the day before. He got his money, but would give no explanation whether he had seen the king's daughter, and he would not take the post again, he said. But after he had got a good breakfast, and tasted well of the king's wines, he undertook to go on guard again the third night, but he would not do it for less than the half of the kingdom, he said, for it was a dangerous post, and the king had to agree, and promise him this.

The remainder of the day went like the previous one. He played the boastful soldier, and the merry smith, and he had comrades and boon-companions in plenty. At eight o'clock he had to put on his uniform again, and was shut up in the church. He had not been there for an hour before he had come to his senses, and thought, ' It's best to stop now, while the game is going well.' The third night, he was sure, would be the worst ; he had been drunk when he promised it, and the half of the kingdom, the king could never have been in earnest about *that !* So he decided to leave, without waiting so long as on the previous nights. In that way he would escape the little man who had watched him before. All the doors and posterns were locked, but he finally thought of creeping up to a window, and opening that, and as the clock struck nine, he crept out there. It was fairly high in the wall, but he got to the ground with no bones broken, and started to run. He got down to the shore without meeting anyone, and there he got into a boat, and pushed off from land. He laughed immensely to himself at the thought of how cleverly he had managed and how he had cheated the little man. Just then he heard a voice from the shore, ' Good evening, Christian, where are *you* going ? ' He gave no answer. ' To-night your legs will be too short,' he thought, and pulled at the oars. But he then felt something lay hold of the boat, and drag it straight in to shore, for all that he sat and struggled with the oars.

The man then laid hold of him, and said, ' You must remain at your post, as you have promised,' and whether he liked it or not, Christian had just to go back with him the whole way to the church.

He could never get in at that window again, Christian said ; it was far too high up.

' You *must* go in there, and you *shall* go in there,' said the little man, and with that he lifted him up on to the window-sill. Then he said to him : ' Notice well now what you have to do. This evening you must stretch yourself out on the left-hand side of her chest. The lid opens to the right, and she comes out to the left. When she has got out of the chest and passed over you, you must get into it and lie there, and *that* in a hurry, without

her seeing you. There you must remain lying until day
dawns, and whether she threatens or entreats you, you
must not come out of it, or give her any answer. Then
she has no power over you, and both you and she are
freed.'

The smith then had to go in at the window, just as he
came out, and went and laid himself all his length on the
left side of the princess's chest, close up to it, and there
he lay as stiff as a rock until the clock struck twelve.
Then the lid sprang up to the right, and the princess
came out, straight over him, and rushed round the church,
howling and shrieking 'Sentry, where are you? Sentry,
where are you?' She went towards the altar, and
right up to it, but there was no one there; then she
screamed again,

> My father has set no sentry in,
> War and Pest will now begin.

Then she went round the whole church, both up and
down, sighing and weeping,

> My father has set no sentry in,
> War and Pest will now begin.

Then she went away again, and at the same moment the
clock in the tower struck one.

Then the smith heard in the church a soft music,
which grew louder and louder, and soon filled the whole
building. He heard also a multitude of footsteps, as if
the church was being filled with people. He heard the
priest go through the service in front of the altar, and
there was singing more beautiful than he had ever heard
before. Then he also heard the priest offer up a prayer
of thanksgiving because the land had been freed from
war and pestilence, and from all misfortune, and the
king's daughter was delivered from the evil one. Many
voices joined in, and a hymn of praise was sung; then
he heard the priest again, and heard his own name and

that of the princess, and thought that he was being wedded to her. The church was packed full, but he could see nothing. Then he heard again the many footsteps as of folk leaving the church, while the music sounded fainter and fainter, until it altogether died away. When it was silent, the light of day began to break in through the windows.

The smith sprang up out of the chest and fell on his knees and thanked God. The church was empty, but up in front of the altar lay the princess, white and red, like a human being, but sobbing and crying, and shaking with cold in her white shroud. The smith took his sentry coat and wrapped it round her; then she dried her tears, and took his hand and thanked him, and said that he had now freed her from all the sorcery that had been in her from her birth, and which had come over her again when her father broke the command against seeing her until she had completed her fourteenth year.

She said further, that if he who had delivered her would take her in marriage, she would be his. If not, she would go into a nunnery, and he could marry no other as long as she lived, for he was wedded to her with the service of the dead, which he had heard.

She was now the most beautiful young princess that anyone could wish to see, and he was now lord of half the kingdom, which had been promised him for standing on guard the third night. So they agreed that they would have each other, and love each other all their days.

With the first sunbeam the watch came and opened the church, and not only was the colonel there, but the king in person, come to see what had happened to the sentinel. He found them both sitting hand in hand on the step in front of the altar, and immediately knew his daughter again, and took her in his arms, thanking God and her deliverer. He made no objections to what they had arranged, and so Christian the smith held his wedding

HE WRAPT HER IN HIS SOLDIER'S CLOAK.

with the princess, and got half the kingdom at once, and the whole of it when the king died.

As for the other sentries, with so many doors and windows open, no doubt they had run away, and gone into the Prussian service. And as for what Christian said he saw, he had been drinking more wine than was good for him.

THE WOUNDED LION [1]

THERE was once a girl so poor that she had nothing to live on, and wandered about the world asking for charity. One day she arrived at a thatched cottage, and inquired if they could give her any work. The farmer said he wanted a cowherd, as his own had left him, and if the girl liked the place she might take it. So she became a cowherd.

One morning she was driving her cows through the meadows when she heard near by a loud groan that almost sounded human. She hastened to the spot from which the noise came, and found it proceeded from a lion who lay stretched upon the ground.

You can guess how frightened she was! But the lion seemed in such pain that she was sorry for him, and drew nearer and nearer till she saw he had a large thorn in one foot. She pulled out the thorn and bound up the place, and the lion was grateful, and licked her hand by way of thanks with his big rough tongue.

When the girl had finished she went back to find the cows, but they had gone, and though she hunted everywhere she never found them ; and she had to return home and confess to her master, who scolded her bitterly, and afterwards beat her. Then he said, ' Now you will have to look after the asses.'

So every day she had to take the asses to the woods to feed, until one morning, exactly a year after she had

[1] *Cuentos Populars Catalans.*

found the lion, she heard a groan which sounded quite human. She went straight to the place from which the noise came, and, to her great surprise, beheld the same lion stretched on the ground with a deep wound across his face.

This time she was not afraid at all, and ran towards him, washing the wound and laying soothing herbs upon it ; and when she had bound it up the lion thanked her in the same manner as before.

After that she returned to her flock, but they were nowhere to be seen. She searched here and she searched there, but they had vanished completely !

Then she had to go home and confess to her master, who first scolded her and afterwards beat her. ' Now go,' he ended, ' and look after the pigs ! '

So the next day she took out the pigs, and found them such good feeding grounds that they grew fatter every day.

Another year passed by, and one morning when the maiden was out with her pigs she heard a groan which sounded quite human. She ran to see what it was, and found her old friend the lion, wounded through and through, fast dying under a tree.

She fell on her knees before him and washed his wounds one by one, and laid healing herbs upon them. And the lion licked her hands and thanked her, and asked if she would not stay and sit by him. But the girl said she had her pigs to watch, and she must go and see after them.

So she ran to the place where she had left them, but they had vanished as if the earth had swallowed them up. She whistled and called, but only the birds answered her.

Then she sank down on the ground and wept bitterly, not daring to return home until some hours had passed away.

And when she had had her cry out she got up and

THE WOUNDED LION.

searched all up and down the wood. But it was no use ; there was not a sign of the pigs.

At last she thought that perhaps if she climbed a tree she might see further. But no sooner was she seated on the highest branch than something happened which put the pigs quite out of her head. This was a handsome young man who was coming down the path; and when he had almost reached the tree he pulled aside a rock and disappeared behind it.

The maiden rubbed her eyes and wondered if she had been dreaming. Next she thought, 'I will not stir from here till I see him come out, and discover who he is.' Accordingly she waited, and at dawn the next morning the rock moved to one side and a lion came out.

When he had gone quite out of sight the girl climbed down from the tree and went to the rock, which she pushed aside, and entered the opening before her. The path led to a beautiful house. She went in, swept and dusted the furniture, and put everything tidy. Then she ate a very good dinner, which was on a shelf in the corner, and once more clambered up to the top of her tree.

As the sun set she saw the same young man walking gaily down the path, and, as before, he pushed aside the rock and disappeared behind it.

Next morning out came the lion. He looked sharply about him on all sides, but saw no one, and then vanished into the forest.

The maiden then came down from the tree and did exactly as she had done the day before. Thus three days went by, and every day she went and tidied up the palace. At length, when the girl found she was no nearer to discovering the secret, she resolved to ask him, and in the evening when she caught sight of him coming through the wood she came down from the tree and begged him to tell her his name.

The young man looked very pleased to see her, and said he thought it must be she who had secretly kept

his house for so many days. And he added that he was
a prince enchanted by a powerful giant, but was only
allowed to take his own shape at night, for all day he was
forced to appear as the lion whom she had so often helped ;
and, more than this, it was the giant who had stolen the
oxen and the asses and the pigs in revenge for her
kindness.

And the girl asked him, 'What can I do to disenchant
you ? '

But he said he was afraid it was very difficult, because
the only way was to get a lock of hair from the head of a
king's daughter, to spin it, and to make from it a cloak
for the giant, who lived up on the top of a high mountain.

'Very well,' answered the girl, 'I will go to the city,
and knock at the door of the king's palace, and ask
the princess to take me as a servant.'

So they parted, and when she arrived at the city she
walked about the streets crying, 'Who will hire me for a
servant? Who will hire me for a servant?' But, though
many people liked her looks, for she was clean and neat,
the maiden would listen to none, and still continued
crying, 'Who will hire me for a servant? Who will hire
me for a servant?'

At last there came the waiting-maid of the princess.

'What can you do?' she said ; and the girl was forced
to confess that she could do very little.

'Then you will have to do scullion's work, and wash
up dishes,' said she ; and they went straight back to the
palace.

Then the maiden dressed her hair afresh, and made
herself look very neat and smart, and everyone admired
and praised her, till by-and-bye it came to the ears of the
princess. And she sent for the girl, and when she saw
her, and how beautifully she had dressed her hair, the
princess told her she was to come and comb out hers.

Now the hair of the princess was very thick and
long, and shone like the sun. And the girl combed it and

combed it till it was brighter than ever. And the princess was pleased, and bade her come every day and comb her hair, till at length the girl took courage, and begged leave to cut off one of the long, thick locks.

The princess, who was very proud of her hair, did not like the idea of parting with any of it, so she said no. But the girl could not give up hope, and each day she entreated to be allowed to cut off just one tress. At length the princess lost patience, and exclaimed, ' You may have it, then, on condition that you shall find the handsomest prince in the world to be my bridegroom ! '

And the girl answered that she would, and cut off the lock, and wove it into a coat that glittered like silk, and brought it to the young man, who told her to carry it straight to the giant. But that she must be careful to cry out a long way off what she had with her, or else he would spring upon her and run her through with his sword.

So the maiden departed and climbed up the mountain, but before she reached the top the giant heard her footsteps, and rushed out breathing fire and flame, having a sword in one hand and a club in the other. But she cried loudly that she had brought him the coat, and then he grew quiet, and invited her to come into his house.

He tried on the coat, but it was too short, and he threw it off, and declared it was no use. And the girl picked it up sadly, and returned quite in despair to the king's palace.

The next morning, when she was combing the princess's hair, she begged leave to cut off another lock. At first the princess said no, but the girl begged so hard that at length she gave in on condition that she should find her a prince as bridegroom.

The maiden told her that she had already found him, and spun the lock into shining stuff, and fastened it on to the end of the coat. And when it was finished she carried it to the giant.

THE MAIDEN BRINGS THE COAT OF HAIR TO THE GIANT.

This time it fitted him, and he was quite pleased, and asked her what he could give her in return. And she said that the only reward he could give her was to take the spell off the lion and bring him back to his own shape.

For a long time the giant would not hear of it, but in the end he gave in, and told her exactly how it must all be done. She was to kill the lion herself and cut him up very small; then she must burn him, and cast his ashes into the water, and out of the water the prince would come free from enchantment for ever.

But the maiden went away weeping, lest the giant should have deceived her, and that after she had killed the lion she would find she had also slain the prince.

Weeping she came down the mountain, and weeping she joined the prince, who was awaiting her at the bottom ; and when he had heard her story he comforted her, and bade her be of good courage, and to do the bidding of the giant.

And the maiden believed what the prince told her ; and in the morning when he put on his lion's form she took a knife and slew him, and cut him up very small, and burnt him, and cast his ashes into the water, and out of the water came the prince, beautiful as the day, and as glad to look upon as the sun himself.

Then the young man thanked the maiden for all she had done for him, and said she should be his wife and none other. But the maiden only wept sore, and answered that that she could never be, for she had given her promise to the princess when she cut off her hair that the prince should wed her and her only.

But the prince replied, ' If it is the princess, we must go quickly. Come with me.'

So they went together to the king's palace. And when the king and queen and princess saw the young man a great joy filled their hearts, for they knew him for the eldest son, who had long ago been enchanted by a giant and lost to them.

And he asked his parents' consent that he might marry the girl who had saved him, and a great feast was made, and the maiden became a princess, and in due time a queen, and she richly deserved all the honours showered upon her.

THE GRATEFUL PRINCE

ONCE upon a time the king of the Goldland lost himself in a forest, and try as he would he could not find the way out. As he was wandering down one path which had looked at first more hopeful than the rest he saw a man coming towards him.

'What are you doing here, friend?' asked the stranger; 'darkness is falling fast, and soon the wild beasts will come from their lairs to seek for food.'

'I have lost myself,' answered the king, 'and am trying to get home.'

'Then promise me that you will give me the first thing that comes out of your house, and I will show you the way,' said the stranger.

The king did not answer directly, but after awhile he spoke: 'Why should I give away my *best* sporting dog. I can surely find my way out of the forest as well as this man.'

So the stranger left him, but the king followed path after path for three whole days, with no better success than before. He was almost in despair, when the stranger suddenly appeared, blocking up his way.

'Promise you will give me the first thing that comes out of your house to meet you?'

But still the king was stiff-necked and would promise nothing.

For some days longer he wandered up and down the forest, trying first one path, then another, but his courage at last gave way, and he sank wearily on the ground under

a tree, feeling sure his last hour had come. Then for the
third time the stranger stood before the king, and said :

'Why are you such a fool? What can a dog be to
you, that you should give your life for him like this?
Just promise me the reward I want, and I will guide you
out of the forest.'

'Well, my life is worth more than a thousand dogs,'
answered the king, 'the welfare of my kingdom depends
on me. I accept your terms, so take me to my palace.'
Scarcely had he uttered the words than he found himself
at the edge of the wood, with the palace in the dim
distance. He made all the haste he could, and just as he
reached the great gates out came the nurse with the
royal baby, who stretched out his arms to his father.
The king shrank back, and ordered the nurse to take the
baby away at once. Then his great boarhound bounded
up to him, but his caresses were only answered by a
violent push.

When the king's anger was spent, and he was able to
think what was best to be done, he exchanged his baby,
a beautiful boy, for the daughter of a peasant, and the
prince lived roughly as the son of poor people, while the
little girl slept in a golden cradle, under silken sheets.
At the end of a year, the stranger arrived to claim his
property, and took away the little girl, believing her to
be the true child of the king. The king was so delighted
with the success of his plan that he ordered a great
feast to be got ready, and gave splendid presents to the
foster parents of his son, so that he might lack nothing.
But he did not dare to bring back the baby, lest the trick
should be found out. The peasants were quite contented
with this arrangement, which gave them food and money
in abundance.

By-and-by the boy grew big and tall, and seemed to
lead a happy life in the house of his foster parents. But
a shadow hung over him which really poisoned most of
his pleasure, and that was the thought of the poor

innocent girl who had suffered in his stead, for his foster
father had told him in secret, that he was the king's son.
And the prince determined that when he grew old enough
he would travel all over the world, and never rest till he
had set her free. To become king at the cost of a maiden's
life was too heavy a price to pay. So one day he put
on the dress of a farm servant, threw a sack of peas on
his back, and marched straight into the forest where
eighteen years before his father had lost himself. After
he had walked some way he began to cry loudly: ' Oh,
how unlucky I am ! Where can I be ? Is there no one to
show me the way out of the wood ? '

Then appeared a strange man with a long grey
beard, with a leather bag hanging from his girdle. He
nodded cheerfully to the prince, and said : ' I know this
place well, and can lead you out of it, if you will promise
me a good reward.'

' What can a beggar such as I promise you ? '
answered the prince. ' I have nothing to give you save
my life ; even the coat on my back belongs to my master,
whom I serve for my keep and my clothes.'

The stranger looked at the sack of peas, and said,
' But you must possess something ; you are carrying this
sack, which seems to be very heavy.'

' It is full of peas,' was the reply. ' My old aunt died
last night, without leaving money enough to buy peas
to give the watchers, as is the custom throughout the
country. I have borrowed these peas from my master,
and thought to take a short cut across the forest ; but I
have lost myself, as you see.'

' Then you are an orphan ? ' asked the stranger.
' Why should you not enter my service ? I want a sharp
fellow in the house, and you please me.'

' Why not, indeed, if we can strike a bargain ? ' said
the other. ' I was born a peasant, and strange bread is
always bitter, so it is the same to me whom I serve ! What
wages will you give me ? '

'Every day fresh food, meat twice a week, butter and vegetables, your summer and winter clothes, and a portion of land for your own use.'

The Prince meets a strange man in the wood

'I shall be satisfied with that,' said the youth. 'Somebody else will have to bury my aunt. I will go with you!'

Now this bargain seemed to please the old fellow so much that he spun round like a top, and sang so loud that the whole wood rang with his voice. Then he set out with his companion, and chattered so fast that he never noticed that his new servant kept dropping peas out of the sack. At night they slept under a fig tree, and when the sun rose started on their way. About noon they came to a large stone, and here the old fellow stopped, looked carefully round, gave a sharp whistle, and stamped three times on the ground with his left foot. Suddenly there appeared under the stone a secret door, which led to what looked like the mouth of a cave. The old fellow seized the youth by the arm, and said roughly, ' Follow me ! '

Thick darkness surrounded them, yet it seemed to the prince as if their path led into still deeper depths. After a long while he thought he saw a glimmer of light, but the light was neither that of the sun nor of the moon. He looked eagerly at it, but found it was only a kind of pale cloud, which was all the light this strange underworld could boast. Earth and water, trees and plants, birds and beasts, each was different from those he had seen before ; but what most struck terror into his heart was the absolute stillness that reigned everywhere. Not a rustle or a sound could be heard. Here and there he noticed a bird sitting on a branch, with head erect and swelling throat, but his ear caught nothing. The dogs opened their mouths as if to bark, the toiling oxen seemed about to bellow, but neither bark nor bellow reached the prince. The water flowed noiselessly over the pebbles, the wind bowed the tops of the trees, flies and chafers darted about, without breaking the silence. The old greybeard uttered no word, and when his companion tried to ask him the meaning of it all he felt that his voice died in his throat.

How long this fearful stillness lasted I do not know, but the prince gradually felt his heart turning to ice, his

hair stood up like bristles, and a cold chill was creeping
down his spine, when at last—oh, ecstasy!—a faint noise
broke on his straining ears, and this life of shadows
suddenly became real. It sounded as if a troop of horses
were ploughing their way over a moor.

Then the greybeard opened his mouth, and said : ' The
kettle is boiling ; we are expected at home.'

They walked on a little further, till the prince thought
he heard the grinding of a saw-mill, as if dozens of saws
were working together, but his guide observed, ' The
grandmother is sleeping soundly ; listen how she snores.'

When they had climbed a hill which lay before them
the prince saw in the distance the house of his master,
but it was so surrounded with buildings of all kinds
that the place looked more like a village or even a small
town. They reached it at last, and found an empty
kennel standing in front of the gate. ' Creep inside this,'
said the master, ' and wait while I go in and see my
grandmother. Like all very old people, she is very
obstinate, and cannot bear fresh faces about her.'

The prince crept tremblingly into the kennel, and
began to regret the daring which had brought him into
this scrape.

By-and-by the master came back, and called him
from his hiding-place. Something had put out his temper,
for with a frown he said, ' Watch carefully our ways in
the house, and beware of making any mistake, or it will
go ill with you. Keep your eyes and ears open, and your
mouth shut, obey without questions. Be grateful if you
will, but never speak unless you are spoken to.'

When the prince stepped over the threshold he caught
sight of a maiden of wonderful beauty, with brown eyes
and fair curly hair. ' Well!' the young man said to
himself, ' if the old fellow has many daughters like that
I should not mind being his son-in-law. This one is just
what I admire'; and he watched her lay the table, bring
in the food, and take her seat by the fire as if she had

never noticed that a strange man was present. Then she took out a needle and thread, and began to darn her stockings. The master sat at table alone, and invited neither his new servant nor the maid to eat with him. Neither was the old grandmother anywhere to be seen. His appetite was tremendous : he soon cleared all the dishes, and ate enough to satisfy a dozen men. When at last he could eat no more he said to the girl, ' Now you can pick up the pieces, and take what is left in the iron pot for your own dinner, but give the bones to the dog.'

The prince did not at all like the idea of dining off scraps, which he helped the girl to pick up, but, after all, he found that there was plenty to eat, and that the food was very good. During the meal he stole many glances at the maiden, and would even have spoken to her, but she gave him no encouragement. Every time he opened his mouth for the purpose she looked at him sternly, as· if to say, ' Silence,' so he could only let his eyes speak for him. Besides, the master was stretched on a bench by the oven after his huge meal, and would have heard everything.

After supper that night, the old man said to the prince, ' For two days you may rest from the fatigues of the journey, and look about the house. But the day after to-morrow you must come with me, and I will point out the work you have to do. The maid will show you where you are to sleep.'

The prince thought, from this, he had leave to speak, but his master turned on him with a face of thunder and exclaimed :

' You dog of a servant ! If you disobey the laws of the house you will soon find yourself a head shorter ! Hold your tongue, and leave me in peace.'

The girl made a sign to him to follow her, and, throwing open a door, nodded to him to go in. He would have lingered a moment, for he thought she looked sad, but dared not do so, for fear of the old man's anger.

' It is impossible that she can be his daughter ! ' he said to himself, ' for she has a kind heart. I am quite sure she must be the same girl who was brought here instead of me, so I am bound to risk my head in this mad adventure.' He got into bed, but it was long before he fell asleep, and even then his dreams gave him no rest. He seemed to be surrounded by dangers, and it was only the power of the maiden who helped him through it all.

When he woke his first thoughts were for the girl, whom he found hard at work. He drew water from the well and carried it to the house for her, kindled the fire under the iron pot, and, in fact, did everything that came into his head that could be of any use to her. In the afternoon he went out, in order to learn something of his new home, and wondered greatly not to come across the old grandmother. In his rambles he came to the farm-yard, where a beautiful white horse had a stall to itself ; in another was a black cow with two white-faced calves, while the clucking of geese, ducks, and hens reached him from a distance.

Breakfast, dinner, and supper were as savoury as before, and the prince would have been quite content with his quarters had it not been for the difficulty of keeping silence in the presence of the maiden. On the evening of the second day he went, as he had been told, to receive his orders for the following morning.

' I am going to set you something very easy to do to-morrow,' said the old man when his servant entered. ' Take this scythe and cut as much grass as the white horse will want for its day's feed, and clean out its stall. If I come back and find the manger empty it will go ill with you. So. beware ! '

The prince left the room, rejoicing in his heart, and saying to himself, ' Well, I shall soon get through that ! If I have never yet handled either the plough or the scythe, at least I have often watched the country people work them, and know how easy it is.'

He was just going to open his door, when the maiden glided softly past and whispered in his ear: ' What task has he set you ? '

' For to-morrow,' answered the prince, ' it is really nothing at all! Just to cut hay for the horse, and to clean out his stall ! '

' Oh, luckless being ! ' sighed the girl; ' how will you ever get through with it. The white horse, who is our master's grandmother, is always hungry : it takes twenty men always mowing to keep it in food for one day, and another twenty to clean out its stall. How, then, do you expect to do it all by yourself? But listen to me, and do what I tell you. It is your only chance. When you have filled the manger as full as it will hold you must weave a strong plait of the rushes which grow among the meadow hay, and cut a thick peg of stout wood, and be sure that the horse sees what you are doing. Then it will ask you what it is for, and you will say, ' With this plait I intend to bind up your mouth so that you cannot eat any more, and with this peg I am going to keep you still in one spot, so that you cannot scatter your corn and water all over the place ! ' After these words the maiden went away as softly as she had come.

Early the next morning he set to work. His scythe danced through the grass much more easily than he had hoped, and soon he had enough to fill the manger. He put it in the crib, and returned with a second supply, when to his horror he found the crib empty. Then he knew that without the maiden's advice he would certainly have been lost, and began to put it into practice. He took out the rushes which had somehow got mixed up with the hay, and plaited them quickly.

' My son, what are you doing ? ' asked the horse wonderingly.

' Oh, nothing ! ' replied he. ' Just weaving a chin strap to bind your jaws together, in case you might wish to eat any more ! '

The white horse sighed deeply when it heard this, and made up its mind to be content with what it had eaten.

The youth next began to clean out the stall, and the horse knew it had found a master; and by mid-day there was still fodder in the manger, and the place was as clean as a new pin. He had barely finished when in walked the old man, who stood astonished at the door.

'Is it really you who have been clever enough to do that?' he asked. 'Or has some one else given you a hint?'

'Oh, I have had no help,' replied the prince, 'except what my poor weak head could give me.'

The old man frowned, and went away, and the prince rejoiced that everything had turned out so well.

In the evening his master said, 'To-morrow I have no special task to set you, but as the girl has a great deal to do in the house you must milk the black cow for her. But take care you milk her dry, or it may be the worse for you.'

'Well,' thought the prince as he went away, 'unless there is some trick behind, this does not sound very hard. I have never milked a cow before, but I have good strong fingers.'

He was very sleepy, and was just going toward his room, when the maiden came to him and asked: 'What is your task to-morrow?'

'I am to help you,' he answered, 'and have nothing to do all day, except to milk the black cow dry.'

'Oh, you *are* unlucky,' cried she. 'If you were to try from morning till night you couldn't do it. There is only one way of escaping the danger, and that is, when you go to milk her, take with you a pan of burning coals and a pair of tongs. Place the pan on the floor of the stall, and the tongs on the fire, and blow with all your might, till the coals burn brightly. The black cow will ask you what is the meaning of all this, and you must answer what I will whisper to you.' And she stood on tip-toe and whispered something in his ear, and then went away.

The dawn had scarcely reddened the sky when the prince jumped out of bed, and, with the pan of coals in one hand and the milk pail in the other, went straight to the cow's stall, and began to do exactly as the maiden had told him the evening before.

The black cow watched him with surprise for some time, and then said : 'What are you doing, sonny?'

HOW THE BLACK COW WAS TRICKED

'Oh, nothing,' answered he ; 'I am only heating a pair of tongs in case you may not feel inclined to give as much milk as I want.'

The cow sighed deeply, and looked at the milkman with fear, but he took no notice, and milked briskly into the pail, till the cow ran dry.

Just at that moment the old man entered the stable, and sat down to milk the cow himself, but not a drop of milk could he get. 'Have you really managed it all yourself, or did somebody help you?'

'I have nobody to help me,' answered the prince, 'but

my own poor head.' The old man got up from his seat and went away.

That night, when the prince went to his master to hear what his next day's work was to be, the old man said : ' I have a little hay-stack out in the meadow which must be brought in to dry. To-morrow you will have to stack it all in the shed, and, as you value your life, be careful not to leave the smallest strand behind.' The prince was overjoyed to hear he had nothing worse to do.

'To carry a little hay-rick requires no great skill,' thought he, ' and it will give me no trouble, for the horse will have to draw it in. I am certainly not going to spare the old grandmother.'

By-and-by the maiden stole up to ask what task he had for the next day.

The young man laughed, and said : ' It appears that I have got to learn all kinds of farmer's work. To-morrow I have to carry a hay-rick, and leave not a stalk in the meadow, and that is my whole day's work ! '

' Oh, you unlucky creature ! ' cried she ; ' and how do you think you are to do it. If you had all the men in the world to help you, you could not clear off this one little hay-rick in a week. The instant you have thrown down the hay at the top, it will take root again from below. But listen to what I say. You must steal out at day-break to-morrow and bring out the white horse and some good strong ropes. Then get on the hay-stack, put the ropes round it, and harness the horse to the ropes. When you are ready, climb up the hay-stack and begin to count one, two, three. The horse will ask you what you are counting, and you must be sure to answer what I whisper to you.'

So the maiden whispered something in his ear, and left the room. And the prince knew nothing better to do than to get into bed.

He slept soundly, and it was still almost dark when he

got up and proceeded to carry out the instructions given him by the girl. First he chose some stout ropes, and then he led the horse out of the stable and rode it to the hay-stack, which was made up of fifty cartloads, so that it could hardly be called 'a little one.' The prince did all that the maiden had told him, and when at last he was seated on top of the rick, and had counted up to twenty, he heard the horse ask in amazement: 'What are you counting up there, my son?'

'Oh, nothing,' said he, 'I was just amusing myself with counting the packs of wolves in the forest, but there are really so many of them that I don't think I should ever be done.'

The word 'wolf' was hardly out of his mouth than the white horse was off like the wind, so that in the twinkling of an eye it had reached the shed, dragging the hay-stack behind it. The master was dumb with surprise as he came in after breakfast and found his man's day's work quite done.

'Was it really you who were so clever?' asked he. 'Or did some one give you good advice?'

'Oh, I have only myself to take counsel with,' said the prince, and the old man went away, shaking his head.

Late in the evening the prince went to his master to learn what he was to do next day.

'To-morrow,' said the old man, 'you must bring the white-headed calf to the meadow, and, as you value your life, take care it does not escape from you.'

The prince answered nothing, but thought, 'Well, most peasants of nineteen have got a whole herd to look after, so surely I can manage one.' And he went towards his room, where the maiden met him.

'To-morrow I have got an idiot's work,' said he; 'nothing but to take the white-headed calf to the meadow.'

'Oh, you unlucky being!' sighed she. 'Do you know

that this calf is so swift that in a single day he can run three times round the world? Take heed to what I tell you. Bind one end of this silk thread to the left fore-leg of the calf, and the other end to the little toe of your left foot, so that the calf will never be able to leave your side, whether you walk, stand, or lie.' After this the prince went to bed and slept soundly.

The next morning he did exactly what the maiden had told him, and led the calf with the silken thread to the meadow, where it stuck to his side like a faithful dog.

By sunset, it was back again in its stall, and then came the master and said, with a frown, ' Were you really so clever yourself, or did somebody tell you what to do?'

' Oh, I have only my own poor head,' answered the prince, and the old man went away growling, ' I don't believe a word of it! I am sure you have found some clever friend!'

In the evening he called the prince and said: ' To-morrow I have no work for you, but when I wake you must come before my bed, and give me your hand in greeting.'

The young man wondered at this strange freak, and went laughing in search of the maiden.

' Ah, it is no laughing matter,' sighed she. ' He means to eat you, and there is only one way in which I can help you. You must heat an iron shovel red hot, and hold it out to him instead of your hand.'

So next morning he wakened very early, and had heated the shovel before the old man was awake. At length he heard him calling, ' You lazy fellow, where are you? Come and wish me good morning.' But when the prince entered with the red-hot shovel his master only said, ' I am very ill to-day, and too weak even to touch your hand. You must return this evening, when I may be better.'

The prince loitered about all day, and in the evening went back to the old man's room. He was received in the most friendly manner, and, to his surprise, his master exclaimed, 'I am very well satisfied with you. Come to me at dawn and bring the maiden with you. I know you have long loved each other, and I wish to make you man and wife.'

The young man nearly jumped into the air for joy, but, remembering the rules of the house, he managed to keep still. When he told the maiden, he saw to his astonishment that she had become as white as a sheet, and she was quite dumb.

'The old man has found out who was your counsellor,' she said when she could speak, 'and he means to destroy us both.' We must escape somehow, or else we shall be lost. Take an axe, and cut off the head of the calf with one blow. With a second, split its head in two, and in its brain you will see a bright red ball. Bring that to me. Meanwhile, I will do what is needful here.

And the prince thought to himself, 'Better kill the calf than be killed ourselves. If we can once escape, we will go back home. The peas which I strewed about must have sprouted, so that we shall not miss the way.'

Then he went into the stall, and with one blow of the axe killed the calf, and with the second split its brain. In an instant the place was filled with light, as the red ball fell from the brain of the calf. The prince picked it up, and, wrapping it round with a thick cloth, hid it in his bosom. Mercifully, the cow slept through it all, or by her cries she would have awakened the master.

He looked round, and at the door stood the maiden, holding a little bundle in her arms.

'Where is the ball?' she asked.

'Here,' answered he.

'We must lose no time in escaping, she went on, and uncovered a tiny bit of the shining ball, to light them on their way.

As the prince had expected, the peas had taken root, and grown into a little hedge, so that they were sure they

would not lose the path. As they fled, the girl told him
that she had overheard a conversation between the old
man and his grandmother, saying that she was a king's
daughter, whom the old fellow had obtained by cunning
from her parents. The prince, who knew all about the
affair, was silent, though he was glad from his heart that

it had fallen to his lot to set her free. So they went on
till the day began to dawn.

The old man slept very late that morning, and rubbed
his eyes till he was properly awake. Then he remembered
that very soon the couple were to present themselves
before him. After waiting and waiting till quite a long
time had passed, he said to himself, with a grin, ' Well,
they are not in much hurry to be married,' and waited again.

At last he grew a little uneasy, and cried loudly, 'Man and maid! what has become of you?'

After repeating this many times, he became quite frightened, but, call as he would, neither man nor maid appeared. At last he jumped angrily out of bed to go in search of the culprits, but only found an empty house, and beds that had never been slept in. Then he went straight to the stable, where the sight of the dead calf told him all. Swearing loudly, he opened the door of the third stall quickly, and cried to his goblin servants to go and chase the fugitives. 'Bring them to me, however you may find them, for have them I must!' he said. So spake the old man, and the servants fled like the wind.

The runaways were crossing a great plain, when the maiden stopped. 'Something has happened!' she said. 'The ball moves in my hand, and I'm sure we are being followed!' and behind them they saw a black cloud flying before the wind. Then the maiden turned the ball thrice in her hand, and cried,

> 'Listen to me, my ball, my ball.
> Be quick and change me into a brook,
> And my lover into a little fish.'

And in an instant there was a brook with a fish swimming in it. The goblins arrived just after, but, seeing nobody, waited for a little, then hurried home, leaving the brook and the fish undisturbed. When they were quite out of sight, the brook and the fish returned to their usual shapes and proceeded on their journey.

When the goblins, tired and with empty hands, returned, their master inquired what they had seen, and if nothing strange had befallen them.

'Nothing,' said they; 'the plain was quite empty, save for a brook and a fish swimming in it.'

'Idiots!' roared the master; 'of course it was they!' And dashing open the door of the fifth stall, he told the goblins inside that they must go and drink up the brook, and catch the fish. And the goblins jumped up, and flew like the wind.

The young pair had almost reached the edge of the wood, when the maiden stopped again. 'Something has happened,' said she. 'The ball is moving in my hand,' and looking round she beheld a cloud flying towards them, large and blacker than the first, and striped with red. 'Those are our pursuers,' cried she, and turning the ball three times in her hand she spoke to it thus:

> 'Listen to me, my ball, my ball.
> Be quick and change us both.
> Me into a wild rose bush,
> And him into a rose on my stem.'

And in the twinkling of an eye it was done. Only just in time too, for the goblins were close at hand, and looked round eagerly for the stream and the fish. But neither stream nor fish was to be seen ; nothing but a rose bush. So they went sorrowing home, and when they were out of sight the rose bush and rose returned to their proper shapes and walked all the faster for the little rest they had had.

'Well, did you find them ?' asked the old man when his goblins came back.

'No,' replied the leader of the goblins, 'we found neither brook nor fish in the desert.'

'And did you find nothing else at all ?'

'Oh, nothing but a rose tree on the edge of a wood, with a rose hanging on it.'

'Idiots !' cried he. 'Why, that was they.' And he threw open the door of the seventh stall, where his mightiest goblins were locked in. 'Bring them to me, however you find them, dead or alive !' thundered he, ' for I will have them ! Tear up the rose tree and the roots too, and don't leave anything behind, however strange it may be !'

The fugitives were resting in the shade of a wood, and

were refreshing themselves with food
and drink. Suddenly the maiden
looked up. 'Something has happened,' said she. 'The ball has
nearly jumped out of my bosom!
Some one is certainly following us,
and the danger is near, but the trees
hide our enemies from us.'

As she spoke she took the ball
in her hand, and said :

'Listen to me, my ball, my ball.
 Be quick and change me into a breeze,
 And make my lover into a midge.'

An instant,
and the girl
was dissolved
into thin air,
while the
prince darted

DANGERS FOLLOWING

about like a midge. The next moment a crowd of goblins
rushed up, and looked about in search of something
strange, for neither a rose bush nor anything else was to
be seen. But they had hardly turned their backs to go
home empty-handed when the prince and the maiden
stood on the earth again.

'We must make all the haste we can,' said she, ' before
the old man himself comes to seek us, for he will know
us under any disguise.'

They ran on till they reached such a dark part of
the forest that, if it had not been for the light shed by the
ball, they could not have made their way at all. Worn
out and breathless, they came at length to a large stone,
and here the ball began to move restlessly. The maiden,
seeing this, exclaimed :

> 'Listen to me, my ball, my ball.
> Roll the stone quickly to one side,
> That we may find a door.'

And in a moment the stone had rolled away, and they
had passed through the door to the world again.

'Now we are safe,' cried she. 'Here the old wizard
has no more power over us, and we can guard ourselves
from his spells. But, my friend, we have to part! You
will return to your parents, and I must go in search of
mine.'

'No! no!' exclaimed the prince. 'I will never
part from you. You must come with me and be my wife.
We have gone through many troubles together, and now
we will share our joys.' The maiden resisted his words
for some time, but at last she went with him.

In the forest they met a woodcutter, who told them
that in the palace, as well as in all the land, there had
been great sorrow over the loss of the prince, and many
years had now passed away during which they had found
no traces of him. So, by the help of the magic ball, the
maiden managed that he should put on the same clothes

that he had been wearing at the time he had vanished, so that his father might know him more quickly. She herself stayed behind in a peasant's hut, so that father and son might meet alone.

But the father was no longer there, for the loss of his son had killed him ; and on his deathbed he confessed to his people how he had contrived that the old wizard should carry away a peasant's child instead of the prince, wherefore this punishment had fallen upon him.

The prince wept bitterly when he heard this news, for he had loved his father well, and for three days he ate and drank nothing. But on the fourth day he stood in the presence of his people as their new king, and, calling his councillors, he told them all the strange things that had befallen him, and how the maiden had borne him safe through all.

And the councillors cried with one voice, ' Let her be your wife, and our liege lady.'

And that is the end of the story.

[Ehstnische Märchen.]

AN IMPOSSIBLE ENCHANTMENT

THERE once lived a king who was much loved by his people, and he, too, loved them warmly. He led a very happy life, but he had the greatest dislike to the idea of marrying, nor had he ever felt the slightest wish to fall in love. His subjects begged him to marry, and at last he promised to try to do so. But as, so far, he had never cared for any woman he had seen, he made up his mind to travel in hopes of meeting some lady he could love.

So he arranged all the affairs of state in an orderly manner, and set out, attended by only one equerry, who, though not very clever, had most excellent good sense. These people indeed generally make the best fellow-travellers.

The king explored several countries, doing all he could to fall in love, but in vain; and at the end of two years' journeys he turned his face towards home, with as free a heart as when he set out.

As he was riding along through a forest he suddenly heard the most awful miawing and shrieking of cats you can imagine. The noise drew nearer, and nearer, and at last they saw a hundred huge Spanish cats rush through the trees close to them. They were so closely packed together that you could easily have covered them with a large cloak, and all were following the same track. They were closely pursued by two enormous apes, dressed in purple suits, with the prettiest and best made boots you ever saw.

The apes were mounted on superb mastiffs, and spurred them on in hot haste, blowing shrill blasts on little toy trumpets all the time.

The king and his equerry stood still to watch this strange hunt, which was followed by twenty or more little dwarfs, some mounted on wolves, and leading relays, and others with cats in leash. The dwarfs were all dressed in purple silk liveries like the apes.

A moment later a beautiful young woman mounted on a tiger came in sight. She passed close to the king, riding at full speed, without taking any notice of him ; but he was at once enchanted by her, and his heart was gone in a moment.

To his great joy he saw that one of the dwarfs had fallen behind the rest, and at once began to question him.

The dwarf told him that the lady he had just seen was the Princess Mutinosa, the daughter of the king in whose country they were at that moment. He added that the princess was very fond of hunting, and that she was now in pursuit of rabbits.

The king then asked the way to the court, and having been told it, hurried off, and reached the capital in a couple of hours.

As soon as he arrived, he presented himself to the king and queen, and on mentioning his own name and that of his country, was received with open arms. Not long after, the princess returned, and hearing that the hunt had been very successful, the king complimented her on it, but she would not answer a word.

Her silence rather surprised him, but he was still more astonished when he found that she never spoke once all through supper-time. Sometimes she seemed about to speak, but whenever this was the case her father or mother at once took up the conversation. However, this silence did not cool the king's affection, and when he retired to his rooms at night he confided his feelings to

The King sees
Princess Mutinosa
out hunting

his faithful equerry.   But the equerry was by no means delighted at his king's love affair, and took no pains to hide his disappointment.

'But why are you vexed?' asked the king.   'Surely the princess is beautiful enough to please anyone?'

'She is certainly very handsome,' replied the equerry, ' but to be really happy in love something more than beauty is required.   To tell the truth, sire,' he added, ' her expression seems to me hard.'

'That is pride and dignity,' said the king, 'and nothing can be more becoming.'

'Pride or hardness, as you will,' said the equerry ; ' but to my mind the choice of so many fierce creatures for her amusements seems to tell of a fierce nature, and I also think there is something suspicious in the care taken to prevent her speaking.'

The equerry's remarks were full of good sense ; but as opposition is only apt to increase love in the hearts of men, and especially of kings who hate being contradicted, this king begged, the very next day, for the hand of the Princess Mutinosa.   It was granted him on two conditions.

The first was that the wedding should take place the very next day ; and the second, that he should not speak to the princess till she was his wife ; to all of which the king agreed, in spite of his equerry's objections, so that the first word he heard his bride utter was the ' Yes ' she spoke at their marriage.

Once married, however, she no longer placed any check on herself, and her ladies-in-waiting came in for plenty of rude speeches—even the king did not escape scolding ; but as he was a good-tempered man, and very much in love, he bore it patiently.   A few days after the wedding the newly married pair set out for their kingdom without leaving many regrets behind.

The good equerry's fears proved only too true, as the king found out to his cost.   The young queen made herself most disagreeable to all her court, her spite and bad temper knew no bounds, and before the end of a month she was known far and wide as a regular vixen.

One day, when riding out, she met a poor old woman walking along the road, who made a curtsy and was going on, when the queen had her stopped, and cried: 'You are a very impertinent person; don't you know that I am the queen? And how dare you not make me a deeper curtsy?'

'Madam,' said the old woman, 'I have never learnt how to measure curtsies; but I had no wish to fail in proper respect.'

'What!' screamed the queen; 'she dares to answer! Tie her to my horse's tail and I'll just carry her at once to the best dancing-master in the town to learn how to curtsy.'

The old woman shrieked for mercy, but the queen would not listen, and only mocked when she said she was protected by the fairies. At last the poor old thing submitted to be tied up, but when the queen urged her horse on he never stirred. In vain she spurred him, he seemed turned to bronze. At the same moment the cord with which the old woman was tied changed into wreaths of flowers, and she herself into a tall and stately lady.

Looking disdainfully at the queen, she said, 'Bad woman, unworthy of your crown; I wished to judge for myself whether all I heard of you was true. I have now no doubt of it, and you shall see whether the fairies are to be laughed at.'

So saying the fairy Placida (that was her name) blew a little gold whistle, and a chariot appeared drawn by six splendid ostriches. In it was seated the fairy queen, escorted by a dozen other fairies mounted on dragons.

All having dismounted, Placida told her adventures, and the fairy queen approved all she had done, and proposed turning Mutinosa into bronze like her horse.

Placida, however, who was very kind and gentle, begged for a milder sentence, and at last it was settled that Mutinosa should become her slave for life unless she should have a child to take her place.

The king was told of his wife's fate and submitted to it, which, as he could do nothing to help it, was the only course open to him.

The fairies then all dispersed, Placida taking her slave with her, and on reaching her palace she said : 'You ought by rights to be scullion, but as you have been delicately brought up the change might be too great for you. I shall therefore only order you to sweep my rooms carefully, and to wash and comb my little dog.'

Mutinosa felt there was no use in disobeying, so she did as she was bid and said nothing.

After some time she gave birth to a most lovely little girl, and when she was well again the fairy gave her a good lecture on her past life, made her promise to behave better in future, and sent her back to the king, her husband.

Placida now gave herself up entirely to the little princess who was left in her charge. She anxiously thought over which of the fairies she would invite to be godmothers, so as to secure the best gift, for her adopted child.

At last she decided on two very kindly and cheerful fairies, and asked them to the christening feast. Directly it was over the baby was brought to them in a lovely crystal cradle hung with red silk curtains embroidered with gold.

The little thing smiled so sweetly at the fairies that they decided to do all they could for her. They began by naming her Graziella, and then Placida said : 'You know, dear sisters, that the commonest form of spite or punishment amongst us consists of changing beauty to ugliness, cleverness to stupidity, and oftener still to change a person's form altogether. Now, as we can only each bestow one gift, I think the best plan will be for one of you to give her beauty, the other good understanding, whilst I will undertake that she shall never be changed into any other form.'

The two godmothers quite agreed, and as soon as the little princess had received their gifts, they went home, and Placida gave herself up to the child's education. She succeeded so well with it, and little Graziella grew so lovely, that when she was still quite a child her fame was spread abroad only too much, and one day Placida was surprised by a visit from the Fairy Queen, who was attended by a very grave and severe-looking fairy.

The queen began at once: 'I have been much surprised by your behaviour to Mutinosa; she had insulted our whole race, and deserved punishment. You might forgive your own wrongs if you chose, but not those of others. You treated her very gently whilst she was with you, and I come now to avenge our wrongs on her daughter. You have ensured her being lovely and clever, and not subject to change of form, but I shall place her in an enchanted prison, which she shall never leave till she finds herself in the arms of a lover whom she herself loves. It will be my care to prevent anything of the kind happening.'

The enchanted prison was a large high tower in the midst of the sea, built of shells of all shapes and colours. The lower floor was like a great bathroom, where the water was let in or off at will. The first floor contained the princess's apartments, beautifully furnished. On the second was a library, a large wardrobe-room filled with beautiful clothes and every kind of linen, a music-room, a pantry with bins full of the best wines, and a store-room with all manner of preserves, bonbons, pastry and cakes, all of which remained as fresh as if just out of the oven.

The top of the tower was laid out like a garden, with beds of the loveliest flowers, fine fruit trees, and shady arbours and shrubs, where many birds sang amongst the branches.

The fairies escorted Graziella and her governess, Bonnetta, to the tower, and then mounted a dolphin which was waiting for them. At a little distance from the tower the queen waved her wand and summoned two thousand great fierce sharks, whom she ordered to keep close guard, and not to let a soul enter the tower.

The good governess took such pains with Graziella's education that when she was nearly grown up she was not only most accomplished, but a very sweet, good girl.

One day, as the princess was standing on a balcony, she saw the most extraordinary figure rise out of the sea. She quickly called Bonnetta to ask her what it could be. It looked like some kind of man, with a bluish face and long sea-green hair. He was swimming towards the tower, but the sharks took no notice of him.

'It must be a merman,' said Bonnetta.

'A *man*, do you say?' cried Graziella; 'let us hurry down to the door and see him nearer.'

When they stood in the doorway the merman stopped to look at the princess and made many signs of admiration. His voice was very hoarse and husky, but when he found that he was not understood he took to signs. He carried a little basket made of osiers and filled with rare shells, which he presented to the princess.

She took it with signs of thanks; but as it was getting dusk she retired, and the merman plunged back into the sea.

When they were alone, Graziella said to her governess: 'What a dreadful-looking creature that was! Why do those odious sharks let him come near the tower? I suppose all men are not like him?'

'No, indeed,' replied Bonnetta. 'I suppose the sharks look on him as a sort of relation, and so did not attack him.'

A few days later the two ladies heard a strange sort

of music, and looking out of the window, there was the merman, his head crowned with water plants, and blowing a great sea-shell with all his might.

They went down to the tower door, and Graziella politely accepted some coral and other marine curiosities he had brought her. After this he used to come every evening, and blow his shell, or dive and play antics under the princess's window. She contented herself with bowing to him from the balcony, but she would not go down to the door in spite of all his signs.

Some days later he came with a person of his own kind, but of another sex. Her hair was dressed with great taste, and she had a lovely voice. This new arrival induced the ladies to go down to the door. They were surprised to find that, after trying various languages, she at last spoke to them in their own, and paid Graziella a very pretty compliment on her beauty.

The mermaid noticed that the lower floor was full of water. 'Why,' cried she, 'that is just the place for us, for we can't live quite out of water.' So saying, she and her brother swam in and took up a position in the bathroom, the princess and her governess seating themselves on the steps which ran round the room.

'No doubt, madam,' said the mermaid, 'you have given up living on land so as to escape from crowds of lovers; but I fear that even here you cannot avoid them, for my brother is already dying of love for you, and I am sure that once you are seen in our city he will have many rivals.'

She then went on to explain how grieved her brother was not to be able to make himself understood, adding: 'I interpret for him, having been taught several languages by a fairy.'

'Oh, then, you have fairies, too?' asked Graziella, with a sigh.

'Yes, we have,' replied the mermaid; 'but if I am not mistaken you have suffered from the fairies on earth.'

The princess, on this, told her entire history to the mermaid, who assured her how sorry she felt for her, but begged her not to lose courage; adding, as she took her

The Sea-People visit Graziella

leave: 'Perhaps, some day, you may find a way out of your difficulties.'

The princess was delighted with this visit and with the hopes the mermaid held out. It was something to meet some one fresh to talk to.

'We will make acquaintance with several of these

people,' she said to her governess, ' and I dare say they are not all as hideous as the first one we saw. Anyhow, we shan't be so dreadfully lonely.'

' Dear me,' said Bonnetta, ' how hopeful young people are to be sure! As for me I feel afraid of these folk. But what do you think of the lover you have captivated?'

' Oh, I could never love him,' cried the princess ; ' I can't bear him. But, perhaps, as his sister says they are related to the fairy Marina, they may be of some use to us.'

The mermaid often returned, and each time she talked of her brother's love, and each time Graziella talked of her longing to escape from her prison, till at length the mermaid promised to bring the fairy Marina to see her, in hopes she might suggest something.

Next day the fairy came with the mermaid, and the princess received her with delight. After a little talk she begged Graziella to show her the inside of the tower and let her see the garden on the top, for with the help of crutches she could manage to move about, and being a fairy could live out of water for a long time, provided she wetted her forehead now and then.

Graziella gladly consented, and Bonnetta stayed below with the mermaid.

When they were in the garden the fairy said : ' Let us lose no time, but tell me how I can be of use to you.' Graziella then told all her story and Marina replied : ' My dear princess, I can do nothing for you as regards dry land, for my power does not reach beyond my own element. I can only say that if you will honour my cousin by accepting his hand, you could then come and live amongst us. I could teach you in a moment to swim and dive with the best of us. I can harden your skin without spoiling its colour. My cousin is one of the best matches in the sea, and I will bestow so many gifts on him that you will be quite happy.'

The fairy talked so well and so long that the princess was rather impressed, and promised to think the matter over.

Just as they were going to leave the garden they saw a ship sailing nearer the tower than any other had done before. On the deck lay a young man under a splendid awning, gazing at the tower through a spy-glass; but before they could see anything clearly the ship moved away, and the two ladies parted, the fairy promising to return shortly.

As soon as she was gone Graziella told her governess what she had said. Bonnetta was not at all pleased at the turn matters were taking, for she did not fancy being turned into a mermaid in her old age. She thought the matter well over, and this was what she did. She was a very clever artist, and next morning she began to paint a picture of a handsome young man, with beautiful curly hair, a fine complexion, and lovely blue eyes. When it was finished she showed it to Graziella, hoping it would show her the difference there was between a fine young man and her marine suitor.

The princess was much struck by the picture, and asked anxiously whether there could be any man so good-looking in the world. Bonnetta assured her that there were plenty of them; indeed, many far handsomer.

'I can hardly believe that,' cried the princess; 'but, alas! if there are, I don't suppose I shall ever see them or they me, so what is the use? Oh, dear, how unhappy I am!'

She spent the rest of the day gazing at the picture, which certainly had the effect of spoiling all the merman's hopes or prospects.

After some days, the fairy Marina came back to hear what was decided; but Graziella hardly paid any attention to her, and showed such dislike to the idea of the proposed marriage that the fairy went off in a regular huff.

Without knowing it, the princess had made another

conquest. On board the ship which had sailed so near was the handsomest prince in the world. He had heard of the enchanted tower, and determined to get as near it as he could. He had strong glasses on board, and whilst looking through them he saw the princess quite clearly, and fell desperately in love with her at once. He wanted to steer straight for the tower and to row off to it in a small boat, but his entire crew fell at his feet and begged him not to run such a risk. The captain, too, urged him not to attempt it. 'You will only lead us all to certain death,' he said. 'Pray anchor nearer land, and I will then seek a kind fairy I know, who has always been most obliging to me, and who will, I am sure, try to help your Highness.'

The prince rather unwillingly listened to reason. He landed at the nearest point, and sent off the captain in all haste to beg the fairy's advice and help. Meantime he had a tent pitched on the shore, and spent all his time gazing at the tower and looking for the princess through his spyglass.

After a few days the captain came back, bringing the fairy with him. The prince was delighted to see her, and paid her great attention. 'I have heard about this matter,' she said; 'and, to lose no time, I am going to send off a trusty pigeon to test the enchantment. If there is any weak spot he is sure to find it out and get in. I shall bid him bring a flower back as a sign of success, and if he does so I quite hope to get you in too.'

'But,' asked the prince, 'could I not send a line by the pigeon to tell the princess of my love?'

'Certainly,' replied the fairy, 'it would be a very good plan.'

So the prince wrote as follows :—

'Lovely Princess,—I adore you, and beg you to accept my heart, and to believe there is nothing I will not do to end your misfortunes.—BLONDEL.'

This note was tied round the pigeon's neck, and he

flew off with it at once.   He flew fast till he got near the tower, when a fierce wind blew so hard against him that he could not get on.   But he was not to be beaten, but flew carefully round the top of the tower till he came to one spot which, by some mistake, had not been enchanted like the rest.   He quickly slipped into the arbour and waited for the princess.

Before long Graziella appeared alone, and the pigeon at once fluttered to meet her, and seemed so tame that she stopped to caress the pretty creature.   As she did so she saw it had a pink ribbon round its neck, and tied to the ribbon was a letter.   She read it over several times and then wrote this answer :—

'You say you love me ; but I cannot promise to love you without seeing you.   Send me your portrait by this faithful messenger.   If I return it to you, you must give up hope ; but if I keep it you will know that to help me will be to help yourself.—GRAZIELLA.'

Before flying back the pigeon remembered about the flower, so, seeing one in the princess's dress, he stole it and flew away.

The prince was wild with joy at the pigeon's return with the note.   After an hour's rest the trusty little bird was sent back again, carrying a miniature of the prince, which by good luck he had with him.

On reaching the tower the pigeon found the princess in the garden,   She hastened to untie the ribbon, and on opening the miniature case what was her surprise and delight to find it very like the picture her governess had painted for her.   She hastened to send the pigeon back, and you can fancy the prince's joy when he found she had kept his portrait.

'Now,' said the fairy, 'let us lose no more time.   I can only make you happy by changing you into a bird, but I will take care to give you back your proper shape at the right time.'

The prince was eager to start, so the fairy, touching

him with her wand, turned him into the loveliest humming-bird you ever saw, at the same time letting him keep the power of speech. The pigeon was told to show him the way.

Graziella was much surprised to see a perfectly strange bird, and still more so when it flew to her saying, 'Good-morning, sweet princess.'

She was delighted with the pretty creature, and let him perch on her finger, when he said, 'Kiss, kiss, little birdie,' which she gladly did, petting and stroking him at the same time.

After a time the princess, who had been up very early, grew tired, and as the sun was hot she went to lie down on a mossy bank in the shade of the arbour. She held the pretty bird near her breast, and was just falling asleep, when the fairy contrived to restore the prince to his own shape, so that as Graziella opened her eyes she found herself in the arms of a lover whom she loved in return!

At the same moment her enchantment came to an end. The tower began to rock and to split. Bonnetta hurried up to the top so that she might at least perish with her dear princess. Just as she reached the garden, the kind fairy who had helped the prince arrived with the fairy Placida, in a car of Venetian glass drawn by six eagles.

'Come away quickly,' they cried, 'the tower is about to sink!' The prince, princess, and Bonnetta lost no time in stepping into the car, which rose in the air just as, with a terrible crash, the tower sank into the depths of the sea, for the fairy Marina and the mermen had destroyed its foundations to avenge themselves on Graziella. Luckily their wicked plans were defeated, and the good fairies took their way to the kingdom of Graziella's parents.

They found that Queen Mutinosa had died some years ago, but her kind husband lived on peaceably,

The Fairy-Car Arrives.

ruling his country well and happily. He received his daughter with great delight, and there were universal rejoicings at the return of the lovely princess.

The wedding took place the very next day, and, for many days after, balls, dinners, tournaments, concerts and all sorts of amusements went on all day and all night.

All the fairies were carefully invited, and they came in great state, and promised the young couple their protection and all sorts of good gifts. Prince Blondel and Princess Graziella lived to a good old age, beloved by every one, and loving each other more and more as time went on.

DORANI

ONCE upon a time there lived in a city of Hindustan a seller of scents and essences, who had a very beautiful daughter named Dorani. This maiden had a friend who was a fairy, and the two were high in favour with Indra, the king of fairyland, because they were able to sing so sweetly and dance so deftly that no one in the kingdom could equal them for grace and beauty. Dorani had the most lovely hair in the world, for it was like spun gold, and the smell of it was like the smell of fresh roses. But her locks were so long and thick that the weight of it was often unbearable, and one day she cut off a shining tress, and wrapping it in a large leaf, threw it in the river which ran just below her window. Now it happened that the king's son was out hunting, and had gone down to the river to drink, when there floated towards him a folded leaf, from which came a perfume of roses. The prince, with idle curiosity, took a step into the water and caught the leaf as it was sailing by. He opened it, and within he found a lock of hair like spun gold, and from which came a faint, exquisite odour.

When the prince reached home that day he looked so sad and was so quiet that his father wondered if any ill had befallen him, and asked what was the matter. Then the youth took from his breast the tress of hair which he had found in the river, and holding it up to the light, replied :

'See, my father, was ever hair like this ? Unless I may win and marry the maiden that owns that lock I must die ! '

" *He never could persuade her to say a single word* "

So the king immediately sent heralds throughout all
his dominions to search for the damsel with hair like spun
gold; and at last he learned that she was the daughter
of the scent-seller. The object of the herald's mission
was quickly noised abroad, and Dorani heard of it with
the rest; and, one day, she said to her father :

'If the hair is mine, and the king requires me to
marry his son I must do so; but, remember, you must
tell him that if, after the wedding, I stay all day at the
palace, every night will be spent in my old home.'

The old man listened to her with amazement, but
answered nothing, as he knew she was wiser than he.
Of course the hair was Dorani's, and the heralds soon
returned and informed the king, their master, who summoned the scent-seller, and told him that he wished for
his daughter to be given in marriage to the prince. The
father bowed his head three times to the ground, and
replied :

'Your highness is our lord, and all that you bid us we
will do. The maiden asks this only—that if, after the
wedding, she stays all day at the palace, she may go back
each night to her father's house.'

The king thought this a very strange request; but
said to himself it was, after all, his son's affair, and the
girl would surely soon get tired of going to and fro.
So he made no difficulty, and everything was speedily
arranged and the wedding was celebrated with great
rejoicings.

At first, the condition attaching to his wedding with
the lovely Dorani troubled the prince very little, for he
thought that he would at least see his bride all day.
But, to his dismay, he found that she would do nothing
but sit the whole time upon a stool with her head bowed
forward upon her knees, and he could never persuade her
to say a single word. Each evening she was carried in a
palanquin to her father's house, and each morning she
was brought back soon after daybreak; and yet never a

sound passed her lips, nor did she show by any sign that she saw, or heard, or heeded her husband.

One evening the prince, very unhappy and troubled, was wandering in an old and beautiful garden near the palace. The gardener was a very aged man, who had served the prince's great grandfather; and when he saw the prince he came and bowed himself to him, and said :

' Child ! child ! why do you look so sad—is aught the matter ? ' Then the prince replied, ' I am sad, old friend, because I have married a wife as lovely as the stars, but she will not speak to me, and I know not what to do. Night after night she leaves me for her father's house, and day after day she sits in mine as though turned to stone, and utters no word, whatever I may do or say.'

The old man stood thinking for a moment, and then he hobbled off to his own cottage. A little later he came back to the prince with five or six small packets, which he placed in his hands and said :

' To-morrow, when your bride leaves the palace, sprinkle the powder from one of these packets upon your body, and while seeing clearly, you will become yourself invisible. More I cannot do for you, but may all go well ! '

And the prince thanked him, and put the packets carefully away in his turban.

The next night, when Dorani left for her father's house in her palanquin, the prince took out a packet of the magic powder and sprinkled it over himself, and then hurried after her. He soon found that, as the old man had promised, he was invisible to everyone, although he felt as usual, and could see all that passed. He speedily overtook the palanquin and walked beside it to the scent-seller's dwelling. There it was set down, and, when his bride, closely veiled, left it and entered the house, he, too, entered unperceived.

At the first door Dorani removed one veil; then she entered another doorway at the end of a passage where she removed another veil; next she mounted the stairs, and at the door of the women's quarters removed a third veil. After this she proceeded to her own room where were set two large basins, one of attar of roses and one of water; in these she washed herself, and afterwards called for food. A servant brought her a bowl of curds, which she ate hastily, and then arrayed herself in a robe of silver, and wound about her strings of pearls, while a wreath of roses crowned her hair. When fully dressed, she seated herself upon a four-legged stool over which was a canopy with silken curtains, these she drew around her, and then called out:

'Fly, stool, to the palace of rajah Indra.'

Instantly the stool rose in the air, and the invisible prince, who had watched all these proceedings with great wonder, seized it by one leg as it flew away, and found himself being borne through the air at a rapid rate.

In a short while they arrived at the house of the fairy who, as I told you before, was the favourite friend of Dorani. The fairy stood waiting on the threshold, as beautifully dressed as Dorani herself was, and when the stool stopped at her door she cried in astonishment:

'Why, the stool is flying all crooked to-day! What is the reason of that, I wonder? I suspect that you have been talking to your husband, and so it will not fly straight.'

But Dorani declared that she had not spoken one word to him, and she couldn't think why the stool flew as if weighed down at one side. The fairy still looked doubtful, but made no answer, and took her seat beside Dorani, the prince again holding tightly one leg. Then the stool flew on through the air until it came to the palace of Indra the rajah.

All through the night the women sang and danced before the rajah Indra, whilst a magic lute played of itself the most bewitching music; till the prince, who sat watching it all, was quite entranced. Just before dawn the rajah gave the signal to cease; and again the two women seated themselves on the stool, and, with the prince clinging to the leg, it flew back to earth, and bore Dorani and her husband safely to the scent-seller's shop.

THE INVISIBLE PRINCE GOES WITH THE LADIES

Here the prince hurried away by himself past Dorani's palanquin with its sleepy bearers, straight on to the palace; and as he passed the threshold of his own rooms he became visible again. Then he lay down upon a couch and waited for Dorani's arrival.

As soon as she arrived she took a seat and remained as silent as usual, with her head bowed on her knees. For a while not a sound was heard, but presently the prince said :

'I dreamed a curious dream last night, and as it was all about you I am going to tell it you, although you heed nothing.'

The girl, indeed, took no notice of his words, but in spite of that he proceeded to relate every single thing that had happened the evening before, leaving out no detail of all that he had seen or heard. And when he praised her singing—and his voice shook a little—Dorani just looked at him ; but she said naught, though, in her own mind, she was filled with wonder. 'What a dream !' she thought. 'Could it have been a dream? How could he have learnt in a dream all she had done or said?' Still she kept silent ; only she looked that once at the prince, and then remained all day as before, with her head bowed upon her knees.

When night came the prince again made himself invisible and followed her. The same things happened again as had happened before, but Dorani sang better than ever. In the morning the prince a second time told Dorani all that she had done, pretending that he had dreamt of it. Directly he had finished Dorani gazed at him, and said :

'Is it true that you dreamt this, or were you really there ?'

'I was there,' answered the prince.

'But why do you follow me ?' asked the girl.

'Because,' replied the prince, 'I love you, and to be with you is happiness.'

This time Dorani's eyelids quivered ; but she said no more, and was silent the rest of the day. However, in the evening, just as she was stepping into her palanquin, she said to the prince :

'If you love me, prove it by not following me to-night."

And so the prince did as she wished, and stayed at home.

That evening the magic stool flew so unsteadily that they could hardly keep their seats, and at last the fairy exclaimed :

'There is only one reason that it should jerk like this ! You have been talking to your husband !'

And Dorani replied : 'Yes, I have spoken ; oh, yes, I have spoken !' But no more would she say.

That night Dorani sang so marvellously that at the end the rajah Indra rose up and vowed that she might ask what she would and he would give it to her. At first she was silent ; but, when he pressed her, she answered :

'Give me the magic lute.'

The rajah, when he heard this, was displeased with himself for having made so rash a promise, because this lute he valued above all his possessions. But as he had promised, so he must perform, and with an ill grace he handed it to her.

'You must never come here again,' said he, 'for, once having asked so much, how will you in future be content with smaller gifts ?'

Dorani bowed her head silently as she took the lute, and passed with the fairy out of the great gate, where the stool awaited them. More unsteadily than before, it flew back to earth.

When Dorani got to the palace that morning she asked the prince whether he had dreamt again. He laughed with happiness, for this time she had spoken to him of her own free will ; and he replied :

'No ; but I begin to dream now—not of what *has* happened in the past, but of what *may* happen in the future.'

That day Dorani sat very quietly, but she answered the prince when he spoke to her ; and when evening fell, and with it the time for her departure, she still sat on. Then the prince came close to her and said softly :

'Are you not going to your house, Dorani?'

At that she rose and threw herself weeping into his arms, whispering gently :

'Never again, my lord, never again would I leave thee!'

So the prince won his beautiful bride; and though they neither of them dealt any further with fairies and their magic, they learnt more daily of the magic of Love, which one may still learn, although fairy magic has fled away.

[Punjâbi story, Major Campbell, Feroshepcre.]

THE STORY OF LITTLE KING LOC

Two or three miles from the coast of France, anyone sailing in a ship on a calm day can see, deep, deep down, the trunks of great trees standing up in the water. Many hundreds of years ago these trees formed part of a large forest, full of all sorts of wild animals, and beyond the forest was a fine city, guarded by a castle in which dwelt the Dukes of Clarides. But little by little the sea drew nearer to the town; the foundations of the houses became undermined and fell in, and at length a shining sea flowed over the land. However, all this happened a long time after the story I am going to tell you.

The Dukes of Clarides had always lived in the midst of their people, and protected them both in war and peace.

At the period when this tale begins the Duke Robert was dead, leaving a young and beautiful duchess who ruled in his stead. Of course everyone expected her to marry again, but she refused all suitors who sought her hand, saying that having only one soul she could have only one husband, and that her baby daughter was quite enough for her.

One day she was sitting in the tower, which looked out over a rocky heath, covered in summer with purple and yellow flowers, when she beheld a troop of horsemen riding towards the castle. In the midst, seated on a white horse with black and silver trappings, was a lady whom the duchess at once knew to be her friend the

Countess of Blanchelande, a young widow like herself, mother of a little boy two years older than Abeille des Clarides. The duchess hailed her arrival with delight, but her joy was soon turned into weeping when the countess sank down beside her on a pile of cushions, and told the reason of her visit.

'As you know,' she said, taking her friend's hand and pressing it between her own, 'whenever a Countess of Blanchelande is about to die she finds a white rose lying on her pillow. Last night I went to bed feeling unusually happy, but this morning when I woke the rose was resting against my cheek. I have no one to help me in the world but you, and I have come to ask if you will take Youri my son, and let him be a brother to Abeille?'

Tears choked the voice of the duchess, but she flung herself on the countess's neck, and pressed her close. Silently the two women took leave of each other, and silently the doomed lady mounted her horse and rode home again. Then, giving her sleeping boy into the care of Francœur, her steward, she laid herself quietly on her bed, where, the next morning, they found her dead and peaceful.

So Youri and Abeille grew up side by side, and the duchess faithfully kept her promise, and was a mother to them both. As they got bigger she often took them with her on her journeys through her duchy, and taught them to know her people, and to pity and to aid them.

It was on one of these journeys that, after passing through meadows covered with flowers, Youri caught sight of a great glittering expanse lying beneath some distant mountains.

'What is that, godmother?' he asked, waving his hand. 'The shield of a giant, I suppose.'

'No; a silver plate as big as the moon!' said Abeille, twisting herself round on her pony.

'It is neither a silver plate nor a giant's shield,' replied the duchess; 'but a beautiful lake. Still, in spite of its beauty, it is dangerous to go near it, for in its depths dwell some Undines, or water spirits, who lure all passers-by to their deaths.'

Nothing more was said about the lake, but the children did not forget it, and one morning, after they had returned to the castle, Abeille came up to Youri.

'The tower door is open,' whispered she; 'let us go up. Perhaps we shall find some fairies.'

But they did not find any fairies; only, when they reached the roof, the lake looked bluer and more enchanting than ever. Abeille gazed at it for a moment, and then she said:

'Do you see? I mean to go there!'

'But you mustn't,' cried Youri. 'You heard what your mother said. And, besides, it is so far; how could we get there?'

'*You* ought to know that,' answered Abeille scornfully. 'What is the good of being a man, and learning all sorts of things, if you have to ask me. However, there are plenty of other men in the world, and I shall get one of them to tell me.'

Youri coloured; Abeille had never spoken like this before, and, instead of being two years younger than himself, she suddenly seemed many years older. She stood with her mocking eyes fixed on him, till he grew angry at being outdone by a girl, and taking her hand he said boldly:

'Very well, we will *both* go to the lake.'

The next afternoon, when the duchess was working at her tapestry surrounded by her maidens, the children went out, as usual, to play in the garden. The moment they found themselves alone, Youri turned to Abeille, and holding out his hand, said:

'Come.'

'Come where?.' asked Abeille, opening her eyes very wide.

'To the lake, of course,' answered the boy.

Abeille was silent. It was one thing to pretend you meant to be disobedient some day, a long time off, and quite another to start for such a distant place without anyone knowing that you had left the garden. 'And in satin shoes, too! How stupid boys were, to be sure!'

'Stupid or not, I am going to the lake, and you are going with me!' said Youri, who had not forgotten or forgiven the look she had cast on him the day before. 'Unless,' added he, 'you are afraid, and in that case I shall go alone.'

This was too much for Abeille. Bursting into tears, she flung herself on Youri's neck, and declared that wherever he went she would go too. So, peace having been made between them, they set out.

It was a hot day, and the townspeople were in-doors waiting till the sun was low in the sky before they set out either to work or play, so the children passed through the streets unperceived, and crossed the river by the bridge into the flowery meadows along the road by which they had ridden with the duchess. By-and-by Abeille began to feel thirsty, but the sun had drunk up all the water, and not a drop was left for her. They walked on a little further, and by good luck found a cherry-tree covered with ripe fruit, and after a rest and a refreshing meal, they were sure that they were strong enough to reach the lake in a few minutes. But soon Abeille began to limp and to say that her foot hurt her, and Youri had to untie the ribbons that fastened her shoe and see what was the matter. A stone had got in, so this was easily set right, and for a while they skipped along the path singing and chattering, till Abeille stopped again. This time her shoe had come off, and turning to pick it up she caught sight of the towers of the castle,

ABEILLE FINDS HERSELF AMONG THE LITTLE MEN

looking such a long way off that her heart sank, and she burst into tears.

'It is getting dark, and the wolves will eat us,' sobbed she. But Youri put his arms round her and comforted her.

'Why, we are close to the lake now. There is nothing to be afraid of! We shall be home again to supper,' cried he. And Abeille dried her eyes, and trotted on beside him.

Yes, the lake was there, blue and silvery with purple and gold irises growing on its banks, and white water-lilies floated on its bosom. Not a trace was there of a man, or of one of the great beasts so much feared by Abeille, but only the marks of tiny forked feet on the sand. The little girl at once pulled off her torn shoes and stockings and let the water flow over her, while Youri looked about for some nuts or strawberries. But none were to be found.

'I noticed, a little way back, a clump of blackberry bushes,' said he. 'Wait here for me, and I will go and gather some fruit, and after that we will start home again.' And Abeille, leaning her head drowsily against a cushion of soft moss, murmured something in reply, and soon fell asleep. In her dream a crow, bearing the smallest man that ever was seen, appeared hovering for a moment above her, and then vanished. At the same instant Youri returned and placed by her side a large leaf-full of strawberries.

'It is a pity to wake her just yet,' thought he, and wandered off beyond a clump of silvery willows to a spot from which he could get a view of the whole lake. In the moonlight, the light mist that hung over the surface made it look like fairyland. Then gradually the silver veil seemed to break up, and the shapes of fair women with outstretched hands and long green locks floated towards him. Seized with a sudden fright, the boy turned to fly. But it was too late.

Unconscious of the terrible doom that had befallen her foster-brother, Abeille slept on, and did not awake even when a crowd of little men with white beards down to their knees came and stood in a circle round her.

'What shall we do with her?' asked Pic, who seemed older than any of them, though they were all very old.

'Build a cage and put her into it,' answered Rug.

'No! No! What should such a beautiful princess do in a cage?' cried Dig. And Tad, who was the kindest of them all, proposed to carry her home to her parents. But the other gnomes were too pleased with their new toy to listen to this for a moment.

'Look, she is waking,' whispered Pau. And as he spoke Abeille slowly opened her eyes. At first she imagined she was still dreaming; but as the little men did not move, it suddenly dawned upon her that they were real, and starting to her feet, she called loudly:

'Youri! Youri! Where are you?'

At the sound of her voice the gnomes only pressed more closely round her, and, trembling with fear, she hid her face in her hands. The gnomes were at first much puzzled to know what to do; then Tad, climbing on a branch of the willow tree that hung over her, stooped down, and gently stroked her fingers. The child understood that he meant to be kind, and letting her hands fall, gazed at her captors. After an instant's pause she said:

'Little men, it is a great pity that you are so ugly. But, all the same, I will love you if you will only give me something to eat, as I am dying of hunger.'

A rustle was heard among the group as she spoke. Some were very angry at being called ugly, and said she deserved no better fate than to be left where she was. Others laughed, and declared that it did not matter what a mere mortal thought about them; while Tad bade Bog, their messenger, fetch her some milk and honey and the

finest white bread that was made in their ovens under
the earth.   In less time than Abeille would have taken
to tie her shoe he was back again, mounted on his crow.
And by the time she had eaten the bread and honey and
drunk the milk, Abeille was not frightened any more,
and felt quite ready to talk.

'Little men,' she said, looking up with a smile,
'your supper was very good, and I thank you for it.
My name is Abeille, and my brother is called Youri.
Help me to find him, and tell me which is the path that
leads to the castle, for mother must think something
dreadful has happened to us!'

'But your feet are so sore that you cannot walk,'
answered Dig.   'And we may not cross the bounds into
your country.   The best we can do is to make a litter of
twigs and cover it with moss, and we will bear you into
the mountains, and present you to our king.'

Now, many a little girl would have been terrified at
the thought of being carried off alone, she did not know
where.   But Abeille, when she had recovered from her
first fright, was pleased at the notion of her strange
adventure.

'How much she would have to tell her mother and
Youri on her return home!   Probably *they* would never
go inside a mountain, if they lived to be a hundred.'   So
she curled herself comfortably on her nest of moss, and
waited to see what would happen.

Up, and up, and up, they went; and by-and-by Abeille
fell asleep again, and did not wake till the sun was shining.
Up, and up, and up, for the little men could only walk very
slowly, though they could spring over rocks quicker than
any mortal.   Suddenly the light that streamed through
the branches of the litter began to change.   It seemed
hardly less bright, but it was certainly different; then
the litter was put down, and the gnomes crowded round
and helped Abeille to step out of it.

Before her stood a little man not half her size, but

splendidly dressed and full of dignity. On his head was a crown of such huge diamonds that you wondered how his small body could support it. A royal mantle fell from his shoulders, and in his hand he held a lance.

'King Loc,' said one of the forest gnomes, 'we found this beautiful child asleep by the lake, and have brought her to you. She says that her name is Abeille, and her mother is the Duchesse des Clarides.'

'You have done well,' answered the king; 'she shall be one of us.' And standing on tiptoe, so that he could kiss her hand, he told her that they would all take care of her and make her happy, and that anything she wished for she should have at once.

'I want a pair of shoes,' replied Abeille.

'Shoes!' commanded the king, striking the ground with his lance; and immediately a lovely pair of silver shoes embroidered with pearls were slipped on her feet by one of the gnomes.

'They are beautiful shoes,' said Abeille rather doubtfully; 'but do you think they will carry me all the way back to my mother?'

'No, they are not meant for rough roads,' replied the king, 'but for walking about the smooth paths of the mountain, for we have many wonders to show you.'

'Little King Loc,' answered Abeille, 'take away these beautiful slippers and give me a pair of wooden shoes instead, and let me go back to my mother.' But King Loc only shook his head.

'Little King Loc,' said Abeille again—and this time her voice trembled—'let me go back to my mother and Youri, and I will love you with all my heart, nearly as well as I love them.'

'Who is Youri?' asked King Loc.

'Why—Youri—who has lived with us since I was a baby,' replied Abeille; surprised that he did not know what everyone else was aware of, and never guessing that by mentioning the boy she was sealing her own fate. For King Loc had already thought what a good wife she would make in a few years' time, and he did not want Youri to come between them. So he was silent, and Abeille, seeing he was not pleased, burst into tears.

'Little King Loc,' she cried, taking hold of a corner of his mantle, 'think how unhappy my mother will be. She will fancy that wild beasts have eaten me, or that I have got drowned in the lake.'

'Be comforted,' replied King Loc; 'I will send her a dream, so that she shall know that you are safe.'

At this Abeille's sad face brightened. 'Little King Loc,' she said, smiling, 'how clever you are! But you must send her a dream every night, so that she shall see *me*—and *me* a dream, so that I may see her.'

And this King Loc promised to do.

When Abeille grew accustomed to do without her mother and Youri, she made herself happy enough in her new home. Everyone was kind to her, and petted her, and then there were such quantities of new things for her to see. The gnomes were always busy, and knew how to fashion beautiful toys as well or better than the people who lived on the earth; and now and then, wandering with Tad or Dig in the underground passages, Abeille would catch a glimpse of blue sky through a rent in the rocks, and this she loved best of all. In this manner six years passed away.

'His Highness King Loc wishes to see you in his presence chamber,' said Tad, one morning, to Abeille, who was singing to herself on a golden lute; and Abeille, wondering why the king had grown so formal all of a sudden, got up obediently. Directly she appeared, King Loc opened a door in the wall which led into his treasure chamber. Abeille had never been there before, and was amazed at the splendid things heaped up before her. Gold, jewels, brocades, carpets, lay round the walls, and she walked about examining one glittering object after another, while King Loc mounted a throne of gold and

ivory at one end of the hall, and watched her. 'Choose
whatever you wish,' he said at last. A necklace of most
lovely pearls was hanging from the wall, and after
hesitating for a moment between that and a circlet of
diamonds and sapphires, Abeille stretched up her hand
towards it. But before she touched it her eyes lighted
on a tiny piece of sky visible through a crack of the rock,
and her hand dropped by her side. 'Little King Loc,
let me go up to the earth once again,' she said.

Then King Loc made a sign to the treasurer, who
opened a coffer full of nothing but precious stones, larger
and more dazzling than were worn by any earthly
monarch. 'Choose what you will, Abeille,' whispered
King Loc.

But Abeille only shook her head.

'A drop of dew in the garden at Clarides is brighter
to me than the best of those diamonds,' she answered,
'and the bluest of the stones are not as blue as the eyes
of Youri.' And as she spoke a sharp pain ran through the
heart of King Loc. For an instant he said nothing, then
he lifted his head and looked at her. 'Only those who
despise riches should possess them. Take this crown,
from henceforth you are the Princess of the Gnomes.'

During thirty days no work was done in those underground regions, for a feast was held in honour of the new
princess. At the end of that period the king appeared
before Abeille, clad in his most splendid garments, and
solemnly asked her to be his wife.

'Little King Loc,' answered the girl, 'I love you as
you are, for your goodness and kindness to me; but
never, never can I love you as anything else.'

The king sighed. It was only what he had expected;
still, his disappointment was great, though he tried bravely
to hide it, and even to smile as he said: 'Then, Abeille,
will you promise me one thing? If there should come a
day when you find that there is somebody whom you
could love, will you tell me?'

And in her turn Abeille promised.

After this, in spite of the fact that everyone was just as kind to her as before, Abeille was no longer the merry child who passed all her days playing with the little gnomes. People who dwell under the earth grow up much faster than those who live on its surface, and, at thirteen, the girl was already a woman. Besides, King Loc's words had set her thinking; she spent many hours by herself, and her face was no longer round and rosy, but thin and pale. It was in vain that the gnomes did their best to entice her into her old games, they had lost their interest, and even her lute lay unnoticed on the ground.

But one morning a change seemed to come over her. Leaving the room hung with beautiful silks, where she usually sat alone, she entered the king's presence, and taking his hand she led him through long corridors till they came to a place where a strip of blue sky was to be seen.

'Little King Loc,' she said, turning her eyes upon him, ' let me behold my mother again, or I shall surely die.' Her voice shook, and her whole body trembled. Even an enemy might have pitied her ; but the king, who loved her, answered nothing. All day long Abeille stayed there, watching the light fade, and the sky grow pale. By-and-by the stars came out, but the girl never moved from her place. Suddenly a hand touched her. She looked round with a start, and there was King Loc, covered from head to foot in a dark mantle, holding another over his arm. ' Put on this and follow me,' was all he said. But Abeille somehow knew that she was going to see her mother.

On, and on, and on they went, through passages where Abeille had never been before, and at length she was out in the world again. Oh! how beautiful it all was! How fresh was the air, and how sweet was the smell of the flowers ! She felt as if she should die with joy ; but at that moment King Loc lifted her off the ground, and, tiny though he was, carried her quite easily across the garden and through an open door into the silent castle.

'Listen, Abeille,' he whispered softly. 'You have guessed where we are going, and you know that every night I send your mother a vision of you, and she talks to it in her dream, and smiles at it. To-night it will be no vision she sees, but you yourself; only remember, that if you touch her or speak to her my power is lost, and never more will she behold either you or your image.'

By this time they had reached the room which Abeille knew so well, and her heart beat violently as the gnome carried her over the threshold. By the light of a lamp hanging over the bed Abeille could see her mother, beautiful still, but with a face that had grown pale and sad. As she gazed the sadness vanished, and a bright smile came in its stead. Her mother's arms were stretched out towards her, and the girl, her eyes filled with tears of joy, was stooping to meet them, when King Loc hastily snatched her up, and bore her back to the realm of the gnomes.

If the king imagined that by granting Abeille's request he would make her happy, he soon found out his mistake, for all day long the girl sat weeping, paying no heed to the efforts of her friends to comfort her.

'Tell me what is making you so unhappy?' said King Loc, at last. And Abeille answered:

'Little King Loc, and all my friends here, you are so good and kind that I know that you are miserable when I am in trouble. I would be happy if I could, but it is stronger than I. I am weeping because I shall never see again Youri de Blanchelande, whom I love with all my heart. It is a worse grief than parting with my mother, for at least I know where she is and what she

KING LOC CARRIES ABEILLE AWAY FROM HER MOTHER.

is doing; while, as for Youri, I cannot tell if he is dead
or alive.'

The gnomes were all silent. Kind as they were, they
were not mortals, and had never felt either great joys or
deep sorrows. Only King Loc dimly guessed at something of both, and he went away to consult an old, old
gnome, who lived in the lowest depth of the mountain,
and had spectacles of every sort, that enabled him to see
all that was happening, not only on the earth, but under
the sea.

Nur, for such was his name, tried many of these
spectacles before he could discover anything about Youri
de Blanchelande.

'There he is!' he cried at last. 'He is sitting in the
palace of the Undines, under the great lake; but he does
not like his prison, and longs to be back in the world,
doing great deeds.'

It was true. In the seven years that had passed
since he had left the castle of Clarides to go with
Abeille to the blue lake, Youri in his turn had become a
man.

The older he grew the more weary he got of the
petting and spoiling he received at the hands of the
green-haired maidens, till, one day, he flung himself at
the feet of the Undine queen, and implored permission
to return to his old home.

The queen stooped down and stroked his hair.

'We cannot spare you,' she murmured gently. 'Stay
here, and you shall be king, and marry me.'

'But it is Abeille I want to marry,' said the youth
boldly. But he might as well have talked to the winds,
for at last the queen grew angry, and ordered him to be
put in a crystal cage which was built for him round a
pointed rock.

It was here that King Loc, aided by the spectacles of
Nur, found him after many weeks' journey. As we know,
the gnomes walk slowly, and the way was long and

difficult. Luckily, before he started, he had taken with him his magic ring, and the moment it touched the wall the crystal cage split from top to bottom.

'Follow that path, and you will find yourself in the world again,' he said to Youri ; and without waiting to listen to the young man's thanks, set out on the road he had come.

'Bog,' he cried to the little man on the crow, who had ridden to meet him, 'hasten to the palace and inform the Princess Abeille that Youri de Blanchelande, for seven years a captive in the kingdom of the Undines, has now returned to the castle of Clarides.'

The first person whom Youri met as he came out of the mountain was the tailor who had made all his clothes from the time that he came to live at the castle. Of this old friend, who was nearly beside himself with joy at the sight of the little master, lost for so many years, the count begged for news of his foster-mother and Abeille.

'Alas ! my lord, where can you have been that you do not know that the Princess Abeille was carried off by the gnomes on the very day that you disappeared yourself ? At least, so we guess. Ah ! that day has left many a mark on our duchess ! Yet she is not without a gleam of hope that her daughter is living yet, for every night the poor mother is visited by a dream which tells her all that the princess is doing.'

The good man went on to tell of all the changes that seven years had brought about in the village, but Youri heard nothing that he said, for his mind was busy with thoughts of Abeille.

At length he roused himself, and ashamed of his delay, he hastened to the chamber of the duchess, who held him in her arms as if she would never let him go. By-and-by, however, when she became calmer, he began to question her about Abeille, and how best to deliver

her from the power of the gnomes. The duchess then
told him that she had sent out men in all directions
to look for the children directly they were found to be
missing, and that one of them had noticed a troop of
little men far away on the mountains, evidently carrying
a litter. He was hastening after them, when, at his feet,
he beheld a tiny satin slipper, which he stooped to pick
up. But as he did so a dozen of the gnomes had
swarmed upon him like flies, and beat him about the
head till he dropped the slipper, which they took away
with them, leaving the poor man dizzy with pain. When
he recovered his senses the group on the mountain had
disappeared.

That night, when everyone was asleep, Youri and his
old servant Francœur stole softly down into the armoury,
and dressed themselves in light suits of chain armour,
with helmets and short swords, all complete. Then
they mounted two horses that Francœur had tied up in
the forest, and set forth for the kingdom of the gnomes.
At the end of an hour's hard riding, they came to the
cavern which Francœur had heard from childhood led
into the centre of the earth. Here they dismounted, and
entered cautiously, expecting to find darkness as thick as
what they had left outside. But they had only gone
a few steps when they were nearly blinded by a sudden
blaze of light, which seemed to proceed from a sort of
portcullis door which barred the way in front of them.

'Who are you?' asked a voice. And the count
answered:

'Youri de Blanchelande, who has come to rescue
Abeille des Clarides.' And at these words the gate
slowly swung open, and closed behind the two strangers.

Youri listened to the clang with a spasm of fear in
his heart; then the desperate position he was in gave
him courage. There was no retreat for him now, and
in front was drawn up a large force of gnomes, whose

arrows were falling like hail about him.   He raised his
shield to ward them off, and as he did so his eyes fell on
a little man standing on a rock above the rest, with a
crown on his head and a royal mantle on his shoulders.
In an instant Youri had flung away his shield and sprung

'IS THIS THE MAN THAT YOU WISH TO MARRY ? '

forward, regardless of the arrows that still fell about
him.

   'Oh, is it you, is it *really* you, my deliverer?   And is
it your subjects who hold as a captive Abeille whom I
love?'

   'I am King Loc,' was the answer.   And the figure

with the long beard bent his eyes kindly on the eager youth. 'If Abeille has lived with us all these years, for many of them she was quite happy. But the gnomes, of whom you think so little, are a just people, and they will not keep her against her will. Beg the princess to be good enough to come hither,' he added, turning to Rug.

Amidst a dead silence Abeille entered the vast space and looked around her. At first she saw nothing but a vast host of gnomes perched on the walls and crowding on the floor of the big hall. Then her eyes met those of Youri, and with a cry that came from her heart she darted towards him, and threw herself on his breast.

'Abeille,' said the king, when he had watched her for a moment, with a look of pain on his face, 'is this the man that you wish to marry?'

'Yes, Little King Loc, this is he and nobody else! And see how I can laugh now, and how happy I am!' And with that she began to cry.

'Hush, Abeille! there must be no tears to-day,' said Youri, gently stroking her hair. 'Come, dry your eyes, and thank King Loc, who rescued me from the cage in the realm of the Undines.'

As Youri spoke Abeille lifted her head, and a great light came into her face. At last she understood.

'You did that for me?' she whispered. 'Ah, Little King Loc——!'

So, loaded with presents, and followed by regrets, Abeille went home. In a few days the marriage took place; but however happy she was, and however busy she might be, never a month passed by without a visit from Abeille to her friends in the kingdom of the gnomes.

[Adapted and shortened from the story of *Abeille*, by M. Anatole France.]

THE GREEN KNIGHT

THERE lived once a king and queen who had an only daughter, a charming and beautiful girl, dearer to them than anything else in the world. When the princess was twelve years old the queen fell sick, and nothing that could be done for her was of any use. All the doctors in the kingdom did their best to cure her, but in spite of their efforts she grew worse and worse. As she was about to die, she sent for the king and said to him:

'Promise me that whatever our daughter asks, you will do, no matter whether you wish to or not.'

The king at first hesitated, but as she added:

'Unless you promise this I cannot die in peace,' he at length did as she desired, and gave the promise, after which she became quite happy and died.

It happened that near the king's palace lived a noble lady, whose little girl was of about the same age as the princess, and the two children were always together. After the queen's death the princess begged that this lady should come to live with her in the palace. The king was not quite pleased with this arrangement, for he distrusted the lady; but the princess wished so much for it that he did not like to refuse.

'I am lonely, father,' she said, 'and all the beautiful presents you give me cannot make up to me for the loss of my mother. If this lady comes to live here I shall almost feel as if the queen had come back to me.'

So a magnificent suite of rooms was prepared and set aside for the new-comers and the little princess was wild with joy at the thought of having her friends so near her. The lady and her daughter arrived, and for a long time all went well. They were very kind to the motherless princess, and she almost began to forget how dull she had been before they came. Then, one day, as she and the other girl were playing together in the gardens of the palace, the lady came to them, dressed for a journey, and kissed the princess tenderly, saying :

'Farewell, my child ; my daughter and I must leave you and go far away.'

The poor princess began to cry bitterly. 'Oh! you must not leave me!' she sobbed. 'What shall I do without you? Please, oh! please stay.'

The lady shook her head.

'It almost breaks my heart to go, dear child,' she said, 'but, alas! it must be.'

'Is there nothing that can keep you here?' asked the princess.

'Only one thing,' answered the lady, 'and as that is impossible, we will not speak of it.'

'Nothing is impossible,' persisted the princess. 'Tell me what it is, and it shall be done.'

So at last her friend told her.

'If the king, your father, would make me his queen I would stay,' she said ; 'but that he would never do.'

'Oh, yes! *that* is easy enough!' cried the princess, delighted to think that, after all, they need not be parted. And she ran off to find her father, and beg him to marry the lady at once. He had done everything she asked, and she was quite certain he would do it.

'What is it, my daughter?' he asked, when he saw her. 'You have been crying—are you not happy?'

'Father,' she said, 'I have come to ask you to marry the countess'—(for that was the lady's real title)—'if you do not she will leave us, and then I shall be as lonely as before. You have never refused me what I have asked before, do not refuse me now.'

The king turned quite pale when he heard this. He did not like the countess, and so, of course, he did not wish to marry her; besides, he still loved his dead wife.

' No that I cannot do, my child,' he said at last.

At these words the princess began to cry once more, and the tears ran down her cheeks so fast, and she sobbed so bitterly, that her father felt quite miserable too. He remembered the promise he had given always to do what his daughter asked him, and in the end he gave way, and promised to marry the countess. The princess at once was all smiles, and ran away to tell the good news.

Soon after, the wedding was celebrated with great festivities, and the countess became queen; but, in spite of all the joy and merriment that filled the palace, the king looked pale and sad, for he was certain that ill would come of the marriage. Sure enough, in a very short time the queen's manner towards the princess began to change. She was jealous of her because she, instead of her own daughter, was heir to the throne, and very soon she could no longer hide her thoughts. Instead of speaking kindly and lovingly as before, her words became rough and cruel, and once or twice she even slapped the princess's face.

The king was very unhappy at seeing his dearly loved daughter suffer, and at last she became so wretched that he could no longer bear it. Calling her to him one day he said :

' My daughter, you are no longer merry as you should be, and I fear that it is the fault of your step-mother. It will be better for you to live with her no longer ; therefore I have built you a castle on the island in the lake, and that is to be your home in future. There you can do just as you like, and your step-mother will never enter it.'

The princess was delighted to hear this, and still more pleased when she saw the castle, which was full of beautiful things, and had a great number of windows looking out on the lovely blue water. There was a boat in which she might row herself about, and a garden where she could walk whenever she wished without fear of meeting the unkind queen ; and the king promised to visit her every day.

For a long time she dwelt in peace, and grew more and more beautiful every day. Everyone who saw her said 'The princess is the loveliest lady in the land.' And this was told to the queen, who hated her step-daughter still more because her own daughter was ugly and stupid.

One day it was announced that a great meeting of knights and nobles was to be held in a neighbouring kingdom distant about two days' journey. There were to be all kinds of festivities, and a tournament was to be fought and a banquet held, in honour of the coming of age of the prince of the country.

The princess's father was amongst those invited, but before he set out he went to take leave of his daughter. Although she had such a beautiful home, and was no longer scolded by the queen, the poor princess was dreadfully lonely, and she told her father that it would be better if she were dead. He did his best to comfort her and promised that he would soon return. Was there anything he could do to help her ?

'Yes,' she said. 'You may greet the Green Knight from me.'

Now the king wondered a little at these words, for he had never heard of the Green Knight ; but there was no time to ask questions, therefore he gave the promise, and rode off on his journey. When he came to the palace where the festivities were to take place, the first thing he did was to ask :

'Can anyone tell me where I may find the Green Knight ? '

No, they were very sorry ; but none had ever heard of such a person either—certainly he was not to be found there. At this the king grew troubled, and not even the banquet or the tournament could make him feel happier.

He inquired of everyone he saw, ' Do you know the Green Knight ? ' but the only answer he got was :

' No, your majesty, we have never heard of him.'

At length he began to believe that the princess was mistaken, and that there was no such person ; and he started on his homeward journey sorrowfully enough, for this was the first time for many months that the princess had asked him to do anything for her and he could not do it. He thought so much about it that he did not notice the direction his horse was taking, and presently he found himself in the midst of a dense forest where he had never been before. He rode on and on, looking for the path, but as the sun began to set he realised that he was lost. At last, to his delight, he saw a man driving some pigs, and riding up to him, he said :

' I have lost my way. Can you tell me where I am ? '

' You are in the Green Knight's forest,' answered the man, ' and these are his pigs.'

At that the king's heart grew light. ' Where does the Green Knight live ? ' he asked.

' It is a very long way from here,' said the swine-herd ; ' but I will show you the path.' So he went a little farther with the king and put him on the right road, and the king bade him farewell.

Presently he came to a second forest, and there he met another swineherd driving pigs.

' Whose beasts are those, my man ? ' he asked.

' They are the Green Knight's,' said the man.

' And where does he live ? ' inquired the king.

' Oh, not far from here,' was the reply.

Then the king rode on, and about midday he reached a beautiful castle standing in the midst of the loveliest garden you can possibly imagine, where fountains played in marble basins, and peacocks walked on the smooth lawns. On the edge of a marble basin sat a young and handsome man, who was dressed from head to foot in a suit of green armour, and was feeding the goldfish which swam in the clear water.

'This must be the Green Knight,' thought the king ; and going up to the young man he said courteously :

' I have come, sir, to give you my daughter's greeting. But I have wandered far, and lost my way in your forest.'

The knight looked at him for a moment as though puzzled.

' I have never met either you or your daughter,' he said at last ; 'but you are very welcome all the same.' And he waved his hand towards the castle. However, the king took no notice, and told him that his daughter had sent a message to the Green Knight, and as he was the only Green Knight in the kingdom this message must be for him.

' You must pass the night with me here,' said the knight ; and as the sun was already set, the king was thankful to accept the invitation. They sat down in the castle hall to a magnificent banquet, and although he had travelled much and visited many monarchs in their palaces, the king had never fared better than at the table of the Green Knight, whilst his host himself was so clever and agreeable, that he was delighted, and thought ' what a charming son-in-law this knight would make ! '

Next morning, when he was about to set forth on his journey home, the Green Knight put into his hand a jewelled casket, saying :

' Will your highness graciously condescend to carry this gift to the princess, your daughter ? It contains my portrait, that when I come she may know me ; for I feel certain that she is the lady I have seen night after night in a dream, and I must win her for my bride.'

The king gave the knight his blessing, and promised to take the gift to his daughter. With that he set off, and ere long reached his own country.

The princess was awaiting him anxiously when he

arrived, and ran to his arms in her joy at seeing her dear father again.

'And did you see the Green Knight?' she asked.

'Yes,' answered the king, drawing out the casket the knight had sent, 'and he begged me to give you this that you may know him when he arrives and not mistake him for somebody else.'

When the princess saw the portrait she was delighted, and exclaimed: 'It is indeed the man whom I have seen in my dreams! Now I shall be happy, for he and no other shall be my husband.'

Very soon after the Green Knight arrived, and he looked so handsome in his green armour, with a long green plume in his helmet, that the princess fell still more in love with him than before, and when he saw her, and recognised her as the lady whom he had so often dreamt of, he immediately asked her to be his bride. The princess looked down and smiled as she answered him :

'We must keep the secret from my step-mother until the wedding-day,' said she, 'for otherwise she will find a way to do us some evil.'

'As you please,' replied the prince ; 'but I must visit you daily, for I can live no longer without you! I will come early in the morning and not leave until it is dark ; thus the queen will not see me row across the lake.'

For a long time, the Green Knight visited the princess every day, and spent many hours wandering with her through the beautiful gardens where they knew the queen could not see them. But secrets, as you know, are dangerous things, and at last, one morning, a girl who was in service at the palace happened to be walking by the lake early in the morning and beheld a wonderfully handsome young man, in a beautiful suit of green satin, come down to the edge of the lake. Not guessing that he was watched, he got into a little boat that lay moored to the bank, and rowed himself over to the island where the princess's castle stood. The girl went home wondering who the knight could be; and as she was brushing the queen's hair, she said to her:

'Does your majesty know that the princess has a suitor?'

THE POISONED NAIL

'Nonsense!' replied the queen crossly. But she was dreadfully vexed at the mere idea, as her own daughter was still unmarried, and was likely to remain so, because she was so ill-tempered and stupid that no one wanted her.

'It is true,' persisted the girl. 'He is dressed all in green, and is very handsome. I saw him myself, though he did not see me, and he got into a boat and rowed over to the island, and the princess was waiting for him at the castle door.'

'I must find out what this means,' thought the queen. But she bade her maid of honour cease chattering and mind her own business.

Early next morning the queen got up and went down to the shore of the lake, where she hid herself behind a tree. Sure enough there came a handsome knight dressed in green, just as the maid of honour had said, and he got into a boat and rowed over to the island where the princess awaited him. The angry queen remained by the lake all day, but it was not until the evening that the knight returned, and leaping on shore, he tied the boat to its moorings and went away through the forest.

'I have caught my step-daughter nicely,' thought the queen. 'But she shall not be married before my own sweet girl. I must find a way to put a stop to this.'

Accordingly she took a poisoned nail and stuck it in the handle of the oar in such a way that the knight would be sure to scratch his hand when he picked up the oar. Then she went home laughing, very much pleased with her cleverness.

The next day the Green Knight went to visit the princess as usual; but directly he took up the oars to row over to the island he felt a sharp scratch on his hand.

'Oof!' he said, dropping the oars from pain, 'what can have scratched so?' But, look as he might, only a tiny mark was to be seen.

'Well, it's strange how a nail could have come here since yesterday,' he thought. 'Still, it is not very serious, though it hurts a good deal.' And, indeed, it seemed such a little thing that he did not mention it to

the princess. However, when he reached home in the
evening, he felt so ill he was obliged to go to bed, with
no one to attend on him except his old nurse. But of
this, of course, the princess knew nothing; and the poor
girl, fearing lest some evil should have befallen him,
or some other maiden more beautiful than she should
have stolen his heart from her, grew almost sick with
waiting. Lonely indeed she was, for her father, who
would have helped her, was travelling in a foreign
country, and she knew not how to obtain news of her
lover.

In this manner time passed away, and one day, as
she sat by the open window crying and feeling very sad,
a little bird came and perched on the branch of a tree
that stood just underneath. It began to sing, and so
beautifully that the princess was obliged to stop crying
and listen to it, and very soon she found out that the
bird was trying to attract her attention.

'*Tu-whit, tu-whit!* your lover is sick!' it sang.

'Alas!' cried the princess. 'What can I do?'

'*Tu-whit, tu-whit!* you must go to your father's
palace!'

'And what shall I do there?' she asked.

'*Tu-whit!* there you will find a snake with nine
young ones.'

'Ugh!' answered the princess with a shiver, for she
did not like snakes. But the little bird paid no heed.

'Put them in a basket and go to the Green Knight's
palace,' said she.

'And what am I to do with them when I get there?'
she cried, blushing all over, though there was no one to
see her but the bird.

'Dress yourself as a kitchen-maid and ask for a place.
Tu-whit! Then you must make soup out of the snakes.
Give it three times to the knight and he will be cured.
Tu-whit!'

'But what has made him ill?' asked the princess. The bird, however, had flown away, and there was nothing for it but to go to her father's palace and look for the snakes. When she came there she found the mother snake with the nine little snakes all curled up so that you could hardly tell their heads from their tails. The princess did not like having to touch them, but when the old snake had wriggled out of the nest to bask a little in the sun, she picked up the young ones and put them in a basket as the bird had told her, and ran off to find the Green Knight's castle. All day she walked along, sometimes stopping to pick the wild berries, or to gather a nosegay; but though she rested now and then, she would not lie down to sleep before she reached the castle. At last she came in sight of it, and just then she met a girl driving a flock of geese.

'Good day!' said the princess; 'can you tell me if this is the castle of the Green Knight?'

'Yes, that it is,' answered the goose-girl, 'for I am driving his geese. But the Green Knight is very ill, and they say that unless he can be cured within three days he will surely die.'

At this news the princess grew as white as death. The ground seemed to spin round, and she closed her hand tight on a bush that was standing beside her. By-and-by, with a great effort, she recovered herself and said to the goose-girl:

'Would you like to have a fine silk dress to wear?'

The goose-girl's eyes glistened.

'Yes, that I would!' answered she.

'Then take off your dress and give it to me, and I will give you mine,' said the princess.

The girl could scarcely believe her ears, but the princess was already unfastening her beautiful silk dress, and taking off her silk stockings and pretty red shoes; and the goose-girl lost no time in slipping out of her rough linen skirt and tunic. Then the princess put on

The Princess changes clothes with the Goose-girl

the other's rags and let down her hair, and went to the kitchen to ask for a place.

'Do you want a kitchen-maid?' she said.

'Yes, we do,' answered the cook, who was too busy to ask the new-comer many questions.

The following day, after a good night's rest, the princess set about her new duties. The other servants were speaking of their master, and saying to each other how ill he was, and that unless he could be cured within three days he would surely die.

The princess thought of the snakes, and the bird's advice, and lifting her head from the pots and pans she was scouring, she said: 'I know how to make a soup that has such a wonderful power that whoever tastes it is sure to be cured, whatever his illness may be. As the doctors cannot cure your master shall I try?'

At first they all laughed at her.

'What! a scullion cure the knight when the best physicians in the kingdom have failed?'

But at last, just because all the physicians *had* failed, they decided that it would do no harm to try; and she ran off joyfully to fetch her basket of snakes and make them into broth. When this was ready she carried some to the knight's room and entered it boldly, pushing aside all the learned doctors who stood beside his bed. The poor knight was too ill to know her, besides, she was so ragged and dirty that he would not have been likely to do so had he been well; but when he had taken the soup he was so much better that he was able to sit up.

The next day he had some more, and then he was able to dress himself.

'That is certainly wonderful soup!' said the cook.

The third day, after he had eaten his soup, the knight was quite well again.

'Who are you?' he asked the girl; 'was it you who made this soup that has cured me?'

'Yes,' answered the princess.

'Choose, then, whatever you wish as a reward,' said the knight, 'and you shall have it.'

'I would be your bride!' said the princess.

The knight frowned in surprise at such boldness, and shook his head.

'That is the one thing I cannot grant,' he said, 'for I am pledged to marry the most beautiful princess in the world. Choose again.'

Then the princess ran away and washed herself and mended her rags, and when she returned the Green Knight recognised her at once.

You can think what a joyful meeting that was!

Soon after, they were married with great splendour. All the knights and princes in the kingdom were summoned to the wedding, and the princess wore a dress that shone like the sun, so that no one had ever beheld a more gorgeous sight. The princess's father, of course, was present, but the wicked queen and her daughter were driven out of the country, and as nobody has seen them since, very likely they were eaten by wild beasts in the forest. But the bride and bridegroom were so happy that they forgot all about them, and they lived with the old king till he died, when they succeeded him.

[From "*Eventyr fra Jylland,*" *samlede og optegnede af Evald Tang Kristensen.* Translated from the Danish by Mrs. Skovgaard-Pedersen.]

THE STORY OF THE YARA

Down in the south, where the sun shines so hotly that everything and everybody sleeps all day, and even the great forests seem silent, except early in the morning and late in the evening — down in this country there once lived a young man and a maiden. The girl had been born in the town, and had scarcely ever left it; but the young man was a native of another country, and had only come to the city near the great river because he could find no work to do where he was.

A few months after his arrival, when the days were cooler, and the people did not sleep so much as usual, a great feast was held a little way out of the town, and to this feast everyone flocked from thirty miles and more. Some walked and some rode, some came in beautiful golden coaches; but all had on splendid dresses of red or blue, while wreaths of flowers rested on their hair.

It was the first time that the youth had been present on such an occasion, and he stood silently aside watching the graceful dances and the pretty games played by the young people. And as he watched, he noticed one girl, dressed in white with scarlet pomegranates in her hair, who seemed to him lovelier than all the rest.

When the feast was over, and the young man returned home, his manner was so strange that it drew the attention of all his friends.

Through his work next day the youth continued to see the girl's face, throwing the ball to her companions, or threading her way between them as she danced. At night sleep fled from him, and after tossing for hours on his bed, he would get up and plunge into a deep pool that lay a little way in the forest.

This state of things went on for some weeks, then at last chance favoured him. One evening, as he was passing near the house where she lived, he saw her standing with her back to the wall, trying to beat off with her fan the attacks of a savage dog that was leaping at her throat. Alonzo, for such was his name, sprang forward, and with one blow of his fist stretched the creature dead upon the road. He then helped the frightened and half-fainting girl into the large cool verandah where her parents were sitting, and from that hour he was a welcome guest in the house, and it was not long before he was the promised husband of Julia.

Every day, when his work was done, he used to go up to the house, half hidden among flowering plants and brilliant creepers, where humming-birds darted from bush to bush, and parrots of all colours, red and green and grey, shrieked in chorus. There he would find the maiden waiting for him, and they would spend an hour or two under the stars, which looked so large and bright that you felt as if you could almost touch them.

'What did you do last night after you went home?' suddenly asked the girl one evening.

'Just the same as I always do,' answered he. 'It was too hot to sleep, so it was no use going to bed, and I walked straight off to the forest and bathed in one of those deep dark pools at the edge of the river. I have been there constantly for several months, but last night a strange thing happened. I was taking my last plunge, when I heard — sometimes from one side, and sometimes from another — the sound of a voice singing more sweetly than any nightingale, though I could not catch any words. I left the pool, and, dressing myself as fast as I could, I searched every bush and tree round the water, as I fancied that perhaps it was my friend who was playing a trick on me, but there was not a creature to be seen; and when I reached home I found my friend fast asleep.'

As Julia listened her face grew deadly white, and her whole body shivered as if with cold. From her childhood she had heard stories of the terrible beings that lived in the forests and were hidden under the banks of the rivers, and could only be kept off by powerful charms. Could the voice which had bewitched Alonzo have come from one of these? Perhaps, who knows, it might be the voice of the dreaded Yara herself, who sought young men on the eve of their marriage as her prey.

For a moment the girl sat choked with fear, as these thoughts rushed through her; then she said: 'Alonzo, will you promise me something?'

'What is that?' asked he.

'It is something that has to do with our future happiness.'

'Oh! it is serious, then? Well, of course, I promise. Now tell me!'

'I want you to promise,' she answered, lowering her voice to a whisper, 'never to bathe in those pools again.'

'But why not, queen of my soul; have I not gone there always, and nothing has harmed me, flower of my heart?'

'No; but perhaps something will. If you will not promise I shall go mad with fright. Promise me.'

'Why, what is the matter? You look so pale! Tell me, why you are so frightened?'

'Did you not hear the song?' she asked, trembling.

'Suppose I did, how could that hurt me? It was the loveliest song I ever heard!'

'Yes, and after the song will come the apparition; and after that — after that ——'

'I don't understand. Well — after that?'

'After that — death.'

Alonzo stared at her. Had she really gone mad?

Such talk was very unlike Julia, but before he could collect his senses the girl spoke again:

'That is the reason why I implore you never to go there again; at any rate till after we are married.'

'And what difference will our marriage make?'

'Oh, there will be no danger then; you can go to bathe as often as you like!'

'But tell me why you are so afraid?'

'Because the voice you heard — I know you will laugh, but it is quite true — it was the voice of the Yara.'

At these words Alonzo burst into a shout of laughter; but it sounded so harsh and loud that Julia shrank away shuddering. It seemed as if he could not stop himself, and the more he laughed the paler the poor girl became, murmuring to herself as she watched him:

'Oh, heaven! you have seen her! you have seen her! what shall I do?'

Faint as was her whisper, it reached the ears of Alonzo, who, though he still could not speak for laughing, shook his head.

'You may not know it, but it is true. Nobody who has not seen the Yara laughs like that.' And Julia flung herself on the ground weeping bitterly.

At this sight Alonzo became suddenly grave, and kneeling by her side, gently raised her up.

'Do not cry so, my angel,' he said, 'I will promise anything you please. Only let me see you smile again.'

With a great effort Julia checked her sobs, and rose to her feet.

'Thank you,' she answered. 'My heart grows lighter as you say that! I know you will try to keep your word and to stay away from the forest. But — the power of the Yara is very strong, and the sound of her voice is apt to make men forget everything else in the world. Oh, I have seen it, and more than one betrothed maiden lives alone, broken-hearted. If ever you should return to the pool where you first heard the voice, promise me that you

will at least take this with you.'   And opening a curiously
carved box, she took out a sea-shell shot with many

Julia sings her song into the shell

colours, and sang a song softly into it. 'The moment
you hear the Yara's voice,' said she, 'put this to your

ear, and you will hear my song instead. Perhaps — I do not know for certain — but perhaps, I may be stronger than the Yara.'

It was late that night when Alonzo returned home. The moon was shining on the distant river, which looked cool and inviting, and the trees of the forest seemed to stretch out their arms and beckon him near. But the young man steadily turned his face in the other direction, and went home to bed.

The struggle had been hard, but Alonzo had his reward next day in the joy and relief with which Julia greeted him. He assured her that having overcome the temptation once the danger was now over; but she, knowing better than he did the magic of the Yara's face and voice, did not fail to make him repeat his promise when he went away.

For three nights Alonzo kept his word, not because he believed in the Yara, for he thought that the tales about her were all nonsense, but because he could not bear the tears with which he knew that Julia would greet him, if he confessed that he had returned to the forest. But, in spite of this, the song rang in his ears, and daily grew louder.

On the fourth night the attraction of the forest grew so strong that neither the thought of Julia nor the promises he had made her could hold him back. At eleven o'clock he plunged into the cool darkness of the trees, and took the path that led straight to the river. Yet, for the first time, he found that Julia's warnings, though he had laughed at her at the moment, had remained in his memory, and he glanced at the bushes with a certain sense of fear which was quite new to him.

When he reached the river he paused and looked round for a moment to make sure that the strange feeling of someone watching him was fancy, and he was really alone. But the moon shone brightly on every tree, and nothing was to be seen but his own shadow; nothing was to be heard but the sound of the rippling stream.

He threw off his clothes, and was just about to dive in headlong, when something — he did not know what — suddenly caused him to look round. At the same instant the moon passed from behind a cloud, and its rays fell on a beautiful golden-haired woman standing half hidden by the ferns.

With one bound he caught up his mantle, and rushed headlong down the path he had come, fearing at each step to feel a hand laid on his shoulder. It was not till he had left the last trees behind him, and was standing in the open plain, that he dared to look round, and then he thought a figure in white was still standing there waving her arms to and fro. This was enough; he ran along the road harder than ever, and never paused till he was safe in his own room.

With the earliest rays of dawn he went back to the forest to see whether he could find any traces of the Yara, but though he searched every clump of bushes, and looked up every tree, everything was empty, and the only voices he heard were those of parrots, which are so ugly that they only drive people away.

'I think I must be mad,' he said to himself, 'and have dreamt all that folly'; and going back to the city he began his daily work. But either that was harder than usual, or he must be ill, for he could not fix his mind upon it, and everybody he came across during the day inquired if anything had happened to give him that white, frightened look.

'I must be feverish,' he said to himself; 'after all, it is rather dangerous to take a cold bath when one is feeling so hot.' Yet he knew, while he said it, that he was counting the hours for night to come, that he might return to the forest.

In the evening he went as usual to the creeper-covered house. But he had better have stayed away, as his face was so pale and his manner so strange, that the poor girl saw that something terrible had occurred. Alonzo, how-

THE YARA DEFEATED

ever, refused to answer any of her questions, and all she
could get was a promise to hear everything next day.

On pretence of a violent headache, he left Julia much
earlier than usual and hurried quickly home.   Taking
down a pistol he loaded it and put it in his belt, and a
little before midnight he stole out on the tips of his toes,
so as to disturb nobody.   Once outside he hastened down
the road which led to the forest.

He did not stop till he had reached the river pool,
when, holding the pistol in his hand, he looked about
him. At every little noise — the falling of a leaf, the rustle
of an animal in the bushes, the cry of a night-bird — he
sprang up and cocked his pistol in the direction of the
sound.   But though the moon still shone he saw nothing,
and by-and-by a kind of dreamy state seemed to steal
over him as he leant against a tree.

How long he remained in this condition he could not
have told, but suddenly he awoke with a start, on hearing
his name uttered softly.

'Who is that?' he cried, standing upright instantly;
but only an echo answered him.   Then his eyes grew
fascinated with the dark waters of the pool close to his
feet, and he looked at it as if he could never look
away.

He gazed steadily into the depths for some minutes,
when he became aware that down in the darkness was
a bright spark, which got rapidly bigger and brighter
Again that feeling of awful fear took possession of him,
and he tried to turn his eyes from the pool.   But it was
no use; something stronger than himself compelled him
to keep them there.

At last the waters parted softly, and floating on the
surface he saw the beautiful woman whom he had fled
from only a few nights before.   He turned to run, but his
feet were glued to the spot.

She smiled at him and held out her arms, but as she
did so there came over him the remembrance of Julia,

as he had seen her a few hours earlier, and her warnings and fears for the very danger in which he now found himself.

Meanwhile the figure was always drawing nearer, nearer; but, with a violent effort, Alonzo shook off his stupor, and taking aim at her shoulder he pulled the trigger. The report awoke the sleeping echoes, and was repeated all through the forest, but the figure smiled still, and went on advancing. Again Alonzo fired, and a second time the bullet whistled through the air, and the figure advanced nearer. A moment more, and she would be at his side.

Then, his pistol being empty, he grasped the barrel with both hands, and stood ready to use it as a club should the Yara approach any closer. But now it seemed her turn to feel afraid, for she paused for an instant while he pressed forward, still holding the pistol above his head, prepared to strike.

In his excitement he had forgotten the river, and it was not till the cold water touched his feet that he stood still by instinct. The Yara saw that he was wavering, and suffering herself to sway gently backwards and forwards on the surface of the river, she began to sing. The song floated through the trees, now far and now near; no one could tell whence it came, the whole air seemed full of it. Alonzo felt his senses going and his will failing. His arms dropped heavily to his side, but in falling struck against the sea shell, which, as he had promised Julia, he had always carried in his coat.

His dimmed mind was just clear enough to remember what she had said, and with trembling fingers, that were almost powerless to grasp, he drew it out. As he did so the song grew sweeter and more tender than before, but he shut his ears to it and bent his head over the shell. Out of its depths arose the voice of Julia singing to him as she had sung when she gave him the shell, and though the notes sounded faint at first, they swelled louder and louder till the mist which had gathered about him was blown away.

Then he raised his head, feeling that he had been through strange places, where he could never wander any more; and he held himself erect and strong, and looked about him. Nothing was to be seen but the shining of the river, and the dark shadows of the trees; nothing was to be heard but the hum of the insects, as they darted through the night.

[Adapted from *Folklore Brésilien.*]

THE PRINCE AND THE THREE FATES

ONCE upon a time a little boy was born to a king who ruled over a great country through which ran a wide river. The king was nearly beside himself with joy, for he had always longed for a son to inherit his crown, and he sent messages to beg all the most powerful fairies to come and see this wonderful baby. In an hour or two, so many were gathered round the cradle, that the child seemed in danger of being smothered; but the king, who was watching the fairies eagerly, was disturbed to see them looking grave. 'Is there anything the matter?' he asked anxiously.

The fairies looked at him, and all shook their heads at once.

'He is a beautiful boy, and it is a great pity; but what *is* to happen *will* happen,' said they. 'It is written in the books of fate that he must die, either by a crocodile, or a serpent, or by a dog. If we could save him we would; but that is beyond our power.'

And so saying they vanished.

For a time the king stood where he was, horror-stricken at what he had heard; but, being of a hopeful nature, he began at once to invent plans to save the prince from the dreadful doom that awaited him. He instantly sent for his master builder, and bade him construct a strong castle on the top of a mountain, which should be fitted with the most precious things from the king's own palace, and every kind of toy a child could wish to play with. And, besides, he gave the strictest orders that a guard should walk round the castle night and day.

For four or five years the baby lived in the castle alone with his nurses, taking his airings on the broad terraces, which were surrounded by walls, with a moat beneath them, and only a drawbridge to connect them with the outer world.

One day, when the prince was old enough to run quite fast by himself, he looked from the terrace across the moat, and saw a little soft fluffy ball of a dog jumping and playing on the other side. Now, of course, all dogs had been kept from him for fear that the fairies' prophecy should come true, and he had never even beheld one before. So he turned to the page who was walking behind him, and said:

'What is that funny little thing which is running so fast over there?'

'That is a dog, prince,' answered the page.

'Well, bring me one like it, and we will see which can run the faster.' And he watched the dog till it had disappeared round the corner.

The page was much puzzled to know what to do. He had strict orders to refuse the prince nothing; yet he remembered the prophecy, and felt that this was a serious matter. At last he thought he had better tell the king the whole story, and let him decide the question.

'Oh, get him a dog if he wants one,' said the king, 'he will only cry his heart out if he does not have it.' So a puppy was found, exactly like the other; they might have been twins, and perhaps they were.

Years went by, and the boy and the dog played together till the boy grew tall and strong. The time came at last when he sent a message to his father, saying:

'Why do you keep me shut up here, doing nothing? I know all about the prophecy that was made at my birth, but I would far rather be killed at once than live an idle, useless life here. So give me arms, and let me go, I pray you; me and my dog too.'

And again the king listened to his wishes, and he and his dog were carried in a ship to the other side of the river, which was so broad here it might almost have been the sea. A black horse was waiting for him, tied to a tree, and he mounted and rode away wherever his fancy took him, the dog always at his heels. Never was any prince so happy as he, and he rode and rode till at length he came to a king's palace.

The king who lived in it did not care about looking after his country, and seeing that his people lived cheerful and contented lives. He spent his whole time in making riddles, and inventing plans which he had much better have let alone. At the period when the young prince reached the kingdom he had just completed a wonderful house for his only child, a daughter. It had seventy windows, each seventy feet from the ground, and he had sent the royal herald round the borders of the neighbouring kingdoms to proclaim that whoever could climb up the walls to the window of the princess should win her for his wife.

The fame of the princess's beauty had spread far and wide, and there was no lack of princes who wished to try their fortune. Very funny the palace must have looked each morning, with the dabs of different colour on the white marble as the princes were climbing up the walls. But though some managed to get further than others, nobody was anywhere near the top.

They had already been spending several days in this manner when the young prince arrived, and as he was pleasant to look upon, and civil to talk to, they welcomed him to the house which had been given to them, and saw that his bath was properly perfumed after his long journey. 'Where do you come from?' they said at last. 'And whose son are you?'

But the young prince had reasons for keeping his own secret, and he answered:

'My father was master of the horse to the king of my

country, and after my mother died he married another wife. At first all went well, but as soon as she had babies of her own she hated me, and I fled, lest she should do me harm.'

The hearts of the other young men were touched as soon as they heard this story, and they did everything they could think of to make him forget his past sorrows.

'What are you doing here?' said the youth, one day.

'We spend our whole time climbing up the walls of the palace, trying to reach the windows of the princess,' answered the young men; 'but, as yet, no one has reached within ten feet of them.'

'Oh, let me try too,' cried the prince; 'but to-morrow I will wait and see what you do before I begin.'

So the next day he stood where he could watch the young men go up, and he noted the places on the wall that seemed most difficult, and made up his mind that when his turn came he would go up some other way.

Day after day he was to be seen watching the wooers, till, one morning, he felt that he knew the plan of the walls by heart, and took his place by the side of the others. Thanks to what he had learned from the failure of the rest, he managed to grasp one little rough projection after another, till at last, to the envy of his friends, he stood on the sill of the princess's window. Looking up from below, they saw a white hand stretched forth to draw him in.

Then one of the young men ran straight to the king's palace, and said: 'The wall has been climbed, and the prize is won!'

'By whom?' cried the king, starting up from his throne; 'which of the princes may I claim as my son-in-law?'

'The youth who succeeded in climbing to the princess's window is not a prince at all,' answered the young man. 'He is the son of the master of the horse to the **great**

king who dwells across the river, and he fled from his
own country to escape from the hatred of his stepmother.'

At this news the king was very angry, for it had
never entered his head that anyone *but* a prince would
seek to woo his daughter.

'Let him go back to the land whence he came,' he
shouted in wrath; ' does he expect me to give my daughter
to an exile ? '   And he began to smash the drinking vessels
in his fury ; indeed, he quite frightened the young man,
who ran hastily home to his friends, and told the youth
what the king had said.

Now the princess, who was leaning from her window,
heard his words and bade the messenger go back to the
king her father and tell him that she had sworn a vow
never to eat or drink again if the youth was taken from
her.   The king was more angry than ever when he
received this message, and ordered his guards to go at
once to the palace and put the successful wooer to death ;
but the princess threw herself between him and his
murderers.

'Lay a finger on him, and I shall be dead before
sunset,' said she; and as they saw that she meant it, they
left the palace, and carried the tale to her father.

By this time the king's anger was dying away, and he
began to consider what his people would think of him
if he broke the promise he had publicly given. So he
ordered the princess to be brought before him, and the
young man also, and when they entered the throne room
he was so pleased with the noble air of the victor that
his wrath quite melted away, and he ran to him and
embraced him.

'Tell me who you are?' he asked, when he had
recovered himself a little, ' for I will never believe that
you have not royal blood in your veins.'

But the prince still had his reasons for being silent,
and only told the same story. However, the king had
taken such a fancy to the youth that he said no more,

and the marriage took place the following day, and great herds of cattle and a large estate were given to the young couple.

After a little while the prince said to his wife: 'My life is in the hands of three creatures—a crocodile, a serpent, and a dog.'

'Ah, how rash you are!' cried the princess, throwing her arms round his neck. 'If you know that, how can you have that horrid beast about you? I will give orders to have him killed at once.'

But the prince would not listen to her.

'Kill my dear little dog, who has been my playfellow since he was a puppy?' exclaimed he. 'Oh, never would I allow that.' And all that the princess could get from him was that he would always wear a sword, and have somebody with him when he left the palace.

When the prince and princess had been married a few months, the prince heard that his stepmother was dead, and his father was old and ill, and longing to have his eldest son by his side again. The young man could not remain deaf to such a message, and he took a tender farewell of his wife, and set out on his journey home. It was a long way, and he was forced to rest often on the road, and so it happened that, one night, when he was sleeping in a city on the banks of the great river, a huge crocodile came silently up and made its way along a passage to the prince's room. Fortunately one of his guards woke up as it was trying to steal past them, and shut the crocodile up in a large hall, where a giant watched over it, never leaving the spot except during the night, when the crocodile slept. And this went on for more than a month.

Now, when the prince found that he was not likely to leave his father's kingdom again, he sent for his wife, and bade the messenger tell her that he would await her coming in the town on the banks of the great river.

This was the reason why he delayed his journey so long, and narrowly escaped being eaten by the crocodile. During the weeks that followed the prince amused himself as best he could, though he counted the minutes to the arrival of the princess, and when she did come, he at once prepared to start for the court. That very night, however, while he was asleep, the princess noticed something strange in one of the corners of the room. It was a dark patch, and seemed, as she looked, to grow longer and longer, and to be moving slowly towards the cushions on which the prince was lying. She shrank in terror, but, slight as was the noise, the thing heard it, and raised its head to listen. Then she saw it was the long flat head of a serpent, and the recollection of the prophecy rushed into her mind. Without waking her husband, she glided out of bed, and taking up a heavy bowl of milk which stood on a table, laid it on the floor in the path of the serpent — for she knew that no serpent in the world can resist milk. She held her breath as the snake drew near, and watched it throw up its head again as if it was smelling something nice, while its forky tongue darted out greedily. At length its eyes fell upon the milk, and in an instant it was lapping it so fast that it was a wonder the creature did not choke, for it never took its head from the bowl as long as a drop was left in it. After that it dropped on the ground and slept heavily. This was what the princess had been waiting for, and, catching up her husband's sword, she severed the snake's head from its body.

The morning after this adventure the prince and princess set out for the king's palace, but found, when they reached it, that he was already dead. They gave him a magnificent burial, and then the prince had to examine the new laws which had been made in his absence, and do a great deal of business besides, till he grew quite ill from fatigue, and was obliged to go away to one of his palaces on the banks of the river, in order to rest. Here he soon got better, and began to hunt, and to shoot wild duck with his bow; and wherever he went, his dog, now grown very old, went with him.

One morning the prince and his dog were out as usual, and in chasing their game they drew near the bank of the river. The prince was running at full speed after his dog when he almost fell over something that looked like a log of wood, which was lying in his path. To his surprise a voice spoke to him, and he saw that the thing which he had taken for a branch was really a crocodile.

'You cannot escape from me,' it was saying, when he had gathered his senses again. 'I am your fate, and wherever you go, and whatever you do, you will always find me before you. There is only one means of shaking off my power. If you can dig a pit in the dry sand which will remain full of water, my spell will be broken. If not death will come to you speedily. I give you this one chance. Now go.'

The young man walked sadly away, and when he reached the palace he shut himself into his room, and for the rest of the day refused to see anyone, not even his wife. At sunset, however, as no sound could be heard through the door, the princess grew quite frightened, and made such a noise that the prince was forced to draw back the bolt and let her come in. 'How pale you look,' she cried, 'has anything hurt you? Tell me, I pray you, what is the matter, for perhaps I can help!'

So the prince told her the whole story, and of the impossible task given him by the crocodile.

'How can a sand hole remain full of water?' asked he. 'Of course it will all run through. The crocodile called it a "chance"; but he might as well have dragged me into the river at once. He said truly that I cannot escape him.'

'Oh, if *that* is all,' cried the princess, 'I can set you free myself, for my fairy godmother taught me to know the use of plants, and in the desert not far from here there

grows a little four-leaved herb which will keep the water
in the pit for a whole year. I will go in search of it at
dawn, and you can begin to dig the hole as soon as you
like.'

To comfort her husband, the princess had spoken
lightly and gaily; but she knew very well she had no light
task before her. Still, she was full of courage and energy,
and determined that, one way or another, her husband
should be saved.

It was still starlight when she left the palace on a
snow-white donkey, and rode away from the river straight
to the west. For some time she could see nothing before
her but a flat waste of sand, which became hotter and
hotter as the sun rose higher and higher. Then a dreadful thirst seized her and the donkey, but there was no
stream to quench it, and if there had been she would
hardly have had time to stop, for she still had far to go,
and must be back before evening, or else the crocodile
might declare that the prince had not fulfilled his conditions. So she spoke cheering words to her donkey, who
brayed in reply, and the two pushed steadily on.

Oh! how glad they both were when they caught sight
of a tall rock in the distance. They forgot that they were
thirsty, and that the sun was hot; and the ground seemed
to fly under their feet, till the donkey stopped of its own
accord in the cool shadow. But though the donkey might
rest the princess could not, for the plant, as she knew, grew
on the very top of the rock, and a wide chasm ran round the
foot of it. Luckily she had brought a rope with her, and
making a noose at one end, she flung it across with all
her might. The first time it slid back slowly into the
ditch, and she had to draw it up, and throw it again, but
at length the noose caught on something, the princess
could not see what, and had to trust her whole weight to
this little bridge, which might snap and let her fall deep
down among the rocks. And in that case her death was
as certain as that of the prince.

But nothing so dreadful happened. The princess got safely to the other side, and then came the worst part of her task. As fast as she put her foot on a ledge of the rock the stone broke away from under her, and left her in the same place as before. Meanwhile the hours were passing, and it was nearly noon.

The heart of the poor princess was filled with despair, but she would not give up the struggle. She looked round till she saw a small stone above her which seemed rather stronger than the rest, and by only poising her foot lightly on those that lay between, she managed by a great effort to reach it. In this way, with torn and bleeding hands, she gained the top; but here such a violent wind was blowing that she was almost blinded with dust, and was obliged to throw herself on the ground, and feel about after the precious herb.

For a few terrible moments she thought that the rock was bare, and that her journey had been to no purpose. Feel where she would, there was nothing but grit and stones, when, suddenly, her fingers touched something soft in a crevice. It was a plant, that was clear; but was it the right one? See she could not, for the wind was blowing more fiercely than ever, so she lay where she was and counted the leaves. One, two, three — yes! yes! there were four! And plucking a leaf she held it safe in her hand while she turned, almost stunned by the wind, to go down the rock.

When once she was safely over the side all became still in a moment, and she slid down the rock so fast that it was only a wonder that she did not land in the chasm. However, by good luck, she stopped quite close to her rope bridge and was soon across it. The donkey brayed joyfully at the sight of her, and set off home at his best speed, never seeming to know that the earth under his feet was nearly as hot as the sun above him.

On the bank of the great river he halted, and the princess rushed up to where the prince was standing by

the pit he had digged in the dry sand, with a huge water
pot beside it.   A little way off the crocodile lay blinking
in the sun, with his sharp teeth and whity-yellow jaws
wide open.

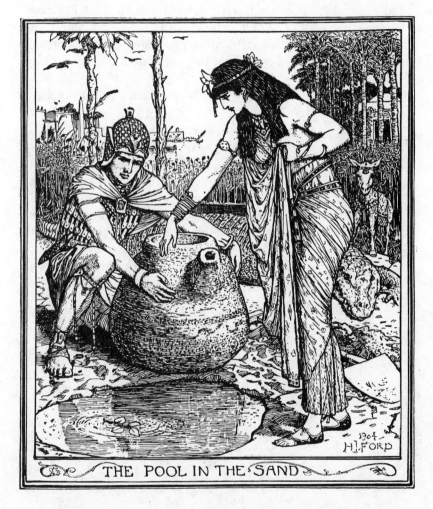

THE POOL IN THE SAND

At a signal from the princess the prince poured the
water in the hole, and the moment it reached the brim
the princess flung in the four-leaved plant.   Would the

charm work, or would the water trickle away slowly through the sand, and the prince fall a victim to that horrible monster ? For half an hour they stood with their eyes rooted to the spot, but the hole remained as full as at the beginning, with the little green leaf floating on the top. Then the prince turned with a shout of triumph, and the crocodile sulkily plunged into the river.

The prince had escaped forever the second of his three fates !

He stood there looking after the crocodile, and rejoicing that he was free, when he was startled by a wild duck which flew past them, seeking shelter among the rushes that bordered the edge of the stream. In another instant his dog dashed by in hot pursuit, and knocked heavily against his master's legs. The prince staggered, lost his balance and fell backwards into the river, where the mud and the rushes caught him and held him fast. He shrieked for help to his wife, who came running; and luckily brought her rope with her. The poor old dog was drowned, but the prince was pulled to shore. 'My wife,' he said, 'has been stronger than my fate.'

[Adapted from *Les Contes Populaires de l' Egypte Ancienne.*]

RÜBEZAHL

OVER all the vast under-world the mountain Gnome Rübezahl was lord; and busy enough the care of his dominions kept him. There were the endless treasure chambers to be gone through, and the hosts of gnomes to be kept to their tasks. Some built strong barriers to hold back the fiery rivers in the earth's heart, and some had scalding vapours to change dull stones to precious metal, or were hard at work filling every cranny of the rocks with diamonds and rubies; for Rübezahl loved all pretty things. Sometimes the fancy would take him to leave those gloomy regions, and come out upon the green earth for a while, and bask in the sunshine and hear the birds sing. And as gnomes live many hundreds of years he saw strange things. For, the first time he came up, the great hills were covered with thick forests, in which wild animals roamed, and Rübezahl watched the fierce fights between bear and bison, or chased the grey wolves, or amused himself by rolling great rocks down into the desolate valleys, to hear the thunder of their fall echoing among the hills. But the next time he ventured above ground, what was his surprise to find everything changed! The dark woods were hewn down, and in their place appeared blossoming orchards surrounding cosy-looking thatched cottages; from every chimney the blue smoke curled peacefully into the air, sheep and oxen fed in the flowery meadows, while from the shade of the hedges came the music of the shepherd's pipe. The strangeness

and pleasantness of the sight so delighted the gnome
that he never thought of resenting the intrusion of these
unexpected guests, who, without saying 'by your leave' or
'with your leave,' had made themselves so very much at
home upon his hills; nor did he wish to interfere with
their doings, but left them in quiet possession of their
homes, as a good householder leaves in peace the
swallows who have built their nests under his eaves.
He was indeed greatly minded to make friends with this
being called 'man,' so, taking the form of an old field
labourer, he entered the service of a farmer. Under his
care all the crops flourished exceedingly, but the master
proved to be wasteful and ungrateful, and Rübezahl soon
left him, and went to be shepherd to his next neighbour.
He tended the flock so diligently, and knew so well where
to lead the sheep to the sweetest. pastures, and where
among the hills to look for any who strayed away, that
they too prospered under his care, and not one was lost
or torn by wolves; but this new master was a hard man,
and begrudged him his well-earned wages. So he ran
away and went to serve the judge. Here he upheld the
law with might and main, and was a terror to thieves and
evildoers; but the judge was a bad man, who took bribes,
and despised the law. Rübezahl would not be the tool
of an unjust man, and so he told his master, who thereupon ordered him to be thrown into prison. Of course
that did not trouble the gnome at all, he simply got out
through the key-hole, and went away down to his underground palace, very much disappointed by his first
experience of mankind. But, as time went on, he forgot
the disagreeable things that had happened to him, and
thought he would take another look at the upper world.

So he stole into the valley, keeping himself carefully
hidden in copse or hedgerow, and very soon met with
an adventure; for, peeping through a screen of leaves,
he saw before him a green lawn where stood a charming
maiden, fresh as the spring, and beautiful to look upon.

The Gnome falls in love with the Princess

Around her upon the grass lay her young companions, as if they had thrown themselves down to rest after some merry game. Beyond them flowed a little brook, into which a waterfall leapt from a high rock, filling the air with its pleasant sound, and making a coolness even in the sultry noontide. The sight of the maiden so pleased the gnome that, for the first time, he wished himself a mortal; and, longing for a better view of the gay company, he changed himself into a raven and perched upon an oak-tree which overhung the brook. But he soon found that this was not at all a good plan. He could only see with a raven's eyes, and feel as a raven feels; and a nest of field-mice at the foot of the tree interested him far more than the sport of the maidens. When he understood this he flew down again in a great hurry into the thicket, and took the form of a handsome young man — that was the best way — and he fell in love with the girl then and there. The fair maiden was the daughter of the king of the country, and she often wandered in the forest with her playfellows gathering the wild flowers and fruits, till the midday heat drove the merry band to the shady lawn by the brook to rest, or to bathe in the cool waters. On this particular morning the fancy took them to wander off again into the wood. This was Master Rübezahl's opportunity. Stepping out of his hiding-place he stood in the midst of the little lawn, weaving his magic spells, till slowly all about him changed, and when the maidens returned at noon to their favourite resting-place they stood lost in amazement, and almost fancied that they must be dreaming. The red rocks had become white marble and alabaster; the stream that murmured and struggled before in its rocky bed, flowed in silence now in its smooth channel, from which a clear fountain leapt, to fall again in showers of diamond drops, now on this side now on that, as the wandering breeze scattered it.

Daisies and forget-me-nots fringed its brink, while tall hedges of roses and jasmine ringed it round, making the sweetest and daintiest bower imaginable. To the right and left of the waterfall opened out a wonderful grotto, its walls and arches glittering with many-coloured rock crystals, while in every niche were spread out strange fruits and sweetmeats, the very sight of which made the princess long to taste them. She hesitated awhile, however, scarcely able to believe her eyes, and not knowing if she should enter the enchanted spot or fly from it. But at length curiosity prevailed, and she and her companions explored to their hearts' content, and tasted and examined everything, running hither and thither in high glee, and calling merrily to each other.

At last, when they were quite weary, the princess cried out suddenly that nothing would content her but to bathe in the marble pool, which certainly did look very inviting; and they all went gaily to this new amusement. The princess was ready first, but scarcely had she slipped over the rim of the pool when down — down — down she sank, and vanished in its depths before her frightened playmates could seize her by so much as a lock of her floating golden hair!

Loudly did they weep and wail, running about the brink of the pool, which looked so shallow and so clear, but which had swallowed up their princess before their eyes. They even sprang into the water and tried to dive after her, but in vain; they only floated like corks in the enchanted pool, and could not keep under water for a second.

They saw at last that there was nothing for it but to carry to the king the sad tidings of his beloved daughter's disappearance. And what great weeping and lamentation there was in the palace when the dreadful news was told! The king tore his robes, dashed his golden crown from his head, and hid his face in his purple mantle for grief and anguish at the loss of the princess. After the first outburst of wailing, however, he took heart and hurried off to see for himself the scene of this strange adventure,

thinking, as people will in sorrow, that there might be
some mistake after all. But when he reached the spot,
behold, all was changed again! The glittering grotto
described to him by the maidens had completely
vanished, and so had the marble bath, the bower of
jasmine; instead, all was a tangle of flowers, as it had
been of old. The king was so much perplexed that he
threatened the princess's playfellows with all sorts of
punishments if they would not confess something about
her disappearance; but as they only repeated the same
story he presently put down the whole affair to the work
of some sprite or goblin, and tried to console himself for
his loss by ordering a grand hunt; for kings cannot bear
to be troubled about anything long.

Meanwhile the princess was not at all unhappy in the
palace of her elfish lover.

When the water-nymphs, who were hiding in readiness,
had caught her and dragged her out of the sight of her
terrified maidens, she herself had not had time to be
frightened. They swam with her quickly by strange
underground ways to a palace so splendid that her
father's seemed but a poor cottage in comparison with it,
and when she recovered from her astonishment she found
herself seated upon a couch, wrapped in a wonderful robe
of satin fastened with a silken girdle, while beside her
knelt a young man who whispered the sweetest speeches
imaginable in her ear. The gnome, for he it was, told
her all about himself and his great underground kingdom,
and presently led her through the many rooms and halls
of the palace, and showed her the rare and wonderful
things displayed in them till she was fairly dazzled at the
sight of so much splendour. On three sides of the castle
lay a lovely garden with masses of gay, sweet flowers, and
velvet lawns all cool and shady, which pleased the eye
of the princess. The fruit trees were hung with golden
and rosy apples, and nightingales sang in every bush, as
the gnome and the princess wandered in the leafy alleys,

sometimes gazing at the moon, sometimes pausing to gather the rarest flowers for her adornment. And all the time he was thinking to himself that never, during the hundreds of years he had lived, had he seen so charming a maiden. But the princess felt no such happiness; in spite of all the magic delights around her she was sad, though she tried to seem content for fear of displeasing the gnome. However, he soon perceived her melancholy, and in a thousand ways strove to dispel the cloud, but in vain. At last he said to himself: 'Men are sociable creatures, like bees or ants. Doubtless this lovely mortal is pining for company. Who is there I can find for her to talk to?'

Thereupon he hastened into the nearest field and dug up a dozen or so of different roots — carrots, turnips, and radishes — and laying them carefully in an elegant basket brought them to the princess, who sat pensive in the shade of the rose-bower.

'Loveliest daughter of earth,' said the gnome, 'banish all sorrow; no more shall you be lonely in my dwelling. In this basket is all you need to make this spot delightful to you. Take this little many-coloured wand, and with a touch give to each root the form you desire to see.'

With this he left her, and the princess, without an instant's delay, opened the basket, and touching a turnip, cried eagerly: 'Brunhilda, my dear Brunhilda! come to me quickly!' And sure enough there was Brunhilda, joyfully hugging and kissing her beloved princess, and chattering as gaily as in the old days.

This sudden appearance was so delightful that the princess could hardly believe her own eyes, and was quite beside herself with the joy of having her dear playfellow with her once more. Hand in hand they wandered about the enchanted garden, and gathered the golden apples from the trees, and when they were tired of this amusement the princess led her friend through all the

wonderful rooms of the palace, until at last they came to
the one in which were kept all the marvellous dresses and
ornaments the gnome had given to his hoped-for bride.
There they found so much to amuse them that the hours
passed like minutes. Veils, girdles, and necklaces were
tried on and admired, the imitation Brunhilda knew so
well how to behave herself, and showed so much taste
that nobody would ever have suspected that she was
nothing but a turnip after all. The gnome, who had
secretly been keeping an eye upon them, was very pleased
with himself for having so well understood the heart of
a woman; and the princess seemed to him even more
charming than before. She did not forget to touch the rest
of the roots with her magic wand, and soon had all her
maidens about her, and even, as she had two tiny radishes
to spare, her favourite cat, and her little dog whose name
was Beni.

And now all went cheerfully in the castle. The princess
gave to each of the maidens her task, and never was
mistress better served. For a whole week she enjoyed
the delight of her pleasant company undisturbed. They
all sang, they danced, they played from morning to night;
only the princess noticed that day by day the fresh young
faces of her maidens grew pale and wan, and the mirror
in the great marble hall showed her that she alone still
kept her rosy bloom, while Brunhilda and the rest faded
visibly. They assured her that all was well with them;
but, nevertheless, they continued to waste away, and day
by day it became harder to them to take part in the
games of the princess, till at last, one fine morning, when
the princess started from bed and hastened out to join
her gay playfellows, she shuddered and started back at
the sight of a group of shrivelled crones, with bent backs
and trembling limbs, who supported their tottering steps
with staves and crutches, and coughed dismally. A
little nearer to the hearth lay the once frolicsome Beni,
with all four feet stretched stiffly out, while the sleek

cat seemed too weak to raise his head from his velvet cushion.

The horrified princess fled to the door to escape from the sight of this mournful company, and called loudly for the gnome, who appeared at once, humbly anxious to do her bidding.

'Malicious Sprite,' she cried, 'why do you begrudge me my playmates — the greatest delight of my lonely hours? Isn't this solitary life in such a desert bad enough without your turning the castle into a hospital for the aged? Give my maidens back their youth and health this very minute, or I will never love you!'

'Sweetest and fairest of damsels,' cried the gnome, 'do not be angry; everything that is in my power I will do — but do not ask the impossible. So long as the sap was fresh in the roots the magic staff could keep them in the forms you desired, but as the sap dried up they withered away. But never trouble yourself about that, dearest one, a basket of fresh turnips will soon set matters right, and you can speedily call up again every form you wish to see. The great green patch in the garden will provide you with a more lively company.'

So saying the gnome took himself off. And the princess with her magic wand touched the wrinkled old women, and left them the withered roots they really were, to be thrown upon the rubbish heap; and with light feet skipped off across to the meadow to take possession of the freshly filled basket. But to her surprise she could not find it anywhere. Up and down the garden she searched, spying into every corner, but not a sign of it was to be found. By the trellis of grape vines she met the gnome, who was so much embarrassed at the sight of her that she became aware of his confusion while he was still quite a long way off.

'You are trying to tease me,' she cried, as soon as she saw him. 'Where have you hidden the basket? I have been looking for it at least an hour.'

'Dear queen of my heart,' answered he, 'I pray you to forgive my carelessness. I promised more than I could perform. I have sought all over the land for the roots you desire; but they are gathered in, and lie drying in musty cellars, and the fields are bare and desolate, for below in the valley winter reigns, only here in your presence spring is held fast, and wherever your foot is set the gay flowers bloom. Have patience for a little, and then without fail you shall have your puppets to play with.'

Almost before the gnome had finished, the disappointed princess turned away, and marched off to her own apartments, without deigning to answer him.

The gnome, however, set off above ground as speedily as possible, and disguising himself as a farmer, bought an ass in the nearest market-town, and brought it back loaded with sacks of turnip, carrot, and radish seed. With this he sowed a great field, and sent a vast army of his goblins to watch and tend it, and to bring up the fiery rivers from the heart of the earth near enough to warm and encourage the sprouting seeds. Thus fostered they grew and flourished marvellously, and promised a goodly crop.

The princess wandered about the field day by day, no other plants or fruits in all her wonderful garden pleased her as much as these roots; but still her eyes were full of discontent. And, best of all, she loved to while away the hours in a shady fir-wood, seated upon the bank of a little stream, into which she would cast the flowers she had gathered and watch them float away.

The gnome tried hard by every means in his power to please the princess and win her love, but little did he guess the real reason of his lack of success. He imagined that she was too young and inexperienced to care for him; but that was a mistake, for the truth was that another image already filled her heart. The young Prince Ratibor, whose lands joined her father's, had won the heart of

the princess; and the lovers had been looking forward
to the coming of their wedding-day when the bride's
mysterious disappearance took place. The sad news
drove Ratibor distracted, and as the days went on, and
nothing could be heard of the princess, he forsook his
castle and the society of men, and spent his days in the
wild forests, roaming about and crying her name aloud
to the trees and rocks. Meanwhile, the maiden, in her
gorgeous prison, sighed in secret over her grief, not wishing to arouse the gnome's suspicions. In her own mind
she was wondering if by any means she might escape
from her captivity, and at last she hit upon a plan.

By this time spring once more reigned in the valley,
and the gnome sent the fires back to their places in
the deeps of the earth, for the roots which they had
kept warm through all the cruel winter had now come to
their full size. Day by day the princess pulled up some
of them, and made experiments with them, conjuring up
now this longed-for person, and now that, just for the
pleasure of seeing them as they appeared; but she really
had another purpose in view.

One day she changed a tiny turnip into a bee, and
sent him off to bring her some news of her lover.

'Fly, dear little bee, towards the east,' said she, 'to my
beloved Ratibor, and softly hum into his ear that I love
him only, but that I am a captive in the gnome's palace
under the mountains. Do not forget a single word of
my greeting, and bring me back a message from my
beloved.'

So the bee spread his shining wings and flew away to
do as he was bidden; but before he was out of sight a
greedy swallow made a snatch at him, and to the great
grief of the princess her messenger was eaten up then
and there.

After that, by the power of the wonderful wand she
summoned a cricket, and taught him this greeting:

'Hop, little cricket, to Ratibor, and chirp in his ear

that I love him only, but that I am held captive by the gnome in his palace under the mountains.'

So the cricket hopped off gaily, determined to do his best to deliver his message; but, alas! a long-legged stork who was prancing along the same road caught him in her cruel beak, and before he could say a word he had disappeared down her throat.

These two unlucky ventures did not prevent the princess from trying once more.

This time she changed the turnip into a magpie.

'Flutter from tree to tree, chattering bird,' said she, 'till you come to Ratibor, my love. Tell him that I am a captive, and bid him come with horses and men, the third day from this, to the hill that rises from the Thorny Valley.'

The magpie listened, hopped awhile from branch to branch, and then darted away, the princess watching him anxiously as far as she could see.

Now Prince Ratibor was still spending his life in wandering about the woods, and not even the beauty of the spring could soothe his grief.

One day, as he sat in the shade of an oak tree, dreaming of his lost princess, and sometimes crying her name aloud, he seemed to hear another voice reply to his, and, starting up, he gazed around him, but he could see no one, and he had just made up his mind that he must be mistaken, when the same voice called again, and, looking up sharply, he saw a magpie which hopped to and fro among the twigs. Then Ratibor heard with surprise that the bird was indeed calling him by name.

'Poor chatterpie,' said he; 'who taught you to say that name, which belongs to an unlucky mortal who wishes the earth would open and swallow up him and his memory for ever?'

Thereupon he caught up a great stone, and would have hurled it at the magpie, if it had not at that moment uttered the name of the princess.

This was so unexpected that the prince's arm fell helplessly to his side at the sound, and he stood motionless.

But the magpie in the tree, who, like all the rest of his family, was not happy unless he could be for ever chattering, began to repeat the message the princess had taught him; and as soon as he understood it, Prince Ratibor's heart was filled with joy. All his gloom and misery vanished in a moment, and he anxiously questioned the welcome messenger as to the fate of the princess.

But the magpie knew no more than the lesson he had learnt, so he soon fluttered away; while the prince hurried back to his castle to gather together a troop of horsemen, full of courage for whatever might befall.

The princess meanwhile was craftily pursuing her plan of escape. She left off treating the gnome with coldness and indifference; indeed, there was a look in her eyes which encouraged him to hope that she might some day return his love, and the idea pleased him mightily. The next day, as soon as the sun rose, she made her appearance decked as a bride, in the wonderful robes and jewels which the fond gnome had prepared for her. Her golden hair was braided and crowned with myrtle blossoms, and her flowing veil sparkled with gems. In these magnificent garments she went to meet the gnome upon the great terrace.

'Loveliest of maidens,' he stammered, bowing low before her, 'let me gaze into your dear eyes, and read in them that you will no longer refuse my love, but will make me the happiest being the sun shines upon.'

So saying he would have drawn aside her veil; but the princess only held it more closely about her.

'Your constancy has overcome me,' she said; 'I can no longer oppose your wishes. But believe my words, and suffer this veil still to hide my blushes and tears.'

'Why tears, beloved one?' cried the gnome anxiously; 'every tear of yours falls upon my heart like a drop of molten gold. Greatly as I desire your love, I do not ask a sacrifice.'

'Ah!' cried the false princess, 'why do you misunderstand my tears? My heart answers to your tenderness, and yet I am fearful. A wife cannot always charm, and though *you* will never alter, the beauty of mortals is as a flower that fades. How can I be sure that you will always be as loving and charming as you are now?'

'Ask some proof, sweetheart,' said he. 'Put my obedience and my patience to some test by which you can judge of my unalterable love.'

'Be it so,' answered the crafty maiden. 'Then give me just one proof of your goodness. Go! count the turnips in yonder meadow. My wedding feast must not lack guests. They shall provide me with bride-maidens too. But beware lest you deceive me, and do not miss a single one. That shall be the test of your truth towards me.'

Unwilling as the gnome was to lose sight of his beautiful bride for a moment, he obeyed her commands without delay, and hurried off to begin his task. He skipped along among the turnips as nimbly as a grasshopper, and had soon counted them all; but, to be quite certain that he had made no mistake, he thought he would just run over them again. This time, to his great annoyance, the number was different; so he reckoned them for the third time, but now the number was not the same as either of the previous ones! And this was hardly to be wondered at, as his mind was full of the princess's pretty looks and words.

As for the maiden, no sooner was her deluded lover fairly out of sight than she began to prepare for flight. She had a fine fresh turnip hidden close at hand, which she changed into a spirited horse, all saddled and bridled, and, springing upon its back, she galloped away over hill and dale till she reached the Thorny Valley, and flung herself into the arms of her beloved Prince Ratibor.

Meanwhile the toiling gnome went through his task over and over again till his back ached and his head swam, and he could no longer put two and two together; but as he felt tolerably certain of the exact number of turnips in the field, big and little together, he hurried back eager to prove to his beloved one what a delightful and submissive husband he would be. He felt very well satisfied with himself as he crossed the mossy lawn to the place where he had left her; but, alas! she was no longer there.

He searched every thicket and path, he looked behind every tree, and gazed into every pond, but without success; then he hastened into the palace and rushed from room to room, peering into every hole and corner and calling her by name; but only echo answered in the marble halls — there was neither voice nor footstep.

Then he began to perceive that something was amiss, and, throwing off the mortal form that encumbered him, he flew out of the palace, and soared high into the air, and saw the fugitive princess in the far distance just as the swift horse carried her across the boundary of his dominions.

Furiously did the enraged gnome fling two great clouds together, and hurl a thunderbolt after the flying maiden, splintering the rocky barriers which had stood a thousand years. But his fury was vain, the thunder-clouds melted away into a soft mist, and the gnome, after flying about for a while in despair, bewailing to the four winds his unhappy fate, went sorrowfully back to the palace, and stole once more through every room, with many sighs and lamentations. He passed through the gardens which for him had lost their charm, and the sight of the princess's footprints on the golden sand of the pathway renewed his grief. All was lonely, empty, sorrowful; and the forsaken gnome resolved that he would have no more dealings with such false creatures as he had found men to be.

Thereupon he stamped three times upon the earth, and the magic palace, with all its treasures, vanished away into the nothingness out of which he had called it; and the gnome fled once more to the depths of his underground kingdom.

While all this was happening, Prince Ratibor was hurrying away with his prize to a place of safety. With great pomp and triumph he restored the lovely princess to her father, and was then and there married to her, and took her back with him to his own castle.

But long after she was dead, and her children too, the villagers would tell the tale of her imprisonment underground, as they sat carving wood in the winter nights.

[*Volksmährchen der Deutschen.*]

STORY OF THE KING WHO WOULD BE STRONGER THAN FATE

ONCE upon a time, far away in the east country, there lived a king who loved hunting so much that, when once there was a deer in sight, he was careless of his own safety. Indeed, he often became quite separated from his nobles and attendants, and in fact was particularly fond of lonely adventures. Another of his favourite amusements was to give out that he was not well, and could not be seen; and then, with the knowledge only of his faithful Grand Wazeer, to disguise himself as a pedlar, load a donkey with cheap wares, and travel about. In this way he found out what the common people said about him, and how his judges and governors fulfilled their duties.

One day his queen presented him with a baby daughter as beautiful as the dawn, and the king himself was so happy and delighted that, for a whole week, he forgot to hunt, and spent the time in public and private rejoicing.

Not long afterwards, however, he went out after some deer which were to be found in a far corner of his forests. In the course of the beat his dogs disturbed a beautiful snow-white stag, and directly he saw it the king determined that he would have it at any cost. So he put the spurs to his horse, and followed it as hard as he could gallop. Of course all his attendants followed at the best speed that they could manage; but the king was so splendidly mounted, and the stag was so swift, that, at the end of an hour, the king found that only his favourite hound and himself were in the chase; all the rest were far, far behind and out of sight.

Nothing daunted, however, he went on and on, till he perceived that he was entering a valley with great rocky mountains on all sides, and that his horse was getting very tired and trembled at every stride. Worse than all evening was already drawing on, and the sun would soon set. In vain had he sent arrow after arrow at the beautiful stag. Every shot fell short, or went wide of the mark; and at last, just as darkness was setting in, he lost sight altogether of the beast. By this time his horse could hardly move from fatigue, his hound staggered panting along beside him, he was far away amongst mountains where he had never been before, and had quite missed his way, and not a human creature or dwelling was in sight.

All this was very discouraging, but the king would not have minded if he had not lost that beautiful stag. That troubled him a good deal, but he never worried over what he could not help, so he got down from his horse, slipped his arm through the bridle, and led the animal along the rough path in hopes of discovering some shepherd's hut, or, at least, a cave or shelter under some rock, where he might pass the night.

Presently he heard the sound of rushing water, and made towards it. He toiled over a steep, rocky shoulder of a hill, and there, just below him, was a stream dashing down a precipitous glen, and, almost beneath his feet, twinkling and flickering from the level of the torrent, was a dim light as of a lamp. Towards this light the king with his horse and hound made his way, sliding and stumbling down a steep, stony path. At the bottom the king found a narrow grassy ledge by the brink of the stream, across which the light from a rude lantern in the mouth of a cave shed a broad beam of uncertain light. At the edge of the stream sat an old hermit with a long, white beard, who neither spoke nor moved as the king approached, but sat throwing into the stream dry leaves which lay scattered about the ground near him.

'Peace be upon you,' said the king, giving the usual country salutation.

'And upon you peace,' answered the hermit; but still he never looked up, nor stopped what he was doing.

For a minute or two the king stood watching him. He noticed that the hermit threw two leaves in at a time, and watched them attentively. Sometimes both were carried rapidly down by the stream; sometimes only one leaf was carried off, and the other, after whirling slowly round and round on the edge of the current, would come circling back on an eddy to the hermit's feet. At other times both leaves were held in the backward eddy, and failed to reach the main current of the noisy stream.

'What are you doing?' asked the king at last, and the hermit replied that he was reading the fates of men; everyone's fate, he said, was settled from the beginning, and, whatever it were, there was no escape from it. The king laughed.

'I care little,' he said, 'what my fate may be; but I should be curious to know the fate of my little daughter.'

'I cannot say,' answered the hermit.

'Do you not know, then?' demanded the king.

'I might know,' returned the hermit, 'but it is not always wisdom to know much.'

But the king was not content with this reply, and began to press the old man to say what he knew, which for a long time he would not do. At last, however, the king urged him so greatly that he said:

'The king's daughter will marry the son of a poor slave-girl called Puruna, who belongs to the king of the land of the north. There is no escaping from Fate.'

The king was wild with anger at hearing these words, but he was also very tired; so he only laughed, and answered that he hoped there would be a way out of *that* fate anyhow. Then he asked if the hermit could shelter

him and his beasts for the night, and the hermit said
'Yes'; so, very soon the king had watered and tethered
his horse, and, after a supper of bread and parched peas,
lay down in the cave, with the hound at his feet, and
tried to go to sleep. But instead of sleeping he only lay
awake and thought of the hermit's prophecy; and the
more he thought of it the angrier he felt, until he gnashed
his teeth and declared that it should never, never come
true.

Morning came, and the king got up, pale and sulky,
and, after learning from the hermit which path to take,
was soon mounted and found his way home without
much difficulty. Directly he reached his palace he
wrote a letter to the king of the land of the north,
begging him, as a favour, to sell him his slave girl
Puruna and her son, and saying that, if he consented, he
would send a messenger to receive them at the river
which divided the kingdoms.

For five days he awaited the reply, and hardly slept
or ate, but was as cross as could be all the time. On the
fifth day his messenger returned with a letter to say that
the king of the land of the north would not sell, but he
would give, the king the slave girl and her son. The king
was overjoyed. He sent for his Grand Wazeer and told
him that he was going on one of his lonely expeditions,
and that the Wazeer must invent some excuse to account
for his absence. Next he disguised himself as an ordinary
messenger, mounted a swift camel, and sped away to the
place where the slave girl was to be handed over to him.
When he got there he gave the messengers who brought
her a letter of thanks and a handsome present for their
master and rewards for themselves; and then without
delay he took the poor woman and her tiny boy-baby up
on to his camel and rode off to a wild desert.

After riding for a day and a night, almost without
stopping, he came to a great cave where he made 'the
woman dismount, and, taking her and the baby into the

cave, he drew his sword and with one blow chopped her head off. But although his anger made him cruel enough for anything so dreadful, the king felt that he could not turn his great sword on the helpless baby, who he was sure must soon die in this solitary place without its mother; so he left it in the cave where it was, and, mounting his camel, rode home as fast as he could.

Now, in a small village in his kingdom there lived an old widow who had no children or relations of any kind. She made her living mostly by selling the milk of a flock of goats; but she was very, very poor, and not very strong, and often used to wonder how she would live if she got too weak or ill to attend to her goats. Every morning she drove the goats out into the desert to graze on the shrubs and bushes which grew there, and every evening they came home of themselves to be milked and to be shut up safely for the night.

One evening the old woman was astonished to find that her very best nanny-goat returned without a drop of milk. She thought that some naughty boy or girl was playing a trick upon her and had caught the goat on its way home and stolen all the milk. But when evening after evening the goat remained almost dry she determined to find out who the thief was. So the next day she followed the goats at a distance and watched them while they grazed. At length, in the afternoon, the old woman noticed this particular nanny-goat stealing off by herself away from the herd and she at once went after her. On and on the goat walked for some way, and then disappeared into a cave in the rocks. The old woman followed the goat into the cave and then, what should she see but the animal giving her milk to a little boy-baby, whilst on the ground near by lay the sad remains of the baby's dead mother! Wondering and frightened, the old woman thought at last that this little baby might be a son to her in her old age, and that he would grow up and in time to come be her comfort and support. So she carried home the baby to her hut, and next day she took a spade to the cave and dug a grave where she buried the poor mother.

Years passed by, and the baby grew up into a fine handsome lad, as daring as he was beautiful, and as industrious as he was brave. One day, when the boy, whom the old woman had named Nur Mahomed, was about seventeen years old, he was coming from his day's work in the fields, when he saw a strange donkey eating the cabbages in the garden which surrounded their little cottage. Seizing a big stick, he began to beat the intruder and to drive him out of his garden. A neighbour passing by called out to him — 'Hi! I say! why are you beating the pedlar's donkey like that?'

'The pedlar should keep him from eating my cabbages,' said Nur Mahomed; 'if he comes this evening here again I'll cut off his tail for him!'

Whereupon he went off indoors, whistling cheerfully. It happened that this neighbour was one of those people who make mischief by talking too much; so, meeting the pedlar in the 'serai,' or inn, that evening, he told him what had occurred, and added: 'Yes; and the young spit-fire said that if beating the donkey would not do, he would beat you also, and cut your nose off for a thief!'

A few days later, the pedlar having moved on, two men appeared in the village inquiring who it was who had threatened to ill-treat and to murder an innocent pedlar. They declared that the pedlar, in fear of his life, had complained to the king; and that they had been sent to bring the lawless person who had said these things before the king himself. Of course they soon found out about the donkey eating Nur Mahomed's cabbages, and about the young man's hot words; but although the lad assured them that he had never said anything about murdering anyone, they replied they were ordered to arrest him, and bring him to take his trial before the king. So, in spite of his protests, and the wails of his mother, he was carried off, and in due time brought before the king. Of course Nur Mahomed never guessed that the supposed pedlar happened to have been the king himself, although nobody knew it.

But as he was very angry at what he had been told, he declared that he was going to make an example of this young man, and intended to teach him that even poor travelling pedlars could get justice in *his* country, and be protected from such lawlessness. However, just as he was going to pronounce some very heavy sentence, there was a stir in the court, and up came Nur Mahomed's old mother, weeping and lamenting, and begging to be heard. The king ordered her to speak, and she began to plead for the boy, declaring how good he was, and how he was the support of her old age, and if he were put in prison she would die. The king asked her who she was. She replied that she was his mother.

'His mother?' said the king; 'you are too old, surely, to have so young a son!'

Then the old woman, in her fright and distress, confessed the whole story of how she found the baby, and how she rescued and brought him up, and ended by beseeching the king for mercy.

It is easy to guess how, as the story came out, the king looked blacker and blacker, and more and more grim, until at last he was half fainting with rage and astonishment. This, then, was the baby he had left to die, after cruelly murdering his mother! Surely fate might have spared him this! He wished he had sufficient excuse to put the boy to death, for the old hermit's prophecy came back to him as strongly as ever; and yet the young man had done nothing bad enough to deserve such a punishment. Everyone would call him a tyrant if he were to give such an order — in fact, he dared not try it!

At length he collected himself enough to say : — 'If this young man will enlist in my army I will let him off. We have need of such as him, and a little discipline will do him good.' Still the old woman pleaded that she

could not live without her son, and was nearly as terrified
at the idea of his becoming a soldier as she was at the
thought of his being put in prison.   But at length the
king — determined to get the youth into his clutches —
pacified her by promising her a pension large enough to
keep her in comfort; and Nur Mahomed, to his own
great delight, was duly enrolled in the king's army.

As a soldier Nur Mahomed seemed to be in luck.
He was rather surprised, but much pleased, to find that
he was always one of those chosen when any difficult
or dangerous enterprise was afoot; and, although he had
the narrowest escapes on some occasions, still, the very
desperateness of the situations in which he found himself
gave him special chances of displaying his courage.   And
as he was also modest and generous, he became a favourite
with his officers and his comrades.

Thus it was not very surprising that, before very long,
he became enrolled amongst the picked men of the king's
bodyguard.   The fact is, that the king had hoped to have
got him killed in some fight or another; but, seeing that,
on the contrary, he throve on hard knocks, he was now
determined to try more direct and desperate methods.

One day, soon after Nur Mahomed had entered the
bodyguard, he was selected to be one of the soldiers told
off to escort the king through the city.   The procession
was marching on quite smoothly, when a man, armed
with a dagger, rushed out of an alley straight towards the
king.   Nur Mahomed, who was the nearest of the guards,
threw himself in the way, and received the stab that had
been apparently intended for the king.   Luckily the blow
was a hurried one, and the dagger glanced on his breast-
bone, so that, although he received a severe wound, his
youth and strength quickly got the better of it.   The
king was, of course, obliged to take some notice of this
brave deed, and as a reward made him one of his own
attendants.

After this the strange adventures the young man

passed through were endless. Officers of the bodyguard were often sent on all sorts of secret and difficult errands, and such errands had a curious way of becoming necessary when Nur Mahomed was on duty. Once, while he was taking a journey, a foot-bridge gave way under him; once he was attacked by armed robbers; a rock rolled down upon him in a mountain pass; a heavy stone coping fell from a roof at his feet in a narrow city alley. Altogether, Nur Mahomed began to think that, somewhere or other, he had made an enemy; but he was light-hearted, and the thought did not much trouble him. He escaped somehow every time, and felt amused rather than anxious about the next adventure.

It was the custom of that city that the officer for the day of the palace guards should receive all his food direct from the king's kitchen. One day, when Nur Mahomed's turn came to be on duty, he was just sitting down to a delicious stew that had been sent in from the palace, when one of those gaunt, hungry dogs, which, in eastern countries, run about the streets, poked his nose in at the open guard-room door, and looked at Nur Mahomed with mouth watering and nostrils working. The kind-hearted young man picked out a lump of meat, went to the door, and threw it outside to him. The dog pounced upon it, and gulped it down greedily, and was just turning to go, when it staggered, fell, rolled over, and died. Nur Mahomed, who had been lazily watching him, stood still for a moment, then he came back whistling softly. He gathered up the rest of his dinner and carefully wrapped it up to carry away and bury somewhere; and then he sent back the empty plates.

How furious the king was when, at the next morning's durbar, Nur Mahomed appeared before him fresh, alert, and smiling as usual. He was determined, however, to try once more, and bidding the young man come into his presence that evening, gave orders that he was to carry a secret despatch to the governor of a distant province.

'Make your preparations at once,' added he, 'and be ready
to start in the morning. I myself will deliver you the
papers at the last moment.'

Now this province was four or five days' journey from
the palace, and the governor of it was the most faithful
servant the king had. He could be silent as the grave,
and prided himself on his obedience. Whilst he was an
old and tried servant of the king's, his wife had been
almost a mother to the young princess ever since the
queen had died some years before. It happened that, a
little before this time, the princess had been sent away
for her health to another remote province; and whilst she
was there her old friend, the governor's wife, had begged
her to come and stay with them as soon as she could.

The princess accepted gladly, and was actually staying
in the governor's house at the very time when the king
made up his mind to send Nur Mahomed there with the
mysterious despatch.

According to orders Nur Mahomed presented himself
early the next morning at the king's private apartments.
His best horse was saddled, food placed in his saddle-bag,
and with some money tied up in his waistband, he was
ready to start. The king handed over to him a sealed
packet, desiring him to give it himself only into the hands
of the governor, and to no one else. Nur Mahomed hid
it carefully in his turban, swung himself into the saddle,
and five minutes later rode out of the city gates, and set
out on his long journey.

The weather was very hot; but Nur Mahomed
thought that the sooner his precious letter was delivered
the better; so that, by dint of riding most of each night
and resting only in the hottest part of the day, he found
himself, by noon on the third day, approaching the town
which was his final destination.

Not a soul was to be seen anywhere; and Nur
Mahomed, stiff, dry, thirsty, and tired, looked longingly
over the wall into the gardens, and marked the fountains,

the green grass, the shady apricot orchards, and giant mulberry trees, and wished he were there.

At length he reached the castle gates, and was at once admitted, as he was in the uniform of the king's body-guard. The governor was resting, the soldier said, and could not see him until the evening. So Nur Mahomed handed over his horse to an attendant, and wandered down into the lovely gardens he had seen from the road, and sat down in the shade to rest himself. He flung himself on his back and watched the birds twittering and chattering in the trees above him. Through the branches he could see great patches of sky where the kites wheeled and circled incessantly, with shrill whistling cries. Bees buzzed over the flowers with a soothing sound, and in a few minutes Nur Mahomed was fast asleep.

Every day, through the heat of the afternoon, the governor, and his wife also, used to lie down for two or three hours in their own rooms, and so, for the matter of that, did most people in the palace. But the princess, like many other girls, was restless, and preferred to wander about the garden, rather than rest on a pile of soft cushions. What a torment her stout old attendants and servants sometimes thought her when she insisted on staying awake, and making them chatter or do something, when they could hardly keep their eyes open! Some-times, however, the princess would pretend to go to sleep, and then, after all her women had gladly followed her example, she would get up and go out by herself, her veil hanging loosely about her. If she was discovered her old hostess scolded her severely ; but the princess only laughed, and did the same thing next time.

This very afternoon the princess had left all her women asleep, and, after trying in vain to amuse herself indoors, she had slipped out into the great garden, and rambled about in all her favourite nooks and corners, feeling quite safe as there was not a creature to be seen. Suddenly, on turning a corner, she stopped in surprise,

for before her lay a man fast asleep! In her hurry she
had almost tripped over him. But there he was, a young

The Princess steals the King's letter.

man, tanned and dusty with travel, in the uniform of an
officer of the king's guard. One of the few faults of

this lovely princess was a devouring curiosity, and she lived such an idle life that she had plenty of time to be curious. Out of one of the folds of this young man's turban there peeped the corner of a letter! She wondered what the letter was — whom it was for! She drew her veil a little closer, and stole across on tip-toe and caught hold of the corner of the letter. Then she pulled it a little, and just a little more! A great big seal came into view, which she saw to be her father's, and at the sight of it she paused for a minute half ashamed of what she was doing. But the pleasure of taking a letter which was not meant for her was more than she could resist, and in another moment it was in her hand. All at once she remembered that it would be death to this poor officer if he lost the letter, and that at all hazards she must put it back again. But this was not so easy ; and, moreover, the letter in her hand burnt her with longing to read it, and see what was inside. She examined the seal. It was sticky with being exposed to the hot sun, and with a very little effort it parted from the paper. The letter was open and she read it! And this was what was written:

'Behead the messenger who brings this letter secretly and at once. Ask no questions.'

The girl grew pale. What a shame! she thought. *She* would not let a handsome young fellow like that be beheaded; but how to prevent it was not quite clear at the moment. Some plan must be invented, and she wished to lock herself in where no one could interrupt her, as might easily happen in the garden. So she crept softly to her room, and took a piece of paper and wrote upon it: 'Marry the messenger who brings this letter to the princess openly at once. Ask no questions.' And even contrived to work the seals off the original letter and to fix them to this, so that no one could tell, unless they examined it closely, that it had ever been opened. Then she slipped back, shaking with fear and excitement, to where the young officer still lay asleep, thrust the letter into the folds of his turban, and hurried back to her room. It was done!

Late in the afternoon Nur Mahomed woke, and, making sure that the precious despatch was still safe, went off to get ready for his audience with the governor. As soon as he was ushered into his presence he took the letter from his turban and placed it in the governor's hands according to orders. When he had read it the governor was certainly a little astonished; but he was told in the letter to 'ask no questions,' and he knew how to obey orders. He sent for his wife and told her to get the princess ready to be married at once.

'Nonsense!' said his wife, 'what in the world do you mean?'

'These are the king's commands,' he answered; 'go and do as I bid you. The letter says "at once," and "ask no questions." The marriage, therefore, must take place this evening.'

In vain did his wife urge every objection; the more she argued, the more determined was her husband. 'I know how to obey orders,' he said, 'and these are as plain as the nose on my face!' So the princess was summoned, and, somewhat to their surprise, she seemed to take the news very calmly; next Nur Mahomed was informed, and he was greatly startled, but of course he could but be delighted at the great and unexpected honour which he thought the king had done him. Then all the castle was turned upside down; and when the news spread in the town, *that* was turned upside down too. Everybody ran everywhere, and tried to do everything at once; and, in the middle of it all, the old governor went about with his hair standing on end, muttering something about 'obeying orders.'

And so the marriage was celebrated, and there was a great feast in the castle, and another in the soldiers' barracks, and illuminations all over the town and in the beautiful gardens. And all the people declared that such a wonderful sight had never been seen, and talked about it to the ends of their lives.

The next day the governor despatched the princess and her bridegroom to the king, with a troop of horsemen, splendidly dressed, and he sent a mounted messenger on before them, with a letter giving the account of the marriage to the king.

When the king got the governor's letter, he grew so red in the face that everyone thought he was going to have apoplexy. They were all very anxious to know what had happened, but he rushed off and locked himself into a room, where he ramped and raved until he was tired. Then, after a while, he began to think he had better make the best of it, especially as the old governor had been clever enough to send him back his letter, and the king was pretty sure that this was in the princess's handwriting. He was fond of his daughter, and though she had behaved so badly, he did not wish to cut *her* head off, and he did not want people to know the truth because it would make him look foolish. In fact, the more he considered the matter, the more he felt that he would be wise to put a good face on it, and to let people suppose that he had really brought about the marriage of his own free will.

So, when the young couple arrived, the king received them with all state, and gave his son-in-law a province to govern. Nur Mahomed soon proved himself as able and honourable a governor as he was a brave soldier; and, when the old king died, he became king in his place, and reigned long and happily.

Nur Mahomed's old mother lived for a long time in her 'son's' palace, and died in peace. The princess, his wife, although she had got her husband by a trick, found that she could not trick *him*, and so she never tried, but busied herself in teaching her children and scolding her maids. As for the old hermit, no trace of him was ever discovered; but the cave is there, and the leaves lie thick in front of it unto this day.

[Told the writer by an Indian.]

THE LUTE PLAYER

ONCE upon a time there was a king and queen who lived happily and comfortably together. They were very fond of each other and had nothing to worry them, but at last the king grew restless. He longed to go out into the world, to try his strength in battle against some enemy and to win all kinds of honour and glory.

So he called his army together and gave orders to start for a distant country where a heathen king ruled who ill-treated or tormented everyone he could lay his hands on. The king then gave his parting orders and wise advice to his ministers, took a tender leave of his wife, and set off with his army across the seas.

I cannot say whether the voyage was short or long; but at last he reached the country of the heathen king and marched on, defeating all who came in his way. But this did not last long, for in time he came to a mountain pass, where a large army was waiting for him, who put his soldiers to flight, and took the king himself prisoner.

He was carried off to the prison where the heathen king kept his captives, and now our poor friend had a very bad time indeed. All night long the prisoners were chained up, and in the morning they were yoked together like oxen and had to plough the land till it grew dark.

This state of things went on for three years before the king found any means of sending news of himself to his dear queen, but at last he contrived to send this letter: 'Sell all our castles and palaces, and put all our treasures

THE LVTE PLAYER

in pawn and come and deliver me out of this horrible prison.'

The queen received the letter, read it, and wept bitterly as she said to herself, 'How can I deliver my dearest husband? If I go myself and the heathen king sees me he will just take me to be one of his wives. If I were to send one of the ministers!—but I hardly know if I can depend on them.'

She thought, and thought, and at last an idea came into her head. She cut off all her beautiful long brown hair and dressed herself in boy's clothes. Then she took her lute and, without saying anything to anyone, she went forth into the wide world.

She travelled through many lands and saw many cities, and went through many hardships before she got to the town where the heathen king lived. When she got there she walked all round the palace and at the back she saw the prison. Then she went into the great court in front of the palace, and taking her lute in her hand, she began to play so beautifully that one felt as though one could never hear enough.

After she had played for some time she began to sing, and her voice was sweeter than the lark's:

'I come from my own country far
    Into this foreign land,
  Of all I own I take alone
    My sweet lute in my hand.

'Oh! who will thank me for my song,
    Reward my simple lay?
Like lover's sighs it still shall rise
    To greet thee day by day.

'I sing of blooming flowers
    Made sweet by sun and rain;
Of all the bliss of love's first kiss,
    And parting's cruel pain.

'Of the sad captive's longing
    Within his prison wall,
Of hearts that sigh when none are nigh
    To answer to their call.

' My song begs for your pity,
  And gifts from out your store,
And as I play my gentle lay
  I linger near your door.

' And if you hear my singing
  Within your palace, sire,
Oh ! give, I pray, this happy day,
  To me my heart's desire.'

No sooner had the heathen king heard this touching song sung by such a lovely voice, than he had the singer brought before him.

' Welcome, O lute player,' said he. ' Where do you come from ? '

' My country, sire, is far away across many seas. For years I have been wandering about the world and gaining my living by my music.'

' Stay here then a few days, and when you wish to leave I will give you what you ask for in your song— your heart's desire.'

So the lute player stayed on in the palace and sang and played almost all day long to the king, who could never tire of listening and almost forgot to eat or drink or to torment people. He cared for nothing but the music, and nodded his head as he declared, ' That's something like playing and singing. It makes me feel as if some gentle hand had lifted every care and sorrow from me.'

After three days the lute player came to take leave of the king.

' Well,' said the king, ' what do you desire as your reward ? '

' Sire, give me one of your prisoners. You have so many in your prison, and I should be glad of a companion on my journeys. When I hear his happy voice as I travel along I shall think of you and thank you.'

' Come along then,' said the king, ' choose whom you will.' And he took the lute player through the prison himself.

The queen walked about amongst the prisoners, and at length she picked out her husband and took him with her on her journey. They were long on their way, but he never found out who she was, and she led him nearer and nearer to his own country.

When they reached the frontier the prisoner said :

' Let me go now, kind lad ; I am no common prisoner, but the king of this country. Let me go free and ask what you will as your reward.'

' Do not speak of reward,' answered the lute player. ' Go in peace.'

' Then come with me, dear boy, and be my guest.'

' When the proper time comes I shall be at your palace,' was the reply, and so they parted.

The queen took a short way home, got there before the king and changed her dress.

An hour later all the people in the palace were running to and fro and crying out : ' Our king has come back ! Our king has returned to us.'

The king greeted every one very kindly, but he would not so much as look at the queen.

Then he called all his council and ministers together and said to them :

' See what sort of a wife I have. Here she is falling on my neck, but when I was pining in prison and sent her word of it she did nothing to help me.'

And his council answered with one voice, ' Sire, when news was brought from you the queen disappeared and no one knew where she went. She only returned to-day.'

Then the king was very angry and cried, ' Judge my faithless wife ! Never would you have seen your king again, if a young lute player had not delivered him. I shall remember him with love and gratitude as long as I live.'

Whilst the king was sitting with his council, the queen found time to disguise herself. She took her lute,

and slipping into the court in front of the palace she
sang, clear and sweet :

> ' I sing the captive's longing
>   Within his prison wall,
> Of hearts that sigh when none are nigh
>   To answer to their call.

> ' My song begs for your pity,
>   And gifts from out your store,
> And as I play my gentle lay
>   I linger near your door.

> ' And if you hear my singing
>   Within your palace, sire,
> Oh ! give, I pray, this happy day,
>   To me my heart's desire.'

As soon as the king heard this song he ran out to
meet the lute player, took him by the hand and led him
into the palace.

'Here,' he cried, ' is the boy who released me from
my prison. And now, my true friend, I will indeed give
you your heart's desire.'

' I am sure you will not be less generous than the
heathen king was, sire. I ask of you what I asked and
obtained from him. But this time I don't mean to give
up what I get. I want *you*—yourself ! '

And as she spoke she threw off her long cloak and
everyone saw it was the queen.

Who can tell how happy the king was ? In the joy of
his heart he gave a great feast to the whole world, and
the whole world came and rejoiced with him for a whole
week.

I was there too, and ate and drank many good things.
I sha'n't forget that feast as long as I live.

[From the Russian.]

THE HISTORY OF DWARF LONG NOSE

IT is a great mistake to think that fairies, witches, magicians, and such people lived only in Eastern countries and in such times as those of the Caliph Haroun Al-Raschid. Fairies and their like belong to every country and every age, and no doubt we should see plenty of them now—if we only knew how.

In a large town in Germany there lived, some couple of hundred years ago, a cobbler and his wife. They were poor and hard-working. The man sat all day in a little stall at the street corner and mended any shoes that were brought him. His wife sold the fruit and vegetables they grew in their garden in the Market Place, and as she was always neat and clean and her goods were temptingly spread out she had plenty of customers.

The couple had one boy called Jem. A handsome, pleasant-faced boy of twelve, and tall for his age. He used to sit by his mother in the market and would carry home what people bought from her, for which they often gave him a pretty flower, or a slice of cake, or even some small coin.

One day Jem and his mother sat as usual in the Market Place with plenty of nice herbs and vegetables spread out on the board, and in some smaller baskets early pears, apples, and apricots. Jem cried his wares at the top of his voice:

'This way, gentlemen! See these lovely cabbages and these fresh herbs! Early apples, ladies; early pears and apricots, and all cheap. Come, buy, buy!'

As he cried an old woman came across the Market Place. She looked very torn and ragged, and had a small sharp face, all wrinkled, with red eyes, and a thin hooked nose which nearly met her chin. She leant on a tall stick and limped and shuffled and stumbled along as if she were going to fall on her nose at any moment.

In this fashion she came along till she got to the stall where Jem and his mother were, and there she stopped.

'Are you Hannah the herb seller?' she asked in a croaky voice as her head shook to and fro.

'Yes, I am,' was the answer. 'Can I serve you?'

'We'll see; we'll see! Let me look at those herbs. I wonder if you've got what I want,' said the old woman as she thrust a pair of hideous brown hands into the herb basket, and began turning over all the neatly packed herbs with her skinny fingers, often holding them up to her nose and sniffing at them.

The cobbler's wife felt much disgusted at seeing her wares treated like this, but she dared not speak. When the old hag had turned over the whole basket she muttered, 'Bad stuff, bad stuff; much better fifty years ago—all bad.'

This made Jem very angry

'You are a very rude old woman,' he cried out. 'First you mess all our nice herbs about with your horrid brown fingers and sniff at them with your long nose till no one else will care to buy them, and then you say it's all bad stuff, though the duke's cook himself buys all his herbs from us.'

The old woman looked sharply at the saucy boy, laughed unpleasantly, and said:

'So you don't like my long nose, sonny? Well, you shall have one yourself, right down to your chin.'

As she spoke she shuffled towards the hamper of cabbages, took up one after another, squeezed them hard, and threw them back, muttering again, 'Bad stuff, bad stuff.'

'Don't waggle your head in that horrid way,' begged Jem anxiously. 'Your neck is as thin as a cabbage-stalk, and it might easily break and your head fall into the basket, and then who would buy anything?'

'Don't you like thin necks?' laughed the old woman. 'Then you sha'n't have any, but a head stuck close between your shoulders so that it may be quite sure not to fall off.'

JEM FOLLOWS THE OLD WOMAN

'Don't talk such nonsense to the child,' said the mother at last. 'If you wish to buy, please make haste, as you are keeping other customers away.'

'Very well, I will do as you ask,' said the old woman, with an angry look. 'I will buy these six cabbages, but, as you see, I can only walk with my stick and can carry nothing. Let your boy carry them home for me and I'll pay him for his trouble.'

The little fellow didn't like this, and began to cry, for

he was afraid of the old woman, but his mother ordered him to go, for she thought it wrong not to help such a weakly old creature; so, still crying, he gathered the cabbages into a basket and followed the old woman across the Market Place.

It took her more than half an hour to get to a distant part of the little town, but at last she stopped in front of a small tumble-down house. She drew a rusty old hook from her pocket and stuck it into a little hole in the door, which suddenly flew open. How surprised Jem was when they went in! The house was splendidly furnished, the walls and ceiling of marble, the furniture of ebony inlaid with gold and precious stones, the floor of such smooth slippery glass that the little fellow tumbled down more than once.

The old woman took out a silver whistle and blew it till the sound rang through the house. Immediately a lot of guinea pigs came running down the stairs, but Jem thought it rather odd that they all walked on their hind legs, wore nutshells for shoes, and men's clothes, whilst even their hats were put on in the newest fashion.

'Where are my slippers, lazy crew?' cried the old woman, and hit about with her stick. 'How long am I to stand waiting here?'

They rushed upstairs again and returned with a pair of cocoa nuts lined with leather, which she put on her feet. Now all limping and shuffling was at an end. She threw away her stick and walked briskly across the glass floor, drawing little Jem after her. At last she paused in a room which looked almost like a kitchen, it was so full of pots and pans, but the tables were of mahogany and the sofas and chairs covered with the richest stuffs.

'Sit down,' said the old woman pleasantly, and she pushed Jem into a corner of a sofa and put a table close in front of him. 'Sit down, you've had a long walk and a heavy load to carry, and I must give you something for your trouble. Wait a bit, and I'll give you some nice soup, which you'll remember as long as you live.'

So saying, she whistled again. First came in guinea pigs in men's clothing. They had tied on large kitchen aprons, and in their belts were stuck carving knives and sauce ladles and such things. After them hopped in a number of squirrels. They too walked on their hind legs, wore full Turkish trousers, and little green velvet caps on their heads. They seemed to be the scullions, for they clambered up the walls and brought down pots and pans, eggs, flour, butter, and herbs, which they carried to the stove. Here the old woman was bustling about, and Jem could see that she was cooking something very special for him. At last the broth began to bubble and boil, and she drew off the saucepan and poured its contents into a silver bowl, which she set before Jem.

'There, my boy,' said she, 'eat this soup and then you'll have everything which pleased you so much about me. And you shall be a clever cook too, but the real herb—no, the *real* herb you'll never find. Why had your mother not got it in her basket?'

The child could not think what she was talking about, but he quite understood the soup, which tasted most delicious. His mother had often given him nice things, but nothing had ever seemed so good as this. The smell of the herbs and spices rose from the bowl, and the soup tasted both sweet and sharp at the same time, and was very strong. As he was finishing it the guinea pigs lit some Arabian incense, which gradually filled the room with clouds of blue vapour. They grew thicker and thicker and the scent nearly overpowered the boy. He reminded himself that he must get back to his mother, but whenever he tried to rouse himself to go he sank back again drowsily, and at last he fell sound asleep in the corner of the sofa.

Strange dreams came to him. He thought the old woman took off all his clothes and wrapped him up in a squirrel skin, and that he went about with the other squirrels and guinea pigs, who were all very pleasant and well mannered, and waited on the old woman. First he learned to clean her cocoa-nut shoes with oil and to rub them up. Then he learnt to catch the little sun moths and rub them through the finest sieves, and the flour from them he made into soft bread for the toothless old woman.

In this way he passed from one kind of service to another, spending a year in each, till in the fourth year he was promoted to the kitchen. Here he worked his way up from under-scullion to head-pastrycook, and reached the greatest perfection. He could make all the most difficult dishes, and two hundred different kinds of patties, soup flavoured with every sort of herb—he had learnt it all, and learnt it well and quickly.

When he had lived seven years with the old woman she ordered him one day, as she was going out, to kill and pluck a chicken, stuff it with herbs, and have it very nicely roasted by the time she got back. He did this quite according to rule. He wrung the chicken's neck, plunged it into boiling water, carefully plucked out all the feathers, and rubbed the skin nice and smooth. Then he went to fetch the herbs to stuff it with. In the store-room he noticed a half-opened cupboard which he did not remember having seen before. He peeped in and saw a lot of baskets from which came a strong and pleasant smell. He opened one and found a very uncommon herb in it. The stems and leaves were a bluish green, and above them was a little flower of a deep bright red, edged with yellow. He gazed at the flower, smelt it, and found it gave the same strong strange perfume which came from the soup the old woman had made him. But the smell was so sharp that he began to sneeze again and again, and at last—he woke up!

There he lay on the old woman's sofa and stared about him in surprise. 'Well, what odd dreams one does have to be sure!' he said to himself. 'Why, I could have sworn I had been a squirrel, a companion of guinea pigs and such creatures, and had become a great cook, too. How mother will laugh when I tell her! But won't she scold me, though, for sleeping away here in a strange house, instead of helping her at market!'

He jumped up and prepared to go : all his limbs still seemed quite stiff with his long sleep, especially his neck, for he could not move his head easily, and he laughed at his own stupidity at being still so drowsy that he kept knocking his nose against the wall or cupboards. The squirrels and guinea pigs ran whimpering after him, as though they would like to go too, and he begged them to come when he reached the door, but they all turned and ran quickly back into the house again.

The part of the town was out of the way, and Jem did not know the many narrow streets in it and was puzzled by their windings and by the crowd of people, who seemed excited about some show. From what he heard, he fancied they were going to see a dwarf, for he heard them call out: 'Just look at the ugly dwarf!' 'What a long nose he has, and see how his head is stuck in between his shoulders, and only look at his ugly brown hands!' If he had not been in such a hurry to get back to his mother, he would have gone too, for he loved shows with giants and dwarfs and the like.

He was quite puzzled when he reached the market-place. There sat his mother, with a good deal of fruit still in her baskets, so he felt he could not have slept so very long, but it struck him that she was sad, for she did not call to the passers-by, but sat with her head resting on her hand, and as he came nearer he thought she looked paler than usual.

He hesitated what to do, but at last he slipped behind her, laid a hand on her arm, and said: 'Mammy, what's the matter ? Are you angry with me ?'

She turned round quickly and jumped up with a cry of horror.

'What do you want, you hideous dwarf?' she cried; 'get away; I can't bear such tricks.'

'But, mother dear, what's the matter with you?'

HANNAH DOES NOT RECOGNISE JEM

repeated Jem, quite frightened. 'You can't be well. Why do you want to drive your son away?'

'I have said already, get away,' replied Hannah, quite angrily. 'You won't get anything out of me by your games, you monstrosity.'

'Oh dear, oh dear! she must be wandering in her mind,' murmured the lad to himself. 'How can I manage to get her home? Dearest mother, do look at me close. Can't you see I am your own son Jem?'

'Well, did you ever hear such impudence?' asked Hannah, turning to a neighbour. 'Just see that frightful dwarf—would you believe that he wants me to think he is my son Jem?'

Then all the market women came round and talked all together and scolded as hard as they could, and said what a shame it was to make game of Mrs. Hannah, who had never got over the loss of her beautiful boy, who had been stolen from her seven years ago, and they threatened to fall upon Jem and scratch him well if he did not go away at once.

Poor Jem did not know what to make of it all. He was sure he had gone to market with his mother only that morning, had helped to set out the stall, had gone to the old woman's house, where he had some soup and a little nap, and now, when he came back, they were all talking of seven years. And they called him a horrid dwarf! Why, what had happened to him? When he found that his mother would really have nothing to do with him he turned away with tears in his eyes, and went sadly down the street towards his father's stall.

'Now I'll see whether he will know me,' thought he. 'I'll stand by the door and talk to him.'

When he got to the stall he stood in the doorway and looked in. The cobbler was so busy at work that he did not see him for some time, but, happening to look up, he caught sight of his visitor, and letting shoes, thread, and everything fall to the ground, he cried with horror: 'Good heavens! what is that?'

'Good evening, master,' said the boy, as he stepped in. 'How do you do?'

'Very ill, little sir,' replied the father, to Jem's

surprise, for he did not seem to know him. 'Business does not go well. I am all alone, and am getting old, and a workman is costly.'

'But haven't you a son who could learn your trade by degrees?' asked Jem.

'I had one: he was called Jem, and would have been a tall sturdy lad of twenty by this time, and able to help me well. Why, when he was only twelve he was quite sharp and quick, and had learnt many little things, and a good-looking boy too, and pleasant, so that customers were taken by him. Well, well! so goes the world!'

'But where is your son?' asked Jem, with a trembling voice.

'Heaven only knows!' replied the man; 'seven years ago he was stolen from the market-place, and we have heard no more of him.'

'*Seven years ago!*' cried Jem, with horror.

'Yes, indeed, seven years ago, though it seems but yesterday that my wife came back howling and crying, and saying the child had not come back all day. I always thought and said that something of the kind would happen. Jem was a beautiful boy, and everyone made much of him, and my wife was so proud of him, and liked him to carry the vegetables and things to grand folks' houses, where he was petted and made much of. But I used to say, "Take care—the town is large, there are plenty of bad people in it—keep a sharp eye on Jem." And so it happened; for one day an old woman came and bought a lot of things—more than she could carry; so my wife, being a kindly soul, lent her the boy, and—we have never seen him since.'

'And that was seven years ago, you say?'

'Yes, seven years: we had him cried—we went from house to house. Many knew the pretty boy, and were fond of him, but it was all in vain. No one seemed to know the old woman who bought the vegetables either;

only one old woman, who is ninety years old, said it might have been the fairy Herbaline, who came into the town once in every fifty years to buy things.'

As his father spoke, things grew clearer to Jem's mind, and he saw now that he had not been dreaming, but had really served the old woman seven years in the shape of a squirrel. As he thought it over rage filled his heart. Seven years of his youth had been stolen from him, and what had he got in return? To learn to rub up cocoa nuts, and to polish glass floors, and to be taught cooking by guinea pigs! He stood there thinking, till at last his father asked him :

'Is there anything I can do for you, young gentleman? Shall I make you a pair of slippers, or perhaps '— with a smile—' a case for your nose?'

'What have you to do with my nose?' asked Jem. 'And why should I want a case for it?'

'Well, everyone to his taste,' replied the cobbler; 'but I must say if I had such a nose I would have a nice red leather cover made for it. Here is a nice piece; and think what a protection it would be to you. As it is, you must be constantly knocking up against things.'

The lad was dumb with fright. He felt his nose. It was thick, and quite two hands long. So, then, the old woman had changed his shape, and that was why his own mother did not know him, and called him a horrid dwarf!

'Master,' said he, 'have you got a glass that I could see myself in?'

'Young gentleman,' was the answer, 'your appearance is hardly one to be vain of, and there is no need to waste your time looking in a glass. Besides, I have none here, and if you must have one you had better ask Urban the barber, who lives over the way, to lend you his. Good morning.'

So saying, he gently pushed Jem into the street, shut the door, and went back to his work.

Jem stepped across to the barber, whom he had known in old days.

'Good morning, Urban,' said he; 'may I look at myself in your glass for a moment?'

'With pleasure,' said the barber, laughing, and all the people in his shop fell to laughing also. 'You are a pretty youth, with your swan-like neck and white hands and small nose. No wonder you are rather vain; but look as long as you like at yourself.'

So spoke the barber, and a titter ran round the room. Meantime Jem had stepped up to the mirror, and stood gazing sadly at his reflection. Tears came to his eyes.

'No wonder you did not know your child again, dear mother,' thought he; 'he wasn't like this when you were so proud of his looks.'

His eyes had grown quite small, like pigs' eyes, his nose was huge and hung down over his mouth and chin, his throat seemed to have disappeared altogether, and his head was fixed stiffly between his shoulders. He was no taller than he had been seven years ago, when he was not much more than twelve years old, but he made up in breadth, and his back and chest had grown into lumps like two great sacks. His legs were small and spindly, but his arms were as large as those of a well-grown man, with large brown hands, and long skinny fingers.

Then he remembered the morning when he had first seen the old woman, and her threats to him, and without saying a word he left the barber's shop.

He determined to go again to his mother, and found her still in the market-place. He begged her to listen quietly to him, and he reminded her of the day when he went away with the old woman, and of many things in his childhood, and told her how the fairy had bewitched him, and he had served her seven years. Hannah did not know what to think—the story was so strange; and it seemed impossible to think her pretty boy and this hideous dwarf were the same. At last she decided to go and talk to her husband about it. She gathered up her baskets, told Jem to follow her, and went straight to the cobbler's stall.

'Look here,' said she, ' this creature says he is our lost son. He has been telling me how he was stolen seven years ago, and bewitched by a fairy.'

'Indeed!' interrupted the cobbler angrily. 'Did he tell you this? Wait a minute, you rascal! Why I told him all about it myself only an hour ago, and then he goes off to humbug you. So you were bewitched, my son were you? Wait a bit, and I'll bewitch you!'

So saying, he caught up a bundle of straps, and hit out at Jem so hard that he ran off crying.

The poor little dwarf roamed about all the rest of the day without food or drink, and at night was glad to lie down and sleep on the steps of a church. He woke next morning with the first rays of light, and began to think what he could do to earn a living. Suddenly he remembered that he was an excellent cook, and he determined to look out for a place.

As soon as it was quite daylight he set out for the palace, for he knew that the grand duke who reigned over the country was fond of good things.

When he reached the palace all the servants crowded about him, and made fun of him, and at last their shouts and laughter grew so loud that the head steward rushed out, crying, 'For goodness sake, be quiet, can't you. Don't you know his highness is still asleep?'

Some of the servants ran off at once, and others pointed out Jem. Indeed, the steward found it hard to keep himself from laughing at the comic sight, but he ordered the servants off and led the dwarf into his own room.

When he heard him ask for a place as cook, he said : ' You make some mistake, my lad. I think you want to be the grand duke's dwarf, don't you?'

' No, sir,' replied Jem. ' I am an experienced cook,

and if you will kindly take me to the head cook he may find me of some use.'

' Well, as you will ; but believe me, you would have an easier place as the grand ducal dwarf.'

So saying, the head steward led him to the head cook's room.

' Sir,' asked Jem, as he bowed till his nose nearly touched the floor, ' do you want an experienced cook ? '

The head cook looked him over from head to foot, and burst out laughing.

' You a cook! Do you suppose our cooking stoves are so low that you can look into any saucepan on them ? Oh, my dear little fellow, whoever sent you to me wanted to make fun of you.'

But the dwarf was not to be put off.

' What matters an extra egg or two, or a little butter or flour and spice more or less, in such a house as this ? ' said he. ' Name any dish you wish to have cooked, and give me the materials I ask for, and you shall see.'

He said much more, and at last persuaded the head cook to give him a trial.

They went into the kitchen—a huge place with at least twenty fireplaces, always alight. A little stream of clear water ran through the room, and live fish were kept at one end of it. Everything in the kitchen was of the best and most beautiful kind, and swarms of cooks and scullions were busy preparing dishes.

When the head cook came in with Jem everyone stood quite still.

' What has his highness ordered for luncheon ? ' asked the head cook.

' Sir, his highness has graciously ordered a Danish soup and red Hamburg dumplings.'

' Good,' said the head cook. ' Have you heard, and do you feel equal to making these dishes ? Not that you will be able to make the dumplings, for they are a secret receipt.'

'Is that all!' said Jem, who had often made both dishes. 'Nothing easier. Let me have some eggs, a piece of wild boar, and such and such roots and herbs for the soup; and as for the dumplings,' he added in a low voice to the head cook, 'I shall want four different kinds of meat, some wine, a duck's marrow, some ginger, and a herb called heal-well.'

'Why,' cried the astonished cook, 'where did you learn cooking? Yes, those are the exact materials, but we never used the herb heal-well, which, I am sure, must be an improvement.'

And now Jem was allowed to try his hand. He could not nearly reach up to the kitchen range, but by putting a wide plank on two chairs he managed very well. All the cooks stood round to look on, and could not help admiring the quick, clever way in which he set to work. At last, when all was ready, Jem ordered the two dishes to be put on the fire till he gave the word. Then he began to count: 'One, two, three,' till he got to five hundred when he cried, 'Now!' The saucepans were taken off, and he invited the head cook to taste.

The first cook took a golden spoon, washed and wiped it, and handed it to the head cook, who solemnly approached, tasted the dishes, and smacked his lips over them. 'First rate, indeed!' he exclaimed. 'You certainly are a master of the art, little fellow, and the herb heal-well gives a particular relish.'

As he was speaking, the duke's valet came to say that his highness was ready for luncheon, and it was served at once in silver dishes. The head cook took Jem to his own room, but had hardly had time to question him before he was ordered to go at once to the grand duke. He hurried on his best clothes and followed the messenger.

The grand duke was looking much pleased. He had emptied the dishes, and was wiping his mouth as the head cook came in. 'Who cooked my luncheon to-day?' asked he. 'I must say your dumplings are always very good ; but I don't think I ever tasted anything so delicious as they were to-day. Who made them ? '

' It is a strange story, your highness,' said the cook, and told him the whole matter, which surprised the duke so much that he sent for the dwarf and asked him many questions. Of course, Jem could not say he had been turned into a squirrel, but he said he was without parents and had been taught cooking by an old woman.

' If you will stay with me,' said the grand duke, ' you shall have fifty ducats a year, besides a new coat and a couple of pairs of trousers. You must undertake to cook my luncheon yourself and to direct what I shall have for dinner, and you shall be called assistant head cook.'

Jem bowed to the ground, and promised to obey his new master in all things.

He lost no time in setting to work, and everyone rejoiced at having him in the kitchen, for the duke was not a patient man, and had been known to throw plates and dishes at his cooks and servants if the things served were not quite to his taste. Now all was changed. He never even grumbled at anything, had five meals instead of three, thought everything delicious, and grew fatter daily.

And so Jem lived on for two years, much respected and considered, and only saddened when he thought of his parents. One day passed much like another till the following incident happened.

Dwarf Long Nose—as he was always called—made a practice of doing his marketing as much as possible himself, and whenever time allowed went to the market to buy his poultry and fruit. One morning he was in the goose market, looking for some nice fat geese. No one thought of laughing at his appearance now; he was known as the duke's special body cook, and every goose-woman felt honoured if his nose turned her way.

He noticed one woman sitting apart with a number of geese, but not crying or praising them like the rest. He went up to her, felt and weighed her geese, and, finding them very good, bought three and the cage to put them in, hoisted them on his broad shoulders, and set off on his way back.

As he went, it struck him that two of the geese were gobbling and screaming as geese do, but the third sat quite still, only heaving a deep sigh now and then, like a human being. 'That goose is ill,' said he; 'I must make haste to kill and dress her.'

But the goose answered him quite distinctly:

> 'Squeeze too tight
> And I'll bite,
> If my neck a twist you gave
> I'd bring you to an early grave.'

Quite frightened, the dwarf set down the cage, and the goose gazed at him with sad wise-looking eyes and sighed again.

'Good gracious!' said Long Nose. 'So you can speak, Mistress Goose. I never should have thought it! Well, don't be anxious. I know better than to hurt so rare a bird. But I could bet you were not always in this plumage—wasn't I a squirrel myself for a time?'

'You are right,' said the goose, 'in supposing I was not born in this horrid shape. Ah! no one ever thought that Mimi, the daughter of the great Weatherbold, would be killed for the ducal table.'

'Be quite easy, Mistress Mimi,' comforted Jem. 'As sure as I'm an honest man and assistant head cook to his highness, no one shall harm you. I will make a hutch for you in my own rooms, and you shall be well fed, and I'll come and talk to you as much as I can. I'll tell all the other cooks that I am fattening up a goose on very special food for the grand duke, and at the first good opportunity I will set you free.'

The goose thanked him with tears in her eyes, and the dwarf kept his word. He killed the other two geese for dinner, but built a little shed for Mimi in one of his rooms, under the pretence of fattening her under his own eye. He spent all his spare time talking to her and comforting her, and fed her on all the daintiest dishes. They confided their histories to each other, and Jem learnt that the goose was the daughter of the wizard Weatherbold, who lived on the island of Gothland. He fell out with an old fairy, who got the better of him by cunning and treachery, and to revenge herself turned his daughter into a goose and carried her off to this distant place. When Long Nose told her his story she said :

' I know a little of these matters, and what you say shows me that you are under a herb enchantment—that is to say, that if you can find the herb whose smell woke you up the spell would be broken.'

This was but small comfort for Jem, for how and where was he to find the herb ?

About this time the grand duke had a visit from a neighbouring prince, a friend of his. He sent for Long Nose and said to him :

' Now is the time to show what you can really do. This prince who is staying with me has better dinners than any one except myself, and is a great judge of cooking. As long as he is here you must take care that my table shall be served in a manner to surprise him constantly. At the same time, on pain of my displeasure, take care that no dish shall appear twice. Get everything you wish and spare nothing. If you want to melt down gold and precious stones, do so. I would rather be a poor man than have to blush before him.'

The dwarf bowed and answered :

' Your highness shall be obeyed. I will do all in my power to please you and the prince.'

From this time the little cook was hardly seen except in the kitchen, where, surrounded by his helpers, he gave orders, baked, stewed, flavoured and dished up all manner of dishes.

The prince had been a fortnight with the grand duke, and enjoyed himself mightily. They ate five times a day, and the duke had every reason to be content with the dwarf's talents, for he saw how pleased his guest looked. On the fifteenth day the duke sent for the dwarf and presented him to the prince.

'You are a wonderful cook,' said the prince, 'and you certainly know what is good. All the time I have been here you have never repeated a dish, and all were excellent. But tell me why you have never served the queen of all dishes, a Suzeraine Pasty?'

The dwarf felt frightened, for he had never heard of this Queen of Pasties before. But he did not lose his presence of mind, and replied :

'I have waited, hoping that your highness' visit here would last some time, for I proposed to celebrate the last day of your stay with this truly royal dish.'

'Indeed,' laughed the grand duke; 'then I suppose you would have waited for the day of my death to treat me to it, for you have never sent it up to me yet. However, you will have to invent some other farewell dish, for the pasty must be on my table to-morrow.'

'As your highness pleases,' said the dwarf, and took leave.

But it did not please *him* at all. The moment of disgrace seemed at hand, for he had no idea how to make this pasty. He went to his rooms very sad. As he sat there lost in thought the goose Mimi, who was left free to walk about, came up to him and asked what was the matter? When she heard she said:

'Cheer up, my friend. I know the dish quite well : we often had it at home, and I can guess pretty well how it was made.' Then she told him what to put in, adding : 'I think that will be all right, and if some trifle is left out perhaps they won't find it out.'

Sure enough, next day a magnificent pasty all wreathed round with flowers was placed on the table. Jem himself put on his best clothes and went into the dining hall. As he entered the head carver was in the act of cutting up the pie and helping the duke and his guests. The grand duke took a large mouthful and threw up his eyes as he swallowed it.

'Oh! oh! this may well be called the Queen of Pasties, and at the same time my dwarf must be called the king of cooks. Don't you think so, dear friend?'

The prince took several small pieces, tasted and examined carefully, and then said with a mysterious and sarcastic smile:

'The dish is very nicely made, but the Suzeraine is not quite complete—as I expected.'

The grand duke flew into a rage.

'Dog of a cook,' he shouted; 'how dare you serve me so? I've a good mind to chop off your great head as a punishment.'

'For mercy's sake, don't, your highness! I made the pasty according to the best rules; nothing has been left out. Ask the prince what else I should have put in.'

The prince laughed. 'I was sure you could not make this dish as well as my cook, friend Long Nose. Know, then, that a herb is wanting called Relish, which is not known in this country, but which gives the pasty its peculiar flavour, and without which your master will never taste it to perfection.'

The grand duke was more furious than ever.

'But I *will* taste it to perfection,' he roared. 'Either the pasty must be made properly to-morrow or this rascal's head shall come off. Go, scoundrel, I give you twenty-four hours' respite.'

The poor dwarf hurried back to his room, and poured out his grief to the goose.

'Oh, is that all,' said she, 'then I can help you, for my father taught me to know all plants and herbs.

Luckily this is a new moon just now, for the herb only springs up at such times. But tell me, are there chestnut trees near the palace?'

'Oh, yes!' cried Long Nose, much relieved; 'near the lake—only a couple of hundred yards from the palace —is a large clump of them. But why do you ask?'

'Because the herb only grows near the roots of chestnut trees,' replied Mimi; 'so let us lose no time in finding it. Take me under your arm and put me down out of doors, and I'll hunt for it.'

He did as she bade, and as soon as they were in the garden put her on the ground, when she waddled off as fast as she could towards the lake, Jem hurrying after her with an anxious heart, for he knew that his life depended on her success. The goose hunted everywhere, but in vain. She searched under each chestnut tree, turning every blade of grass with her bill—nothing to be seen, and evening was drawing on!

Suddenly the dwarf noticed a big old tree standing alone on the other side of the lake. 'Look,' cried he, 'let us try our luck there.'

The goose fluttered and skipped in front, and he ran after as fast as his little legs could carry him. The tree cast a wide shadow, and it was almost dark beneath it, but suddenly the goose stood still, flapped her wings with joy, and plucked something, which she held out to her astonished friend, saying: 'There it is, and there is more growing here, so you will have no lack of it.'

The dwarf stood gazing at the plant. It gave out a strong sweet scent, which reminded him of the day of his enchantment. The stems and leaves were a bluish green, and it bore a dark, bright red flower with a yellow edge.

'What a wonder!' cried Long Nose. 'I do believe this is the very herb which changed me from a squirrel into my present miserable form. Shall I try an experiment?'

'Not yet,' said the goose. 'Take a good handful of

the herb with you, and let us go to your rooms.   We will
collect all your money and clothes together, and then
we will test the powers of the herb.'

THE GOOSE FINDS THE MAGIC HERB

So they went back to Jem's rooms, and here he
gathered together some fifty ducats he had saved, his
clothes and shoes, and tied them all up in a bundle.
Then he plunged his face into the bunch of herbs, and
drew in their perfume.

As he did so, all his limbs began to crack and stretch;
he felt his head rising above his shoulders; he glanced

down at his nose, and saw it grow smaller and smaller; his chest and back grew flat, and his legs grew long.

The goose looked on in amazement. ' Oh, how big and how beautiful you are ! ' she cried. ' Thank heaven, you are quite changed.'

Jem folded his hands in thanks, as his heart swelled with gratitude. But his joy did not make him forget all he owed to his friend Mimi.

' I owe you my life and my release,' he said, ' for without you I should never have regained my natural shape, and, indeed, would soon have been beheaded. I will now take you back to your father, who will certainly know how to disenchant you.'

The goose accepted his offer with joy, and they managed to slip out of the palace unnoticed by anyone.

They got through the journey without accident, and the wizard soon released his daughter, and loaded Jem with thanks and valuable presents. He lost no time in hastening back to his native town, and his parents were very ready to recognise the handsome, well-made young man as their long-lost son. With the money given him by the wizard he opened a shop, which prospered well, and he lived long and happily.

I must not forget to mention that much disturbance was caused in the palace by Jem's sudden disappearance, for when the grand duke sent orders next day to behead the dwarf, if he had not found the necessary herbs, the dwarf was not to be found. The prince hinted that the duke had allowed his cook to escape, and had therefore broken his word. The matter ended in a great war between the two princes, which was known in history as the ' Herb War.' After many battles and much loss of life, a peace was at last concluded, and this peace became known as the ' Pasty Peace,' because at the banquet given in its honour the prince's cook dished up the Queen of Pasties—the Suzeraine—and the grand duke declared it to be quite excellent.

A TALE OF THE TONTLAWALD

LONG, long ago there stood in the midst of a country covered with lakes a vast stretch of moorland called the Tontlawald, on which no man ever dared set foot. From time to time a few bold spirits had been drawn by curiosity to its borders, and on their return had reported that they had caught a glimpse of a ruined house in a grove of thick trees, and round about it were a crowd of beings resembling men, swarming over the grass like bees. The men were as dirty and ragged as gipsies, and there were besides a quantity of old women and half-naked children.

One night a peasant who was returning home from a feast wandered a little farther into the Tontlawald, and came back with the same story. A countless number of women and children were gathered round a huge fire, and some were seated on the ground, while others danced strange dances on the smooth grass. One old crone had a broad iron ladle in her hand, with which every now and then she stirred the fire, but the moment she touched the glowing ashes the children rushed away, shrieking like night owls, and it was a long while before they ventured to steal back. And besides all this there had once or twice been seen a little old man with a long beard creeping out of the forest, carrying a sack bigger than himself. The women and children ran by his side, weeping and trying to drag the sack from off his back, but he shook them off, and went on his way. There was also a tale of a magnificent black cat as large as a foal, but men could not believe all the wonders told by the peasant, and it was difficult to make out what was true and what was false in his story.   However, the fact remained that strange things did happen there, and the King of Sweden, to whom this part of the country belonged, more than once gave orders to cut down the haunted wood, but there was no one with courage enough to obey his commands.   At length one man, bolder than the rest, struck his axe into a tree, but his blow was followed by a stream of blood and shrieks as of a human creature in pain. The terrified woodcutter fled as fast as his legs would carry him, and after that neither orders nor threats would drive anybody to the enchanted moor.

A few miles from the Tontlawald was a large village, where dwelt a peasant who had recently married a young wife.   As not uncommonly happens in such cases, she turned the whole house upside down, and the two quarrelled and fought all day long.

By his first wife the peasant had a daughter called Elsa, a good quiet girl, who only wanted to live in peace, but this her stepmother would not allow.   She beat and cuffed the poor child from morning till night, but as the stepmother had the whip-hand of her husband there was no remedy.

For two years Elsa suffered all this ill-treatment, when one day she went out with the other village children to pluck strawberries.   Carelessly they wandered on, till at last they reached the edge of the Tontlawald, where the finest strawberries grew, making the grass red with their colour.   The children flung themselves down on the ground, and, after eating as many as they wanted, began to pile up their baskets, when suddenly a cry arose from one of the older boys:

'Run, run as fast as you can! We are in the Tontla-wald!'

Quicker than lightning they sprang to their feet, and

THE WOODCUTTER IN THE TONTLAWALD

rushed madly away, all except Elsa, who had strayed farther than the rest, and had found a bed of the finest strawberries right under the trees. Like the others, she heard the boy's cry, but could not make up her mind to leave the strawberries.

'After all, what does it matter?' thought she. 'The dwellers in the Tontlawald cannot be worse than my stepmother'; and looking up she saw a little black dog with a silver bell on its neck come barking towards her, followed by a maiden clad all in silk.

'Be quiet,' said she; then turning to Elsa she added: 'I am so glad you did not run away with the other children. Stay here with me and be my friend, and we will play delightful games together, and every day we will go and gather strawberries. Nobody will dare to beat you if I tell them not. Come, let us go to my mother'; and taking Elsa's hand she led her deeper into the wood, the little black dog jumping up beside them and barking with pleasure.

Oh! what wonders and splendours unfolded themselves before Elsa's astonished eyes! She thought she really must be in Heaven. Fruit trees and bushes loaded with fruit stood before them, while birds gayer than the brightest butterfly sat in their branches and filled the air with their song. And the birds were not shy, but let the girls take them in their hands, and stroke their gold and silver feathers. In the centre of the garden was the dwelling-house, shining with glass and precious stones, and in the doorway sat a woman in rich garments, who turned to Elsa's companion and asked:

'What sort of a guest are you bringing to me?'

'I found her alone in the wood,' replied her daughter, 'and brought her back with me for a companion. You will let her stay?'

The mother laughed, but said nothing, only she looked Elsa up and down sharply. Then she told the girl to come near, and stroked her cheeks and spoke kindly to

her, asking if her parents were alive, and if she really
would like to stay with them.   Elsa stooped and kissed her
hand, then, kneeling down, buried her face in the woman's
lap, and sobbed out :

'My mother has lain for many years under the ground.
My father is still alive, but I am nothing to him, and my
stepmother beats me all the day long.   I can do nothing
right, so let me, I pray you, stay with you.   I will look
after the flocks or do any work you tell me ; I will obey
your lightest word ; only do not, I entreat you, send me
back to her.   She will half kill me for not having come
back with the other children.'

And the woman smiled and answered, ' Well, we will
see what we can do with you,' and, rising, went into the
house.

Then the daughter said to Elsa, ' Fear nothing, my
mother will be your friend.   I saw by the way she looked
that she would grant your request when she had thought
over it,' and, telling Elsa to wait, she entered the house to
seek her mother.   Elsa meanwhile was tossed about
between hope and fear, and felt as if the girl would never
come.

At last Elsa saw her crossing the grass with a box in
her hand.

'My mother says we may play together to-day, as she
wants to make up her mind what to do about you.   But
I hope you will stay here always, as I can't bear you to
go away.   Have you ever been on the sea ? '

'The sea ? ' asked Elsa, staring ; ' what is that ?   I've
never heard of such a thing ! '

'Oh, I'll soon show you,' answered the girl, taking the
lid from the box, and at the very bottom lay a scrap of a
cloak, a mussel shell, and two fish scales.   Two drops of
water were glistening on the cloak, and these the girl
shook on the ground.   In an instant the garden and lawn
and everything else had vanished utterly, as if the earth
had opened and swallowed them up, and as far as the eye

could reach you could see nothing but water, which seemed at last to touch heaven itself. Only under their feet was a tiny dry spot. Then the girl placed the mussel shell on the water and took the fish scales in her hand. The mussel shell grew bigger and bigger, and turned into a pretty little boat, which would have held a dozen children. The girls stepped in, Elsa very cautiously, for which she was much laughed at by her friend, who used the fish scales for a rudder. The waves rocked the girls softly, as if they were lying in a cradle, and they floated on till they met other boats filled with men, singing and making merry.

'We must sing you a song in return,' said the girl, but as Elsa did not know any songs, she had to sing by herself. Elsa could not understand any of the men's songs, but one word, she noticed, came over and over again, and that was 'Kisika.' Elsa asked what it meant, and the girl replied that it was her name.

It was all so pleasant that they might have stayed there for ever had not a voice cried out to them, 'Children, it is time for you to come home!'

So Kisika took the little box out of her pocket, with the piece of cloth lying in it, and dipped the cloth in the water, and lo! they were standing close to a splendid house in the middle of the garden. Everything round them was dry and firm, and there was no water anywhere. The mussel shell and the fish scales were put back in the box, and the girls went in.

They entered a large hall, where four and twenty richly dressed women were sitting round a table, looking as if they were about to attend a wedding. At the head of the table sat the lady of the house in a golden chair.

Elsa did not know which way to look, for everything that met her eyes was more beautiful than she could have dreamed possible. But she sat down with the rest, and ate some delicious fruit, and thought she must be in heaven. The guests talked softly, but their speech was strange to Elsa, and she understood nothing of what was said. Then the hostess turned round and whispered something to a maid behind her chair, and the maid left the hall, and when she came back she brought a little old man with her, who had a beard longer than himself. He bowed low to the lady and then stood quietly near the door.

'Do you see this girl?' said the lady of the house, pointing to Elsa. 'I wish to adopt her for my daughter. Make me a copy of her, which we can send to her native village instead of herself.'

The old man looked Elsa all up and down, as if he was taking her measure, bowed again to the lady, and left the hall. After dinner the lady said kindly to Elsa, 'Kisika has begged me to let you stay with her, and you have told her you would like to live here. Is that so?'

At these words Elsa fell on her knees, and kissed the lady's hands and feet in gratitude for her escape from her cruel stepmother; but her hostess raised her from the ground and patted her head, saying, 'All will go well as long as you are a good, obedient child, and I will take care of you and see that you want for nothing till you are grown up and can look after yourself. My waiting-maid, who teaches Kisika all sorts of fine handiwork, shall teach you too.'

Not long after the old man came back with a mould full of clay on his shoulders, and a little covered basket in his left hand. He put down his mould and his basket on the ground, took up a handful of clay, and made a doll as large as life. When it was finished he bored a hole in the doll's breast and put a bit of bread inside; then, drawing a snake out of the basket, forced it to enter the hollow body.

'Now,' he said to the lady, 'all we want is a drop of the maiden's blood.'

When she heard this Elsa grew white with horror, for she thought she was selling her soul to the evil one.

'Do not be afraid!' the lady hastened to say; 'we do

not want your blood for any bad purpose, but rather to give you freedom and happiness.'

Then she took a tiny golden needle, pricked Elsa in the arm, and gave the needle to the old man, who stuck it into the heart of the doll. When this was done he placed the figure in the basket, promising that the next day they should all see what a beautiful piece of work he had finished.

When Elsa awoke the next morning in her silken bed, with its soft white pillows, she saw a beautiful dress lying over the back of a chair, ready for her to put on. A maid came in to comb out her long hair, and brought the finest linen for her use; but nothing gave Elsa so much joy as the little pair of embroidered shoes that she held in her hand, for the girl had hitherto been forced to run about barefoot by her cruel stepmother. In her excitement she never gave a thought to the rough clothes she had worn the day before, which had disappeared as if by magic during the night. Who could have taken them? Well, she was to know that by-and-by. But *we* can guess that the doll had been dressed in them, which was to go back to the village in her stead. By the time the sun rose the doll had attained her full size, and no one could have told one girl from the other. Elsa started back when she met herself as she looked only yesterday.

'You must not be frightened,' said the lady, when she noticed her terror; 'this clay figure can do you no harm. It is for your stepmother, that she may beat it instead of you. Let her flog it as hard as she will, it can never feel any pain. And if the wicked woman does not come one day to a better mind your double will be able at last to give her the punishment she deserves.'

From this moment Elsa's life was that of the ordinary happy child, who has been rocked to sleep in her baby-hood in a lovely golden cradle. She had no cares or troubles of any sort, and every day her tasks became easier, and the years that had gone before seemed more and more like a bad dream. But the happier she grew the deeper was her wonder at everything around her, and the more firmly she was persuaded that some great unknown power must be at the bottom of it all.

In the courtyard stood a huge granite block about twenty steps from the house, and when meal times came round the old man with the long beard went to the block, drew out a small silver staff, and struck the stone with it three times, so that the sound could be heard a long way off. At the third blow, out sprang a large golden cock, and stood upon the stone. Whenever he crowed and flapped his wings the rock opened and something came out of it. First a long table covered with dishes ready laid for the number of persons who would be seated round it, and this flew into the house all by itself.

When the cock crowed for the second time, a number of chairs appeared, and flew after the table; then wine, apples, and other fruit, all without trouble to anybody. After everybody had had enough, the old man struck the rock again, the golden cock crowed afresh, and back went dishes, table, chairs, and plates into the middle of the block.

When, however, it came to the turn of the thirteenth dish, which nobody ever wanted to eat, a huge black cat ran up, and stood on the rock close to the cock, while the dish was on his other side. There they all remained, till they were joined by the old man.

He picked up the dish in one hand, tucked the cat under his arm, told the cock to get on his shoulder, and all four vanished into the rock. And this wonderful stone contained not only food, but clothes and everything you could possibly want in the house.

At first a language was often spoken at meals which was strange to Elsa, but by the help of the lady and her daughter she began slowly to understand it, though it was years before she was able to speak it herself.

One day she asked Kisika why the thirteenth dish

HOW THE OLD MAN
DISAPPEARED
after dinner

HJ FORD

came daily to the table and was sent daily away un-
touched, but Kisika knew no more about it than she did.
The girl must, however, have told her mother what Elsa
had said, for a few days later she spoke to Elsa
seriously :

'Do not worry yourself with useless wondering.
You wish to know why we never eat of the thirteenth
dish ?   That, dear child, is the dish of hidden blessings,
and we cannot taste of it without bringing our happy life
here to an end.   And the world would be a great deal
better if men, in their greed, did not seek to snatch everything for themselves, instead of leaving something as a
thankoffering to the giver of the blessings.   Greed is
man's worst fault.'

The years passed like the wind for Elsa, and she grew
into a lovely woman, with a knowledge of many things
that she would never have learned in her native village ;
but Kisika was still the same young girl that she had
been on the day of her first meeting with Elsa.   Each
morning they both worked for an hour at reading and
writing, as they had always done, and Elsa was anxious
to learn all she could, but Kisika much preferred childish
games to anything else.   If the humour seized her, she
would fling aside her tasks, take her treasure box, and go
off to play in the sea, where no harm ever came to her.

'What a pity,' she would often say to Elsa, ' that you
have grown so big, you cannot play with me any more.'

Nine years slipped away in this manner, when one
day the lady called Elsa into her room.   Elsa was surprised at the summons, for it was unusual, and her heart
sank, for she feared some evil threatened her.   As she
crossed the threshold, she saw that the lady's cheeks
were flushed, and her eyes full of tears, which she dried
hastily, as if she would conceal them from the girl.
'Dearest child,' she began, ' the time has come when we
must part.'

'Part ? ' cried Elsa, burying her head in the lady's

lap. 'No, dear lady, that can never be till death parts us. You once opened your arms to me; you cannot thrust me away now.'

'Ah, be quiet, child,' replied the lady; 'you do not know what I would do to make you happy. Now you are a woman, and I have no right to keep you here. You must return to the world of men, where joy awaits you.'

'Dear lady,' entreated Elsa again. 'Do not, I beseech you, send me from you. I want no other happiness but to live and die beside you. Make me your waiting maid, or set me to any work you choose, but do not cast me forth into the world. It would have been better if you had left me with my stepmother, than first to have brought me to heaven and then send me back to a worse place.'

'Do not talk like that, dear child,' replied the lady; 'you do not know all that must be done to secure your happiness, however much it costs me. But it has to be. You are only a common mortal, who will have to die one day, and you cannot stay here any longer. Though we have the bodies of men, we are not men at all, though it is not easy for you to understand why. Some day or other you will find a husband who has been made expressly for you, and will live happily with him till death separates you. It will be very hard for me to part from you, but it has to be, and you must make up your mind to it.' Then she drew her golden comb gently through Elsa's hair, and bade her go to bed; but little sleep had the poor girl! Life seemed to stretch before her like a dark starless night.

Now let us look back a moment, and see what had been going on in Elsa's native village all these years, and how her double had fared. It is a well-known fact that a bad woman·seldom becomes better as she grows older, and Elsa's stepmother was no exception to the rule; but as the figure that had taken the girl's place could feel no

pain, the blows that were showered on her night and day
made no difference. If the father ever tried to come to
his daughter's help, his wife turned upon him, and things
were rather worse than before.

One day the stepmother had given the girl a frightful
beating, and then threatened to kill her outright. Mad
with rage, she seized the figure by the throat with both
hands, when out came a black snake from her mouth and
stung the woman's tongue, and she fell dead without a
sound. At night, when the husband came home, he found
his wife lying dead upon the ground, her body all swollen
and disfigured, but the girl was nowhere to be seen.
His screams brought the neighbours from their cottages,
but they were unable to explain how it had all come
about. It was true, they said, that about mid-day they
had heard a great noise, but as that was a matter of daily
occurrence they did not think much of it. The rest of
the day all was still, but no one had seen anything of the
daughter. The body of the dead woman was then prepared
for burial, and her tired husband went to bed, rejoicing
in his heart that he had been delivered from the firebrand
who had made his home unpleasant. On the table he
saw a slice of bread lying, and, being hungry, he ate it
before going to sleep.

In the morning he too was found dead, and as
swollen as his wife, for the bread had been placed in the
body of the figure by the old man who made it. A few
days later he was placed in the grave beside his wife, but
nothing more was ever heard of their daughter.

All night long after her talk with the lady Elsa had
wept and wailed her hard fate in being cast out from her
home which she loved.

Next morning, when she got up, the lady placed a gold
seal ring on her finger, strung a little golden box on a
ribbon, and placed it round her neck ; then she called the
old man, and, forcing back her tears, took leave of Elsa.
The girl tried to speak, but before she could sob out her

thanks the old man had touched her softly on the head three times with his silver staff.   In an instant Elsa knew that she was turning into a bird : wings sprang from beneath her arms ; her feet were the feet of eagles, with long claws ; her nose curved itself into a sharp beak, and feathers covered her body.   Then she soared high in the air, and floated up towards the clouds, as if she had really been hatched an eagle.

For several days she flew steadily south, resting from time to time when her wings grew tired, for hunger she never felt.   And so it happened that one day she was flying over a dense forest, and below hounds were barking fiercely, because, not having wings themselves, she was out of their reach.   Suddenly a sharp pain quivered through her body, and she fell to the ground, pierced by an arrow.

When Elsa recovered her senses, she found herself lying under a bush in her own proper form.   What had befallen her, and how she got there, lay behind her like a bad dream.

As she was wondering what she should do next the king's son came riding by, and, seeing Elsa, sprang from his horse, and took her by the hand, saying, ' Ah ! it was a happy chance that brought me here this morning.   Every night, for half a year, have I dreamed, dear lady, that I should one day find you in this wood.   And although I have passed through it hundreds of times in vain, I have never given up hope.   To-day I was going in search of a large eagle that I had shot, and instead of the eagle I have found—you.'   Then he took Elsa on his horse, and rode with her to the town, where the old king received her graciously.

A few days later the wedding took place, and as Elsa was arranging the veil upon her hair fifty carts arrived laden with beautiful things which the lady of the Tontlawald had sent to Elsa.   And after the king's death Elsa became queen, and when she was old she told this story.   But that was the last that was ever heard of the Tontlawald.

[From Ehstnische Märchen.]

THE FAIRY OF THE DAWN

ONCE upon a time what should happen *did* happen; and if it had not happened this tale would never have been told.

There was once an emperor, very great and mighty, and he ruled over an empire so large that no one knew where it began and where it ended. But if nobody could tell the exact extent of his sovereignty everybody was aware that the emperor's right eye laughed, while his left eye wept. One or two men of valour had the courage to go and ask him the reason of this strange fact, but he only laughed and said nothing; and the reason of the deadly enmity between his two eyes was a secret only known to the monarch himself.

And all the while the emperor's sons were growing up. And such sons! All three like the morning stars in the sky!

Florea, the eldest, was so tall and broad-shouldered that no man in the kingdom could approach him.

Costan, the second, was quite different. Small of stature, and slightly built, he had a strong arm and stronger wrist.

Petru, the third and youngest, was tall and thin, more like a girl than a boy. He spoke very little, but laughed and sang, sang and laughed, from morning till night. He was very seldom serious, but then he had a way when he was thinking of stroking his hair over his forehead, which made him look old enough to sit in his father's council!

'You are grown up, Florea,' said Petru one day to his eldest brother; 'do go and ask father why one eye laughs and the other weeps.'

THE EMPEROR WHOSE RIGHT EYE
LAUGHED WHILE HIS LEFT EYE WEPT

But Florea would not go. He had learnt by experience that this question always put the emperor in a rage.

Petru next went to Costan, but did not succeed any better with him.

'Well, well, as everyone else is afraid, I suppose I must do it myself,' observed Petru at length. No sooner said than done; the boy went straight to his father and put his question.

'May you go blind!' exclaimed the emperor in wrath; 'what business is it of yours?' and boxed Petru's ears soundly.

Petru returned to his brothers, and told them what had befallen him; but not long after it struck him that his father's left eye seemed to weep less, and the right to laugh more.

'I wonder if it has anything to do with my question,' thought he. 'I'll try again! After all, what do two boxes on the ear matter?'

So he put his question for the second time, and had the same answer; but the left eye only wept now and then, while the right eye looked ten years younger.

'It really *must* be true,' thought Petru. 'Now I know what I have to do. I shall have to go on putting that question, and getting boxes on the ear, till both eyes laugh together.'

No sooner said than done. Petru never, never forswore himself.

'Petru, my dear boy,' cried the emperor, both his eyes laughing together, 'I see you have got this on the brain. Well, I will let you into the secret. My right eye laughs when I look at my three sons, and see how strong and handsome you all are, and the other eye weeps because I fear that after I die you will not be able to keep the empire together, and to protect it from its enemies. But if you can bring me water from the spring of the Fairy of the Dawn, to bathe my eyes, then they will laugh for evermore; for I shall know that my sons are brave enough to overcome any foe.'

Thus spoke the emperor, and Petru picked up his hat and went to find his brothers.

The three young men took counsel together, and talked the subject well over, as brothers should do. And the end of it was that Florea, as the eldest, went to the stables, chose the best and handsomest horse they contained, saddled him, and took leave of the court.

'I am starting at once,' said he to his brothers, 'and if after a year, a month, a week, and a day I have not returned with the water from the spring of the Fairy of the Dawn, you, Costan, had better come after me.' So saying he disappeared round a corner of the palace.

For three days and three nights he never drew rein. Like a spirit the horse flew over mountains and valleys till he came to the borders of the empire. Here was a deep, deep trench that girdled it the whole way round, and there was only a single bridge by which the trench could be crossed. Florea made instantly for the bridge, and there pulled up to look around him once more, to take leave of his native land Then he turned, but before him was standing a dragon—oh! *such* a dragon!—a dragon with three heads and three horrible faces, all with their mouths wide open, one jaw reaching to heaven and the other to earth.

At this awful sight Florea did not wait to give battle. He put spurs to his horse and dashed off, *where* he neither knew nor cared.

The dragon heaved a sigh and vanished without leaving a trace behind him.

A week went by. Florea did not return home. Two passed; and nothing was heard of him. After a month Costan began to haunt the stables and to look out a horse for himself. And the moment the year, the month, the week, and the day were over Costan mounted his horse and took leave of his youngest brother.

'If I fail, then you come,' said he, and followed the path that Florea had taken.

The dragon on the bridge was more fearful and his three heads more terrible than before, and the young hero rode away still faster than his brother had done.

Nothing more was heard either of him or Florea; and Petru remained alone.

'I must go after my brothers,' said Petru one day to his father.

'Go, then,' said his father, 'and may you have better luck than they'; and he bade farewell to Petru, who rode straight to the borders of the kingdom.

The dragon on the bridge was yet more dreadful than the one Florea and Costan had seen, for this one had seven heads instead of only three.

Petru stopped for a moment when he caught sight of this terrible creature. Then he found his voice.

'Get out of the way!' cried he. 'Get out of the way!' he repeated again, as the dragon did not move. 'Get out of the way!' and with this last summons he drew his sword and rushed upon him. In an instant the heavens seemed to darken round him and he was surrounded by fire—fire to right of him, fire to left of him, fire to front of him, fire to rear of him; nothing but fire whichever way he looked, for the dragon's seven heads were vomiting flame.

The horse neighed and reared at the horrible sight, and Petru could not use the sword he had in readiness.

'Be quiet! this won't do!' he said, dismounting hastily, but holding the bridle firmly in his left hand and grasping his sword in his right.

But even so he got on no better, for he could see nothing but fire and smoke.

'There is no help for it; I must go back and get a better horse,' said he, and mounted again and rode homewards.

At the gate of the palace his nurse, old Birscha, was waiting for him eagerly.

'Ah, Petru, my son, I knew you would have to come

back,' she cried.   'You did not set about the matter
properly.'

'How ought I to have set about it?' asked Petru, half
angrily, half sadly.

'Look here, my boy,' replied old Birscha.   'You
can never reach the spring of the Fairy of the Dawn
unless you ride the horse which your father, the emperor,
rode in his youth.   Go and ask where it is to be found,
and then mount it and be off with you.'

Petru thanked her heartily for her advice, and went
at once to make inquiries about the horse.

'By the light of my eyes!' exclaimed the emperor
when Petru had put his question.   'Who has told you
anything about that?   It must have been that old witch
of a Birscha?   Have you lost your wits?   Fifty years have
passed since I was young, and who knows where the
bones of my horse may be rotting, or whether a scrap of
his reins still lie in his stall?   I have forgotten all about
him long ago.'

Petru turned away in anger, and went back to his
old nurse.

'Do not be cast down,' she said with a smile; 'if that
is how the affair stands all will go well.   Go and fetch
the scrap of the reins; I shall soon know what must be
done.'

The place was full of saddles, bridles, and bits of
leather.   Petru picked out the oldest, and blackest, and
most decayed pair of reins, and brought them to the old
woman, who murmured something over them and
sprinkled them with incense, and held them out to the
young man.

'Take the reins,' said she, 'and strike them violently
against the pillars of the house.'

Petru did what he was told, and scarcely had the
reins touched the pillars when something happened—
how I have no idea—that made Petru stare with surprise.
A horse stood before him—a horse whose equal in beauty

PETRU HAS TO TURN BACK

the world had never seen ; with a saddle on him of gold
and precious stones, and with such a dazzling bridle you
hardly dared to look at it, lest you should lose your sight.
A splendid horse, a splendid saddle, and a splendid bridle,
all ready for the splendid young prince !

' Jump on the back of the brown horse,' said the old
woman, and she turned round and went into the house.

The moment Petru was seated on the horse he felt
his arm three times as strong as before, and even his
heart felt braver.

' Sit firmly in the saddle, my lord, for we have a long
way to go and no time to waste,' said the brown horse,
and Petru soon saw that they were riding as no man
and horse had ever ridden before.

On the bridge stood a dragon, but not the same one
as he had tried to fight with, for this dragon had twelve
heads, each more hideous and shooting forth more
terrible flames than the other. But, horrible though he
was, he had met his match. Petru showed no fear, but
rolled up his sleeves, that his arms might be free.

' Get out of the way ! ' he said when he had done, but
the dragon's heads only breathed forth more flames and
smoke. Petru wasted no more words, but drew his sword
and prepared to throw himself on the bridge.

' Stop a moment ; be careful, my lord,' put in the
horse, ' and be sure you do what I tell you. Dig your
spurs in my body up to the rowel, draw your sword, and
keep yourself ready, for we shall have to leap over both
bridge and dragon. When you see that we are right
above the dragon cut off his biggest head, wipe the
blood off the sword, and put it back clean in the sheath
before we touch earth again.'

So Petru dug in his spurs, drew his sword, cut off the
head, wiped the blood, and put the sword back in the
sheath before the horse's hoofs touched the ground
again.

And in this fashion they passed the bridge.

'But we have got to go further still,' said Petru, after he had taken a farewell glance at his native land.

'Yes, forwards,' answered the horse ; ' but you must tell me, my lord, at what speed you wish to go. Like the wind? Like thought? Like desire? or like a curse?'

Petru looked about him, up at the heavens and down again to the earth. A desert lay spread out before him, whose aspect made his hair stand on end.

'We will ride at different speeds,' said he, ' not so fast as to grow tired nor so slow as to waste time.'

And so they rode, one day like the wind, the next like thought, the third and fourth like desire and like a curse, till they reached the borders of the desert.

'Now walk, so that I may look about, and see what I have never seen before,' said Petru, rubbing his eyes like one who wakes from sleep, or like him who beholds something so strange that it seems as if . . . Before Petru lay a wood made of copper, with copper trees and copper leaves, with bushes and flowers of copper also.

Petru stood and stared as a man does when he sees something that he has never seen, and of which he has never heard.

Then he rode right into the wood. On each side of the way the rows of flowers began to praise Petru, and to try and persuade him to pick some of them and make himself a wreath.

'Take me, for I am lovely, and can give strength to whoever plucks me,' said one.

'No, take me, for whoever wears me in his hat will be loved by the most beautiful woman in the world,' pleaded the second ; and then one after another bestirred itself, each more charming than the last, all promising, in soft sweet voices, wonderful things to Petru, if only he would pick them.

Petru was not deaf to their persuasion, and was just stooping to pick one when the horse sprang to one side.

THE BATTLE WITH THE WELWA IN THE COPPER WOOD

'Why don't you stay still?' asked Petru roughly.

'Do not pick the flowers; it will bring you bad luck,' answered the horse.

'Why should it do that?'

'These flowers are under a curse. Whoever plucks them must fight the Welwa [1] of the woods.'

'What kind of a goblin is the Welwa?'

'Oh, do leave me in peace! But listen. Look at the flowers as much as you like, but pick none,' and the horse walked on slowly.

Petru knew by experience that he would do well to attend to the horse's advice, so he made a great effort and tore his mind away from the flowers.

But in vain! If a man is fated to be unlucky, unlucky he will be, whatever he may do!

The flowers went on beseeching him, and his heart grew ever weaker and weaker.

'What must come will come,' said Petru at length; 'at any rate I shall see the Welwa of the woods, what she is like, and which way I had best fight her. If she is ordained to be the cause of my death, well, then it will be so; but if not I shall conquer her though she were twelve hundred Welwas,' and once more he stooped down to gather the flowers.

'You have done very wrong,' said the horse sadly. 'But it can't be helped now. Get yourself ready for battle, for here is the Welwa!'

Hardly had he done speaking, scarcely had Petru twisted his wreath, when a soft breeze arose on all sides at once. Out of the breeze came a storm wind, and the storm wind swelled and swelled till everything around was blotted out in darkness, and darkness covered them as with a thick cloak, while the earth swayed and shook under their feet.

'Are you afraid?' asked the horse, shaking his mane.

'Not yet,' replied Petru stoutly, though cold shivers

[1] A goblin.

were running down his back. 'What must come will
come, whatever it is.'

'Don't be afraid,' said the horse. 'I will help you.
Take the bridle from my neck, and try to catch the
Welwa with it.'

The words were hardly spoken, and Petru had no
time even to unbuckle the bridle, when the Welwa
herself stood before him; and Petru could not bear to
look at her, so horrible was she.

She had not exactly a head, yet neither was she
without one. She did not fly through the air, but neither
did she walk upon the earth. She had a mane like a
horse, horns like a deer, a face like a bear, eyes like a
polecat; while her body had something of each. And
that was the Welwa.

Petru planted himself firmly in his stirrups, and
began to lay about him with his sword, but could feel
nothing.

A day and a night went by, and the fight was still
undecided, but at last the Welwa began to pant for
breath.

'Let us wait a little and rest,' gasped she.

Petru stopped and lowered his sword.

'You must not stop an instant,' said the horse, and
Petru gathered up all his strength, and laid about him
harder than ever.

The Welwa gave a neigh like a horse and a howl like
a wolf, and threw herself afresh on Petru. For another
day and night the battle raged more furiously than
before. And Petru grew so exhausted he could scarcely
move his arm.

'Let us wait a little and rest,' cried the Welwa for
the second time, 'for I see you are as weary as I am.'

'You must not stop an instant,' said the horse.

And Petru went on fighting, though he barely had
strength to move his arm. But the Welwa had ceased
to throw herself upon him, and began to deliver her

blows cautiously, as if she had no longer power to strike.

And on the third day they were still fighting, but as the morning sky began to redden Petru somehow managed—how I cannot tell—to throw the bridle over the head of the tired Welwa. In a moment, from the Welwa sprang a horse—the most beautiful horse in the world.

'Sweet be your life, for you have delivered me from my enchantment,' said he, and began to rub his nose against his brother's. And he told Petru all his story, and how he had been bewitched for many years.

So Petru tied the Welwa to his own horse and rode on. Where did he ride? That I cannot tell you, but he rode on fast till he got out of the copper wood.

'Stay still, and let me look about, and see what I never have seen before,' said Petru again to his horse. For in front of him stretched a forest that was far more wonderful, as it was made of glistening trees and shining flowers. It was the silver wood.

As before, the flowers began to beg the young man to gather them.

'Do not pluck them,' warned the Welwa, trotting beside him, 'for my brother is seven times stronger than I'; but though Petru knew by experience what this meant, it was no use, and after a moment's hesitation he began to gather the flowers, and to twist himself a wreath.

Then the storm wind howled louder, the earth trembled more violently, and the night grew darker, than the first time, and the Welwa of the silver wood came rushing on with seven times the speed of the other. For three days and three nights they fought, but at last Petru cast the bridle over the head of the second Welwa.

'Sweet be your life, for you have delivered me from enchantment,' said the second Welwa, and they all journeyed on as before.

But soon they came to a gold wood more lovely far

than the other two, and again Petru's companions pleaded with him to ride through it quickly, and to leave the flowers alone.   But Petru turned a deaf ear to all they said, and before he had woven his golden crown he felt that something terrible, that he could not see, was coming near him right out of the earth.   He drew his sword and made himself ready for the fight.   ' I will die ! ' cried he, ' or he shall have my bridle over his head.'

He had hardly said the words when a thick fog wrapped itself around him, and so thick was it that he could not see his own hand, or hear the sound of his voice. For a day and a night he fought with his sword, without ever once seeing his enemy, then suddenly the fog began to lighten.   By dawn of the second day it had vanished altogether, and the sun shone brightly in the heavens.   It seemed to Petru that he had been born again.

And the Welwa ?   She had vanished.

' You had better take breath now you can, for the fight will have to begin all over again,' said the horse.

' What was it ? ' asked Petru.

' It was the Welwa,' replied the horse, ' changed into a fog !   Listen !   She is coming ! '

And Petru had hardly drawn a long breath when he felt something approaching from the side, though *what* he could not tell.   A river, yet not a river, for it seemed not to flow over the earth, but to go where it liked, and to leave no trace of its passage.

' Woe be to me ! ' cried Petru, frightened at last.

' Beware, and never stand still,' called the brown horse, and more he could not say, for the water was choking him.

The battle began anew.   For a day and a night Petru fought on, without knowing at whom or what he struck. At dawn on the second, he felt that both his feet were lame.

' Now I am done for,' thought he, and his blows fell thicker and harder in his desperation.   And the sun came

out and the water disappeared, without his knowing how
or when.

'Take breath,' said the horse, 'for you have no time
to lose. The Welwa will return in a moment.'

Petru made no reply, only wondered how, exhausted
as he was, he should ever be able to carry on the fight.
But he settled himself in his saddle, grasped his sword,
and waited.

And then something came to him—*what* I cannot tell
you. Perhaps, in his dreams, a man may see a creature
which has what it has not got, and has not got what it
has. At least, that was what the Welwa seemed like to
Petru. She flew with her feet, and walked with her
wings; her head was in her back, and her tail was on top
of her body; her eyes were in her neck, and her neck in
her forehead, and how to describe her further I do not
know.

Petru felt for a moment as if he was wrapped in a
garment of fear; then he shook himself and took heart,
and fought as he had never yet fought before.

As the day wore on, his strength began to fail, and
when darkness fell he could hardly keep his eyes open.
By midnight he knew he was no longer on his horse, but
standing on the ground, though he could not have told
how he got there. When the grey light of morning came,
he was past standing on his feet, but fought now upon his
knees.

'Make one more struggle; it is nearly over now,'
said the horse, seeing that Petru's strength was waning
fast.

Petru wiped the sweat from his brow with his
gauntlet, and with a desperate effort rose to his feet.

'Strike the Welwa on the mouth with the bridle,'
said the horse, and Petru did it.

The Welwa uttered a neigh so loud that Petru
thought he would be deaf for life, and then, though she
too was nearly spent, flung herself upon her enemy; but

Petru was on the watch and threw the bridle over her head, as she rushed on, so that when the day broke there were three horses trotting beside him.

'May your wife be the most beautiful of women,' said the Welwa, 'for you have delivered me from my enchantment.' So the four horses galloped fast, and by nightfall they were at the borders of the golden forest.

Then Petru began to think of the crowns that he wore, and what they had cost him.

'After all, what do I want with so many? I will keep the best,' he said to himself; and taking off first the copper crown and then the silver, he threw them away.

'Stay!' cried the horse, 'do not throw them away! Perhaps we shall find them of use. Get down and pick them up.' So Petru got down and picked them up, and they all went on.

In the evening, when the sun is getting low, and all the midges are beginning to bite, Peter saw a wide heath stretching before him.

At the same instant the horse stood still of itself.

'What is the matter?' asked Petru.

'I am afraid that something evil will happen to us,' answered the horse.

'But why should it?'

'We are going to enter the kingdom of the goddess Mittwoch,[1] and the further we ride into it the colder we shall get. But all along the road there are huge fires, and I dread lest you should stop and warm yourself at them.'

'And why should I not warm myself?'

'Something fearful will happen to you if you do,' replied the horse sadly.

'Well, forward!' cried Petru lightly, 'and if I have to bear cold, I must bear it!'

With every step they went into the kingdom of Mittwoch, the air grew colder and more icy, till even the

[1] In German 'Mittwoch,' the feminine form of Mercury.

marrow in their bones was frozen. But Petru was no coward; the fight he had gone through had strengthened his powers of endurance, and he stood the test bravely.

Along the road on each side were great fires, with men standing by them, who spoke pleasantly to Petru as he went by, and invited him to join them. The breath froze in his mouth, but he took no notice, only bade his horse ride on the faster.

How long Petru may have waged battle silently with the cold one cannot tell, for everybody knows that the kingdom of Mittwoch is not to be crossed in a day, but he struggled on, though the frozen rocks burst around, and though his teeth chattered, and even his eyelids were frozen.

At length they reached the dwelling of Mittwoch herself, and, jumping from his horse, Petru threw the reins over his horse's neck and entered the hut.

' Good-day, little mother ! ' said he.

' Very well, thank you, my frozen friend ! '

Petru laughed, and waited for her to speak.

'You have borne yourself bravely,' went on the goddess, tapping him on the shoulder. ' Now you shall have your reward,' and she opened an iron chest, out of which she took a little box.

' Look ! ' said she ; ' this little box has been lying here for ages, waiting for the man who could win his way through the Ice Kingdom. Take it, and treasure it, for some day it may help you. If you open it, it will tell you anything you want, and give you news of your fatherland.'

Petru thanked her gratefully for her gift, mounted his horse, and rode away.

When he was some distance from the hut, he opened the casket.

' What are your commands ? ' asked a voice inside.

' Give me news of my father,' he replied, rather nervously.

' He is sitting in council with his nobles,' answered the casket.

' Is he well ? '

' Not particularly, for he is furiously angry.'

' What has angered him ? '

' Your brothers Costan and Florea,' replied the casket. ' It seems to me they are trying to rule him and the kingdom as well, and the old man says they are not fit to do it.'

' Push on, good horse, for we have no time to lose ! ' cried Petru ; then he shut up the box, and put it in his pocket.

They rushed on as fast as ghosts, as whirlwinds, as vampires when they hunt at midnight, and how long they rode no man can tell, for the way is far.

' Stop ! I have· some advice to give you,' said the horse at last.

' What is it ? ' asked Petru.

' You have known what it is to suffer cold ; you will have to endure heat, such as you have never dreamed of. Be as brave now as you were then. Let no one tempt you to try to cool yourself, or evil will befall you.'

' Forwards ! ' answered Petru. ' Do not worry yourself. If I have escaped without being frozen, there is no chance of my melting.'

' Why not ? This is a heat that will melt the marrow in your bones—a heat that is only to be felt in the kingdom of the Goddess of Thunder.'[1]

And it *was* hot. The very iron of the horse's shoes began to melt, but Petru gave no heed. The sweat ran down his face, but he dried it with his gauntlet. What heat could be he never knew before, and on the way, not a stone's throw from the road, lay the most delicious valleys, full of shady trees and bubbling streams. When Petru looked at them his heart burned within him, and

---

[1] In the German ' Donnerstag '—the day of the Thunder God, *i.e.* Jupiter.

Among the flowers
were lovely maidans
calling to him with
~soft voices~

his mouth grew parched. And standing among the flowers were lovely maidens who called to him in soft voices, till he had to shut his eyes against their spells.

'Come, my hero, come and rest; the heat will kill you,' said they.

Petru shook his head and said nothing, for he had lost the power of speech.

Long he rode in this awful state, how long none can tell. Suddenly the heat seemed to become less, and, in the distance, he saw a little hut on a hill. This was the dwelling of the Goddess of Thunder, and when he drew rein at her door the goddess herself came out to meet him.

She welcomed him, and kindly invited him in, and bade him tell her all his adventures. So Petru told her all that had happened to him, and why he was there, and then took farewell of her, as he had no time to lose. 'For,' he said, 'who knows how far the Fairy of the Dawn may yet be?'

'Stay for one moment, for I have a word of advice to give you. You are about to enter the kingdom of Venus;[1] go and tell her, as a message from me, that I hope she will not tempt you to delay. On your way back, come to me again, and I will give you something that may be of use to you.'

So Petru mounted his horse, and had hardly ridden three steps when he found himself in a new country. Here it was neither hot nor cold, but the air was warm and soft like spring, though the way ran through a heath covered with sand and thistles.

'What can that be?' asked Petru, when he saw a long, long way off, at the very end of the heath, something resembling a house.

'That is the house of the goddess Venus,' replied the horse, 'and if we ride hard we may reach it before dark'; and he darted off like an arrow, so that as twilight fell

[1] 'Vineri' is Friday, and also 'Venus.'

they found themselves nearing the house. Petru's heart leaped at the sight, for all the way along he had been followed by a crowd of shadowy figures who danced about him from right to left, and from back to front, and Petru, though a brave man, felt now and then a thrill of fear.

'They won't hurt you,' said the horse; 'they are just the daughters of the whirlwind amusing themselves while they are waiting for the ogre of the moon.'

Then he stopped in front of the house, and Petru jumped off and went to the door.

'Do not be in such a hurry,' cried the horse. 'There are several things I must tell you first. You cannot enter the house of the goddess Venus like that. She is always watched and guarded by the whirlwind.'

'What am I to do then?'

'Take the copper wreath, and go with it to that little hill over there. When you reach it, say to yourself, "Were there ever such lovely maidens! such angels! such fairy souls!" Then hold the wreath high in the air and cry, "Oh! if I knew whether any one would accept this wreath from me . . . if I knew! if I knew!" and throw the wreath from you!'

'And why should I do all this?' said Petru.

'Ask no questions, but go and do it,' replied the horse. And Petru did.

Scarcely had he flung away the copper wreath than the whirlwind flung himself upon it, and tore it in pieces.

Then Petru turned once more to the horse.

'Stop!' cried the horse again. 'I have other things to tell you. Take the silver wreath and knock at the windows of the goddess Venus. When she says, "Who is there?" answer that you have come on foot and lost your way on the heath. She will then tell you to go your way back again; but take care not to stir from the spot. Instead, be sure you say to her, "No, indeed I shall do nothing of the sort, as from my childhood I have heard stories of the beauty of the goddess Venus, and it was not for nothing that I had shoes made of leather with soles of steel, and have travelled for nine years and nine months, and have won in battle the silver wreath, which I hope you may allow me to give you, and have done and suffered everything to be where I now am." This is what you must say. What happens after is your affair.'

Petru asked no more, but went towards the house.

By this time it was pitch dark, and there was only the ray of light that streamed through the windows to guide him, and at the sound of his footsteps two dogs began to bark loudly.

'Which of those dogs is barking? Is he tired of life?' asked the goddess Venus.

'It is I, O goddess!' replied Petru, rather timidly. 'I have lost my way on the heath, and do not know where I am to sleep this night.'

'Where did you leave your horse?' asked the goddess sharply.

Petru did not answer. He was not sure if he was to lie, or whether he had better tell the truth.

'Go away, my son, there is no place for you here,' replied she, drawing back from the window.

Then Petru repeated hastily what the horse had told him to say, and no sooner had he done so than the goddess opened the window, and in gentle tones she asked him :

'Let me see this wreath, my son,' and Petru held it out to her.

'Come into the house,' went on the goddess; 'do not fear the dogs, they always know my will.' And so they did, for as the young man passed they wagged their tails to him.

'Good evening,' said Petru as he entered the house, and, seating himself near the fire, listened comfortably to whatever the goddess might choose to talk about, which was for the most part the wickedness of men, with whom she was evidently very angry. But Petru agreed with her in everything, as he had been taught was only polite.

But was anybody ever so old as she! I do not know why Petru devoured her so with his eyes, unless it was to count the wrinkles on her face; but if so he would have had to live seven lives, and each life seven times the length of an ordinary one, before he could have reckoned them up.

But Venus was joyful in her heart when she saw Petru's eyes fixed upon her.

'Nothing was that is, and the world was not a world when I was born,' said she. 'When I grew up and the world came into being, everyone thought I was the most beautiful girl that ever was seen, though many hated me for it. But every hundred years there came a wrinkle on my face. And now I am old.' Then she went on to tell Petru that she was the daughter of an emperor, and their nearest neighbour was the Fairy of the Dawn, with whom she had a violent quarrel, and with that she broke out into loud abuse of her.

Petru did not know what to do. He listened in silence for the most part, but now and then he would say, 'Yes, yes, you must have been badly treated,' just for politeness' sake; what more could he do?

'I will give you a task to perform, for you are brave, and will carry it through,' continued Venus, when she had talked a long time, and both of them were getting sleepy. 'Close to the Fairy's house is a well, and whoever drinks from it will blossom again like a rose. Bring me a flagon of it, and I will do anything to prove my gratitude. It is not easy! no one knows that better than I do! The kingdom is guarded on every side by wild beasts and horrible dragons; but I will tell you more about that, and I also have something to give you.'

Then she rose and lifted the lid of an iron-bound chest, and took out of it a very tiny flute.

'Do you see this?' she asked. 'An old man gave it to me when I was young: whoever listens to this flute goes to sleep, and nothing can wake him. Take it and play on it as long as you remain in the kingdom of the Fairy of the Dawn, and you will be safe.

At this, Petru told her that he had another task to fulfil at the well of the Fairy of the Dawn, and Venus was still better pleased when she heard his tale.

So Petru bade her good-night, put the flute in its case, and laid himself down in the lowest chamber to sleep.

Before the dawn he was awake again, and his first care was to give to each of his horses as much corn as he could eat, and then to lead them to the well to water. Then he dressed himself and made ready to start.

'Stop,' cried Venus from her window, 'I have still a piece of advice to give you. Leave one of your horses here, and only take three. Ride slowly till you get to the fairy's kingdom, then dismount and go on foot. When you return, see that all your three horses remain on the road, while you walk. But above all beware never to look the Fairy of the Dawn in the face, for she has eyes that will bewitch you, and glances that will befool you. She is hideous, more hideous than anything you can imagine, with owl's eyes, foxy face, and cat's claws. Do you hear? do you hear? Be sure you never look at her.'

Petru thanked her, and managed to get off at last.

Far, far away, where the heavens touch the earth, where the stars kiss the flowers, a soft red light was seen, such as the sky sometimes has in spring, only lovelier, more wonderful.

That light was behind the palace of the Fairy of the Dawn, and it took Petru two days and nights through flowery meadows to reach it. And besides, it was neither hot nor cold, bright nor dark, but something of them all, and Petru did not find the way a step too long.

After some time Petru saw something white rise up out of the red of the sky, and when he drew nearer he saw it was a castle, and so splendid that his eyes were dazzled when they looked at it. He did not know there was such a beautiful castle in the world.

But no time was to be lost, so he shook himself, jumped down from his horse, and, leaving him on the dewy grass, began to play on his flute as he walked along.

He had hardly gone many steps when he stumbled over a huge giant, who had been lulled to sleep by the music. This was one of the guards of the castle! As he lay there on his back, he seemed so big that in spite of Petru's haste he stopped to measure him.

The further went Petru, the more strange and terrible were the sights he saw—lions, tigers, dragons with seven heads, all stretched out in the sun fast asleep. It is needless to say what the dragons were like, for nowadays everyone knows, and dragons are not things to joke about. Petru ran through them like the wind. Was it haste or fear that spurred him on?

At last he came to a river, but let nobody think for a moment that this river was like other rivers? Instead of water, there flowed milk, and the bottom was of precious stones and pearls, instead of sand and pebbles. And it ran neither fast nor slow, but both fast and slow together. And the river flowed round the castle, and on its banks slept lions with iron teeth and claws; and beyond were gardens such as only the Fairy of the Dawn can have, and on the flowers slept a fairy! All this saw Petru from the other side.

But how was he to get over? To be sure there was a bridge, but, even if it had not been guarded by sleeping lions, it was plainly not meant for man to walk on. Who could tell what it was made of ?   It looked like soft little woolly clouds !

So he stood thinking what was to be done, for get across he must.   After a while, he determined to take the

PETRU WAKES THE GIANT UP

risk, and strode back to the sleeping giant.   'Wake up, my brave man !' he cried, giving him a shake.

The giant woke and stretched out his hand to pick up Petru, just as we should catch a fly.   But Petru played on his flute, and the giant fell back again. Petru tried this three times, and when he was satisfied that the giant was really in his power he took out a handkerchief, bound the two little fingers of the giant together, drew his sword, and cried for the fourth time, 'Wake up, my brave man.'

When the giant saw the trick which had been played on him he said to Petru, 'Do you call this a fair fight? Fight according to rules, if you really are a hero!'

'I will by-and-by, but first I want to ask you a question! Will you swear that you will carry me over the river if I fight honourably with you?' And the giant swore.

When his hands were freed, the giant flung himself upon Petru, hoping to crush him by his weight. But he had met his match. It was not yesterday, nor the day before, that Petru had fought his first battle, and he bore himself bravely.

For three days and three nights the battle raged, and sometimes one had the upper hand, and sometimes the other, till at length they both lay struggling on the ground, but Petru was on top, with the point of his sword at the giant's throat.

'Let me go! let me go!' shrieked he. 'I own that I am beaten!'

'Will you take me over the river?' asked Petru.

'I will,' gasped the giant.

'What shall I do to you if you break your word?'

'Kill me, any way you like! But let me live now.'

'Very well,' said Petru, and he bound the giant's left hand to his right foot, tied one handkerchief round his mouth to prevent him crying out, and another round his eyes, and led him to the river.

Once they had reached the bank he stretched one leg over to the other side, and, catching up Petru in the palm of his hand, set him down on the further shore.

'That is all right,' said Petru. Then he played a few

notes on his flute, and the giant went to sleep again.
Even the fairies who had been bathing a little lower
down heard the music and fell asleep among the flowers
on the bank.   Petru saw them as he passed, and thought,
' If they are so beautiful, why should the Fairy of the
Dawn be so ugly? '   But he dared not linger, and pushed
on.

And now he was in the wonderful gardens, which
seemed more wonderful still than they had done from
afar.   But Petru could see no faded flowers, nor any
birds, as he hastened through them to the castle.   No
one was there to bar his way, for all were asleep.   Even
the leaves had ceased to move.

He passed through the courtyard, and entered the castle
itself.

What he beheld there need not be told, for all the
world knows that the palace of the Fairy of the Dawn is
no ordinary place.   Gold and precious stones were as
common as wood with us, and the stables where the
horses of the sun were kept were more splendid than
the palace of the greatest emperor in the world.

Petru went up the stairs and walked quickly through
eight-and-forty rooms, hung with silken stuffs, and all
empty.   In the forty-ninth he found the Fairy of the
Dawn herself.

In the middle of this room, which was as large as a
church, Petru saw the celebrated well that he had come
so far to seek.   It was a well just like other wells, and it
seemed strange that the Fairy of the Dawn should have
it in her own chamber; yet anyone could tell it had been
there for hundreds of years.   And by the well slept the
Fairy of the Dawn—the Fairy of the Dawn—herself !

And as Petru looked at her the magic flute dropped by
his side, and he held his breath.

Near the well was a table, on which stood bread
made with does' milk, and a flagon of wine.   It was the
bread of strength and the wine of youth, and Petru

longed for them. He looked once at the bread and once at the wine, and then at the Fairy of the Dawn, still sleeping on her silken cushions.

As he looked a mist came over his senses. The fairy opened her eyes slowly and looked at Petru, who lost his head still further; but he just managed to remember his flute, and a few notes of it sent the Fairy to sleep again, and he kissed her thrice. Then he stooped and laid his golden wreath upon her forehead, ate a piece of the bread and drank a cupful of the wine of youth, and this he did three times over. Then he filled a flask with water from the well, and vanished swiftly.

As he passed through the garden it seemed quite different from what it was before. The flowers were lovelier, the streams ran quicker, the sunbeams shone brighter, and the fairies seemed gayer. And all this had been caused by the three kisses Petru had given the Fairy of the Dawn.

He passed everything safely by, and was soon seated in his saddle again. Faster than the wind, faster than thought, faster than longing, faster than hatred rode Petru. At length he dismounted, and, leaving his horses at the roadside, went on foot to the house of Venus.

The goddess Venus knew that he was coming, and went to meet him, bearing with her white bread and red wine.

'Welcome back, my prince,' said she.

'Good day, and many thanks,' replied the young man, holding out the flask containing the magic water. She received it with joy, and after a short rest Petru set forth, for he had no time to lose.

He stopped a few minutes, as he had promised, with the Goddess of Thunder, and was taking a hasty farewell of her, when she called him back.

'Stay, I have a warning to give you,' said she. 'Beware of your life; make friends with no man; do not ride fast, or let the water go out of your hand; believe

no one, and flee flattering tongues. Go, and take care,
for the way is long, the world is bad, and you hold something very precious. But I will give you this cloth to
help you. It is not much to look at, but it is enchanted,
and whoever carries it will never be struck by lightning,
pierced by a lance, or smitten with a sword, and the
arrows will glance off his body.'

Petru thanked her and rode off, and, taking out his
treasure box, inquired how matters were going at home.
Not well, it said. The emperor was blind altogether
now, and Florea and Costan had besought him to give the
government of the kingdom into their hands; but he
would not, saying that he did not mean to resign the
government till he had washed his eyes from the well of
the Fairy of the Dawn. Then the brothers had gone to
consult old Birscha, who told them that Petru was already
on his way home bearing the water. They had set out to
meet him, and would try to take the magic water from
him, and then claim as their reward the government of
the emperor.

'You are lying!' cried Petru angrily, throwing the
box on the ground, where it broke into a thousand
pieces.

It was not long before he began to catch glimpses of
his native land, and he drew rein near a bridge, the better
to look at it. He was still gazing, when he heard a sound
in the distance as if some one was calling him by his
name.

'You, Petru!' it said.

'On! on!' cried the horse; 'it will fare ill with you
if you stop.'

'No, let us stop, and see who and what it is!' answered
Petru, turning his horse round, and coming face to face
with his two brothers. He had forgotten the warning
given him by the Goddess of Thunder, and when Costan
and Florea drew near with soft and flattering words he
jumped straight off his horse, and rushed to embrace them.

He had a thousand questions to ask, and a thousand things to tell. But his brown horse stood sadly hanging his head.

'Petru, my dear brother,' at length said Florea, 'would it not be better if we carried the water for you? Some one might try to take it from you on the road, while no one would suspect us.'

'So it would,' added Costan. 'Florea speaks well.' But Petru shook his head, and told them what the Goddess of Thunder had said, and about the cloth she had given him. And both brothers understood there was only one way in which they could kill him.

At a stone's throw from where they stood ran a rushing stream, with clear deep pools.

'Don't you feel thirsty, Costan?' asked Florea, winking at him.

'Yes,' replied Costan, understanding directly what was wanted. 'Come, Petru, let us drink now we have the chance, and then we will set out on our way home. It is a good thing you have us with you, to protect you from harm.'

The horse neighed, and Petru knew what it meant, and did not go with his brothers.

No, he went home to his father, and cured his blindness; and as for his brothers, they never returned again.

[From Rümänische Märchen.]

THE NUNDA, EATER OF PEOPLE

ONCE upon a time there lived a sultan who loved his garden dearly, and planted it with trees and flowers and fruits from all parts of the world. He went to see them three times every day : first at seven o'clock, when he got up, then at three, and lastly at half-past five. There was no plant and no vegetable which escaped his eye, but he lingered longest of all before his one date tree.

Now the sultan had seven sons. Six of them he was proud of, for they were strong and manly, but the youngest he disliked, for he spent all his time among the women of the house. The sultan had talked to him, and he paid no heed ; and he had beaten him, and he paid no heed ; and he had tied him up, and he paid no heed, till at last his father grew tired of trying to make him change his ways, and let him alone.

Time passed, and one day the sultan, to his great joy, saw signs of fruit on his date tree. And he told his vizir, ' My date tree is bearing ; ' and he told the officers, ' My date tree is bearing ; ' and he told the judges, ' My date tree is bearing ; ' and he told all the rich men of the town.

He waited patiently for some days till the dates were nearly ripe, and then he called his six sons, and said : ' One of you must watch the date tree till the dates are ripe, for if it is not watched the slaves will steal them, and I shall not have any for another year.'

And the eldest son answered, ' I will go, father,' and he went.

The first thing the youth did was to summon his slaves, and bid them beat drums all night under the date tree, for he feared to fall asleep. So the slaves beat the drums, and the young man danced till four o'clock, and then it grew so cold he could dance no longer, and one of the slaves said to him : ' It is getting light ; the tree is safe ; lie down, master, and go to sleep.'

So he lay down and slept, and his slaves slept likewise.

A few minutes went by, and a bird flew down from a neighbouring thicket, and ate all the dates, without leaving a single one. And when the tree was stripped bare, the bird went as it had come. Soon after, one of the slaves woke up and looked for the dates, but there were no dates to see. Then he ran to the young man and shook him, saying :

' Your father set you to watch the tree, and you have not watched, and the dates have all been eaten by a bird.'

The lad jumped up and ran to the tree to see for himself, but there was not a date anywhere. And he cried aloud, ' What am I to say to my father ? Shall I tell him that the dates have been stolen, or that a great rain fell and a great storm blew ? But he will send me to gather them up and bring them to him, and there are none to bring ! Shall I tell him that Bedouins drove me away, and when I returned there were no dates ? And he will answer, " You had slaves, did they not fight with the Bedouins ? " It is the truth that will be best, and that will I tell him.'

Then he went straight to his father, and found him sitting in his verandah with his five sons round him ; and the lad bowed his head.

' Give me the news from the garden,' said the sultan.

And the youth answered, ' The dates have all been eaten by some bird : there is not one left.'

The sultan was silent for a moment : then he asked, 'Where were you when the bird came?'

The lad answered : 'I watched the date tree till the cocks were crowing and it was getting light; then I lay down for a little, and I slept. When I woke a slave was standing over me, and he said, "There is not one date left on the tree!" And I went to the date tree, and saw it was true; and that is what I have to tell you.'

And the sultan replied, 'A son like you is only good for eating and sleeping. I have no use for you. Go your way, and when my date tree bears again, I will send another son; perhaps he will watch better.'

So he waited many months, till the tree was covered with more dates than any tree had ever borne before. When they were near ripening he sent one of his sons to the garden : saying, 'My son, I am longing to taste those dates : go and watch over them, for to-day's sun will bring them to perfection.'

And the lad answered : 'My father, I am going now, and to-morrow, when the sun has passed the hour of seven, bid a slave come and gather the dates.'

'Good,' said the sultan.

The youth went to the tree, and lay down and slept. And about midnight he arose to look at the tree, and the dates were all there—beautiful dates, swinging in bunches.

'Ah, my father will have a feast, indeed,' thought he. 'What a fool my brother was not to take more heed! Now he is in disgrace, and we know him no more. Well, I will watch till the bird comes. I should like to see what manner of bird it is.'

And he sat and read till the cocks crew and it grew light, and the dates were still on the tree.

'Oh my father will have his dates; they are all safe now,' he thought to himself. 'I will make myself comfortable against this tree,' and he leaned against the trunk, and sleep came on him, and the bird flew down and ate all the dates.

When the sun rose, the head-man came and looked for the dates, and there were no dates. And he woke the young man, and said to him, ' Look at the tree.'

And the young man looked, and there were no dates. And his ears were stopped, and his legs trembled, and his tongue grew heavy at the thought of the sultan. His slave became frightened as he looked at him, and asked, ' My master, what is it ? '

He answered, ' I have no pain anywhere, but I am ill everywhere. My whole body is well, and my whole body is sick I fear my father, for did I not say to him, " To-morrow at seven you shall taste the dates " ? And he will drive me away, as he drove away my brother ! I will go away myself, before he sends me.'

Then he got up and took a road that led straight past the palace, but he had not walked many steps before he met a man carrying a large silver dish, covered with a white cloth to cover the dates. And the young man said, ' The dates are not ripe yet ; you must return to-morrow.'

And the slave went with him to the palace, where the sultan was sitting with his four sons.

' Good greeting, master ! ' said the youth.

And the sultan answered, ' Have you seen the man I sent ? '

' I have, master ; but the dates are not yet ripe.'

But the sultan did not believe his words, and said : ' This second year I have eaten no dates, because of my sons. Go your ways, you are my son no longer ! '

And the sultan looked at the four sons that were left him, and promised rich gifts to whichever of them would bring him the dates from the tree. But year by year passed, and he never got them. One son tried to keep himself awake with playing cards ; another mounted a horse and rode round and round the tree, while the two others, whom their father as a last hope sent together, lit bonfires. But whatever they did, the result was always the same. Towards dawn they fell asleep, and the bird ate the dates on the tree.

The sixth year had come, and the dates on the tree were thicker than ever. And the head-man went to the palace and told the sultan what he had seen. But the sultan only shook his head, and said sadly, ' What is that to me ? I have had seven sons, yet for five years a bird has devoured my dates; and this year it will be the same as ever.'

Now the youngest son was sitting in the kitchen, as was his custom, when he heard his father say those words. And he rose up, and went to his father, and knelt before him. 'Father, this year you shall eat dates,' cried he. ' And on the tree are five great bunches, and each bunch I will give to a separate nation, for the nations in the town are five. This time, I will watch the date tree myself.' But his father and his mother laughed heartily, and thought his words idle talk.

One day, news was brought to the sultan that the dates were ripe, and he ordered one of his men to go and watch the tree. His son, who happened to be standing by, heard the order, and he said :

'How is it that you have bidden a man to watch the tree, when I, your son, am left ?'

And his father answered, ' Ah, six were of no use, and where they failed, will you succeed ?'

But the boy replied : 'Have patience to-day, and let me go, and to-morrow you shall see whether I bring you dates or not.'

' Let the child go, Master,' said his wife; ' perhaps we shall eat the dates—or perhaps we shall not—but let him go.'

And the sultan answered : ' I do not refuse to let him go, but my heart distrusts him. His brothers all promised fair, and what did they do ?'

But the boy entreated, saying, 'Father, if you and I
and mother be alive to-morrow, you shall eat the dates.'

'Go then,' said his father.

When the boy reached the garden, he told the slaves
to leave him, and to return home themselves and sleep.
When he was alone, he laid himself down and slept fast
till one o'clock, when he arose, and sat opposite the date
tree. Then he took some Indian corn out of one fold of
his dress, and some sandy grit out of another. And he
chewed the corn till he felt he was growing sleepy,
and then he put some grit into his mouth, and that kept
him awake till the bird came.

It looked about at first without seeing him, and whispering to itself, 'There is no one here,' fluttered lightly on
to the tree and stretched out his beak for the dates. Then
the boy stole softly up, and caught it by the wing.

The bird turned and flew quickly away, but the boy
never let go, not even when they soared high into the air.

'Son of Adam,' the bird said when the tops of the
mountains looked small below them, 'if you fall, you will
be dead long before you reach the ground, so go your
way, and let me go mine.'

But the boy answered, 'Wherever you go, I will go
with you. You cannot get rid of me.'

'I did not eat your dates,' persisted the bird, 'and the
day is dawning. Leave me to go my way.'

But again the boy answered him : 'My six brothers
are hateful to my father because you came and stole the
dates, and to-day my father shall see you, and my brothers
shall see you, and all the people of the town, great and
small, shall see you. And my father's heart will rejoice.'

'Well, if you will not leave me, I will throw you off,'
said the bird.

So it flew up higher still—so high that the earth
shone like one of the other stars.

'How much of you will be left if you fall from here ?'
asked the bird.

'If I die, I die,' said the boy, 'but I will not leave you.'

And the bird saw it was no use talking, and went down to the earth again.

'Here you are at home, so let me go my way,' it begged once more; 'or at least make a covenant with me.'

'What covenant?' said the boy.

'Save me from the sun,' replied the bird, 'and I will save you from rain.'

'How can you do that, and how can I tell if I can trust you?'

'Pull a feather from my tail, and put it in the fire, and if you want me I will come to you, wherever I am.'

And the boy answered, 'Well, I agree; go your way.'

'Farewell, my friend. When you call me, if it is from the depths of the sea, I will come.'

The lad watched the bird out of sight; then he went straight to the date tree. And when he saw the dates his heart was glad, and his body felt stronger and his eyes brighter than before. And he laughed out loud with joy, and said to himself, 'This is *my* luck, mine, Sit-in-the-kitchen! Farewell, date tree, I am going to lie down. What ate you will eat you no more.'

The sun was high in the sky before the head-man, whose business it was, came to look at the date tree, expecting to find it stripped of all its fruit, but when he saw the dates so thick that they almost hid the leaves he ran back to his house, and beat a big drum till everybody came running, and even the little children wanted to know what had happened.

'What is it? What is it, head-man?' cried they.

'Ah, it is not a son that the master has, but a lion! This day Sit-in-the-kitchen has uncovered his face before his father!'

'But how, head-man?'

'To-day the people may eat the dates.'

' Is it true, head-man ? '

' Oh yes, it is true, but let him sleep till each man
has brought forth a present. He who has fowls, let him
take fowls ; he who has a goat, let him take a goat ; he
who has rice, let him take rice.' And the people did as
he had said.

Then they took the drum, and went to the tree where
the boy lay sleeping.

And they picked him up, and carried him away, with
horns and clarionets and drums, with clappings of hands
and shrieks of joy, straight to his father's house.

When his father heard the noise and saw the baskets
made of green leaves, brimming over with dates, and his son
borne high on the necks of slaves, his heart leaped, and he
said to himself ' To-day at last I shall eat dates.' And he
called his wife to see what her son had done, and ordered
his soldiers to take the boy and bring him to his father.

' What news, my son ? ' said he.

' News ? I have no news, except that if you will open
your mouth you shall see what dates taste like.' And
he plucked a date, and put it into his father's mouth.

' Ah ! You are indeed my son,' cried the sultan.
' You do not take after those fools, those good-for-nothings.
But, tell me, what did you do with the bird, for it was you,
and you only who watched for it ? '

' Yes, it was I who watched for it and who saw it.
And it will not come again, neither for its life, nor for
your life, nor for the lives of your children.'

' Oh, once I had six sons, and now I have only one.
It is you, whom I called a fool, who have given me the
dates : as for the others, I want none of them.

But his wife rose up and went to him, and said,
' Master, do not, I pray you, reject them,' and she entreated long, till the sultan granted her prayer, for she
loved the six elder ones more than her last one.

So they all lived quietly at home, till the sultan's cat
went and caught a calf. And the owner of the calf went

and told the sultan, but he answered, 'The cat is mine, and the calf mine,' and the man dared not complain further.

Two days after, the cat caught a cow, and the sultan was told, 'Master, the cat has caught a cow,' but he only said, 'It was my cow and my cat.'

And the cat waited a few days, and then it caught a donkey, and they told the sultan, 'Master, the cat has caught a donkey,' and he said, 'My cat and my donkey.' Next it was a horse, and after that a camel, and when the sultan was told he said, 'You don't like this cat, and want me to kill it. And I shall not kill it. Let it eat the camel: let it even eat a man.'

And it waited till the next day, and caught some one's child. And the sultan was told, 'The cat has caught a child.' And he said, 'The cat is mine and the child mine.' Then it caught a grown-up man.

After that the cat left the town and took up its abode in a thicket near the road. So if any one passed, going for water, it devoured him. If it saw a cow going to feed, it devoured him. If it saw a goat, it devoured him. Whatever went along that road the cat caught and ate.

Then the people went to the sultan in a body, and told him of all the misdeeds of that cat. But he answered as before, 'The cat is mine and the people are mine.' And no man dared kill the cat, which grew bolder and bolder, and at last came into the town to look for its prey.

One day, the sultan said to his six sons, 'I am going into the country, to see how the wheat is growing, and you shall come with me.' They went on merrily along the road, till they came to a thicket, when out sprang the cat, and killed three of the sons.

'The cat! The cat!' shrieked the soldiers who were with him. And this time the sultan said:

'Seek for it and kill it. It is no longer a cat, but a demon!'

And the soldiers answered him, ' Did we not tell you, master, what the cat was doing, and did you not say, " My cat and my people " ? '

And he answered : ' True, I said it.'

Now the youngest son had not gone with the rest, but had stayed at home with his mother ; and when he heard that his brothers had been killed by the cat he said, ' Let me go, that it may slay me also.' His mother entreated him not to leave her, but he would not listen, and he took his sword and a spear and some rice cakes, and went after the cat, which by this time had run off to a great distance.

The lad spent many days hunting the cat, which now bore the name of ' The Nunda, eater of people,' but though he killed many wild animals he saw no trace of the enemy he was hunting for. There was no beast, however fierce, that he was afraid of, till at last his father and mother begged him to give up the chase after the Nunda.

But he answered : What I have said, I cannot take back. If I am to die, then I die, but every day I must go and seek for the Nunda.'

And again his father offered him what he would, even the crown itself, but the boy would hear nothing, and went on his way.

Many times his slaves came and told him, ' We have seen footprints, and to-day we shall behold the Nunda.' But the footprints never turned out to be those of the Nunda. They wandered far through deserts and through forests, and at length came to the foot of a great hill. And something in the boy's soul whispered that here was the end of all their seeking, and to-day they would find the Nunda.

But before they began to climb the mountain the boy ordered his slaves to cook some rice, and they rubbed the stick to make a fire, and when the fire was kindled they cooked the rice and ate it. Then they began their climb.

THE PRINCE FINDS THE NUNDA

Suddenly, when they had almost reached the top, a slave who was on in front cried :

'Master! Master!' And the boy pushed on to where the slave stood, and the slave said :

'Cast your eyes down to the foot of the mountain.' And the boy looked, and his soul told him it was the Nunda.

And he crept down with his spear in his hand, and then he stopped and gazed below him.

'This *must* be the real Nunda,' thought he. 'My mother told me its ears were small, and this one's are small. She told me it was broad and not long, and this is broad and not long. She told me it had spots like a civet-cat, and this has spots like a civet-cat.'

Then he left the Nunda lying asleep at the foot of the mountain, and went back to his slaves.

'We will feast to-day,' he said ; 'make cakes of batter, and bring water,' and they ate and drank. And when they had finished he bade them hide the rest of the food in the thicket, that if they slew the Nunda they might return and eat and sleep before going back to the town. And the slaves did as he bade them.

It was now afternoon, and the lad said : 'It is time we went after the Nunda.' And they went till they reached the bottom and came to a great forest which lay between them and the Nunda.

Here the lad stopped, and ordered every slave that wore two cloths to cast one away and tuck up the other between his legs. 'For,' said he, 'the wood is not a little one. Perhaps we may be caught by the thorns, or perhaps we may have to run before the Nunda, and the cloth might bind our legs, and cause us to fall before it.'

And they answered, 'Good, master,' and did as he bade them. Then they crawled on their hands and knees to where the Nunda lay asleep.

Noiselessly they crept along till they were quite close to it ; then, at a sign from the boy, they threw their spears. The Nunda did not stir: the spears had done their work, but a great fear seized them all, and they ran away and climbed the mountain.

The sun was setting when they reached the top, and glad they were to take out the fruit and the cakes and the water which they had hidden away, and sit down and rest themselves. And after they had eaten and were filled, they lay down and slept till morning.

When the dawn broke they rose up and cooked more rice, and drank more water. After that they walked all round the back of the mountain to the place where they had left the Nunda, and they saw it stretched out where they had found it, stiff and dead. And they took it up and carried it back to the town, singing as they went, 'He has killed the Nunda, the eater of people.'

And when his father heard the news, and that his son was come, and was bringing the Nunda with him, he felt that the man did not dwell on the earth whose joy was greater than his. And the people bowed down to the boy and gave him presents, and loved him, because he had delivered them from the bondage of fear, and had slain the Nunda

[Adapted from Swahili Tales.]